THE DARK LANDS

Also by Markus Heitz

THE DARK LANDS

MARKUS HEITZ

Translated by Charlie Homewood

Jo Fletcher
BOOKS

First published in Great Britain in 2023 by

Jo Fletcher
BOOKS

Jo Fletcher Books, an imprint of
Quercus Editions Ltd,
Carmelite House
50 Victoria Embankment
London EC4Y 0DZ

An Hachette UK company

Typeset by CC Book Production
Printed and bound in Great Britain by Clays Ltd, Elcograf S.p.A.

MIX
Paper from
responsible sources
FSC® C104740
www.fsc.org

Papers used by Jo Fletcher Books are from well-managed forests and other responsible sources.

DRAMATIS PERSONAE

Aenlin Salomé Kane: an adventurer, Solomon Kane's daughter

Agatha Mühlbach, known as Gatchen: an inhabitant of Bamberg

Anna: a witch

Banker Kettler: a banker from the Bank of Hamburg

Barthel Hofmeister: a captain of landsknechts

Caspar von und zu dem Dorffe: a duellist and adventurer

Christian Schwarz: an inhabitant of Magdeburg

Claas de Hertoghe: brother to Hans de Hertoghe II, merchant of the Dutch West India Company

Comte: a black stallion

David: the miller's son

Emperor Ferdinand II: Holy Roman Emperor, King of Bohemia, Hungary and Croatia

Father Hubertus: a priest of the Societas Iesu

Franz: a tavern lad

Grand Duke Mikhail Alexandrovich Fjodorov: a diplomat of the Tsar

Gustavus Adolphus: King of Sweden

Hans de Hertoghe II: brother to Claas de Hertoghe, merchant of the Dutch West India Company

Henry Rich: First Earl of Holland and Baron of Kensington, an English nobleman

Jacobus Maus: a rope-seller of Hamburg

Jakob, known as Jäcklein: a landsknecht

Joss von Cramm: a mercenary recruiter or crimper

Karl Schulzenmüller: an inhabitant of Magdeburg

Katharina and Peter: a mill-owner and his wife

Maria: a villager

Martin Huber: an innkeeper

Master Schneider: a council member from Mühlhausen

Melchior Pieck, also known as Bracke: a bounty hunter, mercenary, spy and assassin

Moritz Mühler: a young landsknecht and Frozen One

Nicolas: a captain of landsknechts

Ōrmozd: a god

Osanna: a tavern maid

Prince-Bishop Johann Georg II Fuchs Baron of Dornheim: ruler of Bamberg

Sebastian: a guard

Solomon Kane: a Puritan adventurer, deceased

Sophia: a witch

Statius, known as Stats: a landsknecht

Tahmina: an Eastern mystic, friend of Aenlin

Tännel: a giant

Ursula Garnhuber, known as Ula: an inhabitant of Bamberg

Valentin: an ensign, or Fähnrichs, a flag-bearer

Valna: a naiad

Vanth: a goddess

Venetian, the: a plague doctor

Veronica Stadler, known as Nica: an inhabitant of Bamberg

GLOSSARY

Ahura Mazda: the Zoroastrian Creator, God

Deva: a fiend

Djinn: a supernatural being; may be good or evil

Dutch West India Company (Geoctroyeerde Westindische Compagnie): a chartered company of Dutch merchants

Fougasse: an improvised mortar hidden in a hollow in the ground, can be fired via a cloth line from afar

Hagzussa: an ancient word for witch

Passau Art: the art of making somebody magically immune to musket balls and blades, also called 'turn frozen'

Tercio: a battlefield formation

Xolotl: a deity or monster

Yatu: an ancient Persian word for magic, spellcraft, sorcery and witchcraft

ADDITIONAL READING
THE REAL STATE OF AFFAIRS IN 1629

Don't worry, this is a fantasy novel and I have no intention of turning it into anything else. However, to make my readers understand the context better, I have decided to supply a little overview of the historical backdrop of the seventeenth century.

The Holy Roman Empire of the German Nation was not a nation at all, but an alliance of three hundred Imperial cities, counties and principalities, from giant electorates to tiny territories consisting only of a few farmsteads ruled by Free Imperial Knights of the Holy Roman Empire. The Emperor was no autocrat but instead was chosen by seven electors: three clerical and four mundane ones of different confessions. Moreover, the ruling Emperor, the staunch Catholic Ferdinand II, had to cooperate with the Imperial Diet consisting of nobles, clerics and citizens. They also belonged to different religious persuasions, and tension grew.

As a result, some of these coreligionist lords, states and cities formed the 'Catholic League' to oppose the Protestant 'Union', while others declared themselves independent and neutral. Both the Catholic League and the Protestant Union mustered troops to defend themselves against attacks by their counterparts.

Foreign powers such as the Dutch, the Danes, the Swedes, the English and the French intervened in the conflicts on German soil; feudal rights even gave some of them a say.

What started with the well-known Defenestration of Prague in 1618 and ended with the Treaty of Westphalia in 1648 has gone down in history as the Thirty Years' War. In fact, it was not a long war at all, but a series of related battles with ever-changing allies and enemies.

When the novel starts, the Battle of White Mountain (1620) is already over and the Low Saxon War (1625–1629) is about to end.

The Holy Roman Empire was in a state of permanent unrest, triggered by religious disputes and fuelled by the thirst of those already powerful for more power and the belligerence of the mercenary leaders whom the war had already made rich.

To find out more, start reading up on this tumultuous era – and be warned: you will need patience to follow all those tangled conflicts.

Now, however, let me present to you: adventure, intrigues and . . . magic.

Better to reign in Hell, than serve in Heav'n.

John Milton, *Paradise Lost* (1667)

EXORDIUM

Kingdom of England, London, March 1629

'I am sorry for the hubbub and the dirt. However, if you want comfort, you have to suffer through some discomfort first.' At the sound of the voice echoing through the high, panelled room, Melchior Pieck turned towards the entrance he had come through half an hour ago. His host had made him wait; punctuality was the politeness of kings, not of lords.

'I did not notice them at all, your Lordship.' For someone from Hanover, Melchior was not too fluent in English. 'Your servants know how to find the dust, even in the most remote corners and dispose of it.'

'Like you do with your prey, right? No matter if it's human or animal.' Henry Rich, First Earl of Holland and Duke of Kensington, entered the great room.

The various scenes adorning the stucco ceiling clashed with the paintings on the walls, while several oil lamps and candles fought a losing battle against the dark colours; the dying light of the evening falling through the gate-like windows was not enough to illuminate the room.

'That is the reason why you are here, dear Pieck.' The long, tailored brocade jacket that fell past his hips and the puffy sleeves and breeches made the slender man look more sturdily built. He had curly hair and wore a stylish moustache and a goatee. 'Did no one offer you a drink?'

Melchior, who was just past fifty and wore his grey-silver beard and his hair cropped short, bowed slightly, the movement fluid despite his stoutness. 'I declined, your Lordship. My throat is not used to your kind of fine wine.' In his deliberately simple wardrobe and worn leather boots, he looked the exact opposite of the Earl.

'Don't be too modest. I know that you are a man of wealth and taste. Someone who was one of the favourites of the Count of Mansfeld must have earned a fortune.' The Earl gestured at the two armchairs next to the crackling fire. 'Have a seat. I can see that my messenger has brought you here unharmed.'

'Thank you, your Lordship. A charming lady indeed. The coach was extremely comfortable, too.' Melchior took a seat and arranged his baldric with its broad sabre. He carried his flintlock pistol in a holster on his chest.

'You knew the Count?'

'No. It was enough for me to hear about him and his fights. Excellent mercenary leader. His last battle was for the English Crown near Breda. However, things went downhill for him after Dessau and against Wallenstein.'

'Appearances were deceitful,' Melchior replied coolly. He didn't have to put up with imputations and derogatory remarks. Mentally, he added fifty guilders to his fee. 'The Count came up with a new plan.'

'Did he, then? A pity the Ottomans poisoned him, then. Wasn't he about to travel to Venice with you to raise more money for a fresh army?'

'I saw no Turks close to him when he dictated his last will to us, coughing up blood and little pieces of his lungs. It was a haemorrhage, your Lordship.'

'What a pity. Less heroic.'

'If your Lordship prefers, you may imagine an Ottoman behind it. I for one will stick with the affliction.' Melchior took in his surroundings. He didn't like to speak about the past; those memories hurt him as much as the scars on his face and body. He had liked his leader a great deal, and had learned a lot from him. 'Your Lordship has plans for the Holland House?'

'Oh, yes, indeed! That brick building is far too unpretentious for my taste,' he confessed. 'The stucco and stone ornaments are not nearly ornate enough for a man of my standing. After my wife inherited the building, I ordered the addition of wings and colonnades at once. Doric columns will also be a good addition. At the entrance. What do you think, Pieck?'

'They will, your Lordship.'

The Earl gestured for the waiting servants to put victuals and various beverages on the table between them, then he dismissed the lot. He was forty, ten years younger than Melchior, and now he smiled deviously. It was time to talk business. 'Since the Count of Mansfeld's death three years ago, you've made yourself quite a name as—'

'I prefer the word "trader",' Pieck interjected.

'Well, and I prefer to call a spade a spade.' The Earl leaned closer to him. 'Bounty hunter. Mercenary. Spy. Assassin. Schemer.' He took his goblet of port and slurped noisily. 'Did I forget anything, my dear Pieck?'

'The things I offer as a trader are manifold. Would your Lordship like to make use of my talents?' Melchior grabbed his own wine and drank it at a gulp. 'Your Lordship was right.' He put the less intricately adorned cup back down on the serving tray. 'Your port is not too fine for me.'

'Touché.' He laughed softly. 'A man after my fancy.' He reached under the table, pulled forth a portfolio and handed it to Pieck. 'Your mission.'

Full of curiosity, Melchior opened it to find several pencil drawings of a young woman in her mid-twenties, some in profile, some face-on. She had long dark hair, with a midnight-black lock about as wide as a finger that almost absorbed the light; the artist had drawn a white ribbon holding her tresses in place. Her left eyebrow had a striking light streak – a scar, perhaps? In the profile drawing, the lady wore a white hat adorned with a black ribbon and a wide brim tilted up on the right side.

'Pretty. Her face is a little ... long,' Melchior commented. Her features were vaguely familiar, but he could not quite place her. Beneath the drawing was the woman's personal crest, two crossed, burning torches with a rapier and pistols, and the words *Aenlin Salomé Kane*.

'She resembles her father.' The Earl pointed at the crest. 'She knows how to fight with a rapier and a main gauche. Additionally, she always carries two hidden stilettoes on her body. Moreover, she is an exceptionally good shot, or so they say.'

'Kane?' Melchior squinted his eyes shut. The name finally enabled him to place the resemblance. He had seen drawings of this face in many a book. 'Is she ... is she in fact Solomon Kane's daughter, your Lordship? The daughter of *the* Solomon Kane?'

'Does that matter, Pieck?'

It does when it comes to my fee, he thought, studying her features. 'I didn't know that this legendary man had had children.'

'Let's say his mistress Bess waited in vain for him to return, to show him the wonder that he had left her,' the Earl answered sardonically. 'After her death, he saw no need to investigate.' He poured himself some more port. 'I have heard through the grapevine that young Aenlin can already look back on a remarkable career as a swashbuckler. That is why I mentioned her weapons. Do not let her youth fool you. She is said to use her blades with extreme precision.'

Melchior knew all the stories about Solomon Kane, the Puritan adventurer who had fought evil in Europe and Africa and gone on the wildest of journeys there. Most people considered them little more than fairy tales to scare children, but Melchior had fought on battlefields in devastated regions and forlorn villages and knew what darkness could spawn if unopposed – or if someone summoned it.

'What would your Lordship like me to do?'

'You, my dear Pieck, will follow Aenlin Kane to Hamburg and keep her always in sight. Keep her safe. You have to protect her, no matter how you manage to do so, and no matter what it takes – and she cannot learn about you.' He refilled his goblet.

'So, your Lordship is her benefactor?'

'Up to a certain point, yes.'

'And which point would that be, your Lordship?'

'My protection ends as soon as Aenlin Kane leaves the city again.' He looked pensively at the painting to his right, which showed him on a hunt. 'Then – well, then you will kill the woman.'

Melchior raised his grizzled brows and also helped himself to some more of the excellent wine. Again he drank it at one gulp. 'Care to explain?'

'You will crate up all the belongings Aenlin Kane is carrying with her at the time of her death, and everything that she has acquired in Hamburg, and you will send it to London, to an address that I will give you as soon as we have signed this contract.'

Melchior said slowly, 'Your Lordship wants something she's going to pick up in Hamburg, but she will only acquire it if she feels herself unobserved.'

'Exactly, Pieck.'

'Is that reason enough to kill her, your Lordship?'

'Qualms don't fit a man like you, Pieck. She will never surrender the item voluntarily. Moreover, I do not want us to get in trouble because of this. It's a delicate matter.'

'Like your Lordship's affair with the paramour of the Count of Chalais?' Melchior whispered with an innocent look. 'I believe he was executed for conspiracy against Richelieu, but the duchess—'

'—is back in Paris,' the Earl said gruffly, his face reddening. 'Her ban has been lifted; the Duchess of Chevreuse has been forgiven.' He was one of a string of lovers the beautiful French woman had had; as a husband, he had more than one reason for anger when hearing her name.

'Is your Lordship still on friendly terms with the Duchess?' Melchior inconspicuously put one hand on the hilt of the dagger resting next to his sabre in the double sheath.

'That is not important for your mission, Pieck. Do not presume too much.'

'I am asking this only for business reasons. I do not care for gossip and tittle-tattle. For all I care, your Lordship can have as many liaisons as you can manage.' Melchior liked the port. 'Tell me, did Lord Buckingham's life not end in a truly tragic fashion last summer? Stabbed by his own man!'

'May his soul rot in Hell! Buckingham cost us more than four thousand good men at La Rochelle. I should have . . .' He made a fist. 'Turn over the drawing.'

Melchior grinned. He felt he had paid back the Earl for his earlier taunts. The Crown of England had made too many enemies in its wargames and was now paying the price.

He turned the drawing over. 'Another woman? Or a disguise?'

She was obviously younger and more delicate of feature; the artist had darkened her complexion with tiny dots and had written 'brown skin' next to the drawing. Her eyes were dark, too. Her wardrobe was Oriental, a style that Melchior recognised from the Ottoman women he'd met serving in mercenary armies. She held a carved hiking pole in one hand.

'A Persian mystic called Tahmina. She has been at Aenlin Kane's side for a while now. Presumably, Kane saved her life; she has been following her around ever since.'

'So she is a witch?'

'Let's say this child has connections to some exquisite powers that no one wants to investigate any further.' He pointed to the sealed envelope within the portfolio. 'That is why you will slip Tahmina this letter discreetly – after Kane's death.'

'What shall I do if she claims to be Kane's heiress?'

'Knock her out – but *do not* kill her, Pieck.'

'As your Lordship pleases.' Melchior's eyes darted back and forth between the two drawings. He didn't want to fight a witch. She might have cast a protective spell on herself and the murder victim-to-be. This was not looking to be quite so easy a mission after all. 'An unusual team,' he commented.

'Soon, only one horse will remain. See to it.' He had obviously got over his anger about the defeat at La Rochelle and Lord Buckingham. 'Do you think that is feasible?'

'Of course, your Lordship.' Melchior had already calculated his pay. 'That will be two hundred guilders per month, or two hundred English thalers, whatever is easier for your Lordship. First month in advance.'

The Earl inhaled slowly and audibly and the carefully trimmed moustache under his nose quivered.

'These are two missions, your Lordship,' Melchior explained, 'and I will be running a significant risk. This mystic can cause mortal peril for me. Moreover, I must turn down other ladies and gentlemen who—'

He raised his hand to cut him short. 'All right, Pieck. Half of your fee now, the other half later. For my own safety.'

'Forgive me, your Lordship, but I know that the English Crown has financial problems, thanks to your King's belligerence,' Melchior insisted. 'Is it not true that royal demesnes and jewels have been sold and valuable cutlery has been melted down? Also, let us not forget the exaction of forced loans. Did Parliament not grant additional funds?'

'Consider me impressed. For a German mercenary, you are very well informed.'

'I keep an eye on my business acquaintances' solvency. If His Majesty ever considered infringing on his lords' assets . . .'

'Don't worry. I know that Charles is having initial exploratory talks with the French and the Spaniards to end these expensive wars. I heard that Rubens himself may be travelling to London to negotiate on behalf of Madrid.'

'Still, Charles remains a king with an iron crown, not a golden one.' Melchior put the drawing of the two women back into the portfolio. 'Your Lordship could hire someone cheaper than me . . .'

'No, Pieck. You shall get your money.' Rich took the bell. 'Sign the contract in the portfolio. The coin will be here soon enough.'

At the back of the portfolio Melchior found two copies of the agreement for a mission to be agreed orally, and entered the fee they had agreed upon into a space left deliberately blank.

'One more thing,' the Earl said, as Melchior signed the parchments. 'If you should not be able to complete your task, if you should warn those women, or if you should fail to send me all that Kane acquires in Hamburg, Pieck, you will not have much longer to live.'

'Heavens!' Melchior perused the agreement once more, deliberately exaggerating his study. 'Where do I find that clause here, your Lordship?'

'These are the details agreed upon by word of mouth.' He signed and sealed his copy and handed it to Melchior. 'Now you know the clauses. If it should take you more than two weeks, let me know. Is that clear, Pieck?'

'Very clear, your Lordship.'

'Do you know Hamburg?'

'I have been there once or twice. It thinks itself invulnerable; it is full of merchants, diplomats and agents of all nations.' As Melchior recited his list, he considered whether he should have demanded a higher fee. 'I will find them quickly, your Lordship and carry out your orders, as we have discussed.'

The Earl scribbled something on a scrap of paper and waved it to dry the ink. As he folded the paper to seal it shut, his servants returned. 'This is the address to where you will deliver Aenlin Kane's belongings. Do not open it before her death.'

'Very well.' Melchior pocketed the scrap of paper, shoved his own copy of the agreement under his doublet and picked up the heavy sack full of thalers. Under the eyes of the Earl, he opened it and counted. 'Two hundred.'

'Do you not trust me?' the Earl asked dryly.

'Your Lordship would be surprised how many coins grow legs, even on short distances.' He looked at the servants standing by the doors, gazing at the ornate linenfold panelling. They looked unfazed. 'Not this time, though. Your servants are honest.'

'Well, good hunting then, Pieck. Now be off.' He didn't rise, just waved him off. 'I will see you soon. I hope.'

Melchior got up and bowed. 'Your Lordship.'

Without another word he went to the door, straightening his baldric and taking his floppy hat with its two kinked grey feathers from a servant. The retainer also handed him his large bag, which bore a lock to protect against unauthorised opening.

Melchior left Holland House, which could have housed dozens of families, without even considering the extensive estates, which were quite big enough for a good day's hunting.

They made him walk to the gate, where the coach awaited him. Another small insult.

As he had hoped, the woman who had picked him up near the docks was waiting inside. Angelique was almost thirty years old, and he had already noticed the French accessories she wore with her English dress.

'Good evening. Will you take care for my safety, Milady?' He put the bag of silver in his satchel.

She inclined her head slightly, her blonde curls moving and bobbing in the light of the small lamp. 'I will.' She knocked against the roof of the coach and the one-horse carriage started moving. 'The Earl wants to make sure that you board the *Ivy* right away. She leaves London with the flood tide. She will get you to Calais swiftly.'

Melchior was happy to hear that there was nothing to stop him from leaving. 'My luggage is already on board?'

'Of course.' She smiled. 'You have—'

Melchior drew his hardened dagger from its sheath next to the sabre and drove it into the woman's chest. On the battlefield, the armour-piercing weapon served as a tool against harnesses and cuirasses; it easily pierced the soft skin and the bones. As the blow found her heart, the woman opened her eyes wide.

'Cardinal Richelieu sends his regards, Countess Henriette,' he said. 'You couldn't fool me.'

Smoke billowed up from the margins of the wound and her skin burned with a hiss wherever the silver touched it.

The noblewoman wanted to reply, but the pain allowed her only to gasp. The paralysing effect of the Argentum stopped her from using her self-healing powers. Softly snarling, she stared at the handle of the dagger protruding from her chest. Her fingers turned into claws, her fingernails becoming long and sharp.

'Before visiting Holland House, I took the precaution of familiarising myself with the Earl's activities – who he hosts and to whom he offers protection,' Melchior explained, drawing his pistol. 'You are the Huguenot friend of the pardoned Duchess of Chevreuse – you felt safe in London.' He leaned into her. 'It appears the rumours are true, Countess. You are a shifter.'

Henriette growled and tried to bite Melchior with teeth that had become long fangs. 'You fiend!' She grabbed the hilt of the dagger impaling her, but she wasn't strong enough. 'I have done nothing wrong!'

'Unlike the Duchess, who has many powerful friends at court, your low title doesn't save you from Richelieu's revenge,' Melchior said. 'London can thank me later. The fewer beasts like you prowling around, the better.'

'You will ...' Henriette began, but her eyes flared red and half a breath later, the Countess died – and turned back into a normal woman. Nothing was left to hint at what she had truly been in life.

'*Excusez-moi.*' Melchior pulled his dagger from the dead body and wiped it clean on her dress. Then he laid the body on the bench seat in a position that better enabled him to behead her with his sabre, which took him three tries, thanks to the shaking of the coach. 'A deal is a deal.'

Working swiftly now, he opened his capacious satchel and took out the large glass vessel holding the liquid honey.

He cut off the longest curls, then immersed her head in the honey to preserve it. At Calais, he would hand over the head to a messenger. He'd soon get his reward: Richelieu paid well.

The coach rumbled through the deserted area around Holland House while Melchior stripped Henriette of her jewellery. He considered his list of prey: there was Benjamin de Rohan, Duc de Frontenay, and Baron de Soubise, the Huguenots' military leader, who had fled to London after the fall of La Rochelle, and who was allegedly pondering his return to France.

As far as Melchior knew, de Rohan was also a shifter. It was rumoured the Duc had a pet jaguar from the New World, however, de Rohan and the jaguar had never appeared in public together. Melchior had no doubts that the nobleman was himself the beast.

However, the two hundred thalers in his bag meant the Earl took priority. He could deal with de Rohan after he'd delivered Aenlin Kane's belongings to London.

As they rolled across a small bridge, Melchior called out,

'Coachman, stop!' and produced his primed pistol. 'Her ladyship feels sick. She would like to vomit.'

As soon the man stopped the coach and peered anxiously over the side to look for his mistress, Melchior fired.

With a bang, the propelling charge ignited. Whitish gun smoke riddled with sparks shot out like angry mist, while the musket ball hit the man right between the eyes, tearing away half of his skull and his hat. He slumped on the box seat, blood trickling down the coachwork.

Quickly, Melchior got out and threw the headless corpse of the Countess into the stream below; it ran into the Thames, and on into the open sea.

To make it look even more like an assault, he hit the coach a few times with his sabre, then slathered the coachman's rapier with the fellow's own blood before putting the weapon into his hand. Then he threw one of the Countess' rings back into the coach to make it look as if the robbers had dropped it; he dropped another one next to the coach. The rest he pocketed.

He unhitched the horse and without a backwards look, he rode towards the harbour, pondering what he might expect when he encountered Aenlin Kane and Tahmina: a fighter and a mystic.

It surely would not be as simple a task as killing the Huguenot.

The first thing he would do in Hamburg would be to find the executioner or someone who was skilled at the Passau Art to buy a magical writ of protection that would save him from various hardships. Just in case.

The earth, whose custom it is to cover the dead, was there itself covered with them and those variously distinguished: some had their bowels hanging out in most ghastly and pitiful fashion and others had their heads cleft and their brains scattered.

Hans Jakob Christoffel von Grimmelshausen,
Simplicius Simplicissimus (1668)
about the Battle of Wittstock on 4 October 1636

CAPITULUM I

Free Imperial city of Hamburg, April 1629

Aenlin stood out amongst the bustle and flurry of the lower harbour – for various reasons.

One was that she was standing still amid all the ado, which was involving a stack of crates holding cannonballs. Another was that she wore bright, expensively tailored clothes, including a light grey, wide-brimmed hat adorned with a black ribbon which partly covered her long dark hair. But mostly she stood out because she was a woman wearing men's clothing. Moreover, she wore her coat open, letting everyone see the weapons she carried.

She didn't mind the looks the bustling servants, house cleaners, hucksters, merchants and peasants gave her as she absentmindedly read her father's letter, which had reached her mother a long, long time ago.

Beloved Bess,

There may come a day when I do not return. When I lose my life fighting evil. Do not grieve me. I have taken care that you will be set up for life, should that happen.

In these hours I write this letter, I have no idea how you have spent those last years, nor you I. You should know, though, that every time my task dragged me away from you, you were always on my mind. Bess, together with my faith, you have given me the strength to oppose the beasts of darkness.

I have been able to gather some artefacts and amass a small fortune, which I hope you will be able to multiply. I bequeath them to thee. As they are of considerable value, I have taken precautions to protect them against unauthorised access.

To claim what is yours, and what you deserve, go to Hamburg. Find a man called Jacobus Maus in Niederhafen, the lower harbour, and show him your signet ring. He owns a rope shop. Maus will tell you how to proceed from there.

Should Jacobus Maus be dead by the time you arrive in Hamburg, he will have taken steps to ensure you have access to your treasure.

I do not want to go into any more details in this letter. Should somebody read what kind of riches await you, even kings and queens might become jealous.

I am looking forward to seeing you again, be it in this life or in Paradise, where God will reunite us.

May the Righteous bless you.

Deeply in love and forever yours,

Solomon

Aenlin lowered the letter and took a deep breath, watching the constant loading and unloading of the huge ships moored in the harbour. Their masts jutted skywards, punctuated by the reefed sails tied to the halyards. Here and there, sailors were climbing in the shrouds, checking ropes and spars for damage before the ships set sail again.

Aenlin's thoughts and emotions slowly adjusted to the fact that she was awfully close to her destination: Jacobus Maus' shop was only a stone's throw away.

However, she did not want to take this last step alone. She wanted her friend Tahmina by her side. She waited anxiously for her.

The shouting and the clamour, the rattling of the derricks and the runners keeping the machines going, the hoofbeats of the working teams and the grinding of the wheels resounded across the quay and echoed from the counting houses and warehouses. Trade across the Elbe never slept; even the sporadic embargoes and controls by the Danes, the English and the Dutch could not stop the keels.

Every day, ships set sail from Hamburg, several thousand each year, to every nook and cranny of the known world. In times of peace or in times of no matter which war, the city catered to all conflicting parties alike. Hamburg could afford this approach, having declared its own neutrality while at the same time erecting fortifications that stopped everyone from attacking the city.

Aenlin liked the bustle of the harbour; her bright eyes scanned the façades of the brick and half-timbered buildings. She had found the letter folded between the pages of her mother's Bible. Elisabeth Kane had died in poverty from typhus at the age of forty-five. The fever hit the inhabitants of London, taking turn and turn about with the Black Death.

Other cities suffered from those afflictions, too. On her way to Hamburg, Aenlin had heard about the plague ravaging nearby Altona, and Hamburg itself had had to cope with typhus recently. On one hand, the citizens were happy about its prosperity, even as large parts of the surrounding countryside fell victim to wandering armies. On the other hand, they were ranting against the fugitives who took shelter behind their walls thanks to the war and, according to rumour, brought those afflictions with them.

Aenlin had been to Hamburg before, but this was the first time she'd seen the massive works completed: the walls, the bastions with the defensive works and the cannon that were able to fire in all directions. No matter how long this war between Catholics and Protestants, nations and interests would rage, this city would survive – unless an affliction or a conflagration should overtake it. Her father's treasure for her mother was safe here.

'Hey! Where do you think you're going with my purse?' shouted a merchant in expensive clothing He waved his foppish hat at a ragged boy who was running across the quay. The merchant unleashed his grey mastiff and the dog barked darkly. 'Brutus, attack! Attack! Tear the little thief to pieces!'

Aenlin saw the boy, who was about eleven years old, weave through the obstacles and jump over sacks and crates. He might have lost an adult this way, but the mastiff refused to give up its prey. Whenever it lost sight of the little thief, the animal dropped his nose and followed his scent.

Aenlin's heart quickened in her chest. Intervening would be tricky, but she could not simply watch this hunt come to a bad end. She picked up an empty sack from the ground and walked towards the boy. *Lucifer help me.*

'That's the spirit! Cut him off, woman,' the merchant shouted, gleeful with anticipation. 'But be careful: don't let Brutus attack you.'

The crowd laughed. Some onlookers showed their sympathy for the child by whistling loudly to distract the dog.

The little thief tried to evade Aenlin, but she had foreseen his route correctly. Just before the mastiff could bite down on the boy's neck, she tripped him, so he hit the ground at full pelt and went head over heels several times across the cobblestones.

Deftly, she threw the open sack over the raging dog's head and the beast's aggressive barking stopped at once. Blind and taken off-guard, Brutus crashed into the crates and shook himself with a yowl, trying to shred the coarse fabric with his claws.

Aenlin went over to the boy, who was just getting up, and

grabbed him by the shoulder. 'Give me that,' she demanded and held out her gloved left hand.

'But it's my due,' he protested. 'It belongs to me and my people.'

The merchant approached. 'Miserable lugworm!'

A crowd formed around Aenlin and the boy, who kicked at her and at the man in turn, as if he had any chance to escape.

'You won't steal from me ever again!' The merchant told his dog to sit and freed it from the sack. The mastiff sat down next to him with a snarl, closely watching the humans in front of it. 'Give me back your loot.'

'You betrayed us, Master Fischer!' The boy grabbed his waist-band. 'You owe us money – for a month's work.'

'Shut your cheeky mouth, you thief,' the merchant snarled.

Undaunted, the boy continued, 'We loaded the carts and pushed them from the lower harbour up to the weigh station, all March long. You gave us nothing!'

Aenlin admired his courage. Neither the crowd nor the merchant – nor even the giant dog, which was eye to eye with the boy as it sat upright – intimidated him. 'Is that true, Master Fischer?'

'How is this your business?' The merchant grabbed for the boy, but Aenlin pushed his shoulder and the man's fingers grasped nothing.

'Is what the boy says true?'

A soft babble echoed throughout the crowd.

'Brutus!' The mastiff rose with a growl as the merchant shouted at Aenlin, 'Unhand that thief so I can get my money back, you strange, foolish woman. Why are you out in public like this at all, wearing man's clothes?'

'What's the wage he owes you, boy?' Aenlin looked at him, her manner friendly, yet stern.

'A ducat. For both of us.'

'Then take one from the purse and give the rest back.'

'Are you mad?' Fischer said, obviously pondering an attack.

Meanwhile, the boy took the proper coin from the purse and pocketed it, then handed the purse to Aenlin. His conqueror still did not let go of him.

'Here. Your purse, Master Fischer.' Aenlin gave it to the theft victim and the crowd laughed softly. 'And here is a guilder. From me.' She took a coin from her coat pocket. 'Now the world is no longer out of kilter.'

'Not out of kilter any more?' Fischer grabbed the purse and the coin. Both disappeared beneath his cape. 'My world is out of kilter until this mangy thief has been punished.' From his belt he pulled a bludgeon that looked worn from frequent use. 'I'll smash his hand – that'll stop him from stealing other people's belongings.' He raised his bludgeon. 'Give me his arm!'

Aenlin let go of the boy, who ran away at once.

'Brutus, attack!' Fischer called.

Aenlin stepped onto the dog's lead as the mastiff tried to dash off and yanked the animal around so it crashed yelping to the ground. She was sorry she had had to hurt the beast. 'Brutus, stop,' she ordered.

Now the onlookers laughed.

'You dare protect a thief?' Fischer raised his bludgeon against her. 'I'm going to beat the living daylights out of you, woman. You'll never forget this beating – you'll be picking up your teeth from the gutter.'

Aenlin took a deep breath and put her hands on her hips, in the same movement, pushing open her coat to reveal her two flintlock pistols and the rapier. 'Pay your people so they don't have to rob you to get their wages.' She slowly took her foot from the lead. 'Then you and your Brutus wouldn't have to get so overexcited running around the docks.'

Fischer scrutinised the intrepid young woman, his wavering gaze giving away his indecision. 'I will not forget this!'

He turned around and walked through the cordon of onlookers to the stack of crates and the old cog he had loaded. When he whistled loudly, the mastiff slunk off after its angry master.

Aenlin smiled, her gaze following the thief. Hopefully, this would teach him a lesson.

The crowd dispersed; there were ships to load and unload. The entertaining diversion was over.

Aenlin's heartbeat slowly returned to normal. She sat down on a crate. A long sip of ale would have been very welcome.

By showing off her impressive collection of weapons, unusual for a woman, she had sought to intimidate her opponent so she would not have to use her arsenal. Of course, she knew how to fight with the rapier. She also was a surprisingly good shot and knew how to use her stilettos – during training sessions.

But she had never used her blades or balls against another human being.

Her mother had set immense value upon her education. Gaining knowledge and skill with weapons had been equally important. Aenlin leaned heavily towards knowledge, but the times favoured those who were proficient with instruments of death.

Moreover, as Solomon Kane's daughter, a certain reputation preceded her in England – not in Hamburg, though. She was sure that nobody in the Free Imperial city had known her father, and she surely would not go about flaunting her inheritance.

She also kept her beliefs to herself. In a pub in England, Aenlin remembered, she had shared some interesting conversations on religion, Heaven and Earth and demons with a student. Young John Milton he had been deeply impressed by her opinions, but she knew better than to voice them openly, not in these days when Catholics, Protestants, Calvinists, Quakers and other Christian sects were all fighting each other for pre-eminence.

'There you are!' Tahmina came running towards her.

People might have mistaken her for some exotic monk from the Caribbean or the East, thanks to her darker skin. The loose garment of midnight blue, cinched by a loose belt around her hips, gave no hint of the shape of her body. In her right hand, she carried a carved walking staff that came up to her chest; it looked quite ordinary, unless examined more closely.

'Have you been the reason for this uproar?' Tahmina asked.

'No – a thief. I might've saved his life.'

'Found a friend doing so?' Tahmina looked at the merchant standing in front of his old cog, who was gazing angrily at them. The mastiff lying on the ground beside him was watching people at work. 'Now that was quick. We have only just arrived in Hamburg and already you are making life awkward for yourself. Which means for both of us.' The Persian was five years younger than Aenlin. A cap hid her long brown hair, but her eyes shone blue like the open sea on a bright, sunny day, even if there was disapproval in them. 'Did I not say we need to keep a low profile on our little journey?'

Aenlin laughed softly. 'We both stand out, even in Hamburg, which is crawling with people from other countries.' She pointed to the quay wall of the lower harbour, where the larger sailing ships were moored. New ones arrived constantly; once winter ended and the ice on the Elbe melted, trade gained momentum. 'Look: Frenchmen, Englishmen, Spaniards, Portuguese, Dutchmen – even people from the West Indies and Asia. I think all skin colours and languages of the world are gathered here.'

'It was your idea to claim your father's inheritance,' Tahmina said. 'And to dress conspicuously.'

'I thought being armed would discourage villains.' Aenlin gestured towards the merchant. 'It worked with him. But you might be right, I should dress more discreetly. A burlap sack would do, yes?'

'Don't use your sharp tongue against your servant,' Tahmina

replied. They had agreed that the Persian would pose as Aenlin's servant, even though that was not the case. Tahmina introducing herself as a mystic would be the straw to break the camel's back when it came to tolerance, even in neutral Hamburg, where people tended to ignore questions of faith. Witchcraft and similar arts were no laughing matters anywhere. Brushwood and logs were easy to find and burning witches at the stake promised great entertainment for locals and visitors alike.

Aenlin put a hand on her friend's shoulder. 'What have you been up to while I was busy saving a boy from the teeth of the beast?'

'I found us lodgings. Our luggage is already there.' Tahmina pointed at the smallest inn: The Thirsty Roper. 'We can rest our weary heads there once we have found this man. What was he called? Some rodent name. Hamster? Rat?'

'Maus.' Aenlin glanced at the shop. 'Jacobus Maus. That is his store.'

'You haven't been in there yet?'

'I want you by my side when I'm finding out about my inheritance.'

Tahmina batted her eyelashes as she put her left hand to her chest. 'O my gracious mistress. You are so kindly to let me—'

'Stop it.' Aenlin got up, ignoring her rumbling stomach. All day long she had been too excited to eat. 'All right. Let's solve this riddle, shall we?'

Together, they approached the rope-trader's shop, which was wedged between two tall, narrow and well-frequented buildings. The women were surrounded by various languages; people struck deals while walking and judging by the hand gestures, there was a lot of negotiating going on. According to the faces, not all of the negotiations were going well.

Aenlin knew Hamburg was bustling with spies, agents and diplomats and that various of the nations even had embassies

here, where it was possible to talk to emissaries of their kings –
to get subsidies, to suggest deals, or to discuss other things.

She crossed the threshold with very mixed feelings.

Altona, near the Free Imperial city of Hamburg, April 1629

'Damn, get me that beer,' Statius hollered across the tavern. It
carried the beautiful name Rogue Wave and stood on the bank
of the Elbe, right next to the ferry he and his two companions
had used to cross the river. 'Wifey, how long will we keep on
waiting? Don't you know that it's dangerous to let warriors
suffer want?'

'Coming up, coming up,' replied the barmaid, who couldn't
have been much older than fourteen. She poured his drink from
a large pitcher into a tankard.

As the other patrons hid behind their own tankards and
talked quietly, four card players tried to discard their hands
softly, to avoid the attention and displeasure of the mercenaries.

'What about that food?' said Statius, whose garb was as
colourful as that of the two friends with whom he shared his
table. Their beards were meticulously trimmed and the tips
of Statius' moustaches were dashingly waxed horizontal. They
wore colourfully striped shirts with puffy sleeves; puffed slashed
breeches and large floppy hats with long coloured feathers,
proudly advertising the fact that they were not ordinary people.

'Yes, Mother is at it,' the girl reassured him, lugging more
tankards to the table. 'There you are.' She hurried away to avoid
being dragged onto one of the men's laps. 'I hope you like it,'
she added.

'I hope so, too. Otherwise, I'll see how much I like you
tonight.' Statius distributed the mugs. 'A toast to this life, my
friends!'

Jacob, the smallest and skinniest of them, whom the others always called Jäcklein, raised his mug and touched it to Statius'. 'Yes! May our enemies' blades always be blunt.' His blond hair and beard always managed to stick out in all directions, making him look a little scruffy.

Nicolas, the oldest of them, a towering fellow of almost thirty years, looked at the tendrils of smoke drifting lazily out the window from the room's numerous glowing pipes. He kept an eye on the cart holding their tent, their armour and their pole weapons – and on the horse tethered next to it. He would rather have put the cart and the animal into a livery stable, but when Jacob and Statius had seen the inn, they would not budge. They assumed that no one would dare to touch what was theirs, and anyway, no one wanted to confront landsknechts, especially not drunk ones.

In the end, Altona was just a pitiful collection of farmsteads, fishermen's huts and inns, unloved by its thriving sister Hamburg. The Counts of Schauenburg had allowed prosecuted Protestants from the Spanish Netherlands – as well as Mennonites and German and Portuguese Jews – to settle here. After the Danes had conquered Altona, the Imperial troops had ravaged the village. Then the Black Death had come. Several houses now stood empty; some were still marked as haunted by the plague.

Nicolas had visited other places like this. He grabbed his mug without looking at it. 'May their blades be blunt,' he repeated, and emptied it in one gulp. The beer tasted bitter and watered-down, but it quenched his thirst. He turned to his friends again. 'Can we resume our conversation now?'

'You can always have a conversation with me,' Jäcklein said, wiping the foam from his upper lip.

'Not until I've eaten.' Statius banged his fist on the table rhythmically, making his shoulder-length brown hair bounce, and shouted, 'Food! Food! Food!'

'Stop that,' Nicolas barked at him. 'The little one is scared to death by you.'

'Well, then she'll be more pliable later when I—' He stopped as he saw his leader's angry look. 'All right, all right, I'll let her be. But I'll bet you your meal that she's had more than a dozen cocks inside her.' He gestured about the taproom. 'That's good money for a sweet little thing like her. Who knows how much longer she'll stay pretty?'

Nicolas didn't react. Statius was a rough guy, often too loud and too coarse, exactly like the generally accepted landsknecht cliché. However, he was extremely dependable on the battlefield and that was essential for survival when Nicolas stood in a tercio, fighting for his life. When the cavalry approached, firing into the ranks, when the enemy came marching on, the musket balls flying and the pikes jabbing like oversized thorns, when gun smoke obscured Nicolas' view – that was when Statius stood by his side. So the mercenary leader tolerated some of the excesses Statius allowed himself off the battlefield.

Jäcklein took another sip and looked at Nicolas. 'What do you think? Will we be able to enter Hamburg?'

'Depends on his behaviour.' Nicolas pointed at Statius. 'They say the Council doesn't particularly like errant landsknechts.'

'Oh, I can be as godly as a lamb.'

Jäcklein laughed. 'You'd be the first lamb with claws and fangs.'

'Yet still pious.' Statius got up and threw his tankard behind the counter, where it clattered noisily to the floor. 'Fill it up, girl, or I'll fill you up.'

The gamblers pocketed their cards and left the small inn, grumbling, smoking and protesting – quietly.

Nicolas looked out of the window to ensure they were not tampering with the cart. One of them pissed against the wheel, but that, Nicolas didn't mind. He would have intervened only if the urine had hit their cargo.

'Are people behaving nicely?' he heard Jäcklein ask. 'We should have installed a fougasse outside to protect our stuff. Click, bang – and over.'

'A mortar would have been pretty extreme.' Nicolas returned his gaze to the taproom and the much-notched bidenhänder resting against the wall next to him. The huge sword was his. In combat, he wore it on his back while wielding a halberd against cuirassiers and musketeers. Only when the enemy formation was close enough would he break from the tercio to plough through the ranks of pikemen and musketeers with the bidenhänder. The heavy blade cracked wooden poles, bones and skulls alike.

In his head, he relived the cruel memories of their last battle. 'Brandy, girl,' he quickly called, knowing he had to fight off those images or he would mope all day. Slowly he took the colourful hat from his ash-blond hair.

Every mercenary dealt with his memories in their own unique way. Jäcklein resorted to jokes and mischief, Statius to obscenity and constant brawls. To Nicolas, intoxication was soothing.

'Coming right up, sir.' The serving maid brought the beer, setting it down carefully in front of Jäcklein to avoid getting too close to Statius, then she returned with a tray bearing a bottle and bowls of steaming stew, little more than greasy meat in porridge.

'Enjoy your meal,' she said, turning to go.

With a lightning-quick movement, Statius grabbed her left wrist. 'Tell me, little one, what's your name? Wouldn't you like to see the world? I need somebody to stitch me up, cook for me and look after my affairs while we're on the battlefield.'

'No, no. I like the world in Altona,' she stammered. Her gaze implored the other two mercenaries to help her. She had tucked her light brown hair under a greasy kerchief; an old scar marred her cheek. She said nervously, 'My name is Osanna.'

'Eat now, Stats,' Nicolas ordered. 'We'll find some willing souls.'

'A pity, child. I would have liked you all right.' Statius let her go and started eating. 'I've had worse,' he mumbled between the bites he wolfed down. This way of eating was a habit acquired in the field: no one could take from you what you already had in your belly.

Jäcklein resumed the conversation. 'So, we are going to Hamburg? Ask around for the next battle, find a crimper to recruit us? Maybe that cut-throat Joss von Cramm is in town? He always knows who needs capable warriors.' Unlike Statius, he ate slowly, chewing every mouthful more than twenty times. Food was more filling that way.

Nicolas nodded. 'Let's make the moneybags get us up to speed. Those in port will know where our pikes and blades are needed. The Danes can piss off, but the Swedes, they're trustworthy people. They don't betray their Protestants and the Union.' Ladling food into his mouth, he looked around. 'How about your savings? Does one of you have enough for a musket? A pistol?'

'I'd be glad if I could afford to have my harness repaired,' Statius replied, then he belched noisily.

'A musket would be nice! But not one of those with the dumb fuses. The damned flying sparks keep burning my beard. I heard there's new ones again. With a matchlock like the wheel lock, just less inconvenient.' Jäcklein's face lit up with delight. 'I'd gladly exchange my pike for one of those.'

'Who would accept an old piece of iron on a wooden pole for a gun?' Statius laughed at him. 'We have it good, don't we?'

Nicolas heard the message loud and clear: they were all in need of money. His purse held ten lousy ducats, a few hellers and batzes and kreutzers from assorted principalities and states that felt lighter to him than they should have. He had heard that some nobles had ordered their mints to secretly reduce the amount of metal in their coins. Treachery was everywhere.

'Beggars can't be choosers,' he said to the others. 'As soon as we're in Hamburg, we'll look for a proper battle. Even in Bohemia, for all I care. I don't mind walking.'

'Against the Catholics or against the Protestants?' Statius threw his wooden spoon at the girl. It clattered against the bar next to her. 'Hey! Bring that back to me, together with another bowl of stew and some beer.'

Osanna got to work.

'My steel doesn't care whom it pierces.' Jäcklein had not even finished half of his stew. 'I'd love to fight for Wallenstein. A pity Mansfeld is dead. He was skilled at fighting and trickery. He got a hundred thousand thalers for not joining the battle at the White Mountain! What a fox!'

'Still, he's dead,' Nicolas mused. 'Wallenstein. Why not? Yes, let's see if he's hiring. Otherwise, Tilly. Guard duty would also be a possibility. Or Bohemia. We could also set sail for the South Sea, where other countries fight their battles.' He scraped up the last of his food while Statius tucked into his second bowlful.

'Across the sea? No, not for a hundred thousand guilders! A witch told me I would die at sea. No, I'd rather not.' Jäcklein watched their leader and shook his spoon at him. 'Tell me, what was that? A while ago?'

'I don't know what you're talking about.' Actually, Nicolas knew exactly.

'When we went into battle.' The small, wiry man scratched a line into the roughly hewn tabletop with the round edge of his spoon. 'You cut a swathe through the enemy's entire tercio as if the Devil himself was on your heels.'

'But you weren't wounded at all.' Statius banged his chest. 'Admit it. You're carrying a Writ of Protection. I have one, too. Always helpful.'

Nicolas only dimly remembered it. He had been frenzied in the heat of the battle, like one of those berserkers the Romans used to talk about. He had attacked his enemies like a demon unleashed, although he didn't fully remember any of it. In his head, he relived the cruel memories of their last battle. 'More brandy, girl,' he called quickly. He had to fight those images, or he'd be miserable all day.

'The Reaper himself, Nicolas. I'd never seen you that way before, not in all these years.' Jäcklein didn't sound worried. 'You should ask for a bigger fee for yourself.'

'For all of us,' Statius interjected at once. 'Because, never forget, we follow him.' His voice turned conspiratorial. 'Did you ever notice that some of the men we beheaded stank awfully? Like . . . the dead?'

'They were dead.' Nicolas remembered this detail vividly.

'They tore the dead from their graves and imbued them with unholy life,' Jäcklein confirmed. 'Upon my soul! This must be the resurrection everyone is talking about. I envisioned it differently. We are not in Paradise, gentlemen!'

The three mercenaries laughed.

'How does that work?' Statius pushed back his empty bowl and twirled the tips of his moustache back into shape. 'How do you resurrect corpses? That can't be a Christian spell.'

'I have heard that it's possible to command victims of the plague if you cut out their tongues.' Jäcklein shrugged. 'Or perhaps the men didn't know that they were dead and just fulfilled their duty.'

'Plague.' Nicolas thought of the many marked houses in Altona where the Black Death had wreaked – or was still wreaking – havoc.

'The villages of the dead,' said a soft female voice next to them, and the mercenaries turned in astonishment to see Osanna holding a broadsheet. 'Some people talk about them – places full of malice where darkness and demons reign – and that's only the beginning.'

Jäcklein looked at the stained piece of paper, which had obviously passed through many hands. 'Ah. Penned by a priest,' he said. 'Who else would write such a thing?'

'Demons,' Statius repeated. He shuddered and crossed himself. He could not read the words, but the illustrations made it easy enough to understand what it was about. He looked at Osanna. 'Villages full of dead people?'

'Yes, sir. They – the corpses – roam around, some of them attack the living, others sign up for the army, or they say.'

'For money?' Jäcklein laughed. 'Zounds! What do these walking dead eat and drink?'

'The living. That is their greatest motivation. The freshly fallen belong to them, too.' Osanna stacked the empty bowls and carried them back to the bar.

'Someone fart me in the face,' Statius said after a brief silence. 'Now the little woman has me scared. God, she is a sly dog!' He laughed. It sounded loud, but hollow. It didn't chase away his discomfort.

Nicolas looked at Jäcklein, who looked worried, too.

It was not the first time they had met weirdness on their way through the realms, principalities and cities of the land. Nicolas clearly remembered the crazed itinerant preacher in motley garb who was followed by a flock of children with their skin painted green. He had called out to them that the Dark Lands, where the thralldom of humankind originated, were spreading, where demons, witches, wizards and the beasts of darkness ruled. In the next city they reached, they heard that the madman had been incarcerated for heresy. He had abducted the children.

'The Dark Lands,' Nicolas said quietly. The term had stuck in his head.

They had seen demons fighting, spectres on fiery horses or bat-winged creatures that appeared under cover of gun smoke and turmoil. Nicolas, Statius and Jäcklein had spotted the red eyes of a colonel who had bared his fangs before attacking his enemies with a snarl.

'We urgently need money,' Nicolas told his friends, 'for bigger and better weapons.'

'Yes and for Writs of Protection.' Again, Statius banged his chest, making the tips of his moustaches quiver. 'I'll also buy a painted amulet of St Christopher and of St Jude to wear around my neck.'

'St Jude?' Jäcklein laughed. 'Oh dear – do I have to watch my back in battle from now on, man?'

'He was an assassin – fought with a sickle. He will protect me just right.' Statius pointed at the pamphlet about the villages of the dead. 'I'd better have his name carved into my skin and across my heart, so I won't lose his succour.'

The door of the Rogue Wave opened and a giant silhouette filled the doorframe, before bowing his head to step inside. Only after the newcomer had crossed the threshold was he able to stand at his full height. He was more than six feet tall.

'Good day,' he said in a friendly manner, looking around. He wore a threadbare shepherd's coat over shirt and trousers, all that protected him from the cold. His shoes were mended and on his back he carried a sack.

All conversations died down as everyone stared at the new guest.

'Shit me in the boots,' Statius exclaimed. 'That guy looks not even fifteen – but he's as tall and broad as a little giant.'

'He's eaten his siblings and then his parents,' Jäcklein said with conviction, pulling out his pipe. 'For the first time I see a man who could easily take you on, Nicolas.'

'And he's not even a man yet,' Nicolas pointed out.

'Ah, you must be the owners of the cart with pikes and the tents.' With two steps of his long legs, the young man reached the mercenaries' table. 'I am Moritz Mühler, from the beautiful city of Bremen. I want to become proficient at warcraft. Will you take me in and teach me? I'll give you half of my pay for it.'

'Heaven must have sent you,' Statius muttered, staring at him in fascination.

'Or Hell,' Jäcklein added as he stuffed some tobacco into his pipe.

Nicolas gestured to the other two men in turn, briefly introducing his friends and himself. 'How old are you, Moritz Mühler?'

'Fifteen, sir.'

'Forget the sir,' he said, keeping his tone friendly. 'Why would you like to be a landsknecht?'

'I want to make money – experience things. Be a war hero.' The towering lad wore a smile as wide as his prodigious chest. He quickly took off his cap, and black locks tumbled to his shoulders. 'I couldn't stand it at home anymore. Too placid for my taste.'

'Placid!' Jäcklein blurted. 'Hell's bells! He wants to exchange peace for hewing and stabbing.'

Moritz just laughed. It was the friendliest laugh Nicolas had ever heard his life. The boy would soon lose it on the battlefield. It wasn't yet clear whether he was dim, or just a reckless fellow who didn't think about death.

'What have you done before, Moritz Mühler?'

'I was a logger, but the trees didn't bother trying to avoid my blows. That's too boring for me.'

Statius snorted his beer across the table. 'Holy Moses, we need this fellow! He'll keep joking even on the most awful of days.'

'I wasn't joking. I was serious.' Moritz looked imploringly at the men in turn. 'Take me with you. I want to be a landsknecht!'

'Have you ever fought before?' Nicolas asked, although he already knew the answer.

'Only against spruces and firs. A few oaks will probably have been among my victims, too,' Moritz told him with a grin. 'Oh, yes, I have! I threw flour bags until no one knew what had hit them.'

'He's too good for the carnage.' Jäcklein raised his pipe and the serving maid brought him a smouldering splint. 'Stay away from the war. You're too nice, child. Find yourself another craft, take a pretty wife like this flower of the bar and have some children.' He lit the tobacco and puffed quickly.

Moritz remained adamant. 'I still can do that as a landsknecht.'

'Take the bidenhänder, boy.' Nicolas handed him the heavy blade. 'Now show us your strength.'

'Will you take me if I smash through the table?' The boy's brown eyes glittered.

'Agreed,' Statius said without hesitation. 'I'll take him if neither of you want to teach him.'

'You heard the man. If you manage this blow, you'll be one of us.' Nicolas put on his cap. Jäcklein just kept puffing, feeling uncomfortable. To be on the safe side, the three mercenaries took their mugs from the table.

Moritz didn't even take a big swing, instead wielding the two-handed blade with his right hand as if it were no heavier than a cane.

The sword hit the table, smashing the thick wooden slab in half – but Moritz didn't stop at that. Cockily, he grabbed one of the halves and held it upright, easily splitting it in half again, this time with his equally powerful left hand.

The three mercenaries had jumped to their feet as the guests of the inn shouted in surprise and excitement. They had never seen anything like this before in Altona.

'Looks like I'm in,' Moritz said. He tried to give the bidenhänder back to Nicolas.

'Keep it as a gift,' the mercenary leader said, and he shook Moritz's hand. 'Welcome, Moritz Mühler.' He winked at the terrified Osanna. 'I'll pay for the damage.'

'By my immortal soul! You can slice up a cuirassier from head to horse! They'll soon be calling you the man-splitter,' Jäcklein said. 'Well, unless a musket ball takes you down first.' He shook the giant's hand, and Statius followed suit.

'That won't happen,' Moritz replied offhandedly.

A boy entered the taproom and walked straight over to the conspicuous little group. His shirt and breeches were threadbare and instead of shoes, he wore woven willow twigs on his feet to protect against stones.

'Here, an invitation,' he announced. He held out a sealed letter to them.

'For us?' Jäcklein looked around. 'Are you sure, boy?'

'How could I mistake your cart and garb?' the boy replied.

'Don't ask,' Statius hissed. 'That smells of money. Why should we care if it was originally addressed to another bunch?'

'Thanks, little one.' Nicolas took the letter. There were no names; it said only *To the landsknechts in Altona.*

He agreed with Statius: they needed money, and they were landsknechts. In Altona. If any other landsknechts were around and they were stealing a job from them, well, that was Providence.

'You owe me a kreutzer,' the boy stated and sniffled. 'That's what I was promised.'

'Statius, pay him,' Nicolas ordered.

'Why me?'

'Because you'll soon be getting half of Moritz's pay – you'll be the richest of us all.' He cracked the seal. As he perused the lines, he grinned broadly. 'This sounds like a fat payday, gentlemen.'

Statius threw the messenger a kreutzer, then lightly clapped him round the back of his head to chase him away.

With a curse, the boy ran out.

'So who needs our blades? A lovely damsel in distress?' Jäcklein stood on his tiptoes and glanced at the parchment. Unlike Statius, he could read. 'Or a king?'

'Even better. Someone who has lots of coin.'

Nicolas held up the missive so his friends could see the seal that half-covered the signature. 'The West India Company.'

'I will devastate Bavaria and burn it to the ground so that the marauding Imperial soldiery will drain itself there.'

Gustav Adolf, King of Sweden, Spring, 1632

CAPITULUM II

Near the Free Imperial city of Hamburg, April 1629

'Up there! That must be him.' Aenlin ran along the road leading past Altona to catch up with the man riding a donkey. She was sweating, though the sun was only weak. They'd not been able to buy a cart or horse, so she and Tahmina had been forced to walk.

'Just like all the other Jacobus Mauses before him, this will not be the right one either.' The mystic walked beside her at a brisk pace, swinging her engraved staff, which somehow enabled her to match Aenlin's long strides without becoming as exhausted as she was. Unlike Aenlin, no perspiration marred her midnight-blue robe. 'Or is it Mauses? Mäuse? Mouses? Mice?'

'As if that mattered,' Aenlin said impatiently. Gathering all her courage, she had entered the rope shop and asked for Mr Maus, only to be told that Mr Maus had left for nearby Altona on personal business. The man had had no idea when his employer would be back.

'It must be him,' Aenlin added. 'The coat, the grey black-tailed donkey . . .'

'Then why did he not enter that village but rode past it?'

'Let us ask him.' Aenlin sped up a little. She felt the weight of her weapons, but her training paid off. She took off her hat and let the air caress her dark hair.

Around her, spring was rippling across the landscape: the grass grew green and the first cornstalks were already peeking through the soil. Leaves were clothing every twig and branch, while the birds chased buzzing insects through the foliage.

Jacobus Maus, if it was he, guided his steed onto a trail that ran into the lush willows bordering the fertile fields. He kicked the donkey on towards a thick grove.

'Personal business, hm?' Tahmina was not sounding too convinced. 'A rope-trader riding into a grove? What is he up to?'

'Maybe a tryst? Mr Maus is married, after all. A well-known shop owner like him has to be cautious.'

'In April? In this heat? In a forest?' Tahmina's doubts were unmistakeable. 'We should be the ones to be more cautious.'

Aenlin looked at her in surprise. 'I don't expect him to try to ambush us.'

'Couldn't he be looking for the treasure? Suppose the news that Solomon Kane's daughter has shown up to put forward her claim is already all over Hamburg . . .'

'No one knows me here.'

'But what if I am right, that he has buried the treasure in this grove and is now unearthing it to hide it somewhere else and pretend someone has stolen it?'

That sounded too far-fetched for Aenlin. 'Well, we'll soon find out.'

They turned onto the trail and hurried after Maus, who had just reached the grove.

'Mr Maus!' Aenlin called and waved her hat to attract his attention. 'Mr Maus, wait!'

The elderly man wearing a jerkin, knee-length breeches, stockings and buckled shoes, reined in the donkey and turned in the saddle. He looked surprised to see the two women. 'Good day to you, young ladies,' he said them in a friendly voice, tipping his broad-brimmed hat. 'Have we met?'

'I told you: no trap,' Aenlin whispered to Tahmina. To him she said, 'No, you don't know us, Mr Maus.' She took a deep breath and wiped the sweat from her brow. 'We are here about an inheritance.' She kept her hat in her hand for now.

Jacobus Maus obviously didn't believe her, for he had spotted the rapier and the pistols hanging from Aenlin's baldric. 'Is this to be a robbery?' He touched the hilt of his sword. 'Be warned! I was once—'

'No, no, by ... the angel!' Aenlin had almost said Lucifer's name, which would probably not have made the rope-trader relax. 'I am Aenlin Kane, daughter of Solomon and Elisabeth.' She took the signet ring from her pocket and showed it to him. A sudden ray of sunlight illuminated it, making the crest shine. 'My mother was supposed to identify herself by showing this ring to you. I carry with me papers that prove whose child I am.' She let out another deep breath and stepped to one side of the donkey. Her heart was beating at a normal rate again. 'My father wrote to me – he said that you are the trustee of his estate, dear sir.'

Maus clapped his hands. 'Good gracious! On this day of all days, duty comes calling? How long I have been waiting for this!' He slid from the saddle and took Aenlin's hand. He thoroughly inspected the ring, checking the engravings. 'It does look to be the right one. My condolences – and congratulations, young Miss Kane.' He smiled at Tahmina, probably assuming, like everybody did, that she was Aenlin's maid. 'Come, accompany me while I take care of my business, then we will take care of your inheritance. It will soon be finished.'

Aenlin thought it might be rude to ask what Mr Maus was doing in the forest, far away from all spying eyes and ears, although it didn't sound likely to be indecent or forbidden, else he would not have invited them to watch. Or would he?

'You knew my father?' She threw back the ebony strand of hair and put her hat back on.

'No.'

That was a surprise. 'But ... how did you end up with this task, then?'

'Through *my* father. Our parents knew each other from way back when; some event in the Black Forest. Father didn't like to talk about it, whatever it was.' He turned from the trail onto a path someone else had used recently, judging by the trampled grass.

Soon afterwards, they met three men and two women. Their garb under the open, expensive cloaks showed them to be well off; it was clear none of them had known hunger or hardship. They saluted Maus, tipping their hats as if it were completely normal to meet in a remote part of the forest, then led the way onwards. One of the men carried a flat, oblong box.

'Anyway, he promised to help your father,' Maus continued, 'and thus, my family became the keepers of the inheritance.'

'Ah. Well.' Tahmina kept looking around, tightly gripping the ebony staff covered in carvings. 'Where does this little procession go?'

'We'll soon find out,' Aenlin said, considering it inappropriate to question the rope-trader after he had invited them to join him.

Tahmina rolled her eyes.

'To a small pond. A hidden spot.' Maus led the way into a small clearing from where the enticing scent of flowers arose.

From the grassy floor sprouted the most beautiful blossoms, with bees and other insects buzzing around, collecting pollen. The sun fell through the canopy, glinting on the green and the nearby pond covered in water lilies.

This rural idyll was ruined by a small man in a black cloak who looked to have been put into this tableau by an evil painter specifically to mar the beauty of nature.

Aenlin guessed the man to be in his forties. She noticed his wiry build, which made her think of a professional dancer.

Beneath a fashionable hat with a long black feather, he wore an elaborate wig, like that of a French noble, with thick curls hanging down to his chest. A neat goatee and moustache highlighted his face. The man was incredibly handsome, even at his age.

'By the stars,' said Tahmina, sounding impressed. 'This is the first time I have seen such a man.'

'Probably some nobleman.' Aenlin wondered whether they were to witness some forbidden deal – a relics trade, perhaps, or some obscure occult objects changing ownership.

The noble had tethered a handsome black stallion to a tree so the animal could crop the lush grass. Two sash-like baldrics with slender daggers hung from the saddlebags.

'You are probably wondering what we are doing here.' Maus laughed and made a deprecating gesture. 'No, this is no demon summoning. We are not so desperate in Hamburg to do as other principalities do.'

'Reassuring.' Tahmina leaned on her staff. 'Who is this man, Mr Maus?'

'He calls himself Caspar von und zu dem Dorffe, but I doubt that's his true name.' He raised a hand in greeting.

The man tipped his hat and answered with a perfect courtly bow, then he righted himself again and dropped his cloak flamboyantly, revealing black clothing with silver embroidery that would have befitted a count or some other extraordinarily rich man.

'No nobleman, then?' Aenlin found this behaviour strange. 'What is this all about, Mr Maus?'

A man and a woman who had been in the procession approached the unknown man. Two others stayed with Maus, while the last man put down the flat box and opened it. It held two wheellock pistols, complete with rammer, powder flask, pliers, musket balls – all the accessories to load them.

'A duel?' The rope-trader did not look in the least like a trained killer to Aenlin. 'Mr Maus, what are you up to? You are not even of noble birth.'

'But I have my honour! I know that I'll win against this fop!' The rope-trader's voice was full of anger and resentment.

Aenlin noticed the closed pistol holsters attached to the saddle of the beautiful black horse. Caspar von und zu dem Dorffe looked to be an experienced user of firearms. This was not going to end well for the rope-trader. 'Wouldn't an apology be enough?'

'No.' Maus approached the man with the small box. 'I know you are worried about your inheritance. Do not be. One shot and we can go home.' He took a glove from his pocket and put it on his right hand.

'Have you ever shot before, Mr Maus?' Aenlin hoped to hear that he handled a pistol at least once a week.

'A while ago. Occasionally. It will be more than adequate.'

'Lucifer help him,' Aenlin murmured and crossed herself the wrong way round.

Caspar strode across the clearing, elegantly sidestepping the flowers to avoid crushing them underfoot, which was all the odder since he obviously had no qualms about shooting a man. 'Good day, everyone,' he shouted with exuberant conceit. 'I do not know the two young ladies, my dear Mouse. Whom do we have here?'

'These are Aenlin Kane and her maid, from England,' the rope-trader said. 'We have business to take care of, so suffer your wound and let me make those ladies happy.'

'The Mouse, a philanderer!' Caspar made another scrape and waved his hat as if chasing flies in a perfectly flamboyant manner. 'I apologise should this gentleman soon be unable to speak another word. I am sorry for your concerns. However, that's the way Mouse here wanted it.'

'No more words,' Maus shouted at him, 'or I will forget myself, put a ball through your grin right here and now and turn your stupid beard into the world's smallest rope!'

'You hear that? Now I should be the one demanding satisfaction. However, I'll let Mouse go first.' Caspar gestured invitingly.

Under the watchful eyes of the participants and their seconds, the wheellock pistols were checked.

'Is this your first duel, Mr vom Dorffe?' Aenlin asked.

'Yes – and it is *von und zu dem Dorffe*.' Caspar took the round projectiles and inspected them scrupulously. 'I hope these are not infernal musket balls, Mouse. You're lucky that I can detect neither secret scorings nor markings.'

'They are not necessary for this art,' Tahmina commented offhandedly.

'Oh, so the maid is well-informed.' Caspar looked up and his grey-blue eyes scrutinised first her, then the ebony staff she leaned on. 'No "sir"? No subservience when talking to me?' he remarked pointedly. 'And then there are these symbols on your little staff . . . you're a fascinating maid.'

'So, this is your first duel,' Aenlin said, adjusting her hat. This shooting might yet come to a good end. 'How did it—?'

'My first one in Altona.' Caspar chose a loaded weapon and let the barrel rest easily against his shoulder, his index finger lightly touching the trigger guard.

'How many have you had altogether?' she enquired with a sigh.

Caspar squinted his eyes shut a little and looked up at the clouds drifting above the clearing.

'What's up?' Maus prompted. 'Tell her, so we can begin.'

'I am still counting, Mouse.' Caspar made a strained grimace. 'Here we go. Exactly three hundred and ninety-nine.' He knocked against his chest to prove that he was not wearing metal beneath his jacket. 'Yet here I stand. Not always unharmed, but alive.'

'Heavens!' Maus shouted out in horror. 'Three hundred and ninety-nine? I didn't know that!'

'You challenge a duellist without even knowing it?' Aenlin saw her inheritance disappear with the first shot. 'Mr Maus, cancel the duel. Buy your way out of this, but—'

'Now, now! I want this to be number four hundred,' Caspar said. 'This man sells me incredibly bad ropes, I insult and slight him, he demands satisfaction and refuses to give me my money back.' He pointed to the clearing. 'Voilà. So here we are. One of us will soon be on the ground. Number four hundred.' He grinned. 'Mouse over.' Aenlin knew duels of honour had become a real plague in England, because people reached for their rapiers, swords or other blades far too readily – but first blood as satisfaction was easy to do with bladed weapons without cutting your opponent to pieces, and honour was restored.

A pistol, however, tore bad holes over such a short distance, even if less powder was used in loading the weapons for duels than for battles. Aenlin had shot carcasses during her training sessions and had seen what musket balls could do to fragile flesh.

The rope-trader's hand was trembling like an aspen leaf. He would lose.

'Stay out of this, dear lady.' Caspar stood bolt upright and waited for Maus to turn his back to him. 'Find a place where Mouse cannot hit you accidentally.'

'On my command you will take ten steps forward, turn around and fire at will,' the referee declared. 'If you shoot first and miss, you must wait for your opponent's shot. If someone flees, I'll shoot him.' He drew his own pistol from the holster at his belt. 'If both miss, the procedure will be repeated until someone is wounded. If both opponents suffer wounds, the last man standing is the winner. If both fall at the same time, the one with the more grievous wound loses. Or the one who dies.' He waited until both men had nodded affirmatively. 'Then one . . . two . . .'

Aenlin stood next to Tahmina. 'We need to act! I cannot rely on Lucifer's intervention alone.'

' . . . five . . . six . . .'

'If you stop the duel, Caspar will demand satisfaction from you. It is easy to see that you are an experienced fighter, but that won't help us.' She toyed with her staff. 'By the djinni of Shiraz! None of my powers can stop musket balls. I would be helpful against devas, yatus or common spells, but simple gunpowder and lead? I am no match for that.'

' . . . ten!'

Aenlin held her breath.

Maus whirled around, almost losing his balance, and shot at the duellist. The pistol fired with a bang; billowing gun smoke obscured Aenlin's vision.

When the smoke had cleared, Caspar stood unharmed, his body turned sideways to offer his opponent a smaller target. Aenlin realised again how slender he was: a good precaution, given his chosen profession.

'Now it's my turn, Mouse.'

'No, have mercy,' Maus begged and dropped the pistol.

'Stay where you are,' the duel judge admonished him and he aimed his weapon at the rope-trader. 'You know you may not move until von und zu dem Dorffe has fired.'

'It will not hurt,' Caspar promised and narrowed one eye to a slit to get a better aim. 'Name a body part, Mouse. I do not wish to be uncooperative. I can be generous in my four hundredth duel.'

'My leg. The left one,' Maus whispered and closed his eyes. His lips moved in silent prayer.

The pistol went off with a bang and Maus' hat went flying. He lost a few long strands of hair, but was otherwise unharmed.

'Missed on purpose,' Aenlin happily whispered and flung her arms around Tahmina. 'He missed him on purpose—'

Rustling and cracking noises erupted in the underbrush.

'Stop,' yelled a loud voice. 'No one move a muscle! You are under arrest.' A man carrying a long-barrelled musket stepped into the clearing, his weapon cocked, its fuse burning. He wore a dented, rusty harness and a helmet with a hole from a musket ball in it. The foliage disgorged more men in simple garb with halberds and firearms – villagers from Altona. 'You are wanted, Caspar vom Dorf. Your bounty—'

'The name is *von und zu dem Dorffe*, you Elbe pisser. Well, the odds in this game are too poor for my tastes. Count me out.' With two swift strides Caspar reached his horse, undid the reins from the tree and jumped on its back. 'I do not care what is going on here. I won't have my number four hundred taken from me.'

The first shots rang out: the musketeers were resting their heavy guns on branch forks and shooting at the fleeing man.

At once, Tahmina and Aenlin ducked and looked for cover.

Lucifer, if you have sent those people, they are too late, thought Aenlin.

Jacobus Maus cried out and clutched his chest – only to fall down seconds later with blood welling from the hole in his jerkin. One of the heavy balls had pierced his chest.

'No! No, that—' Aenlin stammered and watched the rope-trader breathe his last amidst the flowers, his eyes wide with pain.

'I would recommend the ladies not linger,' Caspar shouted at them as he dodged through a gap between the trees, the trunks providing cover, for the muskets required awkward reloading.

Aenlin and Tahmina heeded his counsel and ran.

Sitting behind the hedge, his sabre drawn, Melchior Pieck watched the more courageous men from Altona chasing the seconds, the referee and Caspar von und zu dem Dorffe. A shepherd had seen the odd group entering the woods and told the village there were strangers worth robbing, or so Melchior had gathered from the attackers' conversations.

He walked slowly backwards, covering Aenlin Kane's and Tahmina's retreat. He could not blame those poor people for trying to seize rich folk from Hamburg and rob them. These were hard times.

'Caspar von und zu dem Dorffe,' Melchior chuckled. He had heard of the man, who was wanted in a number of German principalities, regions and cities. This person wasn't even a nobleman. His trick shot with the pistol, however, was without equal. Melchior was almost tempted to believe that he really did have four hundred duels under his belt. The price on his head also suggested it. Alas, he had no chance to seize and kill the man to earn coin. His Lordship's mission came first, and in any case, it promised to be far more lucrative.

Suddenly a man in threadbare clothing carrying a pitchfork appeared in front of Melchior. 'Here's another one,' he yelled with a start and raised the dirty prongs. 'Hurry up!'

'You should have stayed in your plague hole.' Melchior batted the pitchfork aside and pierced the man's throat with his sabre. His opponent collapsed, gurgling and spitting blood.

Melchior turned around and started jogging, not wanting to lose sight of Aenlin and Tahmina. A mission was a mission. He hurried on and saw the women's silhouettes less than twenty paces ahead. Soon, they would reach Hamburg's city gates and be safe.

But not from him.

Free Imperial City of Hamburg, April 1629

Nicolas sat on one side of the large stained, carved table. In a battle it would have provided great cover, as the heavy oak would have been a good shield. At that moment, the table served as a barrier between him and his potential employers, who were ignoring him and speaking quietly amongst themselves. He heard the name *Barthel* several times, and sometimes one of the two men pointed at him while saying it.

Across from Nicolas sat Claas de Hertoghe and Hans de Hertoghe II, iconic examples of middle-aged Dutch merchants. Their embroidered clothing, jerkins and shirts, puffed breeches and buckled shoes spoke of noble understatement trying to avoid coming across as too wealthy. Nonetheless, the lush interior of the house by the lower port spoke for itself. Members of the Company simply had to be rich.

Behind Nicolas, Jäcklein, Statius and Moritz were leaning against the wall. They remained silent, leaving the negotiation to their leader. None of them wanted to be the reason the merchants found out they were talking to the wrong landsknechts. First, they were not sure how quickly they would be able to find their way out of this house full of nooks and crannies; second, and more importantly, it was still possible that they could get a profitable mission. Third, they had had to leave their weapons at the door.

The blond de Hertoghe brothers had neatly trimmed, light beards that left the cheeks bare. They were talking to each other in their native language so the mercenaries wouldn't know what they were discussing.

'You sent for us,' Nicolas said with a smile, trying keep up the appearance that he was a man called Barthel. He knew that neither he nor his men smelled of roses, which had become especially obvious in these spotlessly clean rooms. The servant had already opened the windows, through which floated the sounds of the busy trading port. 'Well, here we are.'

This prod was intended to start a conversation that, best-case scenario, would end with a contract before the intended recipients of the missive showed up, because then there would be trouble, potentially even a brawl.

Claas de Hertoghe turned to him and clasped his fingers. 'Yes, we have sent for you. Where are your horses, Captain?'

'My horses? Oh, the horses! Yes, they . . . they died.' Nicolas had been afraid there would be complications like this. 'On the way. The nags ate the wrong weed and that was that.'

'I see. Well, we can remedy that. We should be able to procure horses.' Claas reached for quill, ink and paper to make notes. 'I saw that your cart is in pretty bad shape.'

'Yes, after an attack by Danish marauders we had to break camp quicker than planned. That's where we lost a lot of our equipment,' Nicolas said, smelling an opportunity to replenish their worldly goods. He wondered if the merchant was buying the excuses.

'What do you and your men need, Captain?'

'Some harnesses and helmets, a bidenhänder, two muskets and two pistols per man,' he told the merchant, expecting a disapproving glare from Claas or his brother, who was sitting next to Claas unmoving, like a tailor's dummy. Claas' attentive gaze lingered on the landsknechts as if he was trying to read their minds.

'Fucking Danes,' Nicolas added. 'We stood no chance against fifty of them, although we killed or badly wounded thirty.'

Jäcklein, Statius and Moritz quietly muttered their consent and some choice curses.

Claas kept writing, repeatedly dipping the quill in the ink. The tip scratched audibly across the paper. 'What kind?'

'Well, Danes, you know. Ugly and crapulous.'

Statius suppressed a laugh.

Claas looked up, his blond eyebrows twitched briefly. 'I was talking about the pistols and muskets, Captain. What kind? Fuse, wheellock, or this new flintlock?' He caressed the soft feather with the index finger of his other hand. 'I can get any-thing. Harquebuses too, if necessary. However, they will get in the way. You are supposed to be quick – and it would be best if you do not fight at all.'

'Yes, I agree, Trader de Hertoghe.' Nicolas had a hard time hiding his enthusiasm. His principals were willing to give him whatever he wanted! Firearms, horses, armour, new wagon – he had never had a better mission. Normally, landsknechts had to buy their equipment themselves. Strike a light! 'We will take the flintlocks.'

Claas made some more notes. 'I will have everything loaded onto the cart. In two days, you will be set to go.' He nodded at his brother, who leaned to the side and took a ring of keys from his belt. At first, the table hid what Hans was doing, but he could hear clicking and clinking noises. Finally, Hans opened a lid.

Nicolas sat upright when he saw the ironclad chest on the floor, from which the taciturn brother was taking first one, then another and then a third and fourth leather pouch. He put them next to one another on the oak table.

'Four hundred guilders, as agreed,' Claas said airily. 'You will receive the rest of the thousand upon your return, Captain.'

'Yes. As agreed.' Nicolas noticed that his voice sounded higher than usual. *Keep a stiff upper lip*, he told himself sternly, and glanced over his shoulder to give his men an admonishing look as he heard them cheering quietly. They too had to exercise restraint if they were to keep up appearances.

'I will keep this' – Claas took one of the pouches – 'for all the equipment, including gunpowder, musket balls and horses.' He gave the pouch back to his brother, who threw it into the chest, where it landed with a hearty clinking noise.

Nicolas didn't mind losing those one hundred guilders at all. As soon as they came back from their mission, they would get another six hundred on top. But for what kind of work?

He guessed that they were to go somewhere quickly and bring something back to Hamburg.

But would they really?

It would have been possible to grab the guilders and the equipment and disappear, never to be seen again – of course, they'd have to stay clear of Hamburg for a few years, but even then, the West India Company did not forget.

Also, the de Hertoghe brothers might then offer that pouch of one hundred guilders as prize on their heads. There were people in Altona – the barmaid, for one – who would be able to describe them well. They would never be able to work as landsknechts again.

So Nicolas decided not to betray the Hertoghes. He made a second attempt to learn about the mission that was filling their pockets. 'Let's go over the strategy again.'

Claas stroked his blond beard, two golden rings shimmering in the light that came through the windows. 'Now that you mention it, Captain, I do have to inform you about a change in the plan.' His brother handed him a letter. 'This message reached us almost a week ago. You now have to get five people from Bamberg.' He handed the missive across the table to the mercenary. 'These five. Their addresses are listed here. With your money you will be buying a coach. Two of them are too old to ride.'

'I see.' Nicolas didn't understand. *Bamberg?* That was many days' ride away in the far south. They would have to cross regions that belonged to the Catholics one day and Protestant areas the next. 'What do we need to know about these people? The new ones, I mean.' To him, the conversation with the de Hertoghes was as exhausting as walking through a powder chamber with a burning fuse: the smallest mistake, the slightest negligence, and everything would go off.

'Respectable people, we were told.' Claas took a look at his notes. 'They are Protestants afraid of falling victim to the

Emperor's Edict of Restitution. They absolutely do not want to renounce their faith – which is why they will feel more secure in Hamburg.'

Nicolas had heard of the Edict but didn't know exactly what it meant, other than it had led to many Protestant Dukes and Princes, cities and monasteries losing huge parts of their estates and their wealth. It had lit the fuse of the next war, and that was good for his business. 'I will bring them to Hamburg safe and sound.'

'That's what I wanted to hear, Captain.' Hans took a scroll from the inexhaustible desk drawer and handed it to him. It unrolled to reveal two copies of a contract. 'Let us get down to business. Your signature and your seal, and your mission will begin two days hence.'

'Have you hired any others, my dear de Hertoghe?' Nicolas perused the lines in small print to learn from whom they had stolen this mission. He found only that name, which meant nothing to him: Barthel Hofmeister.

However, he found exactly what the second rate looked like: six hundred guilders to share amongst them and two hundred more per person – because the number of people to save had grown.

Nicolas stared at the sum. *Jesus, Mary and Joseph! That would make all of them filthy rich.*

He hid his joy by extensively clearing his throat and signed the contract – as illegibly as possible – as Barthel Hofmeister. For want of a seal, he used the pommel of his dagger, which he pressed forcefully into the wax.

Claas did not comment on this unusual way of sealing. 'I am still negotiating with one or two additional agents. Those negotiations will be resolved before you leave. Here is your copy, Captain.' He pointed at one paragraph with the tip of his quill. 'Don't forget this. I hope it serves as an incentive. Where do I send word about news concerning the mission?' He rose, and his silent brother followed suit. For the de Hertoghes, the conversation was over.

'We will be in the Golden Swan,' Nicolas said, also standing. They had not yet put up anywhere, but with this handsome sum they could easily afford that noble inn. They'd have enough to eat, enough to drink and a soft bed too! With his mind reeling with joy, he was unable to think straight. The bags of coins and the prospect of even more made him dizzy.

'Good. Then come to the Company office in the lower port two days hence, at seven in the morning.' Claas pointed at the door. 'God bless you, Captain.'

Nicolas bowed. 'A good day to you and your brother.' He took the three heavy pouches with fingers that were clumsy from joy and passed one each to Statius and to Jäcklein. His men stood against the panelled wall sharing an astonished grin that no painter in this world could have done justice to.

They muttered their farewells, bowing several times, and went into a dark hallway. After several hallways and junctions and just before they stepped out onto the cobblestones, a servant gave them back their rapiers.

'I'm so happy I could piss myself,' Statius shouted, doing a little dance on the spot. 'We're rich!' He showered the pouch containing the coins with kisses. 'I'll cut a hole into the leather and royally swive these gold coins!'

'We will be even richer once we bring those five people back here. Then we'll be paid again and there will be two hundred more for you, you and you.' Nicolas stabbed his index finger at the chest of each of the three landsknechts. 'Oh, and for me.'

'I'll get a musket. A shiny new one!' Jäcklein exhaled ecstatically. '*Bang, bang!* And it's game over for the enemy!'

'You can't even handle it.' Statius laughed at him. 'None of us can. Except for Nicolas. He can kill with any piece of kit you give him.' He weighed the pouch in his hand and twirled the tips of his moustache. 'That sound soothes my pure white soul. Money. Wealth!'

'Pure white soul? Oh, of course.' Jäcklein sighed and caressed the pouch. 'I would have had to creep through barrages of gunfire for years for this, with holes in my soles and hunger in my belly.'

'It sounds easy.' Young Moritz smiled down at them. 'To Bamberg and back.'

'If the weather stays like this, it will be quick.' Nicolas gave the giant his pouch. 'Our young man gets all the pouches. He will guard them with his life.'

'Yes, of course. No one would dare touch him.' Jäcklein threw Moritz a second pouch, which he caught skilfully, as if the metal inside were weightless.

Statius hesitated. 'I'd like to keep my coins.' He opened the drawstring and took a handful of them out, making them tinkle in his hand.

'Stop it and hand them over. We have to divide them anyway.' Nicolas recognised another of his friend's flaws: avarice. 'You'll get your fair share, Stats.'

With a click of his tongue, Statius threw Moritz the last pouch. 'Take good care of it, my giant child. For every missing coin I'll cut off a circular piece of your skin.'

'You won't have to,' Moritz replied, putting the landsknechts' pay into his bag. 'No one is taking this from me, I swear.'

'I have one more question: what about this paragraph he showed you?' Jäcklein took the contracts from beneath Nicolas' arm. 'That was clearly some kind of threat.' Together, he and Nicolas looked for the passage.

'Who did we steal the mission from?'

Statius had to wait a while, but then Nicolas told him the name.

'Barthel Hofmeister!' Statius laughed out loud.

'You know him?' Moritz put his giant hands on the bag, forming a fortress of flesh and bone for their treasure.

'He fought with Wallenstein's hordes when they chased the last of the Danes from the banks of the Elbe. I thought he had stayed in Altona and died of the plague.' Statius toyed with two coins, looking around for where he might spend them in the port. There were plenty of taverns, inns and low pubs.

'Have we not been to Altona, though? Where the plague was?' Moritz looked terrified.

'The plague is everywhere, lad.' Statius produced a fine-meshed cotton pouch containing dried leaves from under his colourful shirt. 'This helps. A *medico* who had the knowledge from an army surgeon gave it to me – as soon as I feel an itch in my armpit that could grow into a boil, I burn it out and inhale the smoke.'

'What's in there?' Moritz curiously smelled the little pouch.

Statius held up a coin between thumb and index finger. 'Give me a few of those and I'll tell you.'

'Stop teasing the boy,' Nicolas said. 'We'll buy him real landsknecht garb so people can see that he's one of us.' He found the passage that de Hertoghe had indicated and read it.

That's not good.

'Damn it,' Nicolas said.

'To hell with the grocers!' Jäcklein exclaimed after reading the paragraph himself. 'Mind, at least he thinks we're someone else if it all goes wrong.'

'Why? What did we sign?' Statius clutched his coins as if he were afraid the Company would send someone to take them away from him.

'If we fail, it's the gallows for us. In Venice.' Nicolas cursed soundly. His joy melted like ice in the sunshine. No amount of money was worth that. He should have known the job sounded too good to be true.

'You look as if you could use a beer,' Statius said.

'I need two beers,' Jäcklein added sulkily.

'I'll gladly drink with you.' Moritz still exuded confidence and cheerfulness. 'My new garb will look great. I'm looking forward to being dressed like you – like a *real* landsknecht.' He shook his black locks. 'But I won't cut my hair. It's impenetrable to lice – my hair eats them up as if they were tasty snacks.'

The mercenaries laughed.

'Stay exactly as you are, boy.' Nicolas lifted his arm to pat Moritz's broad shoulder. It felt as if he was touching iron. 'We may yet need your merry ways.'

'Off to the Golden Swan – the first round is on me!' Statius leaped onto the cart and grabbed the reins. Moritz sat next to their weapons and equipment to hold them in place while Nicolas and Jäcklein took up position walking on either side the cart.

'Bamberg,' the small landsknecht muttered. 'There was something rotten in that damn city, but I can't call it to mind right now.'

'Ah well,' Nicolas said, 'I don't need to hear it right now. First, I want a beer.'

'You have to pay your colonels very well or they will loot on their own.'

Albrecht von Wallenstein,
military leader during the Thirty Years' War

CAPITULUM III

Free Imperial City of Hamburg, April 1629

Aenlin and Tahmina reached the city gate without any further problems.

The bandits, who looked like they were all desperately poor people from Altona, had focused on seizing the duellist and the wealthy seconds because they promised the best loot. The sight of Aenlin's weapons, however, had dampened the robbers' courage.

Huffing and puffing, but walking slowly to avoid too much attention, the two women entered Hamburg as the spring sun sank beneath the horizon.

'I cannot believe it,' Aenlin said angrily as she stopped by the roadside. She took off her hat, revealing her dark hair, and fanned herself with it. The ebony strand fell into her face. 'This man spares Maus, but some accursed ball from a musket kills him! I almost had my inheritance!'

'Yes and without it, you will not return to England,' Tahmina said predictively. This time, the moist stains on her night-blue gown showed she too was sweating.

Aenlin looked around for an inn. She was incredibly thirsty, but she wouldn't drink the water, not with all those animal-cules in it. Beer was the better choice, as the heating during the brewing process mostly killed them off. 'Let's go to the Catskin.' She pointed at a tavern with open shutters, through which lively music resounded into the street. 'Then I'll go to the rope shop. Maus will most certainly have told his family what to do if he dies and someone with a signet ring drops by.'

What excitement! Aenlin put her hat back on. Her legs felt heavy and she was looking forward to putting them up. The situation had almost turned into her first real fight ... against destitute, impoverished people who could eke out a living only through banditry.

'What if Maus has not taken any precautions?' Tahmina dabbed at her moist face with her loose sleeve. She sounded quite convinced that the merchant had not thought of this circumstance. 'What do we do then?'

Aenlin would have loved to declare that such misfortune could never be the case, but her friend was right, of course: she had to assume the worst. 'We'll search everything. The shop, his flat, every nook and cranny.'

'Against his family's will? No one will believe us, will they?'

Aenlin hated these constant arguments. How could she work this way? 'By Lucifer, then I'll break in!'

'If you get caught, you will be put on trial.' Tahmina clearly enjoyed ripping apart every plan that Aenlin proposed. She spun her staff around her hand several times. 'I do not know what the sentence is for burglary and theft in Hamburg. Maybe it will even turn into robbery if you have to defend yourself.'

'That sounds as if you want me to do this on my own.' Aenlin gave her a mock blow against her upper arm. 'What a great companion you are.'

'The best you will ever get, my dear.'

Briefly, their gazes met and the women exchanged warm smiles from deep within their hearts, from their conjoined souls.

The peaceful moment ended as a horse stopped abruptly in front of them, huffing loudly and prancing. The animal's broad black chest pushed into the mystic, who almost lost her balance until Aenlin steadied her.

From the back of the skittish black horse came a familiar voice. 'Good thing I am a cautious man. This is not a good place to linger.' It was Caspar von und zu dem Dorffe, the black-clad duellist. 'Two pretty women escape the murderous mob from Altona, only to be ridden down by me.' He calmed the nervous stallion and with his right hand, removed his hat from the long, brown-haired wig he wore. 'Miss Kane and her maid: you should pay more attention to your surroundings in the future. Once again, I bid you a good day.' He steered the black horse around them.

Aenlin had an idea. 'Wait!' She grabbed the horse's bridle to stop him from riding away. 'Can I have a word with you?'

'As long as you don't want to duel me like that stupid Mouse . . . ? Wait, I'll join you.' The duellist dismounted and they moved to the side of the road to avoid being shouted at or colliding with oncoming traffic. Commerce in Hamburg waited for no one. 'Were you headed for the Catskin?' he asked as he smoothed his black goatee and moustache with a quick movement of his hand.

'Yes. Can I offer you a drink?'

Caspar shook his head. 'That's a friendly offer, but I'm in this beautiful Hanseatic city on different business and this tavern is not on my list of places to visit. You may, however, have that word you asked for.' The man nodded at Tahmina. 'I'll even grant you two if this weird beauty would like to say something as well.'

Aenlin didn't like him refusing her. Most people became more open and talkative after a beer. But she still wanted to try her luck. 'First I would like to thank you for trying to keep Jacobus Maus alive.'

'A tragedy, yes?' Caspar glanced from Aenlin to Tahmina with a gaze that was full of regret. 'But we were lucky that those predatory peasants couldn't handle muskets. Otherwise, we would now be lying naked in the forest, with foxes and wild dogs eating our cold, dead bodies.' He grinned. 'Was that the word you wanted?'

'No. I had something to discuss with the friendly Mr Maus. His death got in the way, though,' Aenlin said, ignoring Tahmina's warning tug at her coat. 'He was the keeper of my inheritance. You will understand that I am now desperate, thinking that I might have lost that inheritance. Did he mention anything about this?'

'Regrettable, very regrettable. I am afraid I cannot help you. The only business I had with the rope-trader was that I met him at the Company and wanted to buy rope from him. You know the rest of the story.' Caspar remounted his horse. 'He had no family – that's what he told me when we were discussing our duel. I wanted to know whom to notify of his death.'

Aenlin saw her father's last gift vanish, hidden in some secret place she might never find. Artefacts, treasures, jewels, whatever it was her father had amassed for them . . . all lost. 'Then I thank—'

'Not so fast,' Caspar said. 'There is one thing you might try. I advise you to make enquiries with the Company.'

'What company?'

'The West India Company. It has an office in the lower port.' He caressed the black stallion's muscular neck. 'If I understood him correctly, Mr Maus deposited something there. The Dutch have the most secure strongboxes, a vault with the thickest walls and an iron door that many a thief has had a tough time trying to get through. Maybe Maus has stored it there, yes? Then your inheritance wouldn't be completely lost.' He donned his hat atop his wig again. 'Godspeed with your parley. The Comte and I must continue our journey.'

'Your horse is called "Comte"?' Laughing, Tahmina leaned

on her staff. 'The high-and-mighty ladies and gentlemen you encounter will not like this.'

'That's what I'm counting on. I introduce them to the Comte every time, a stylish beast with a noble pedigree, which most of the aristocracy cannot claim to have. Any of them I can shoot is a benefit to humanity. Four hundred duels, two hundred high-borns killed and more than a hundred gravely wounded. Impressive, don't you think?' Caspar set his black horse in motion. 'Better find another inn. Adieu, young ladies! May fortune be in your favour.'

And with that, he disappeared into the warren of streets and alleys.

'There is still hope for my inheritance.' Aenlin tried not to rejoice prematurely. She had never dealt with the West India Company before. *How can I prove to them that Jacobus Maus is dead?* His corpse had probably been looted and was now being carried towards the sea by the Elbe. The notion that people would believe her seemed highly unlikely.

'We have to make a plan for our parley with the merchants. In here.' She entered the Catskin, dragging Tahmina along. 'Come on! I'm still thirsty.'

'But Caspar . . .'

Aenlin ignored her companion's words and dragged her inside.

Most of the patrons of the crowded tavern were travellers. Dust-covered clothes, luggage was piled everywhere and various languages and remarkably diverse styles of attire could be discerned in every corner of the establishment. Aenlin could not place some of the tongues, strange to her ears as they were. The war had brought people of all nationalities to the German lands. Soldiers from all over Europe and Asia had come to join the various armies.

Some young landsknechts, easily recognisable by their flashy garb and the long daggers and rapiers on their belts, were among the patrons. Surely they were in town to look for jobs as guards, sentries or cargo sentinels. After the Danish retreat, there was not much else for mercenaries to do.

The women quickly found two empty spots on a bench.

The odours of sweat; of food, tobacco smoke and herbs burned as protection against fleas, bugs and ailments; of clothing in desperate need of washing, all mixed and assailed their noses.

There was loud storytelling and laughter. Here, someone told a tale of some battle; over there, someone was spreading news from the surrounding countryside; a group sang along to the tunes of three minstrels in the corner, while others played cards.

'Oh, djinni of the desert,' Tahmina moaned. She leaned her ebony staff against the wall, near enough that she could reach it easily. 'What chaos! What a stench!'

'I find it exciting.' Aenlin looked around, working out what to tell the Company. Her famous last name might help. 'If I can find a—'

A woman in a lace dress and a dirty apron put two tankards of beer in front of them, sloshing foam over the rims. 'That's one kreutzer. Don't try to give me sham money: I'll know.' She obviously recited this mantra many times a day.

'But I don't drink . . .' Tahmina started, but Aenlin had already put the coin on the table.

'Thanks,' she said quickly as the woman weighed it in her hand, then pocketed it and left to dispense more tankards. Clearly it was the law that everybody in the Catskin had to drink. Always.

'I will not drink that,' Tahmina said firmly, and she adjusted her hat on her brown hair. 'It tastes awful – and it is alcohol.'

'You can catch any number of diseases from the water here,' Aenlin pointed out.

'Good point. Innkeeper!' Tahmina shouted. 'A cup of hot water, please. Freshly boiled.'

'Coming right up, noble lady,' answered the woman in passing. 'Water from the Elbe or from the port? I could also offer you water from the Inner Alster. That is the tastiest one.'

Other patrons of the inn laughed, but Tahmina ignored them.

Aenlin tasted the beer, which was lighter than the brew she had become used to in London. It would be hard to get drunk on it, which was a good thing. 'All right then: the West India Company. I'll show them my paperwork and the ring and tell them that we were present when Jacobus Maus died. We could check if there is a bookseller who carries a collection of my father's adventures – to make an impression, you know. I will also swear an oath. And so will you. What do you think?'

'An oath.' Tahmina exhaled. 'On the Bible? You probably will not swear this oath.' In a whisper, she added, 'As a follower of Lucifer.'

'Why do you all hate him so much? Without him, there would probably be no Bible.' Aenlin had lowered her voice, too. No one was supposed to know the strange path she had chosen. Her father might have been a Puritan, but that didn't mean she had to share his beliefs and ideas.

Amid peals of laughter, the serving woman brought Tahmina her boiling water, together with some scraps of wood.

'For the taste,' the innkeeper explained, pocketing another kreuzer, for it was as expensive as the beer.

'But the Bible was written by the enemy,' Tahmina said, 'to vilify your Lucifer – isn't that what you told me?'

'More or less,' Aenlin said. 'Adam's and Eve's eviction from Paradise is God's fault. He ordered Lucifer to lead the first two humans into temptation, although he knew exactly what would happen; that they would fail his test.'

'Why?' Tahmina sipped her hot water and shuddered. The heat had not improved the taste.

'Because the trial was too hard for their naïve souls. Any child

would have taken the fruit.' Aenlin took a gulp of beer against
the thirst and the rage she was talking herself into. 'Then God
blamed Lucifer and the humans to make himself look better.'

'Better you should keep this view to yourself in the German
lands.' Soothingly, Tahmina put her hand on Aenlin's forearm.
'Excuse me. I know all that. I only wanted to tease you.'

There were a lot of arguments on the tip of Aenlin's tongue,
but she kept them to herself. She was angry about people's gul-
libility: that they let the claim that Lucifer was the evil one in
this story go unchallenged. *God* was the real tempter. He could
have created Paradise differently if he had cared. Besides, he
was the one who had denied Adam and Eve the tree of knowledge – he'd even made it taboo. They had only wanted to be
mature . . . autonomous.

'The Company,' she said before she could become even more
upset. 'Our goal.'

'I think the Dutch will give you what is yours,' Tahmina said,
taking from her pocket a small pouch of herbs. She sprinkled
them into the water and the smell of mint arose from her cup;
it was fresh – but it had no chance against the odours of the
Catskin. 'You have everything you need to prove who you are.
Why would they deny you?'

'Let's find out.' Aenlin looked through the thick, dirty windowpanes at the darkening streets. People, horses and carts became
fleeting shadows and silhouettes and sometimes glowing spots
rushed by when somebody carried a lit lantern. 'But not today.
We'd better try—'

Next to her, Tahmina cried out and drops of water splattered
the table and the floor.

A girl of maybe eight years, dressed in a simple baggy linen
dress, had grabbed the cup of hot water and thrown it at
Tahmina. Tahmina's right cheek and her neck were already
reddened and painful.

With lightning speed, the girl grabbed the ebony staff and ran between the benches, chairs and tables, then jumped through an open window. Most patrons had not even noticed the theft in the hustle and bustle of the Catskin.

'My staff!' Tahmina jumped to her feet.

'You take the front door,' Aenlin cried as she took the same path the thief had, sending bottles, plates and tankards flying, which provoked a volley of outraged shouts.

'Sorry!' she called out as she jumped through the window into a dark alley that reeked like a cesspit.

A few steps ahead was the girl, racing along the narrow passage, roofed over by the leaning walls of the half-timbered houses.

Aenlin didn't call out but saved her breath and started running. The girl would have to explain why she had stolen the mystic's staff when the taproom had been full of far more valuable and less well-guarded items belonging to other travellers.

Aenlin ran like the wind, despite being encumbered by the weight of her weapons; she was forced to hang on to her rapier to avoid stumbling over it. The thief was keeping her head-start by turning unexpected corners and dodging down dark alleys and through unlikely passages.

Quicker than a mouse, thought Aenlin, looking around for Tahmina every now and then, but she was nowhere to be seen.

It was getting even darker and breathing was becoming an ordeal. The smell reminded Aenlin of rotting plague or typhus corpses; she imagined them festering behind the doors she was passing because no one dared to touch them.

She had long ago lost all sense of direction, but now she began to feel as if she was running straight into a trap. She had sweated out the few gulps of beer she had managed to drink to slake her thirst, but that didn't matter right now: she needed the precious staff, which was incredibly powerful in the right – properly skilled – hands.

Her legs were already hurting from the exertions of the day and she was completely fed up with running. She grabbed some wet ropes, left hanging on a wall to dry, and still pounding over the cobblestones, tied them in knots – then threw them at the girl, who was about to enter an even narrower alley.

The heavy mass entangled the girl's feet and down went the child, cursing vociferously. She opened her right hand. With a wooden clatter, the ebony staff rolled across the ground and into the blackness of the adjacent alley.

'Got you.' Breathing heavily, Aenlin reached the thief, who was cutting the ropes from her legs with a small knife, moaning softly. She wore simple shoes made of burlap.

Aenlin stood in front of her, panting. 'Stay there and tell me what this is all about. What's your name?'

The girl stopped cutting the hemp and glared up at her. 'I liked the staff.' A dirty cap hid most of her reddish hair; she wore a pendant around her neck.

'Do you always take everything you like?' Aenlin looked around for the staff, which had disappeared into the darkness of the alley, illuminated only by a little starlight falling through the gaps between the roofs, along with some faint candlelight from ground-floor windows. The staff would be hard to find.

'Of course. That's how I make my living.' The girl looked at Aenlin. 'What will you do now? Hand me over to the Watch?'

'I assume that would make no sense.' Without taking her eyes off the thief, Aenlin entered the dark alley and felt around for the staff with her foot. The fear of a trap felt unlikely, but Aenlin was wondering why the child was so calm. Yet this was surely not the first time the girl had been caught red-handed; she was clearly used to it.

'Why did you take the staff, of all things?' Aenlin asked.

'It looks weird – as if it came from the Orient or from Africa or the Americas. Exotic. I reckoned it would've brought me quite some money if I sold it.' She was free of the ropes now, but she remained seated on the ground, looking about . . .

As if she was waiting for someone – or afraid of something?

'Do you belong to a gang?'

The girl shook her head.

'What's your name?' Aenlin found the staff at last and bent to retrieve it.

At the same moment, the child leaped to her feet. 'They call me Shayatin,' she hissed, hurling herself against Aenlin. Somehow, she weighed as much an adult man. 'Tahmina cannot keep the staff any longer! She is a renegade – she betrayed us.'

As Aenlin fell to the ground, her hand just missed the staff, and one of her pistols slid from its holster and across the cobblestones. Next thing she knew, Shayatin was half-sitting atop her, pressing her to the floor of the alley so she couldn't reach her other weapons.

Her opponent's embossed pendant swung in front of Aenlin's face. It showed a pair of bird's wings encircled by three snakes. 'What are you?' she demanded.

'Shayat.' The girl watched Aenlin with honey-coloured, glowing eyes. 'Why do you let her guard you? You are much closer to us than to her. Lucifer is on our side. Join us.' She leaned to the right and grabbed the staff. 'Or you will end up like your father, Aenlin Salomé Kane!'

The carvings glowed ruby-red and flickered, then the light turned a golden hue. In the alley, its glare was brighter than ten lanterns. It smelled fiery, of heated wood, as if the artefact was about to combust: the staff was resisting the energies trying to possess it.

'Get off of me!' With some effort, Aenlin pushed Shayatin off her and drew her stiletto. It felt strange to attack a real enemy – her first – and one who looked like a child, at that.

Her hesitant stab missed her opponent. Shayatin rolled over

one shoulder and faced Aenlin. She snarled softly, illuminated by the glowing symbols on the ebony staff.

Aenlin got up. *What does this creature know about my father?* There were rumours about his death, but no one knew for sure exactly what had happened to him.

'You will not get that staff!' she cried, drawing her rapier, and attacked. She knew she could have done better, but she really did have qualms about attacking a little girl.

Shayatin easily dodged the sharp point, then she deflected Aenlin's second, hesitant attack with the solid wood staff. There was a metallic sound and a third of the blade suddenly glowed as if fresh from the forge.

'Join us, Aenlin,' said the fearsome creature in a child's body. 'Follow your destined path – the path you are walking anyway. We—'

A shot rang out and grey smoke filled the alley.

The ball struck Shayatin's slim wrist, separating her hand from her arm. It fell slowly towards the ground, still clutching the staff.

Before the staff hit the cobbles, Tahmina suddenly appeared and grabbed it. At once, the golden glow of the carvings turned back to deep red. She shouted a spell, swung the staff around and hit the pendant hanging around the screaming girl's neck.

The leather that held it broke and the metal pendant fell to the ground.

At the same moment, Shayatin *changed*. Her childlike body grew, becoming bulkier, as the girl turned into a bellowing beast covered in scaly fur standing two feet high, with a gruesome hairless skull and long fangs. The shreds of the shabby dress fell to the floor. The narrow alley stopped the creature spreading the bird-like wings that stretched from its back.

The stench of decay and death exuded by the monster took Aenlin's breath away. *Lucifer, don't leave me!* she prayed. Her training had *theoretically* prepared her for demons and creatures of the night, illustrated with images, descriptions and sketches, but in the absence of actual enemies. Her heartbeat quickened, but she refused to let fear rule her.

'You will die, Tahmina,' yelled the monster as it readied itself to attack the mystic—

'You have to get past me first!' Aenlin shouted, compelled by fear for Tahmina, and pierced Shayatin's heart with her still-glowing rapier. Without the child-like body, Aenlin had no qualms about killing the thing.

The beast howled.

'Perish!' Tahmina grabbed the staff with both hands and smashed the monster's head with a mighty blow. 'Perish forever!'

Its ugly skull shattered, pieces went flying and blood hit the walls to hiss there and dissolve – as did their opponent's body. The terrifying creature dissipated into pale yellow flakes of ash that the wind carried away until every bit were gone without a trace, as if Shayatin had never existed.

Only the shattered pendant remained.

'What in the name of Lucifer was that?' Aenlin wanted to pick up the trinket, but her fingers were trembling a bit. Her very first battle, and she had fought an actual creature of evil!

Tahmina stopped her from picking it up with a gesture of warning. 'That was a Shayatin: a demon older than the Bible, the Koran or any of these other young religions.' She ground the fallen object into the ground under her heel. 'She belongs to the followers of Vanth.'

The stolen staff, the insinuation about her father, the threat against Tahmina, the offer the creature had made her and the attempt on her life all spiralled through Aenlin's head.

This is not how I had imagined my first visit to Hamburg. 'Let's discuss this back at the inn,' she suggested, picking up the pistol Tahmina must have fired, which was lying on the ground between the two women. Aenlin's hand stopped trembling, her anxiety subsided, giving way to the certainty that she was able to face such enemies. Her training had been of use. 'Good shot. I thought you weren't skilled at firearms?'

Tahmina approached her and pulled her into a long embrace. They stood in the alley, heartbeat next to heartbeat. 'I am incredibly glad that you are unharmed.'

After a while, they hesitantly let go of each other.

'Your old master sent her,' Aenlin guessed. 'The one I saved you from in London, right?'

Tahmina took her hand and dragged her away. 'Not here.'

Together, they found their way out of the maze of alleys, back to the lower port and to the Thirsty Roper.

It was impossible for them to sleep . . . especially once Aenlin heard that Tahmina hadn't fired the pistol.

The next day, at sundown, Aenlin and Tahmina stood at the door of the offices of Claas and Hans de Hertoghe II, two strong men of understated wealth that didn't show in their garb, but did in everything else within their intricately decorated house. Aenlin had had to leave her rapier and her pistols at the entrance.

It had taken Aenlin and Tahmina the entire day to get an appointment with the representatives of the West India Company. The brothers de Hertoghe were busy, servants had told them, but at last they would see if their strategies for finding Aenlin's inheritance would pay off.

The neatly bearded merchants were going through mountains of books and lists and signed orders: one gave orders and read the paperwork; the other wrote and checked the other records to make sure everything was in order.

'Come,' Claas said. 'We do not have long.'

Aenlin removed her hat and pushed back her hair, strands

of which kept falling over her forehead. 'Thank you for finding the time to hear me.' She stepped forward and placed her credentials and her father's signet on the last free spot atop the desk, which was overflowing with maps, papers and blotters. Then she bowed slightly and took a seat.

Tahmina, playing the maid, stood silently by the doorway, where the servants of the Dutchmen were marvelling at her extraordinary garb and intricate staff.

'You have exactly five minutes.' Claas took an hourglass from a compartment under the desk and inverted it. Its white grains started falling. 'What do you want?'

Aenlin realised that the brothers had not read her note, so she had to explain her reason for visiting as briefly as possible. 'Jacobus Maus was the custodian of my inheritance, but he died in front of my eyes during an attack not far from Altona. We had no chance to save him.' She pointed at the things she had brought with her. 'But I know he has deposited valuables with you. My inheritance should be among them.'

Claas stopped his constant, practised signing. He reached for the documents she had brought and perused them before examining the signet ring and finally looking up to meet Aenlin's gaze. Slowly, he stroked his beard. 'Poor Maus is dead?'

'Yes.'

'Do you have any proof for your claim? You could have killed him yourself.'

'Begging your pardon, but that would have been stupid, considering the fact that I want to claim my inheritance.'

'He could have denied you. Or you are an impostor and he realised that your proof of descent is false.' Claas spoke calmly and without reproach. 'Do not take exception to my words. My brother and I, we know the tricks to fraudulently obtain a fortune. This wouldn't be the first time that somebody tried to obtain the inheritance of a dead person unjustifiably.'

'I think if you have somebody drag the Elbe, beyond the port towards the sea, you'll find his corpse at some point. If you want, sent outriders to Altona to search the huts and houses for his belongings. His killers will have taken everything, including his boots.' Aenlin spoke calmly; she had expected resistance. *I will not stand falsely accused of a murder.* 'I don't have the time for that, and neither have you, I assume, considering the amount of work that you and your brother are burdened with.'

'Well said. Time truly is money. You do not look like a murderess to me, either.' Claas passed the papers to Hans, who took eyeglasses from a drawer and examined the pages scrupulously, holding them against the light and in front of a lamp. Then he reached for a magnifying glass and kept scrutinising.

'May I have a look at it?' Aenlin gave him a smile. 'At your vault or wherever poor Maus has hidden my valuable inheritance?'

Claas shrugged regretfully. 'I am sorry, but it is not as easy as that, although I can confirm that Jacobus Maus had dealings with us, and that we sometimes reserved a compartment of our vault for him.'

'He has no descendants. No one will lay claim to the rest.' Aenlin realised where this conversation was leading. Businesspeople would be businesspeople, with their minds set on simple profit. All the talk about murder was simply tactics. 'I want only what my mother and I are due.'

'What your mother *was* due,' Claas corrected in a friendly tone. 'I can't just let everybody walk into the Company's inner sanctum to take whatever they want. So, I'll first have to find out what Maus has deposited with us. Until then, I will also find out what happened to the man.'

'Please do that, good sir.' Aenlin was having an increasingly hard time keeping up the friendly façade. She wanted only what was rightfully hers. *You will not get rid of me that easily.*

'The box has been locked,' Claas said, 'by Maus. If you do not carry a key, we will need someone to prise it open, which is no mean feat. It will take a very long time.'

Hans finished his visual inspection and gave the papers back to his brother, muttering his approval.

'We do not doubt your descent or your identity. That is a good start.' Claas kept her paperwork on the table in front of him. 'Solomon Kane's daughter,' he said, obviously impressed. 'That explains your unusual demeanour, your garb – and the arsenal of weapons.' He rose from his armchair and extended his hand across the table. Light glinted on the intricate curlicue brocade embroideries of his jacket; two golden rings flashed at his fingers. 'My pleasure, Milady. Please excuse my rudeness. We are constantly having to deal with people who consider themselves important. You, on the other hand, actually are.'

Hans nodded and even looked up at her.

The sudden friendliness and the change of address surprised Aenlin. A new tactic? 'Thank you.'

'Refreshments? Beer? Some liqueur, or a good port wine?' Claas offered. His behaviour had changed completely. He called a servant and issued some orders in Dutch.

Hans bowed slightly sidewise, watching Tahmina with open curiosity. Then he took his quill and scribbled some lines on a piece of paper that he handed his brother.

'You are an Englishwoman, unaware of the customs of this city,' Claas said. 'The usual procedure would look like this. You explain yourself to the Council and swear an oath that you had nothing to do with the trader's death. Then you prove your claim. The Council, meanwhile, at least has to pretend to investigate Jacobus Maus' death, although I believe that the Hamburg city watch is neither welcome in Altona, nor will it discover anything. Moreover, Altona is not part of Hamburg, so it is not their domain. All this will take time. Then, after weeks or months, the Council will let you know whether you actually have a claim or whether the city will keep the entire inheritance.' He folded his hands. 'Then you bring the sealed—'

Aenlin realised that the merchant's kind words had been nothing more than posturing. *He wants a share.* She cut the conversation short. 'I assume you have an idea how we could work around all this.'

'You are a businesswoman. I like that.' Claas dug for a map that gave a rough overview of the Holy Roman Empire of the German Nation. 'We are here.' His fleshy finger tapped at the word *Hamburg* and drew a line downwards until it rested on the word *Bamberg*. 'But I need you there, dear Aenlin Kane.'

Again, she was surprised. 'I must confess I am not on top of the lands and realms. There are just too many. Who owns Bamberg?'

'It is a bishopric of its own. Catholic. Five of its inhabitants' – Claas' finger retraced the path it had taken before – 'would like to come to the Hanseatic City. As soon as possible.' He looked at her. 'While the Company resolves all legal matters concerning your inheritance and while poor Maus' compartment in the vault is forced open, you will bring these people here.'

Aenlin felt overwhelmed, taken by surprise. This option had not been part of her discussion with Tahmina. Damn! 'Alone, it will be hard to get five—'

'I have hired some good landsknechts to accompany you. It will be simplicity itself.'

She had no argument she could offer: if she wanted her inheritance, she had to make this deal with the de Hertoghes, her own wishes notwithstanding. She had no doubt the merchants were influential enough to make it extremely hard for her to claim her inheritance via the Council of Hamburg. 'Who are the people I'll be escorting?'

'Good folk who are afraid to embark on this long journey

alone. Some of them are old and frail. It is a Christian task, Miss Kane.'

Aenlin sighed. 'Why me?'

'Your famous name and your even more famous father will help you conquer all hardships – hardships that might not be of this world. Landsknechts are fine and dandy, but these days it's an advantage to travel with someone who knows a great deal about the powers of darkness and what to do to thwart them.' He regarded her expectantly. 'I assume you're familiar with these things? Just like your father?'

'I am.' It was no lie, although Aenlin's approach differed from her father's, which showed clearly in her choice of companion, of whom her Puritan father would certainly not have approved. Neither Protestants nor Catholics were counted among the friends of Lucifer.

Claas pointed at Tahmina. 'Your servant. Where did you find her?'

'We met in London, when I was looking for a companion to aid me on my journeys.'

'Oh, I am sorry. I thought you had bought her from her slaver. This kind of woman fascinates my brother to the extreme. Exotic and exciting.' Claas looked at the slip of paper Hans had handed him. 'Where is she from? My brother might want to buy someone like her? We maintain the best relations throughout the world.'

'I am Persian, sir,' Tahmina answered and tapped the end of her staff to the floor lightly to make her pride clear. When it hit the floor, it cracked like a punishing whip. The pendant chandeliers in the room swung to and fro, as if set in motion by the sound.

'Ah, and passionate, too. A mystical pearl from the East, enticing like incense. It's going to be a challenge to find another woman like you.' Claas turned to Aenlin. 'How about you bring the five people to me and upon your return, nothing will stand between you and your inheritance.'

I must agree. 'Since this is a matter of business, I would like to set it down in a contract with the Company.'

'Of course.' Claas gestured and Hans took up a new sheet of paper at once. The tapered tip of the quill flew across it. 'My brother will write down the terms exactly, but concisely. We just need a few paragraphs. And as well, the Company will pay you one hundred guilders for your efforts.' He smiled. 'Proof of my trust in you and, at the same time, a sign of the fact that I do not try to use you. A give-and-take, my honourable Aenlin Kane.'

'But these people really do want to leave Bamberg?' Aenlin enquired. 'I do not want this to turn into an abduction.'

Claas raised a hand. 'I swear that those people will actually throw themselves at you. They want to leave the city.'

Aenlin suspected that these people were intimidated Protestants trying to flee Bamberg, the centre of the Catholic bishopric, before they lost their money and their lives. She had heard of the Emperor's Edict that was going to make life hard for Protestants.

The conversation died down as they watched Hans write incredibly quickly, his razor-sharp letters crossing the page. He managed to sum up the essence of their agreement in a few paragraphs. His practice and knowledge of law was clear.

Aenlin realised that sand had long since run through the hourglass, but the de Hertoghes clearly no longer cared. Her visit was under different auspices now.

Hans handed Aenlin the second copy so she could check the paragraphs he had written down.

'Can you read,' Claas asked, 'in German?'

'Yes,' she said, and although it took her a while to fully understand the details, the wording was brief and she found no back door or trap in the few lines of the agreement. With a flourish, she signed the contract and sealed it with her own ring.

Claas pulled the agreement across the desk, signed it himself, and sealed it as well. 'This one is yours, the other one is ours.' Again, he shook her hand. 'My thanks. You are helping good people. Be in front of the office tomorrow morning. The hired landsknechts will be there, carrying everything you and your maid might need.'

Hans leaned close to his brother and whispered something in his ear.

'I am to ask you,' Claas said to Tahmina, talking past Aenlin, 'if you would like to take service with my brother. A Persian with knowledge and contacts could open new markets for us in the Orient. You will get a share of—'

'No, thank you, gentlemen.' Tahmina laughed loudly as she interrupted him. 'I am happy where I am now. My mistress treats me well and rarely beats me. What more could I want?' She could not help herself.

Aenlin rose with a smile, pocketing her copy of the agreement. She had felt better about business agreements in the past, but she saw no alternative. Even if Claas de Hertoghe had lied to her about the procedures in Hamburg, trying to work around him would mean an enormous effort, plus a great loss of time and potentially of her inheritance in the end.

I will finish this journey as quickly as possible.

'See you tomorrow, then.'

'No, I will not be there,' Claas said. 'It is your meeting. I will inform my people so the landsknechts know that I have sent you. May God bless your journey.'

Tahmina laughed quietly as Aenlin said, 'It cannot hurt. I will take any blessing as long as it's helpful.' *Like yours, Lucifer.* As Aenlin turned to go, a servant appeared with a large leather bag embossed with the symbol of the West India Company. 'What is that?'

'A gift,' Claas said. 'From us. Our finest port, some French wine and the best rum available in all of Hamburg.' As he rose, his taciturn brother also got up from his chair. 'May it make your journey more agreeable.'

The servant handed the bag to Tahmina, who leaned slightly sidewise to balance its weight. The man stared at the Persian. Almost no one was immune to the effect of her blue eyes.

Why would he fare better than I did, back in London? Aenlin wondered.

'Let me thank you again.' She bowed slightly, then she and Tahmina left the office, and the Company offices.

'Now we have something to drink. Or rather, you do.' Tahmina used her staff to counterbalance the weight of the bag. 'If you share these bottles with the landsknechts, we will likely keep losing our way.'

'It will make the gentleman happy and buy their goodwill.' With one hand, Aenlin caressed Tahmina's back, a tender gesture of closeness. 'We will surely need it.'

Melchior Pieck wandered about in the lower port, keeping his light-blue eyes, hidden by the brim of his floppy hat, fixed on the entrance of the Company's house.

After the exciting evening at the Catskin, Kane and her maid were taking things more slowly. They had not left their lodgings since noon, until an hour ago.

Time was running out. Melchior assumed that he would soon have to turn from protector to killer. His pistols were loaded and ready. The night before, for simplicity's sake, he had used Kane's own weapon to shoot that monster. But instead of hitting the abomination's head, his near miss had only sheared off its hand. Before Melchior had had to intervene a second time, however, the maid and Kane had settled the situation between them.

The event had sunk deep into his memory. Despite all his experience and his encounters with shape-changers and other ghastly creatures on battlefields and beyond them, he had never seen anything like that miraculous staff, or the dreadful Shayatin demon.

Wearing a child's body? Perfidious. To be on the safe side, in case he should ever meet a similar creature, and to continue his own studies, Melchior had picked up the pendant from where the maid had pushed it into the ground. It was dirty, but still whole. Once he'd cleaned it, he had tucked it into his right boot for safety.

The sally port within the warehouse gate opened.

Kane stepped out onto the street. Her maid, who was now carrying a heavy leather bag embossed with the Company's crest, followed her. The young mystic looked heavily burdened.

'Look you, look you. Solomon Kane's inheritance,' Melchior muttered to himself. At a booth, Melchior bought little smoked and roasted fish that were supposed to be eaten whole, flesh, skin and bones. They were wrapped in an old newspaper and came with two slices of fried grey bread: greasy and delicious.

Melchior followed the two women across the square, but they went straight back to the inn where they had rented a room.

That suited him very well. He intended to take ship to England from Hamburg. Two captains would be taking that route within the next days, one of whom was setting sail the next day. A perfect fit.

So Melchior decided to change the Earl's plan slightly – after all, why wait until Kane left the city? She was carrying everything with her. He would surprise them both in their lodgings, knock out the mystic and kill the young woman; he'd also slip Tahmina the letter the Earl had given him for her to read when she came round.

Softly humming, finishing the last of the salty, delicious fish, he entered the Thirsty Roper and went to the taproom. The tiny bones crunched between his teeth.

Kane's boots disappeared up the stairs and shortly after-wards, he heard the two women walk along the corridor above him.

Melchior turned to the small bar and produced the letter for Tahmina, signalling with it. 'Excuse me and good day,' he said jovially. 'I have a message for Aenlin Kane – an Englishwoman, travelling with a maid.' He also produced several kreutzers. 'Where can I find her?'

'You just missed her.' The innkeeper, a seasoned woman in nice clothing, pointed up the stairs. 'Room four. If you don't make it down again within five minutes, I'll add a whoring sur-charge to her room rate.' She left him standing there to serve bowls of steaming meat and pickled cabbage.

Melchior was both taken aback and amused. Moneymaking obviously came naturally to the inhabitants of Hamburg. He mounted the stairs, pocketing the envelope again, and went silently along the corridor.

The room numbers, in Roman numerals, were written on the doors with chalk, as if they changed from time to time.

He did not even want to guess the reason.

Melchior pressed his ear against the wood to listen.

The voices were clearly recognisable: Kane and the mystic.

He readied his pistols, then he took the stained fish paper, folded it several times and pushed it under the door so two thirds of it was sticking inside the room. He knocked against the door with the barrel of his pistol to alert the women to the apparent message.

'Oh?' Kane said softly.

'I will get it.' Tahmina's light steps approached the door.

When the piece of paper disappeared inside, Melchior force-fully kicked against the lock.

The door flew open with a crash.

The door and the handle hit the delicate mystic. Gasping,

she stumbled across the room to collapse in front of Kane. Her black staff was leaning against the bunk bed, beyond her reach.

Works like a charm. Melchior raised the pistol. 'The Earl of Holland sends his regards!' He pulled the trigger and the propellant exploded.

Kane had great reflexes; she dodged the musket ball, which crashed through the shutters, sending wooden slivers raining down into the alley below. She produced her rapier and attacked him. 'Whoever you are, you will be sorry for this!'

Melchior deflected the tip of her blade with the barrel of his pistol and tried to ram her with his shoulder. 'You will not win our little fight this way,' he growled, but he missed her again and had to sidestep to avoid losing his balance, thanks to his own momentum.

At once, her elbow hit his face. Blood spurted from his nose, running in two wide rivulets across his lips and chin into the salt-and-pepper beard. 'Bloody Hell!' Melchior kneed her in the groin. 'I will give you the Earl's regards, as true as I'm standing here!'

Cursing, she doubled over and jumped back. 'You're mistaken. I don't know this Earl!'

Melchior drew his second pistol. 'I don't care.' When he pulled the trigger, there was only a spark, but no bang. *Fucking misfire!*

'The tide is turning.' Again Kane jumped towards him, her arm with the rapier stretched out before her to pierce him. 'You will justify yourself to me.'

He dropped the useless weapon, produced his own sabre and parried her attack at the last possible moment. Her blade slid down along his, right into the gap between his blade and the iron edge of his handguard.

There, her rapier caught. 'Got you, little one!' Melchior jerked his sabre around, his opponent's sword shattered noisily and she was left with a finger-length stub.

Kane dropped the rapier and tried to draw her stilettos. 'In your dreams!'

But Melchior hit her cheek with the handguard of his sabre, forcing her back. In her stupor, Kane missed the unconscious Tahmina, stumbled over her – and fell headfirst through the shattered window.

'No!' Melchior ran to the window and looked down. If any passer-by found the woman, things would get complicated.

But Kane was not below him.

'Where the—?'

It was a sound from above that told him where the young woman had gone.

The roof! With a curse, Melchior sheathed his weapons and went after her. *Now she forces me to play the monkey.* But despite his weight, he was a good climber. He pulled himself up onto the ridge of the roof.

Kane was already halfway to the next building. Her long dark hair was flowing in the wind. To the right and to the left, the chimneys jutting up into the air were spewing forth grey smoke from burning peat and wood.

This time I will get her. Melchior cocked his pistol again and took aim. In his line of business, it was a thousand times better to shoot people in the back than to confront them face to face. The breeze stirred the brim of his floppy hat and made his white shirt flutter. 'The Earl's regards, Aenlin Kane. Do not forget them.'

'I cannot believe it!' A male voice suddenly interrupted, yelling in amazement, 'Pieck! How the devil did you find me, you bastard?'

In surprise, he turned his head towards the speaker.

At a wide window in the next building stood the duellist in his fighting stance, naked from the waist up, turned sideways to present a smaller target, the pistol in his extended arm aimed at Melchior. The long-haired brown wig rested on a stand; his own hair was brown and close-cropped; soap covered the part of his face which was not, like the other half, freshly shaven.

Kane had heard his words too, and stopped. She took two steps backwards from the cover of the chimneys and gazed over her shoulder. 'Ah, Caspar,' she called out in relief. 'Good to—'

'Shut up, Kane!' Melchior grumbled. He was afraid the duellist, who might be almost his age, could pull the trigger quick as breathing and spread his head across the roofs of Hamburg. 'This is a misunderstanding, von und zu dem Dorffe,' he said loudly. 'I just want her.'

'Aenlin Kane is a wanted woman?' Caspar sounded amazed. 'What have you done, Aenlin, to make a bounty hunter try to kill you?'

'I don't know. He burst into our room and—'

'Shut up, damn you!' Without dropping his aim, Melchior quickly glanced around again. So far, no one else had noticed them, but it wouldn't be long until someone on the ships or at the docks saw them. *Damn it! This is not what I needed!* In a quick motion, he pulled a kerchief and tied it over his nose and mouth to disguise him. 'She killed somebody,' he lied. 'In London.'

'Nonsense!' Kane protested. 'I do not know this man,' she repeated.

'I do,' Caspar replied. He stood there, still bare-chested, obviously not caring about the remains of the shaving foam. 'We met once – or at least, I saw him, and when I heard who he was I quickly disappeared.' Calmly, he took his second pistol from the table. 'An awkward situation, Pieck. I have more firing power than you. Also, I am afraid I am more on Aenlin's side than on yours, Bracke. Don't they call you that?'

With every passing second, Melchior's situation was growing worse. Tahmina might wake up and start yelling bloody murder in the Thirsty Roper, and that would make the watch appear. He had rarely botched a mission as completely as this one.

'I will offer you one hundred guilders,' Melchior told the duellist as he prepared to fire. He wanted to duck to the other side of the roof to avoid the man's musket balls and finish what his Lordship had paid him to do. 'No, let's make it one hundred and fifty.'

'For me to spare you, so you can shoot me when the auspices are better?' Caspar laughed. 'Do we turn this into a duel? Or how do we—?'

He would shoot. Melchior could hear in his voice. *He is siding with Kane.* He changed his mind and jerked his pistol around, now aiming it at the duellist.

But the moment Melchior moved, Caspar took his shot. Both his weapons discharged with a thundering noise. The first musket ball batted away the hand in which Melchior held the weapon. Wooden slivers of the handle, bone, blood and flesh sailed through the air. The second projectile hit him right in the chest, making him lose his balance.

His suddenly weak legs slid out from under him and he fell from the window, slid down the roof, off the edge and into the alley, where he landed atop of a pile of wet straw reeking of horse manure and dung.

Then, things turned *very* weird.

What . . . what has happened to me? Melchior lay on his back on the soft surface, but he couldn't feel his body any more. He seemed to consist of pure thought; he was able only to see and hear, nothing more. As much as he tried to feel something or to move – he could not. *Damn it! To hell with them all!*

He heard excited voices from the port. People had heard the shots and soon, night-watchmen would appear to find out what was going on.

Great – and I'm lying here in horseshit, unable to move.

Steps approached, someone climbed down the side – then

he saw Kane's features and Caspar's monkey face, still partly covered in shaving foam, hovering above him.

'Is he alive?'

As Kane touched his neck to feel for a pulse, an ebony strand brushed his nose. 'Yes.'

'Not for very much longer. He'll bleed to death, both internally and because of his lost hand. Blood is already filling his lungs. I know what I'm talking about.' Caspar patted him down, cursing all the time. 'What a mess.'

'Let me help you,' Kane said, absentmindedly plaiting her hair.

Melchior would have loved to shout – to grab them, to poke out their eyes and tear off that jet-black lock of hair. He lay there, however, trapped – trapped and dying.

They found the letter addressed to Tahmina, the directions to the warehouse at the docks in London and, finally, his contract with his Lordship.

No – that can't be . . .

'What does all this mean?' Caspar looked over his shoulder and said hastily, 'Someone's coming. Let's go – I have no desire to face the Council. Plus, I'm only half shaved.'

Kane shoved the papers under her coat and rose. 'Let's go!'

The duellist touched a dagger to Melchior's throat. 'Do we put an end to his suffering to make it easier on the scavengers?'

She stopped him from delivering the killing stroke. 'No murder.' She dragged him along by his arm. 'We need to talk.'

'Ah, sadly, I can't. I have an appointment, before which, I need to finish shaving. But it was a pleasure being of assistance.' Caspar disappeared from Melchior's view. 'Adieu, Aenlin. Who knows when we will meet again?'

Kane looked at Melchior thoughtfully. 'I'll unearth your secrets. This Earl will not be able to hide from me.' Then she too ran away.

You bloody cowards! You let me die here like a dog?

Then nothing happened for a long time. No one in Hamburg came looking for him.

But Melchior didn't die – it was as if God wanted to put him on trial, wanted to make him wait for Paradise.

He counted the birds flying above him, listened to the tolling of the bells of the tower and the church clocks.

It was evening when he was finally found. Some stable hands dragged him down from the heap and called for a guard – only after stealing everything save his bloodied clothes and the boots. They closed his eyes so he could see no more, obviously considering him dead.

Melchior accepted it, listening and thinking, *When will it finally be over?*

'Just another thug,' the guard said, 'wearing a kerchief to hide his face. He died in the dung – a fitting death for such a scoundrel.'

Shortly afterwards, a cart approached. Judging by the sounds, they were loading Melchior's body onto it, and according to the smell, he was lying on top of corpses.

'Bury them well,' the guard charged the coughing men. 'His boots will be payment enough.'

'Yes, yes,' replied an old man whose lack of teeth made him hard to understand. 'The Council is bloody stingy.'

Then Melchior stopped thinking. He must have fallen unconscious, but the loud crack of metal against stone woke him up. *What kind of game are you playing with me, Lord? Won't you finally kill me? Kill me before I feel the pain!*

'Here we go,' a younger voice declared. 'That's deep enough – it'll do. Take his boots and chuck him into the hole.'

Melchior would have loved to get up and run away – or to ask for help. But he couldn't; he could still only hear and think. *The horror! The horror!*

'What . . . ? Feel this, George,' a younger voice said. 'He's still warm to the touch.' With a start, the voice added, 'His heart is still beating!'

'Not for very much longer,' the toothless one said. 'Once the good earth covers him, it'll soon be over. Come on, we'll do him first.'

'Hey, look! There was a pendant in his boot.' Fingers rubbed against metal. 'It's worthless, though – just tin. Strange stuff, mind, all those feathers and snakes. A snake angel!' He laughed.

'I don't want it,' the other man said. 'Let him keep it. No, put it under his tongue so he has something to suck on – that'll stop him eating any of the dead. Will you just get rid of him?'

Melchior didn't feel them lift him, but he smelled the metal of the pendant, which was probably in his mouth now. *Off I go to Paradise.*

He smelled freshly dug earth all around, then came the stench of the dead that the skinners or hangman's assistants or whoever they were had collected. He knew where he had ended up: in a mass grave for those who died broke in the city.

Melchior wanted to scream, to cry, to beg and plead – but he could only listen and think. He was barely able to smell anything now the earth covered his face, clogging up his nose. The grave would finish what the two musket balls had not been able to do. *I will suffocate miserably.*

The less air he had to breathe, the clearer his mind became.

His life passed before his eyes, his entire life, lightning-quick, yet still he saw every detail, realised every mistake he had made. He also knew which ones he wouldn't repeat, to make his existence turn out for the better. But Melchior would not get a second chance, even if he would have given anything to have fired a musket ball in that duellist's foppish, moustachioed face.

To the gates of Heaven, he thought, still fighting for air. *Up the ladder and . . .*

Then Melchior smelled fire, smoke and the stench of burning flesh.

That was when he knew that he had ended up in Hell.

'The only things landsknechts do not mess with are millstones and hot iron.'

Common saying

CAPITULUM IV

Free Imperial City of Hamburg, April 1629

Early in the morning, Aenlin and Tahmina reached the offices of the West India Trading Company. Their saddlebags on their newly acquired horses were bulging.

Hamburg had awakened a while ago and was bustling. The city had been busy since its founding, and the docks of the lower port were currently full of carts and wagons, people and pack animals. Aenlin, viewing it from her saddle, was impressed by the hustle and bustle, even though she had rarely been this tired before. Nightmares had haunted her sleep all night.

The battle against Shayatin had left its mark. Without her training, she knew she wouldn't have been able to withstand the attack, mentally or physically. Hopefully, this journey would provide her with some distraction.

From afar, the two women saw the small group of landsknechts standing next to a coach, holding the bridles of their own steeds. The youngest of them was also the tallest. He was more than two feet in height, making the massive bidenhänder at his belt look like a normal sword. He wore no armour.

Strange fellow, she thought, wondering about his story.

As well as the young giant, the band consisted of three more men, who were talking to each other: a small one, a beefy one and a muscular one. They all looked to be in their twenties. At the centre of attention was the one with the long, ash-blond hair, who was holding a map in his hand.

All four of them wore bright clothes: puffy breeches, extravagantly slashed jackets revealing different colours beneath. They sported large, flashy hats adorned with jaunty feathers and metal badges, as if they were members of an estate or their own guild.

Even from where she was, Aenlin could feel the muscular leader's charisma.

Tahmina made a startled sound. 'Do you feel it, too?' The mystic had a very acute sense for the supernatural and extraordinary. 'What kind of man is this? His aura is . . . so many things at once. I cannot place him.'

'What about the others?'

'Simple men, although there is also something unusual about the giant child. And I'm not talking about his size,' she added, pointing at the youngest member towering over the group.

Shortly before the women reached them, the squad gathered around a familiar-looking man in black, a broad-brimmed hat atop his long-haired wig, leading a beautiful black horse by the reins. The horseman was deep in conversation with someone who looked to be an employee of the Company.

'The Comte and his owner,' Tahmina said, looking delighted. 'Will he be coming along?'

'I hope so.' Aenlin felt better at once. She felt she could trust someone who had already saved her life more than she could any of those strangers. 'It's always good to have a marksman like him on side.'

They pulled up when they reached the coach. A canvas tarpaulin covered the roof, shielding the chests and boxes stacked there from ill weather.

'Good day,' Aenlin said to the assembled men in a friendly tone and waved her pale hat. 'Is this the Bamberg travelling party?'

The four landsknechts stopped talking and looked up at Aenlin and Tamara.

'Oh, it's you two again,' Caspar called out merrily. 'My surrogate daughters. I might have guessed that our destinies would be entwined, for a while at least.' He tipped his hat in a flamboyant, courtly gesture. 'Recovered from the scare?'

'What scare?' The leader lowered the map. 'Who are you two?'

'Real eye candy,' commented the beefy man with the chiselled face.

'One of them looks as if she wouldn't like you to graze on her pasture,' added the smallest of the men with a friendly laugh. 'You must excuse my brother-in-arms' boorishness. Statius rarely gets to meet such pretty, cultivated women.'

'That'll change after a few days on the road.' The leader pointed at his men in turn. 'The tall one over there is Moritz, the gawker is Statius, the well-mannered one is Jäcklein and I am Nicolas.' He pointed to the duellist. 'You obviously know Mr von und zu. I understand that he will be travelling with us, to back us up with firepower.'

'Aenlin and Tahmina,' Aenlin said by way of introduction. 'The Company hired us, just like you, to go to Bamberg and save good people.'

The landsknechts laughed.

'They are people, we can agree; I don't care if they are evil or if they are beasts,' Statius commented without taking his eyes off Tahmina. It was clear to see what he was fantasising about. 'Where does your charming maid come from? Russian violet eyes, maroon hair and skin like—'

'I am Persian.' Her voice was as sharp as a sword.

He was so taken aback that he stopped asking questions. The rebuke had succeeded.

The man who had accompanied Caspar from the Company's office seized the moment. 'Good morning to you all.' Although his clothes could never compete with those worn by the brothers de Hertoghe, his velvet puffy breeches worn with a jerkin and an embroidered coat were nonetheless impressive. 'As you are all here, you may begin your journey.' He pointed to Nicolas. 'The captain here will be in command; he will make all necessary decisions on the way to Bamberg. He may assign other ranks as he sees fit.'

Caspar said at once, 'Unless I am mistaken, I am the oldest here. I have also been in more battles than anyone else.' He brandished his hat before putting it back on his long-haired wig. 'Just wanted it noted from the start. I don't like disputes.'

'We'll talk about that later,' Nicolas replied with a grin. 'I have a lot to learn from you, your Aged Cockiness.'

His three men laughed, but the Company employee was still talking.

'Aenlin Kane and her maid will follow the captain's orders as well – unless they have valid objections due to their knowledge of the work of demons, as they are commonly known, of hauntings, visitations, or other things not of the earthly realm.'

'Hear ye, hear ye,' Jäcklein said as he grimaced appreciatively. 'I would not have thought you knowledgeable in such fields.'

'A witch-hunter. Like her father.' Statius spat. 'So young, and already such a celebrity.'

'Your father?' Jäcklein asked. 'Well, who might that be?'

'Solomon Kane,' Aenlin confessed. She was surprised that the most uncouth of the lot had recognised her at once – or at least, he'd correctly guessed who she was. 'He was no witch-hunter. My father hunted down evil in whatever form it took.'

'That's good.' Nicolas gave her a friendly nod. 'You must tell me anytime if you or your maid notice something odd. Strange creatures roam the land and they know how to use war to exploit people's weaknesses to their own benefit.' He put away the map.

He knows about demons! 'I shall.' Aenlin looked at Tahmina, wondering if that had been a hidden hint about his own strong presence. Or did he not even know about his own aura? It was a long way to Bamberg. They would be able to learn a lot on their journey.

The Company employee handed the captain a heavy leather bag. 'In there, you will find letters of safe conduct for the various duchies, principalities and dioceses you will have to traverse. Should they not suffice, the bag also contains coins of high value, in case you need to buy that free passage.'

Aenlin watched as Nicolas stowed them behind a lockable hatch under the coachman's box.

'My thanks,' said the captain.

'The brothers de Hertoghe and the West India Company wish you success,' said the employee, and he turned back towards the office building. 'Godspeed, Captain.'

As Nicolas, Statius and Jäcklein mounted clumsily, Aenlin realised that none of the landsknechts could ride. It was clear none of them were sure about how to use the stirrups, and way they sat could only be called miserable. She guessed it was only the men's pride that stopped them from dismounting again. All their weapons looked new. Only their clothes were worn.

'What a merry band,' Tahmina whispered. 'I hope the horses are docile at least.'

The giant called Moritz clambered onto the coach and took up the reins. 'Giddyup, horsies!' he shouted, and the pair of grey mares broke into a trot.

'Bamberg, here we come!' Nicolas announced, and with that, he awkwardly took the lead.

Jäcklein and Statius took up position flanking the coach.

Caspar waved Aenlin and Tahmina nearer. 'Let us use the journey for some conversation, now that I'm a surrogate father to you. Yesterday, several things happened that have piqued my curiosity. I would have loved to have stayed to chat then, but I had business to attend to.'

The two women followed his lead, dropping back behind the coach and one on either side of the duellist.

'Do you see that?' Caspar asked. 'They don't know how to ride. If you ask me, these foxes have really fleeced the Company.' He pointed at Jäcklein, who was trying to read a small notebook as he rode. 'Do you see this?'

Tahmina realised what he was doing and laughed. 'An instruction manual on how to use a musket! He's not used one before, has he? What kind of mercenaries are they if they can neither ride nor shoot?'

'Landsknechts. Simple landsknechts, who usually carry pikes on the battlefield – except for the captain and Moritz: they wield bidenhänders.' Caspar greeted some passing ladies, who looked up to the handsome duellist and giggled. 'What do you think that means?' he wondered aloud.

'That they lied when they were hired,' Tahmina guessed.

'No.' Aenlin heard amusement as Caspar voiced his suspicion; he had a more charitable theory. 'They're the wrong men.'

This keeps getting better and better. 'You really think they—?'

'I overheard a conversation between them. The beefy one, Statius, wanted to get to Altona quickly, to make sure no one could give them away.' Caspar smoothed his goatee. 'It all fits together.'

'Then they'll probably make off at some point on the road?' Tahmina looked at the mercenaries in front of them. 'Is that their plan?'

'Maybe. They have plenty of money now, as well as equipment, horses and weapons. They could lead a good life far away from Hamburg – and the Company.' He touched the hilt of one of his pistols. 'What do you ladies think – should we form an alliance for mutual protection? Like a father and his daughters. Just in case these people decide to kill us and run away.'

'Count me in.' Aenlin shook his hand, and Tahmina did the same. 'Why didn't you tell the de Hertoghes about your suspicion?'

'Ah, I'm an adventurer. This is going to be a fascinating journey, and a well-paid one at that. What more could I want?' Caspar winked at her and set the tips of his long-haired wig flopping like large dog's ears. 'Especially since you're travelling with me. Think about what we have experienced in only two days – I wonder what will happen on the rest of our journey.'

'It will surely be boring.' Aenlin took the offensive to stop the duellist from asking about the evening in the Catskin and the attempt to kill her in the name of the Earl, whoever he was. Since she was unable to make heads or tails of it herself, she didn't want to talk about it. 'Speaking of impostors and tricksters, why do you pose as a nobleman? Why all the duels?'

Caspar grinned. 'Does the name François de Montmorency ring a bell?' When both women shook their heads, he explained, 'He is an infamous duellist in beautiful France. Over the course of one year, he killed more than forty Princes, Counts and Dukes. I want to do the same: exterminate noblemen.' He knocked on his pistols, the very latest flintlocks. 'These are my weapons.' He lowered his voice and added, 'Between you and me, I'm pretty bad with the rapier and the sword.'

Duels were a favourite pastime of French nobles and officers, despite the ban. Aenlin had heard that more than ten thousand noblemen and military officers were supposed to have lost their lives in duels in the last few years.

'But you're not noble,' she pointed out. 'You invented that title.'

'Damn right. I fool these vain folk who are so proud of their lineage. My name alone – von und zu dem Dorffe – is a challenge to them.' Caspar laughed. 'Of course, it's lucrative, too. I pilfer the corpses. Most of them carry a well-filled purse. If

I can find the time, I also take a look around their homes for more revenue.'

'Is that how you got your equipment?' Tahmina clearly disapproved of what he did.

'Don't pity them, my surrogate daughter. Most of my opponents earned their riches by squeezing the poor and the poorest.'

'Why do you hate the aristocracy so much?' Aenlin leaned a bit closer to Caspar. 'Why risk your own life when you could simply ambush them?'

'Well, listen closely, Aenlin Kane. It is and always has been personal.' A shadow darkened Caspar's face. 'My form of satisfaction. If I die, then ...' He took a few slow breaths. 'Never mind. Let us get back to our exciting evening. Why was Pieck hunting you? In his Lordship's name? He'd made up this murder he was blabbing about, right?'

Aenlin cursed the fact that the duellist hadn't taken the bait. 'You're very welcome to challenge his Lordship to a duel.'

'So it is true?'

'The Earl of Holland would make a nice addition to your list.' She decided not to put him in his place. 'One of the documents Pieck was carrying was an agreement with the Earl on the procurement of worldly goods.'

'Aenlin's worldly goods,' Tahmina interjected. 'I guess it was all about Aenlin's inheritance.'

'It also contained an address at the docks in London where Pieck was supposed to send the stuff.' She didn't mention the letter to Tahmina, inviting the mystic to a meeting of a magical circle in London; it was up to her companion to decide how much she wanted to tell him.

Caspar looked interested. 'What exactly did you inherit?' He caressed his stallion's neck. The horse put up with it with a snort. 'What could the Earl have wanted so badly?'

Aenlin shrugged. 'We don't know.'

'Pieck saw us leave the office with a bag, I guess,' Tahmina added, patting her saddlebags. 'He must have thought it contained Aenlin's inheritance; that's why he tried to kill Aenlin – he wanted to steal it. Which you prevented. You have our eternal gratitude for that, Caspar.'

The duellist waved it off. 'So it seems your father had something this lord wanted. I saw how Pieck's body was taken away. No one cared about how he had died.' Again, he greeted some ladies as they passed by, sitting up straight in the saddle, and again, they giggled and curtsied. 'But what happened to your inheritance? Has it been lost?'

'It is safely stored in the Company's vault, put there by poor Jacobus Maus,' Aenlin said, not bothering to hide her dissatisfaction with this state of affairs.

Caspar laughed. 'So that's why the two of you have joined this endeavour. The de Hertoghes forced you to! Still, I am very happy to be travelling with two ladies who, despite their youth, know how to fight evil.'

'I hope we will not need our skills.' Tahmina had shoved the tip of her ebony staff through a special leather loop on her saddle so it rested on her stirrup, so she didn't have to support its full weight.

The small train rode through the south gate, leaving lively, energetic, bustling Hamburg behind.

'Hey, horsies, giddyup!' Moritz flapped the reins and the horses fell back into a gentle trot. The landsknechts were muttering curses and oaths as they hopped up and down in their saddles like frogs, their equipment clattering and jiggling around them. Before long, the inexperienced riders had to reduce their speed to a walk to avoid plummeting to the dusty road.

'Oh, this journey is going to be long, longer than planned,' Caspar prophesied cheerfully. 'Tonight, these fellows will have glowing arses and sore thighs.'

'Hey, your Snootiness!' Nicolas called to Caspar as if he had heard his derision, 'I have a few questions about our journey – I'd like to know how well-informed you are.'

'Duty calls.' Caspar touched the brim of his hat and rode elegantly past the coach and Statius. The way he sat the horse, guiding his mount by the pressure of his thighs alone, spoke of great skill. *He'll be able to shoot and hit, even at a gallop*, Aenlin thought.

'What do you think of our mercenaries?' she asked Tahmina, suppressing a yawn. She felt tired again now the tension from their first meeting the landsknechts had dissipated.

'Statius will cause problems. He is unpredictable and full of bloodlust: a beast in a man's guise,' Tahmina said thoughtfully. 'Something is wrong with Moritz – in a positive way, though. I have not yet figured it out.' She nodded towards the captain, with his long, ash-blond hair. 'He is . . . a riddle to me. I cannot see through him.'

Aenlin had hoped for a different answer.

South of the Free Imperial City of Hamburg, April 1629

For days, the band made only slow progress, thanks to the landsknechts' non-existent riding skills. Maybe it was pride or greed that stopped them from abandoning the horses for the coach; in any case, they kept riding and suffered intensely, even at walking speed.

Aenlin, Tahmina and Caspar watched the spectacle from the back as they dawdled along the road at a pace that allowed even ox-carts to overtake them. These embarrassing manoeuvres were always accompanied by overly friendly words of greeting to the mercenaries, although Moritz was the only one to respond to the mockers in a friendly manner, laughing with the people who were taunting him. Statius cursed their tormentors and threw stones at them; he had collected them during one of their breaks for that very reason.

Sometimes, the captain ordered Caspar to ride ahead, to determine whether someone was trying to block their way – but of course, that was nonsense. Nicolas bossed Caspar around under the pretext of making him scout because the duellist thought too much of himself.

Aenlin was lost in her thoughts, pondering the events and insights of the last few days, for there was not much else to do. She had never harmed the Earl of Holland; she didn't even know him, so Tahmina must be right. The only conceivable reason for her attempted murder was her inheritance. Which part of it did this lord want? In his letter, her father had mentioned riches and artefacts that would make any king envious. Had the Earl somehow heard about them?

And what was this mysterious circle that so desperately wanted to meet and talk to Tahmina? What had happened in the Kingdom of England that required the services of a Persian mystic?

Then there was the attempted theft of the magic staff by a demonic creature – and its cryptic remarks about Solomon Kane. Who had sent it?

That was an extensive list, but maybe Aenlin would find answers to her many questions after her mission for the brothers de Hertoghe. Once she received her inheritance, some of the mists obscuring everything might lift.

'Do you think about the demon?' Tahmina straightened her back and rolled her slender shoulders, then adjusted her bonnet and wiped a few dandelion seeds from her blue robe.

'Only now that you mention it.' In her mind's eye, Aenlin promptly saw the dark alley. The events had caused her several nightmares, and this uneventful journey wasn't really distracting her. Still, she felt she ought to be able to confront such creatures, just as her father had. It was another kind of legacy. 'Has this happened to you before?'

'Someone trying to steal my staff?' Tahmina held it upright like a flagpole. Next to Aenlin and the men, she looked like a girl in disguise, delicate and weak, but in Hamburg, the mystic had proved how misleading her appearance was. 'The Shayatin was not the first demon to try. After my old master and two of his henchmen betrayed our scola and fled Shiraz with the holy manuscripts, he summoned the Shayatin to stop us from following him. She whom the Etruscans called Vanth heard his summoning and sent her lesser servants.' She paused for a moment, then added, 'I've seen three of them before.'

'So this was the fourth attempt.' *She hasn't mentioned this before.* Aenlin's and Tahmina's paths had crossed in London a year earlier, in an alley in Whitechapel, where the mystic had been having problems with a street gang who coveted Tahmina's possessions – and her body. Aenlin had helped her, and since then, they had been inseparable. Their souls had felt an immediate connection. 'What if your former master is behind this invitation?'

'I have thought about that, too. Or someone who wants to confront him and for that needs the same weapons as he has.' Tahmina looked worried. 'London is the perfect hideaway for him. Our Yatu teachings are too strange for European soil. You have other creatures, other wizards, witches and alchemists, but you have never heard of von Ōrmozd or Anromainyus, and you wouldn't know how to fight a deva or a djinn.' Her gaze followed the birds crossing the sky. 'Vanth and Shayatin are only small parts of this world, but they can upset the equilibrium, like an unknown but deadly fish that turns up in a lake. Before you know it, it has eaten those that were once strong there.'

'And is now the sole power in the lake.' The original reason for

Tahmina's journey to London had been to stop her old master. Aenlin had promised to help her friend until the inheritance issue had cropped up. What had started as a minor distraction on their so-far-unsuccessful search for the man suddenly became relevant to the hunt for the traitor as well. *Fascinating how everything is interconnected.*

'I am sorry,' Tahmina said softly.

'For what?'

'For dragging you into this. The Shayatin knew you – they knew your name. I believe they want to divide us. Do not believe a word they say, whatever it is.' She touched Aenlin's hand and their fingers locked for a heartbeat. 'I am putting you in danger.'

'Nonsense! They have surely known about me since I came to your aid in Whitechapel. We fight together, my dear and we will be victorious together.' *I must distract her.* Aenlin gestured at Nicolas, who was standing up in his stirrups to rub his aching backside. At times like this, he just looked laughable, not strong and authoritative. 'Were you able to figure out his aura?'

'No, he still is a riddle to me.' Tahmina could not help grinning. The periodic pained scowl on the face of their muscular leader was worth a fortune. 'I talked to Jäcklein earlier. He wanted to brag a little about his captain's strength. He told me Nicolas had cut a swathe through an entire tercio without realising it – as if he'd been in a frenzy.' She considered her own words.

'Do you believe that? Or is it a form of possession?' Aenlin had the feeling she was being watched and looked over at Statius.

The brawny man was staring at them, first at her, then at the Persian in turn. His face betrayed his filthy thoughts. She didn't like him one bit. *He will surely land us in trouble. War and carnage has completely depraved and brutalised him.*

'If only I knew.' Tahmina wanted to add something, but Statius had slowed his horse to join them. It looked like he had decided to take Aenlin's disgusted gaze as an invitation.

'Tell me,' he said, 'which one of you wants to come under my blanket tonight? I have a huge cock – we'll have a lot of fun.'

'Then your fist must have a lot of fun beating your meat,' Aenlin replied. She was not afraid of coarseness; someone who spent as much time in London's pubs and taverns as she did could not afford to be.

'You should buy yourself some prostitutes,' Tahmina added, 'now that you have enough coin to pay them.'

'What if I pay you, Persian girl?' Statius laughed coarsely. 'I'd love to fill such a sweet exotic plum – to see if there are differences between your thighs. I like it when the—'

'Stats,' Nicolas yelled sharply from ahead. 'Take up your post.'

'But I'm chatting with the petticoats,' he replied. 'The cinnamon bud and I, we're negotiating the price for her to let me enter her. It won't take long, I promise.'

'There will be no negotiations,' Tahmina replied coldly. 'And should you ever talk to me this way again, you will find your cock much thinner and shorter one of these mornings.'

'Would you like to ride it until it is all thin and short?'

'I prefer to cut it in half. Lengthwise and breadthwise.' Tahmina slightly tilted her head, her blue eyes icy. 'That's all, landsknecht. Pray to whomever you believe in that you will never need my help. It could be delayed.'

Statius laughed, roaring like a fool who had mistaken rejection for a challenge. 'My cock will get you, cinnamon bud. You are so delicate I will skewer you with it and carry you around.' His gaze turned evil and ugly. 'And you will like it.' Then he forced his horse back into position beside the coach, the animal neighing wildly, rebelling against his rough treatment.

With a pinched face Nicolas looked back at the two women and gestured an apology. Jäcklein shook his head and muttered something unintelligible as he drew his hat lower over his brow.

Moritz appeared oblivious to all of this, concentrating on driving the coach along the narrow tree-lined road.

Over the turning of the wheels and the rumbling of the coach, Aenlin heard a soft, crackling sound in the underbrush. *That was no animal—*

But before she could warn anyone, hooded figures jumped from cover. Some wielded spears and pikes; others were drawing notched rapiers and battered old swords. They threatened the travelling band with the long iron tips of their polearms.

'Stop,' their leader commanded. 'Down with the chests. Throw to the ground what you have in your pockets. Then you can keep your lives and travel on. Remember: life is your greatest treasure.'

His men laughed raucously.

Nicolas looked around on the road. 'Only ten?'

The footpads laughed again, this time clearly amused.

'We're not afraid of landsknechts – some of us were landsknechts ourselves, once. We know very well how you fight. When we had enough of marching and looting villages that offered nothing but corn and fleas, we turned to highway robbery. Much more lucrative. Come on, brother! Surrender the money and the chests.'

Tahmina and Aenlin stood ready, having no intention of letting Nicolas and his band give up the money and papers.

Aenlin's palms were sweaty with excitement. She was afraid that would never change. She would soon have her third real fight.

Moritz brought the coach to a jerky halt and surprised everyone by jumping from the box. Instead of surrendering his purse, he untied the ribbon taming his black curls and stepped towards the nearest bandit. Grabbing the top of the man's pike, he said, 'Give me that before you hurt yourself.'

'You were warned,' the leader said. 'Beat that fool to flinders!'

Nicolas signalled his men to hold back and wait.

With great surprise, Aenlin saw a rapier, a spearhead and a club all strike Moritz – but none of them pierced his skin. Laughing, he moved a few feet back to compensate for the impact, but the iron clearly hadn't hurt him.

'By all the djinni of Shiraz! I told you something was wrong with him.' Tahmina stared incredulously.

'Take that, you dung-eaters!' Jäcklein laughed at their attackers. 'You won't be able to kill him – but I wonder what he will do to you!'

'I did tell you not to attack me.' Moritz broke the pike he had taken from the man in two, then drew his bidenhänder, which looked like a normal sword in his huge hand.

With a whirring sound, he slashed the overlong sword in a semicircle – and the group of attackers fell to the dusty ground, cut down by Moritz's blade. The downed footpads had broken bones, open wounds and gaping cuts.

'Let's speed this up, shall we?' When Nicolas slid from his saddle, Statius and Jäcklein came running, too, to join the fight with their own blades.

'I see you don't need me and my skills,' Caspar announced from the back of his black horse, but nevertheless, he drew his pistols as a deterrent. 'Listen, you scoundrels: I give you fair warning: I will shoot down anybody who would attack the ladies or me.'

Aenlin and Tahmina remained in the saddle and left the skirmish to the landsknechts. After the young giant had prepared the ground, the men easily bested their opponents, their fighting styles as individual as their looks.

Moritz's youth was visible in his style. He walked between the attackers, laughing and reckless, not bothering with his enormous blade any more, but knocking them down bare-knuckled. No matter what weapons they turned against him, the gleaming steel couldn't hurt him. It didn't look like he had any intention of killing anyone, but the invincible boy was having a lot of fun venting some steam. He convulsed with laughter whenever he sent an enemy sailing through the air after giving him a sound thump.

Nicolas also attacked only to wound, wanting to make the bandits flee, while Jäcklein responded to attacks against him with equal severity – or mildness.

Statius, however, started rampaging like the Grim Reaper himself. Wielding a rapier in one hand, a sword in the other, he hewed, cut and hacked his way through the footpads nearest him, showing no mercy, killing the wounded even as they begged for mercy in the name of God. He took out the unconscious men Moritz had flattened too, and all the while he laughed, baring his teeth and licking drops of his enemies' blood from his lips.

By Lucifer – I have never seen anything like that. Aenlin, who had barely tasted anything more than shooting targets and fencing matches so far, was deeply impressed by the speed with which the landsknechts had acted. The warriors were demonstrating what it meant to kill: there were no rules; the only thing that mattered was victory. The tormented cries of the wounded haunted her and when she smelled the first stench of blood and excrement, Aenlin had to turn sideways quickly as she vomited in disgust.

This is war in a nutshell. Aenlin's teachers had tried to explain to her what happened when you hit a human being, what blades could do, by using animal carcasses for demonstration purposes. But to actually see it, to smell it, to hear the sounds and the agonised cries, was too much. She vomited again, spitting to clear her mouth.

Tahmina grabbed her bag to stop Aenlin falling off her horse. 'I am afraid this is only the beginning,' she said slowly.

When Aenlin pulled herself upright again, preparing herself

to see the bloody bodies spewing guts and worse, it was all over. All ten of the brigands were lying unmoving in the road beside the coach, dead.

Nicolas and Jäcklein returned to their horses, but Statius was hurrying from corpse to corpse to break out their teeth.

'Give it a rest,' Nicolas ordered, mounting up. 'You've collected enough souvenirs.'

'In a second.' Statius finished his work, not caring that he'd covered himself in filth in the process. 'These are beautiful teeth. I might have a jeweller turn them into a nice necklace. Well, we'll see what use I find for them.' With a bestial grin, he walked over to his horse. 'Ha. I enjoyed that. I was feeling rusty. These idiots' blood has greased my tired joints. I could run into battle now, continue the fight and send another fifty to Hell!' He looked at Tahmina. 'Or have a rut. I am full of exuberance!'

She showed him her raised fist.

Moritz clambered up to the box seat, grinning like a rascal. 'Nice surprise, right?'

'You could say that.' Jäcklein touched Moritz's muscular biceps. 'They pierced your clothes, but you're not harmed. That is madness – demonic power, or God's doing?'

'A hangman,' Moritz said frankly. 'He was skilled in the Passau Art – and the freezing, of course. That's why I'm immune to weapons.' He tied his long curls into a knot on the back of his head. 'I gave him a cow and a chicken for it.'

'Now that's what I call a good deal. You must introduce me to that hangman.' Jäcklein patted his back. 'I knew you'd be worth your salt, little giant.'

'I can still strangle him, or drown him. Or hang him.' Statius had scrambled back on his horse. 'Fortunately, we're on the same side, so this way, you don't have to be afraid of my hands.'

'You'd be welcome to try.' Moritz laughed as he dusted down at his tatty clothes. 'How about a bet? Whoever manages to kill me gets my as-yet unpaid share of this mission. But every time someone tries and fails, he pays me five thalers.'

Jäcklein split his sides laughing. 'Boy, you're a real comedian – you're either dumb or incredibly naïve.'

'I'll gladly take that bet,' Statius grumbled.

'Me too,' Jäcklein declared.

'Count me in,' Caspar said, and aimed at him with his cocked pistol. 'Let's see how well you fare against musket balls.'

Moritz adjusted his hat and spread his arms. 'Go ahead! But don't shoot off one of my curls! I love my hair!'

Can you believe this? Aenlin had been watching with a mix of consternation and amazement. 'They're just like children.'

'Like very young children,' Tahmina added.

'Will you stop the nonsense, please? You will *not* do this!' Nicolas rode off, slowly. 'Moritz is far too valuable – we'd be stuck if one of you damn fools were successful.'

Aenlin silently agreed.

'Listen up,' Nicolas continued. 'There's been a change of plan.' He took out his map. 'We're going west.'

'Why, Captain?' Jäcklein was barely managing to stay in the saddle, so badly was his horse shying at the sight and stench of the dead bodies lying around. He tried desperately to catch the twisted stirrup with his foot.

'We're too slow,' Nicolas said. 'None of us – well, us landsknechts – is a skilled rider, so this is taking too long. We'll find us a ship and travel upstream on the Weser. That way, we'll make better progress – and we'll be able to travel day and night.'

'Good idea.' Aenlin was glad false pride would no longer hamper their journey. She wanted to get her inheritance as quickly as possible, unravel the conspiracy to murder her and rid herself of the mercenaries' company. *I think Statius is capable of the worst deeds conceivable.*

'Are you not going to bury them?' Tahmina moved past the

corpses littering the road. The first vigilant crows had landed around the dead, expecting a feast.

'Nah. I won't get my hands dirty for that rabble.' Jäcklein pointed to the black birds hopping about, picking at the still-warm flesh and rummaging in the wounds. 'Look, the Holy Joes are already there. They'll take care of the requiem. Afterwards, there'll be no trace of those footpads any more.'

His companions laughed. Caspar only nodded.

Nicolas suddenly reined in his horse. 'I almost forgot.' He dismounted, drew the bidenhänder from its sheath and walked towards the corpses. 'Ride on. I'll quickly decapitate the corpses.'

Croaking boisterously, the crows flew up to find shelter in the surrounding trees. They were in no hurry; their food wasn't going to go running away.

'Ah, the living dead the tavern maid told us about,' Statius ventured. 'Clever idea, Captain! That'll stop their revenants following us to get revenge.'

'Exactly.' Nicolas raised his bidenhänder. 'I will not be devoured by corpses.'

Aenlin and Tahmina looked away, exchanging a look as the blade came down. Here they were, in the middle of the harshness of war.

[...] around 800 people, men, women and children from our citizenry died, innocents killed in a most miserable fashion, with neither pregnant women nor under-aged infants, neither old nor afflicted people spared, but all whom the soldiers encountered after their invasion that day, except for those whom God Himself spared as an exception, were struck down with halberds, so that they suffered for a long while before sighing out their soul, and quite some were thrown into hot water and burned, and many were thrown from the tower or other high places; to many, powder was attached to torture them, many were tied up and roasted in the fire, some had ropes tied around their heads, some were hanged, some had their eyes gouged out, ill, weak folk were killed in their sickbeds, young children were stabbed down with pikes and lifted up to thrash around on them; several noble old councilmen of seventy, eighty and more years, and also an ancient mariner of one hundred and eight years who had almost been like a child again, were struck down with the others, several were burnt on the tower next to the city wall with fire and powder, the dead bodies in the alleys were partially naked, amongst them also a pregnant woman, who was dead, but the fruit of her womb, *salva Reverentia*, had been stuck halfway through the process of birth and was still moving; several obese people had their fat stomachs and their entrails cut out of their bodies, others their hearts; some were pushed from the roofs like birds and afterwards, the soldiers sat on the dead corpses and drank a toast to each other. Many had paid their ransom once, twice or even three times, had been promised quarter, but the promise went unkept and such ungodly deeds had been committed against us, beatings, assault, rape, abuse and others, all of them almost ineffable, yet still afterwards, the dead (and this is what pains many heartsick widows the most to this day), citizens and strangers alike, more than 2,260, were tracked and heaps of forty, fifty or more piled at the corners of the alleys, thrown on carts, brought to the bridge and thrown into the water from there, amongst them several wounded who still lived and whose pleas rang out, even the fruit of the womb that also still moved, even when it lay in the water.

translated from a report by Christoff Hüpeden, Alderman, former Mayor and Councillor of Münden, on Bloody Whitsun of Münden in 1626

CAPITULUM V

On the Weser, May 1629

Aenlin sat on the forecastle of the long river barge *Lorelei*, enjoying the evening sun on her skin as she watched the landscape passing by. She had taken off her hat and her baldric, leaving her dark hair loose on her back. Only one ebony strand fell on her face.

They had made satisfactory progress in the last few days and Aenlin was finding the mission unexpectedly quiet, pleasant – even the weather was playing nice. *Who would have thought?*

The large sail on the folding mast caught the wind, letting the *Lorelei* sail south against the current. Birds chirped and sang. Devil's needles, as the people here called dragonflies, visited the ship to land on the railing and ride along for a short way.

It would be wonderful if our journey remained that peaceful. The quiet conversations of the crew and landsknechts gathered behind her reached her ears.

From time to time, there came a ringing sound, Statius and Moritz continuing their fencing lessons. The beefy mercenary had graciously offered not to take half the young giant's pay. He was one of them now. Moritz looked like he'd grown another six inches with pride.

Occasional curses sounded across the water from time to time: Jäcklein was busying himself with his musket, practising what he'd taught himself. It apparently took more than one hundred and forty different movements to load the rifle, and he had to learn them all by himself. He had declined Aenlin's help.

Tahmina approached her, handed her a mug of tea and sat down. 'Here. This will invigorate you.'

'What herbs did you use?'

'Nothing you need to worry about.' She smiled. 'Dried mint.'

Aenlin slid a little closer so that they were able to touch each other without anybody noticing. 'I know it isn't only mint. There are more ingredients in this tea.'

'Oh? Since when are you a trained herbalist?'

'I don't have to be. I feel calmer, less haunted by the nightmares.' She suffered from them only sporadically now, which she attributed to the brew her companion provided.

'Don't worry. It will do you good.'

Aenlin nodded thankfully. 'We're making good progress.'

'That is what the captain said, too.' Tahmina watched the reeds swaying on the left bank as if waving at the barge and its passengers.

The *Lorelei* was a river barge equipped with only a small cargo hold, so most of their equipment had to be stored on deck, but there was space enough for the coach and the horses on board. The boat's crew included two large plough horses to drag the barge along if necessary, should the charitable wind subside.

When the barge's captain had seen the drafts issued and sealed by the West India Company, he had immediately agreed to take the band from Bremen as far as he could go on the Weser and the Werra.

The sailors kept their distance from the landsknechts and stuck with their own kind. No one wanted an altercation with these warriors, which might arise all too quickly.

'Nicolas thinks we might make it to Bamberg within two weeks.' Tahmina sighed happily. 'It is so beautiful here on the river, with the trees and bushes in full bloom; there is life and spring in the air. Very different from drab London.'

Or from the country road with its footpads and marauders. Aenlin looked at the villages lining the Weser. 'Do I hear a trace of homesickness?'

'I do not feel homesick for London.' Tahmina sipped her tea. *But I do . . .*

Nicolas had asked the captain how many borders they'd be crossing on their journey. The answer was, quite a few, and of course, every principality or duchy, no matter how small, would demand some sort of levy – everyone using the Weser and the Werra had to pay these tolls. The *Lorelei* would also have to pass through two Imperial Circles, and to deal with the change of judiciary domains. Some of those along the river were on such bad terms that they diverted the tributaries, literally taking the water – and thus, the income – out of their hated neighbours' mouths.

Aenlin looked over her shoulder at the mercenaries.

Caspar was lying on an improvised cot of coiled ropes, his hat covering his face. The ends of his wig protruded from beneath the felt like floppy ears. Moritz and Statius were still training with rapier and bidenhänder while Nicolas checked the map again, trying to work out what tolls and bribes they'd need to pay to continue their journey. Jäcklein stood at the stern, practising with his musket.

'The slayer is restless,' Tahmina stated. 'His bloodlust haunts him, and he is spoiling for a fight. The battle against the footpads has stirred him up, but on the barge, he is a prisoner who must behave. There is no chance for him to take out his anger on somebody.'

'Do you think he will become a danger for us?'

'As long as Nicolas is around, he will obey.' Tahmina smoothed

Aenlin's wind-tousled hair, smiling warmly at her. 'I will look out for you and you will look out for me.'

'From the bottom of my heart.' Aenlin quickly touched Tahmina's right cheek, a gentle caress. With so many pairs of eyes around, she didn't dare to do more.

A loud curse made the two women whirl around.

'How the hell do you do that?' Jäcklein stood behind Moritz, looking down at his bent rapier. 'The spell is effective even if you don't pay attention?'

Hearing Statius and Moritz laughing, Caspar pushed up his hat to check for the reason behind the merriment.

'It would be bad if it only worked when I see the blow coming,' Moritz declared. 'In combat, you often don't even notice that you are under attack.'

Jäcklein tried to straighten the blade on the planks with his foot, but the steel stayed bent. 'By the Devil! I'll have to have it reforged.'

'You owe me five guilders.' Moritz held out his hand.

'Do you know how much a rapier costs?'

'Hey, don't pike out now,' Caspar said from where he lay. 'We had an arrangement. You tried to kill him. Unsuccessfully. Now pay him, old chap.'

'And after this, I want no one giving it a second try,' Nicolas shouted across the deck, looking up from his papers. 'Is that clear? I will remind you, I ordered you to stop this nonsense.'

'But he provoked me, Captain!' Jäcklein ran his fingers through his unruly hair.

'Me?' Moritz asked, all innocence.

'Yes, you, little giant. You turned your back to me. It was a positive invitation!' Jäcklein shouldered his bent rapier. 'That will cost me a lot.' He took the sum in question from his pocket and counted it into Moritz's palm. 'Next time I'll try it secretly,' he said, 'so Nicolas won't notice.'

'You're welcome to try anything that will make me rich.' Moritz patted his back encouragingly and Jäcklein involuntarily took a step forwards.

Tahmina and Aenlin couldn't hide their grins.

'Silly people,' the mystic muttered, then she turned serious. 'I don't know how long the frozenness will last. Moritz might still die in battle – or during this stupid competition.'

'I'll tell Nicolas to call them to order, stop them from trying again.' Aenlin was enjoying the effects of Tahmina's tea, and she liked ships, with their soft swaying and the liveliness of the water, her favourite element. The pastoral surroundings only added to her feeling of contentment. 'If my inheritance is large enough, we'll buy ourselves a boat.'

'What?' Tahmina laughed. 'What would we do with a boat?'

'Live on the River Thames. And if we get fed up with London, we can set sail for wherever we might like better.' Aenlin sighed and leaned against the mystic. 'But first we need to accomplish this mission and solve the riddle surrounding your old master.'

'Oh, dear. Looks like I used the wrong herbs after all.' Tahmina gently touched her shoulder. 'But I like the idea. You, me, a boat.'

The ship's captain shouted orders across the deck and the *Lorelei* headed towards the bank.

The sailors dropped anchor beside a steep embankment and moored the barge there. There wasn't enough oil on board to fill all the dark-lanterns so they could keep going through the night, as Nicolas had demanded, but they'd be able to rectify that when they reached the next big town or city. Then they would be able to continue their journey at a quicker pace.

'Jäcklein and Moritz, as soon as it's dark, you take the first watch,' Nicolas said loudly. 'Then Statius and me.'

'Yes, sir!' Jäcklein had grabbed his musket and was resting the heavy barrel on the handguard of his rapier. He was still struggling with the handling of the firearm. 'Hey, your Aged

Know-it-allness von und zu dem Dorffe! Would you be so kind to show me this—?'

'He didn't want help from a woman,' Aenlin interposed. 'Men!'

'No, I can't,' Caspar replied, propping himself up on an elbow and watching the mercenary struggle. 'I'm only good with pistols. We should consider ourselves lucky that the de Hertoghes have given us those new flintlock weapons. Even though I'm pretty fond of my old wheellock pistols. Who knows how good this new mechanism is? It seems to me it has not been fully tested in the field. However, a wheellock wouldn't be at all suitable for a musket.'

'Best of luck with your shooting irons. See you later. Take good care.' Statius jumped from the barge and landed almost on top of the embankment. As well as his armour, he wore his rapier, his sword and a crossbow, and carried a quiver filled with bolts. 'I'll go and find us something nice to roast for dinner.' He looked around in anticipation. 'By your leave, Captain?'

'Bring us a tender deer,' Nicolas replied. 'Don't go messing with wild boars, though. That would surely end in tears.'

The beefy Statius raised his hand and disappeared into the underbrush.

Moritz walked up to Aenlin and Tahmina. 'May I ask you a question, mystic?'

Jäcklein was still occupied with the handling of his musket, watched carefully by Nicolas, who was checking everything he did, determined to learn to use it as well.

'I would prefer it if you called me Tahmina.' She discreetly pointed at the sailors who were finishing up the mooring to prevent the *Lorelei* drifting off. 'I would not want them to consider me a witch and burn me at the stake.'

Moritz bowed politely, like a child apologising for a mistake. He sat down, but still towered over the women. 'Your staff is so beautifully carved. Would you like to tell me what it can do?'

Aenlin didn't really want them to discuss the artefact; the fewer people who knew about its special properties, the better, and especially in these German lands, where there was a real hysteria over witches, wizards and the powers of evil. Maybe it would be smarter to wrap the staff in leather. The carvings and the inlaid work were too conspicuous.

'Oh, most definitely,' Tahmina said, and with exaggerated facial expressions, as if she was telling a fairy tale, she started, 'The wood is from a tree long since extinct: the tree of good, which is full of light.' She really wanted Moritz to believe that she was making up her story. Caressing the carvings in the shaft, she went on, 'I can exorcise evil spirits and demons with it, and I can use it to kill witches and wizards by reflecting their own spells and curses back at them.' She tapped her forehead with the palm of her hand. 'Oh, and I almost forgot: it tells me whether I am dealing with supernatural beings. I knew at once that there was something unusual about you – but in a positive way. This is why I didn't have to do anything about you.'

'Oh, how fascinating!' Moritz clapped his hands once. 'Do you detect angels, too?'

Tahmina laughed. 'Definitely.'

'Tell me, how many adventures has it helped you through so far?'

Now she hesitated for a moment. 'A whole bagful.' She cast a sidelong glance at Aenlin. 'You must know that my staff is a loyal companion. Without it, more than one encounter with a demon would have turned out badly. Where I come from, we call them Shayatin, djinni and devas.'

'But what about the angels? Are they always nice?'

They are fucking cowards, Aenlin thought. *So many of them cower instead of rebelling!* But she kept silent, even if doing so was not at all easy. She would have loved to tell Moritz about Lucifer and how God had falsely accused him to cover up his own failure. But if the youth told some religious fanatic about this, she would be brought to trial for heresy, sacrilege, blasphemy – whatever.

'Angels are always nice,' she answered instead, though it hurt her to contradict her own convictions. *For you, Lucifer.*

'What about the Angel of Death? The one God sent to bring the plague and kill the children?' Moritz appeared to have been pondering this issue for a while.

'How do you know that?' Tahmina put both hands on her staff, now resting it across her lap.

'A priest I once met said that the angels are God's army. They come to punish, to reward and to bear tidings, some of them bad, some of them good.' Moritz looked down the Weser. 'The plague has afflicted Altona – did angels appear there to warn the inhabitants?'

Aenlin had to fight to keep her composure. *Lucifer, give me strength not to blurt out a hymn of praise to you!*

'The plague is an affliction, like the catarrh or a cough.' Tahmina gestured with her fingers as she spoke. 'We spread it – and sometimes, it is animals who spread the disease from human to human, for example lice, fleas and other insects. Where I come from, people know that. Here, they don't yet. They believe in . . . other causes.'

'Ah! Then the plague is rather . . . like . . . the rabies in dogs!' He smiled, as if to prove that he understood the concept.

'That is right, Moritz. It has nothing to do with angels or demons.' Tahmina paused for a moment, then admitted, 'Well, I will not exclude the possibility. Some demons do have that kind of power.'

'Thought so.' Moritz gazed across the river, which was turning dark in the rapidly dying light. 'I should have paid that hangman more. Then he would have made me immune against that, too.'

'What exactly did the executioner do to you?' Aenlin was

glad they weren't talking about angels any more. 'Why wasn't he executed for sorcery?'

'Who would hang the hangman?' Moritz laughed.

'Another hangman,' Caspar replied dryly. He had given up lounging around like a nobleman and was standing two paces away.

'Some people might think you had been eavesdropping,' Aenlin pointed out, thinking, *He can be very quiet if he wants to.*

'You were speaking too loudly for me not to overhear your conversation. It was doubly interesting for me: a duellist meeting someone like you, dear Moritz, is fucked.' He put his right hand in his pocket and produced a musket ball with a special engraving. 'Even this won't hurt you, although hitting you would not be a problem, young giant.'

'What is that?' Aenlin remembered the strange expression on his face before the duel. 'An infernal musket ball?'

'Yes. I don't need it – I'm skilled enough at shooting.' Caspar's answer had the well-earned arrogance of an expert. 'But I own it, and I know how to make more. They never miss their mark. However, the Devil himself guides the seventh musket ball – he decides its trajectory the moment it leaves the barrel.'

'Why do you keep it, if there is a chance it might pierce your own head?' Moritz took it from his hand. 'Or do you know that it's not the seventh one?'

'Oh, it's just a keepsake, a reminder of someone who wanted to use it against me.' His grim smile told the trio how that duel had ended. 'He got it from a hangman – or rather, a hang*woman*.'

'I would love to have a chat with that hangwoman,' Tahmina muttered.

'In my case, it was simple,' the giant declared. 'The executioner wrote some words on a page he had torn out of a Bible, sprinkled a little chicken blood over it and drew a cross on the page. He told me to burn the page while saying ten Paternosters and one hundred Hail Marys.' He rubbed his belly. 'But I ate it instead. I wanted it to strengthen me from within.'

Aenlin stifled a laugh while Tahmina grinned broadly.

'How was it?' Caspar enquired. He pinched the back of his nose with thumb and index finger, as if visibly fighting for composure. 'How was the finish? Did you have wine with it – and if so, which one would you recommend as a good accompaniment for the Bible?'

'It was ... dry; I almost choked at the psalm,' Moritz said, 'But as you have seen, neither blade nor ball can kill me.'

He passed the infernal musket ball along, and each of them studied it with some wonder before passing it to the next person.

'Is it really no evil curse?' Moritz suddenly looked worried. 'Did I sell my soul?'

'At the most, you have eaten your soul.' Caspar laughed, his brief show of temper gone. 'I am so happy, my little one, that you are on our side. You are worth as much as a thousand landsknechts, especially with your strength. You and Nicolas, I would bet you could challenge each other when it comes to mowing down an enemy tercio.'

Moritz slapped his thighs. 'Yes, we should! You will be our judge, friend Bang-Bang.'

'Thanks, but no thanks,' the duellist said. 'When the two of you lash out, it's like planets striking each other. I don't like steaming, oozing entrails and split skulls. That mess back there on our journey was quite enough for me.'

'Well, I could eat now.' Moritz gazed across the deck at the crew, gathered around a cauldron in which stew bubbled. They obviously weren't relying on Statius' hunting skills. 'Oh, look there – that looks tasty! I smell bacon.' He got up. 'Come. I—'

Aenlin suddenly noticed that the smoke wasn't coming from

the sailors' brazier. 'Can you smell that, too?' She licked her finger and raised it to the wind to check its direction. 'It's coming from inland.'

'Now, what's this?' Jäcklein stopped loading his musket and sniffed the air. 'I know this stench: wood, stone and meat, burning in hot flames. Someone's burning down a village!'

They all looked around, but because of the slope of the embankment and the thick underbrush beyond, they could see nothing but grey and white swaths of smoke marring the night-blue evening sky.

'Jäcklein, Snootiness, Aenlin and Tahmina, with me,' Nicolas calmly ordered, his voice firm. 'Moritz, you'll stay here and guard the barge.' He grabbed his sword, pulled on his hat and fastened his breastplate. 'It will neither leave without us, nor will anybody come on board.'

'Understood, Captain.' Moritz saluted.

Quickly, Aenlin donned her own baldric and with Tahmina's help, attached her weapons. Her blue eyes looked worried.

'I don't think we need be worried for a fellow like Statius.' Caspar readied his pistols and adjusted his wig so he could don his hat.

'No, not for him,' Nicolas replied. He mounted the slope at a light trot. 'But for the place this smoke is rising from.'

The others followed him.

That was my first thought too. Aenlin hadn't felt suspicious when the brutal mercenary left them, even though she and Tahmina had been discussing his restlessness, but maybe he had found an opportunity to vent his savagery. Maybe this had been his plan all along.

As soon the group reached the top of the slope, they saw the burning village, less than a mile north. The fire had already spread to the neighbouring fields, the flames rising high into the twilight sky. Ash fell like snow, covering them with small grey flakes. The wind blew in their faces, carrying silent cries of men, women. Children.

'Holy shit, Stats,' Nicolas whispered, his face paling. 'What have you done?' He started running.

Jäcklein and Caspar followed the captain, with Aenlin and Tahmina bringing up the rear.

'If this really was him, he needs to be punished,' Aenlin said to Tahmina. Her worry was growing with every step. She hadn't forgotten the images of the fight against the footpads, not nearly. The raging fire and the shrieks that were rising in volume spoke of even more terrible sights to come.

'According to the prevailing law, this would mean death.' Tahmina's darker skin had a pale shine to it. She too was afraid of what they were going to see.

Flames came shooting out of the barns and huts, joining together to form an inferno, a hot vortex turning the flames into one glowing pillar spiralling upwards, forty, fifty paces high, gyrating and hissing as if trying to burn a hole into the night.

'The work of a demon?' Nicolas called over his shoulder.

'No, no demon,' Tahmina answered after a quick glance at her staff. Its symbols remained dark. 'I am afraid the perpetrator is made only of flesh and blood,' she added quietly.

Aenlin found herself rejoicing at Statius' potential demise, but had to calm herself. *It's too early for that.*

Finally, the group reached the village, gasping and coughing.

The continuous rain of ash had turned the light grey, making the surroundings look almost unreal. Heat had cracked the stone walls of the houses; there was no cool air to breathe. Everywhere was covered in corpses, charred and split open and stinking like overcooked meat – but cuts, mutilations and blows were still visible.

Aenlin followed the captain's example, covering her mouth and nose with a cloth and shielding her eyes with one hand to protect them from the heat. 'He has slaughtered them,' she whispered to Tahmina. She would never forget the sight of the conflagration and the dead people. *Never.*

'There are some more over there.' The mystic pointed to some small limbs that had been hacked off. 'Children.'

'Stats,' Nicolas yelled through the hissing, crackling and whispering of the fire, 'Stats, where are you?'

'Let's leave him to burn,' Aenlin muttered. He had earned Hell.

But Jäcklein, crouching low, was already running between the burning buildings, trying to reach the heart of the village. 'Over here,' he shouted. 'He's here.' He turned to the right and disappeared behind flames.

Aenlin had never seen a fire this big up close. Merely breathing burned her lungs; her hair was smouldering, her eyes were dry as a desert. Struggling against her flight instinct with all her might, she followed the group.

Jäcklein was standing by a well at the centre of the village.

'By Lucifer!' The words slipped out of Aenlin's mouth.

Statius sat on the edge of the stone basin, naked to the waist and covered in blood. It dripped from his beard and the sword he held with both hands and leaned against. Flames and shadows alike surrounded him, the dark red shine highlighting the countless scars and fresh wounds adorning his body as ash rained down. His face spoke of triumph and satisfaction, the expression of a cruel god having vented his lust for destruction. A twisted smile played at the corners of his mouth.

Corpses lay at his feet, in the well, draped across its edge and all around Statius. Some of them were intact, some of them looked as if they'd been hacked to pieces in a slaughterhouse. Sparks danced around the landsknecht, who at that moment might well have been a demon.

'Stats!' Nicolas cowered against the heat. 'What have you—?'

'They were hunting me,' Statius whispered without looking

up. His wide pupils were a mirror for the inferno. 'They wanted to eat my flesh and sacrifice my heart. Man-eaters – a village full of cannibals.' He laughed darkly. 'Well, they caught the wrong one this time. I made them eat their own entrails and fingers until they suffocated.'

That is his excuse for this massacre? 'Look around, find out if he speaks the truth,' Aenlin whispered to her companion. 'Search for signs of idolatry – you're the only one who can recognise them. Then go back to the barge.'

Tahmina nodded and separated herself from the group.

Statius fished the severed head of a woman from the well. Her long blonde hair hung down like wet threads. 'Their leader. Lisbeth.' He watched her frozen features, then touched his forehead to hers. 'The witch tried to curse me, but my blade was quicker than her words.' He laughed darkly. 'Little Lis. You felt nice to the touch, you demon.'

'This is the Apocalypse,' Nicolas gasped, shaking his head as if he could not believe what was going on around him. 'This is exactly how the Apocalypse must be!'

Jäcklein, cursing, approached the blood-drenched mercenary. 'Let's get away from here, Stats, otherwise you'll burn alive. There's no one left in the village who wants to eat you. What a waste.' He grabbed the crazed man's arm, which was covered in a layer of ash. 'Get up! You still have some pay to spend.'

When the landsknecht didn't budge, Nicolas came over and helped drag him away.

Statius dropped the woman's head, which rolled across the ground until it came to rest at Aenlin's toes.

With a gasp, she flinched from the head, fighting down the bile rising in her throat. *Lucifer, what is going on here on this earth?*

Tahmina reappeared from the roiling smoke. 'It looks to be true,' she coughed. 'I have found bones and smoked meat – of adults and children alike.'

They really had eaten each other? Aenlin didn't want to believe it any more than she wanted to believe Statius' claim to have acted in self-defence. *We would be better off if he was dead.*

'Hurry up, hurry up,' Nicolas ordered. The landsknechts and Caspar hurried past them, Jäcklein and the captain supporting Statius.

The women followed them back to the barge. On the way, Aenlin looked back several times.

The village was gone. The fire had reached a lush green area bordering the fields and lost its power in the wet grass. But the acrid smoke still blotted out the stars, creating unnatural clouds over the moon.

Aenlin thought she saw a human silhouette, surrounded by flames, lurch from the subsiding inferno, and the scream that followed the group was so loud that it must have been audible across the entire region. Then the figure collapsed, and the fire devoured it.

After two more steps, Aenlin stopped and vomited what little she had eaten into the tall grass. The smell of burnt flesh was still in her nose; it would probably remind her forever of the recent events.

Tahmina dragged her along. 'That's what war does to people, Aenlin. It makes apocalypses on a daily basis.'

Aenlin spat and walked on, but the stench of Statius' blood rose into her nostrils and she heaved again.

That was not how she had imagined coming into her inheritance.

Near Münden, May 1629

Aenlin, Tahmina and the landsknechts sat on the soft grass in the shadow of trees at the edge of the embankment, watching the flowing, glittering waters. From time to time they picked berries from the bushes.

Nicolas was checking their funds. 'So far, the journey has been pretty expensive,' he said. He tied his ash-blond hair back to keep it from falling into his face.

'But at least without nuisance.' Jäcklein ate some berries, which stained his beard around his lips. 'Except for the affair with the village of the man-eaters – oh, and the footpads.' His musket lay across his knees. He had learned to handle it really well since their departure, although not yet in combat conditions; he confessed that it might be possible he would have a harder time with it in battle. Reloading the thing was supposed to take no more than two minutes. It was still taking him more than three.

The *Lorelei* was moored by the riverbank just below them, not far from the placid town of Münden. The barge hadn't continued on to the city because it had collided with a drifting tree, despite all their precautions and poking about with boat hooks.

The captain had made the crew moor up at the riverbank to thoroughly check the keel, as well as the surrounding woodwork, from inside and out. He didn't want to risk his barge springing a leak in the middle of the Weser, especially since the river was full of rocks here. One minor crunch could turn an apparently harmless crack into a gaping hole that would be the end of the *Lorelei*, her cargo and her passengers.

Aenlin plucked some berries from a bush, then pushed her hat back to protect her neck against the sun. *What a beautiful light.*

By day, the lovely weather exorcised the dark images that had taken hold of her thoughts after that gory night in the village. In the darkness, Tahmina's tea and her closeness helped; they held hands secretly under their blankets so none of the men would notice.

'It's not the fastest way to travel, but it's better than wearing down my soles.' Jäcklein patted his belly. 'I've gained weight too. Not enough walking.'

'Why don't you walk ahead of the towing horses from now on,' said Caspar, who was lying on his back with a blade of grass in the corner of his mouth. His behaviour suggested simpler origins at odds with his courtly manner and expensive clothing. 'You'll soon be lithe and lissome.'

'But he's already thin as a straw,' Statius said. He, too, had familiarised himself with the way the muskets worked. During the day, he, Nicolas and Jäcklein liked to stand on the deck of the drifting *Lorelei* and shoot at targets on the shore, with moderate success. 'Look what I built.' He raised the long weapon. With wire and thick cord, he had attached a dagger below the barrel. 'If someone gets too close to me while I'm loading, I'll gut him like I'm used to.'

'Now then: a shooting pike? Consider me enthusiastic.' Caspar mockingly tipped his hat. 'Your invention will soon be everywhere. Build a real locking mechanism into it and you'll be rich.'

Aenlin shuddered. At the word *gut*, images of the night when Statius had taken revenge on the village rose before her eyes. *At least, that was what he called it.*

Even though Tahmina had confirmed to Nicolas that people *had* been eaten in that settlement, she would still have preferred to see Statius on the gallows.

Whether the villagers had tried to bring down a beefy, well-armed landsknecht was a different matter. It was well known that civilians often took vengeance upon mercenaries travelling alone after having been separated from their bunch or the army. *But would they have tried to eat him?*

'You're dead right, your Snootiness. That would bring me money. I think the next war's only a matter of time. The Danes will disappear and the Swedes will land, I bet.' Nicolas stopped counting and consulted the map to get his bearings. 'If our barge makes it, we'll enter the Werra tomorrow and the next part of our journey will begin.'

I would so love to be on the way back already. Aenlin looked down at the *Lorelei.* The captain and some of his sailors were standing on the forecastle. *What are they talking about?* she wondered. A number of the crew had gone to the nearby village to look for beer, brandy and a pig to slaughter and roast over a fire. They hadn't wanted to send the landsknechts, for some reason.

'How long, Captain?' she asked Nicolas.

'Hard to tell – I have no idea about navigation – but since we're travelling day and night now, it shouldn't take too long.'

'Let me tell you, we will never, ever enter Münden.' Jäcklein dropped another berry into his mouth. 'We should sail past the city quick-like, and stay below decks. They would just love to see landsknechts.'

'What about Münden?' Aenlin looked at the mercenary.

'What do you think?' Statius exaggerated a show of being stabbed. 'Three years ago, Tilly looted it. On Pentecost. He weakened the walls in preparation for his attack and took Münden because the idiots didn't want to surrender. He had twenty thousand men, cannon and mortars.' The look on his face showed how much he would have loved to be there.

'*Looted* it is an understatement,' Jäcklein added. 'Tilly's landsknechts killed more than two thousand men, women and children – the elderly, sick and disabled, they even killed babies. They say they threw the corpses from the bridge over the Werra.'

''S what I heard as well. Half of the inhabitants.' Caspar sat upright in the tall grass, brushing stray blades of grass from his black clothes. 'It was one of many towns they sacked. It was the innocent who had to suffer.'

'Well, they should have surrendered.' As always, Statius was on the side of the mercenaries. He hadn't talked about that night at the cannibal village, but ever since, he'd been acting meekly, his thirst for blood apparently quenched, at least for now.

Aenlin and Tahmina considered his change of behaviour too good to last.

'How could they believe they would ever be able to withstand such odds? Without supplies or help?' He stroked his growing moustache and twisted the tips out.

'But that doesn't give them the right to kill the inhabitants.' Aenlin was angry at herself for reacting to his remark at all. The idea that she could do otherwise, however, was in vain – as was her hope that Statius would never again lose his temper.

Tahmina had seen it in him at once.

Jäcklein plucked more berries and promptly pricked his finger on a thorn. 'Killing is not a fitting word for what they did. Those were atrocities. They stopped at nothing.' He looked down at the drop of blood.

'Another apocalypse,' Statius muttered, watching, intrigued, as he allowed a butterfly to land on his outstretched finger. The peacock butterfly gracefully opened and closed its wings. 'We are the riders of the Apocalypse, racing through the Dark Lands.'

'Yes, and our seal of destruction is a butterfly,' Moritz said in an exaggerated whisper as he whittled away at a stick.

'Doesn't the Bible speak of a seven-headed beast?' Caspar looked at Statius. 'This little flying thing must be confused. Why would it visit a man like our butcher?'

'A blind butterfly?' Jäcklein supposed.

'There is nothing good about war. There never is, neither the reason for it nor the fact of it. However, there are excuses for both.' Tahmina ignored Aenlin's pleading look. 'People want peace, but the broadsheets are dripping with blood.'

'And so I will never learn to read. It's what it is.' Statius watched the butterfly rise into the air again and waved his musket, the dagger attached to it making a little whirring noise as it moved. 'I would never have become a farmer. I owe my life to war, strange as it may sound.' He pointed at the whittling Moritz. 'Look at him. I was once like he is now: a runaway in search of a better life.' He first caressed the handle of his rapier, then the butt of his musket. 'Well, I found it – and now more than ever, thanks to the Company.'

'One thing is sure: war is the great equaliser, Aenlin. You are a woman from a loving home. How would you know?' Jäcklein pointed at his companions. 'We once had other professions. In our tercios and squads, we had people of all kinds, from peasants to nobles, from farmers and sailors to impoverished scribes and indebted bakers. They came and still come from all over the world to make a living by killing. War makes the count a pikeman and the innkeeper a captain. They must only be efficient: that's all.'

'Well, they should also have enough money for their own equipment.' Caspar pointed at his black horse, which was grazing nearby. 'I was a mercenary briefly, a cuirassier. Pistols, harness, ammunition, fodder, provisions – all of that is costly.' He spat out his blade of grass. 'No, I prefer to ride my faithful Comte, acting for myself.'

I should have guessed. Now Aenlin knew where the duellist came by his riding skills.

'I don't care what or who they pray to.' Statius opened his mouth and Jäcklein threw a berry inside. 'Tomorrow, I'll be a Protestant, the day after, I'll be a Catholic and back again. It doesn't matter to me: he who pays the piper calls the tune – as long as he does pay.'

'You were not there? When Münden fell?' Moritz kept whittling.

'No, lad. We had to push halberds and pikes through bodies elsewhere.' Statius sighed with remorse. 'But, oh, the loot we could have walked off with.'

Aenlin heard the subtext in his words: *Oh, what cruelties I could have committed*. And without being afraid of a conviction. Rape was prohibited during lootings, under penalty of death, but the truth was, perpetrators were rarely punished. The generals allowed massacres to frighten new enemies and break their resistance more easily. Journals and broadsheets printed extensive reports about such events, with detailed descriptions and drawings for the illiterate.

Nicolas had been keeping conspicuously quiet, but now, after thoroughly studying the map, he said, 'On board the *Lorelei*, we won't make it past the city of Wanfried. The captain said that there are too many mills beyond Wanfried damming the Werra's water, so it becomes unnavigable.'

'Let's switch to small boats,' Statius suggested. 'Or rafts, or something like that.'

'Too much trouble,' Nicolas declared. 'We'll buy another cart in Wanfried to go easy on our arses. Not for all the tea in China will I ride another horse.' He grinned.

His men responded with relieved laughter.

'From there, it's straight on to Bamberg. We can make it there in less than a week.'

Aenlin pointed to some annotations by a shaded area on the map. 'What do they mean?'

'That we'll be forking over more money.' Nicolas pushed the map at her. 'The Company has marked this region as recently belonging to the Landgrave of Hesse-Rotenburg – some nobles and petty rulers who consider themselves Emperor of their little landgraviate.'

The men all laughed.

'Then, for all I know, another Tilly, another Wallenstein, another Emperor – a Dane, a Swede, a Frenchman – comes marching through and shoots their cities to pieces to teach them their proper place. Then it's time to draw up a new map reflecting the recent events.'

'That's pretty confusing,' Tahmina said.

'That's what everyone says. Two armies meeting and fighting until there's a winner doesn't cut it any more.' Nicolas looked over at the *Lorelei*. The captain was arguing loudly with some of the sailors – the group who'd gone to the village had returned with a sack full of bacon, sausages and fresh bread. 'They appear to be arguing about how much the barge can carry.'

'Who do we help?' Statius rose from the grass. He was looking forward to a brawl. 'I'd love to test my invention.' He stabbed with the musket and again, the dagger made a low, whirring noise.

'The group who are in the right,' Jäcklein said, laughing. 'Would anyone like to end up at the bottom of the Weser? Not me, that's for sure.'

'It's not about the barge.' Caspar had the sharpest ears of all of them and he'd been listening. 'It's about where we'll be mooring.'

Aenlin rolled her eyes and took the map. 'Well, it says here that the boundary—'

'Those simple people aren't afraid of mundane things,' the duellist said, looking startled. He turned his head to the wind and put a hand to his ear to better catch the voices. 'They say the villagers advised them to disappear – to continue to Münden before *she* comes. As soon as she appears, it's supposed to be too late; we'd have to join her game.' Caspar took a look around. 'Or go to Hell.'

'*She*.' Nicolas looked at Tahmina. 'That sounds like a job for you, Mystic. What do your senses tell you? Is there something about this piece of land that could send us into Satan's parlour?'

Again, his landsknechts laughed.

Aenlin bit her lips. *There is no Hell, not the way they imagine it – no Purgatory or the like. God and the Church had only invented damnation and the Devil to make the people docile, and to unjustly characterise Lucifer as evil.*

'No,' she replied, as if the question had been directed at her, ignoring Tahmina's look of warning. *I must finally straighten this out.* 'There is no—'

'Hey,' the captain shouted at them, 'come on over. Supper's ready.'

'Looks as if we're staying at this cosy river bend for now.' Caspar stood, brushing grass and petals from his breeches. 'Hopefully, the bread is tasty. The last lot was hard as rock.'

No one asked Aenlin what she had been about to say. The men rose and walked towards the barge, eager to allay their hunger. Only Nicolas watched her for several heartbeats before also heading towards the *Lorelei*.

'I almost did it,' she told Tahmina.

'Don't. We need to be united.' Tahmina raised the staff, turned it in her hand and gazed at its symbols. Two of them were flickering brightly, almost like a warning. 'What they said in the village might be true.'

The Water Nymphs

The waves were plashing against the lone strand,
The moon had risen lately,
The knight was lying upon the white sand,
In vision musing greatly.

The beauteous nymphs arose from the deep,
Their veils around them floated;
They softly approach'd, and fancied that sleep
The youth's repose denoted.

The plume of his helmet the first one felt,
To see if perchance it would harm her;
The second took hold of his shoulder belt,
And handled his heavy chain armour.

The third one laugh'd, and her eyes gleam'd bright,
As the sword from the scabbard drew she;
On the bare sword leaning, she gazed on the knight,
And heartfelt pleasure knew she.

The fourth one danced both here and there,
And breath'd from her inmost bosom:
"O would that I thy mistress were,
"Thou lovely mortal blossom!"

The fifth her kisses with passionate strength
On the hand of the knight kept planting;
The sixth one tarried, and kissed at length
His lips and his cheeks enchanting.

The knight was wise, and far too discreet
To open his eyes midst such blisses;
He let the fair nymphs in the moonlight sweet
Continue their loving kisses.

Heinrich Heine,
Translated by Edgar Alfred Bowring, C.B.

CAPITULUM VI

Altona, near the Free Imperial City of Hamburg, May 1629

Osanna filled a large tankard with beer and carried it from the small brick cellar to the Rogue Wave's taproom. The barrels behind the bar were empty. Neither her constantly drunk father nor her lazy brothers, who were sitting with the locals, had bothered to swap them over – not even with the beer-swilling patrons who had been residing in their establishment for the last two weeks. So Osanna was constantly running back and forth between the taproom and the basement.

The motley crew of landsknechts cheered at her return to the taproom, banged their mugs on the table and sang a frivolous song to honour her.

Barthel, the leader of the three dozen men who had invaded the Rogue Wave's two guest rooms and barn, carried empty mugs to the bar, as did his second-in-command, Valentin. 'There you go, girl. This will quicken your work.' The dark-haired men could have been brothers. Both were in their twenties, of normal build, their unremarkable faces stubbly. Barthel put several kreutzers in a row on the stained wood. 'Another deposit. You'll get the rest when we leave. Run a tab.'

'Yes, Captain Hofmeister.' Osanna didn't believe for a moment he would settle the full tab, but she scratched another notch in the wooden tablet she had started for his unit. They already owed the Rogue Wave a substantial sum for lodging, food and beer. *A lot* of beer.

The mugs were quickly filled and the tankards were emptied again just as quickly, which meant going down to the cellar once again.

'Thank you, girl.' Barthel winked at Osanna. 'Join me later.' He took six of the mugs and left.

'The captain wants you in his bed tonight,' translated Valentin, who had the rank of Fähnrichs – Flag-bearer or Ensign. 'That will be nice extra income for you if you have it off with him nicely. Fondle his balls. The harlots say he likes that.'

'Why don't you have a baggage train with your own women to cook for you and take care of you? I thought that was customary.'

'They're lagging behind. They'll get here eventually. But until then, we need some diversion.' Valentin lifted the other mugs. 'Get cleaned up and rub yourself down with a few fragrant flowers. If he praises you and your tight crevice, you'll soon find yourself pretty busy with us.' He gazed at her breasts, which were only half covered; her apron had slid down, so her cleavage was quite visible. 'Luscious and busty. That's the way I like them.' Laughing, he returned to his comrades.

The gaudy, elaborately dressed landsknechts smoked, rolled dice and played card games; those who were literate read to the others from journals and broadsheets.

Some of them were outside, training with rapiers, pikes and muskets. Sometimes the mercenaries burst into song, singing about drinking, war or love. They didn't sound too bad, but more than anything else, they were loud.

The Altona locals at the small inn kept their distance from these raucous patrons, although they'd got used to them, of necessity. This was the only place around here to find alcohol and company.

I do hope their own women will arrive soon. Sighing, Osanna gazed at the empty tankards and put them on the floor for the time being. She filled small mugs with apple schnapps and carried them to the locals' table. 'Toast my mother and me,' she asked, and clinked her mug against theirs. 'May the Rogue Wave weather this storm without anything getting broken.'

'So be it,' replied the men and women, and they all drank.

'Where are ours?' her father demanded in a slurred voice.

'Get them yourself.' The liquor burned Osanna's throat, but she was as used to that as she was to the hard work.

She had just carried the empty mugs back to the bar when Barthel gestured at her with his feathered hat to bring fresh tankards. The landsknechts were constantly pissing out their anger in thick streams of urine with every trip behind the tavern, while the alcohol soothed their discontent. For a while.

Barthel and his men had been waiting in vain for an answer from the West India Company. When the captain finally heard that another band of landsknechts had intercepted the letter to him just before their arrival, seething with anger, he'd sent a message to Hamburg. Ever since, he and his mercenaries had dug in here. Without news from the Company, they were going nowhere.

Osanna checked the white kerchief that held back her long, dark blonde hair and kept the sweat from dripping in her face. She'd had no time to wash her clothes, although they were in urgent need of scrubbing. She grabbed the tankards by their handles and walked towards the narrow stairway leading down to the cellar. She had lost count of how often she had gone down there in the last few days, and didn't want to think about how many more times she would have to do so. They'd soon be needing to order more beer.

'Fucking Dutchmen,' Osanna cursed softly, a tankard in each hand. 'How much longer will they be staying here?' She toyed with the idea of sending Barthel's tab to the de Hertoghes. Then the merchants would have to act.

The Rogue Wave's door opened slowly, as if it were afraid to let in the next patron. This caution attracted Osanna's attention. It was unusual.

She stopped to see who would step across the threshold. Secretly she hoped for a shy, frightened Company messenger.

But what entered the taproom first, as if to check the air, was a long, silver beak. Then a black brim became visible, followed by a figure in a heavy deep brown leather apron over a long, dark robe. The nose was part of a mask covering the entire face.

Obviously, a plague doctor had come to Altona, probably at the behest of the Counts of Schauenburg, to check the marked houses and the afflicted.

The doctor's mask was different from anything Osanna had ever seen. It was made of silver and adorned with ornaments and symbols. The giant nose protruded from it, almost beak-like, its point shimmering as if sharpened.

The landsknechts had not yet noticed the plague doctor, who was creeping like a shadow into the low room. In his gloved left hand he was carrying a leather suitcase that must hold instruments and medicine for the sick.

Osanna watched the newcomer, fascinated.

The pronounced snout served to keep the man from getting too close to his patients, and it usually contained sponges doused in fragrant oils. She could smell the scent of cloves and cinnamon. The Black Death spread through bad air, the so-called miasma – and it had robbed Osanna of her future husband. She and Heinrich had been looking forward to a life together. After his death, she had become indifferent to many things.

Upon closer inspection, Osanna could see a little smoke rise from the nostrils of the silver mask. Obviously, incense was burning in the protruding part as another counteragent. The reddish glass in the eye sockets had been deliberately shattered, to deflect sick people's evil eye, which some considered the reason for the affliction.

To Osanna, the plague doctor looked like a creature from another world. She could not look away.

'Ho, look who's crept into the Rogue Wave,' Valentin said, alerting the landsknechts to the new arrival. 'Doctor Ravenbeak himself.'

'Looks like a Venetian gone astray,' one of the mercenaries said. 'I heard they wore these things as a carnival masquerade. Hey, are you lost? This is no masquerade ball! We have almost no music, and Venice is far away.'

'Leave him be,' another one said. 'He's looking for the plague.' The mercenary pointed at Osanna. 'But don't push your nose too deep between her legs. You might break her, and we still need her.'

The men laughed and bawled and smashed their mugs together violently. The alcohol was playing its game with the landsknechts.

'Shut your mouths,' Barthel said, calling them to order. 'Don't mock those who help us when the Black Death has us by the scruff of our necks.'

The mockery and the laughter slowly subsided.

'Come on over, my good man,' Barthel said. 'Have a beer.'

The doctor gave him the hint of a majestic bow, as if he required no gratitude.

'Braggarts and quacks,' Valentin said unexpectedly, and planted himself in front of the plague doctor. His garish outfit only emphasised the Venetian's sombreness. 'You and your kind, you know just about as much about the plague as we do.' He tapped the doctor's chest with his index finger. 'What did you do before? Skinner? Unsuccessful trader? Did you simply retrain, or did you really study?'

'What's up with you?' Barthel gave his second-in-command

a startled look. 'You sound like he personally wronged you, Ensign.'

'I hate quacks like him. Keep blabbing about unfortunate constellations of Saturn and Jupiter and blame the stars for the plague haunting us.' Valentin poked him with more force. 'But when sick people are lying right there in front of you, instead of helping them, you flee.'

Osanna suspected that the landsknecht had experienced much the same as she had: he had lost the love of his life to the Black Death. Only his sorrow was still as intense as his anger.

Quickly, she set aside the tankards, took up a new bottle of schnapps and ran towards the men. 'Don't be too hard, Ensign,' Osanna cooed, waving the bottle. She knew she couldn't count on help from her brothers or her father. 'Your captain has promised him a beer and I will give you—'

He ignored her. 'When the plague hit my village and I asked a doctor like you for help for my wife and my parents, you told me to kill them and fled. It was supposed to be a mercy killing.' Valentin was talking himself into a rage, his face reddening. 'You are fucking bunglers! You take the people's money and health and then vanish!'

Barthel grabbed his second-in-command by the shoulder to stop him. 'Valentin, stay calm. That's not the doctor who—'

'A judgement from above, that scoundrel said! A judgement from above! But where were the priests who should have prayed for us? Fled like the doctors!' Drops of Valentin's spittle flew against the shattered red glass. 'God was not involved in all of this.'

'We celebrated with a nice orgy to fuck away the plague,' one landsknecht said, followed by the quiet laughter of his comrades. They had enough beer and brandy and nothing was going to dampen their spirits. 'It worked, too. We all survived, even our crotch-lice.'

'We also killed some – Jews, Moors and Romanies – and the plague went,' interjected another. 'They're behind everything – they're the instigators of death, believe me!'

'Schnapps, Ensign,' Osanna reminded him. She waved the bottle in front of Valentin's heated face. 'Take a seat and—'

'You are a rakish bird, aren't you? With your ostentatious silver beak. Is that why you don't say a word?' Valentin grabbed the nose of the mask. 'Off with it! I want to see who I'm talking to!' He tugged at it.

As his fingers slid along the metal down to the tip, he cried out. The mask had not budged at all.

'What . . . ?' Valentin stared at the heel of his hand, where a deep cut gaped. The tip of the nose was indeed sharpened. 'What kind of a backstabbing medic are you? Do you stab your patients with that?' The commander was still trying to grab Valentin and calm him down, but he shook off Barthel's hands and drew his rapier. 'Let's duel, since you wear your treacherous blade in the middle of your face!'

Barthel pushed Osanna aside to get her out of harm's way. 'Away with the rapier, Ensign,' he shouted at Valentin, pushing him two steps backwards before turning to face the doctor. 'Take off your mask, or you won't be able to drink the beer I promised you, Venetian.' He gestured to Osanna to get some, quickly.

But she didn't budge. For some reason she had to stay and find out who was hidden behind the mask, keeping so tenaciously quiet. *I wonder what he looks like.* Her heart beat faster.

All eyes in the Rogue Wave were now on the doctor. A strained silence had fallen abruptly; there was no laughter, no shouting, not even a soft song to be heard. Her brothers and her father were staring at him, too.

Osanna would have preferred it if the man had simply turned around and left the taproom, for trouble would have left with him.

Instead, the Venetian carefully set down his leather case. 'You are looking for the landsknechts who snatched your mission from under your noses,' he said in a muffled voice. 'I know who they are. I also know where they went.'

The smoke from his nostrils grew thicker. Grey wisps rose up, wafting in small circles and spreading beneath the ceiling, though there was no movement of air inside the inn. From there, the tendrils floated downwards like vines, right into the open mouths of the soldiers.

Osanna also inhaled the fumes. *Oh, what . . . ?* It tickled her nose, triggering nice feelings in her head: lightness, intoxication, indifference and amidst it all came the soothing, healing voice of the doctor.

She quickly huffed out the smoke. This could not be good.

'I need you, Barthel Hofmeister, and your fighters. We will follow the thieves and hunt them down. Leave the two women travelling with them to me – and also the staff the swarthy one carries. Then you can finish the mission owed to you.' Something was glowing behind the shattered red glass of the mask, as if an inferno was burning there. He raised his voice. 'All of you – follow me! In addition to the thalers I'll give you, you will receive a reward that no earthly ruler could ever pay you. Afterwards, you can return to your baggage train and your women.'

With shaking hands, Osanna put down the schnapps bottle. This was getting to be unnerving. *Almighty God, help me.* She remembered the descriptions of witches and demons walking abroad, of the power of Evil, remembered the drawings and illustrations on the broadsheets. Unexpectedly, she had found herself in the very middle of just such an outrageous event.

The landsknechts were listening to the voice of the doctor as if they were ensorcelled, while the people from Altona were looking at each other in bewilderment and softly whispering amongst themselves.

The Venetian gestured and the bag next to him opened by itself. A cloud of black spores rose from it and mixed with the curls of smoke from the mask. He waved, and the mixture wafted into the mouths and nostrils of the soldiers.

'Receive the blessing of your new goddess. She immunises you against illness. Against sadness. Against grief and sorrow.' The masked one spoke unctuously and solemnly, raising both hands as if celebrating a mass. 'Against death. For *she* is Death and you will die only if she wants you to. Please her, and you will live forever – you will be invincible in battle.'

With a quick step forward, he tore the rapier from Valentin's hand and stabbed him through the heart so violently that the handguard hit the landsknecht's chest.

He sucked in the black air and looked down at the hilt protruding from his ribs. Astonishment and fear turned into relief, then laughter.

The Venetian dragged the bloody blade from his body and handed it back to him. The wound closed itself until nothing remained of the massive wound except for the hole in the fabric, with its red fringes. Such a blow would have killed any normal human being instantly. 'From now on, nothing can frighten you any more, as long as you obey. You are the warriors of Vanth!'

'We are.' Barthel dropped quickly to one knee, as if before a mighty king. 'Unto all eternity, we thank you for this gift, Milord!'

'Show me that you have earned this gift.' The doctor turned to the door and opened it. 'No one in this inn who is not part of your group can live. No one must know about our plan – or about your being special. I'll wait for you outside.' Slowly, he left the room and closed the door behind him.

No! Osanna ran for the back door at once while the landsknechts drew their blades and attacked the other patrons. 'Father – run!' She dodged Valentin's bloody rapier and took shelter behind the rough-hewn bar, where she cowered, looking around. 'Mother, run away,' she yelled into the kitchen. 'As fast as you can.'

Her own escape plan would not work: a mercenary was already standing in front of the back door, striking down an old man.

In her distress, Osanna raced down the stairs to the cellar, where she hid in the darkness between the empty beer barrels. She stifled her sobbing with her kerchief, which she pressed against her mouth and nose. Silently, she recited all the psalms she could remember, for herself and for her family. *Almighty God, into your merciful hands I commit my life.*

The noise and the shouting in the taproom subsided.

Blood dripped between the floorboards and down the stairs into Osanna's hideout in the cellar dug into the cold earth. She recognised the last scream: her mother had fallen to the hand of a murderer.

Osanna sobbed into the cloth. The Venetian had to be a sorcerer, a wizard, a devil-worshipper, to be able to give such orders to the soldiers. Or he might even be a demon himself, a cruel seducer.

Above her in the Rogue Wave, the last boots clattered outside and the door fell shut. The carnage was over and the landsknechts had gone, following their new master.

Osanna breathed too quickly, and at once felt dizzy.

She turned the Venetian's words over in her head. *Why is he chasing two women and a staff?*

She thought she knew the answer: this holy staff must be able to kill the plague doctor, the demon, whoever was hidden under this mask. That was how most stories about evil went. Maybe a relic or another holy item was enshrined in the wood – a thorn from the crown of the Saviour, for example.

Osanna cautiously left her hiding place and went up the

blood-slick stairs to the taproom, which stank of death. She had to know what had happened in the Rogue Wave – if there was anyone left to save, what had become of her family.

A quick look was enough. Osanna closed her eyes but already the images were burned into her head: her mother, father, her brothers and all the people from Altona – no one had been spared. They were all part of an image of death now, painted in blood.

'No . . . by the Almighty . . .' Osanna leaned on the bar, gasping in horror. She had to get to those two women the Venetian had talked about – she needed to warn them, and then watch them kill this fiend. There could be no other punishment for his order to the mercenaries!

'Hofmeister and his men might have forgotten about you because they were busy,' the Venetian's voice echoed from a dark corner. 'But I have not, serving wench.'

Osanna cried out in dismay and grabbed a knife from the shelf behind the bar. 'Come and get a piece of this! I will—'

Wisps of smoke wafted from the silver beak and quickly surrounded her.

The first deep breath made Osanna's thoughts easy and happy, the sight of the dead didn't bother her now. Her father, her mother, her brothers – she didn't care for them any more. Nothing mattered, like the time just after the death of her beloved.

She dropped the knife.

The Venetian came over to her and raising his gloved right hand, said, 'I think you can be helpful to my endeavour.' Tiny black specks rose from his hand and into Osanna's nose, causing a brief but intense headache. 'A young woman like you is good bait – a diversion. A nice surprise.' He turned to go. 'Come. Your new life has just begun.'

Osanna was ready and willing to follow the Venetian. She was fed up with living in Altona anyway.

Near the Free Imperial City of Münden, May 1629

'The boards will hold, the captain says. He's added some new planks on the inside and tarred the vessel anew.' Statius bit into his piece of bread and smoked sausage; the skin popped with a soft sound. 'But he wants to wait until tomorrow, to see if it is really safe.'

A bowl lantern shed some indirect light on the landsknechts sitting on the forecastle, together with Caspar, Aenlin and Tahmina. The crew of the *Lorelei* had made themselves comfortable on the flat bank, where they were preparing to light a fire. They still preferred to keep their distance from the passengers. The horses were also on the riverbank, grazing peacefully.

'Agreed. We'll pass Münden without stopping.' Nicolas passed Jäcklein a piece of hard cheese. 'You're right. It's too chancy. If they want us to pay a toll, they'll send a boat.'

'It'll be chancy everywhere we go,' Moritz said. 'Don't you think? After all the stories I've heard about you?'

'Well, we've got you, giant lad.' Jäcklein patted his shoulder. Even seated, the fifteen-year-old was much taller than the other men. 'You can compensate for that.'

Aenlin thought Moritz was right: suffering people tended to catch, torture and kill scattered marauders, lone wolves and small groups of landsknechts, for revenge, for fear – for many reasons that the war had created.

'We won't moor up again before we reach Wanfried,' Nicolas decided. 'We won't be there for any length of time, either, but Tilly's troops probably didn't go to great lengths to spare the city.'

'I'll ask the captain,' said Statius, talking through a mouthful. 'He should know.' He rose, adjusted his baldric and walked across the sagging gangplank towards the barge's crew.

'Do you believe him?' Tahmina asked the captain.

Aenlin looked at her.

'Did he really slaughter that entire village in self-defence?'

'Yes – you yourself found the proof.'

'Proof of cannibalism, yes. But that does not mean they hunted him as he claimed.' The mystic tilted her head slightly, her blue eyes shimmering in the weak light. 'It was the perfect excuse to avoid being punished by you. Or would you have decided differently?'

What's he going to say? Aenlin chewed more slowly and watched Nicolas, who was pulling his fair hair into a knot, as if preparing for a fight.

In the ensuing silence, Jäcklein cleared his throat. 'Maybe I should answer this. The three of us have known each other for a long time, and we've fought together on many a battlefield. I've long forgotten who saved who how often from a deadly blow or a ball, or who cleaned whose wounds after an injury.' He cut a paper-thin slice of ham and sniffed at it before placing it in his mouth. 'Stats is a tough guy. He's coarse, for certain, too loud, too harsh and too uncouth. But I believe him.'

Nicolas nodded, a little hesitantly. 'Anyway, the village had earned its punishment. Eating people is not—'

'What if the people sacrificed themselves of their own free will? To feed the others? Maybe they were the old and the weak?' Moritz dragged his bread through the pot of lard. Roasted onions gave the salted fat some added flavour. 'Then it wouldn't have been a crime. Well, strictly speaking.'

'I told you he got that big because he ate his family,' Jäcklein butted in.

'Excuse me, but I'm eating,' Caspar complained. He took the slices of sausage from his piece of bread and examined it. 'Oh, dear! Now I'm afraid there could have been too much person in this pig.'

'Before or after the slaughter?' Jäcklein made rude gestures. 'In the countryside, people have wild tastes. Where humans and animals live under the same roof, they sometimes get pretty close.'

Moritz and Caspar grinned.

Aenlin took a deep breath. *So he won't get rid of Statius.*

Unsmilingly, Nicolas looked towards the riverbank, where Statius was talking to the crew. 'What's done cannot be undone. I will abide by what he told me. But should I see him, some day or night, doing something that's against everything that is sacred to us, he will be properly punished.'

'Does that include rape?' Tahmina touched her ebony staff. 'You know why I am asking. It is more than obvious that he wants me – no matter what I feel.'

'Statius wants every woman,' Jäcklein said, trying to calm her. 'Don't take it to heart. He talks a lot, and he thinks a real man has to say these things.'

'I always considered myself a real man.' Caspar looked at the clay pot of lard. 'Damn! How do I know that this is not sinners' fat? You and your blasted talk about cannibals.'

'What's sinners' fat?' Aenlin didn't know the expression, though her German had improved a lot over the last few weeks. She kept eating the lard with a healthy appetite. *I will regret this question.*

'Flesh taken from the corpses of executed criminals,' Caspar said. 'After the inspection, the dead are given to the hangman, who takes from the bodies the best these brigands have to offer. They produce ointments and medicines from it.'

'Sinners' fat is good against stabbing wounds.' Jäcklein rubbed his right thigh. 'Without it, I'd have lost this leg long ago.'

Aenlin bit into a roasted onion, feeling the urge to gag.

'Yes, that's exactly the way I looked, too,' Caspar said to her. 'I think this bread is enough for my happiness.'

'You only say that because you have never had to go hungry, your Aged Snootiness,' Jäcklein replied, chewing with relish. 'Is your bodycount still at four hundred and one?'

'Yes, and it's making me cranky. Strictly speaking, this thing with Pieck was no duel of honour, but I'm still counting it. It's bad enough as it is.' Caspar looked around in mock suffering and stroked his moustache and goatee. 'Don't you understand? No Counts, no Dukes, not even a minor aristocrat, officer, or council member who wants to duel me, so it's a pretty annoying river cruise.'

'Why exactly did you decide to use pistols?' Aenlin was glad of this change of topic, especially after the revelations about sinners' fat. From her training she knew that firearms were sometimes unreliable, especially at greater distances. 'What about sabres, swords, rapiers, or . . .'

'I don't know how to use them. I don't even want to know.'

The landsknechts raised their heads in surprise, staring at Caspar as he added, 'I swear. I'm a loser with any blade longer than my forearm used for hacking or stabbing. But anything you can shoot with or throw – that's my thing.'

'Throwing knives against breastplates?' Jäcklein said. 'That won't get you far.'

'That depends. If a helmet has an eye-slit, I have something to aim at. Name a target.'

Jäcklein grinned mischievously. 'Moritz's right eye!'

'No, blast it,' Nicolas said at once. 'I told you to stop wagering on his death.'

'Then right below the lantern,' Aenlin suggested in anticipation. 'At the mast. As close as you—'

Caspar had already drawn one of his slender daggers, which he spun skilfully before throwing it at the mast. Its tip sank into the wood two feet up – just under the lantern. Not even a playing card could have fitted between them.

The mercenaries and the women applauded.

'It's a gift,' Caspar said as he took a bow, making a flourishing movement with his head that sent the curls of his wig whipping around. 'As I said, I am no good at fencing.'

'You would have no reason to fence on these banks, either,' a clear voice unexpectedly rang out from the bow. The group turned to find themselves facing a beautiful young woman. Her conspicuously pale skin had a greenish tint and her long, green hair dampened the simple white dress she wore; droplets were steadily falling from the hem of her skirt. 'Welcome, strangers.'

Tahmina noticed two symbols on her staff glowing warnings. 'She has approached us before to spy on us,' she whispered to Aenlin, 'so be careful. This creature is not mortal.'

My next challenge. Aenlin's heart rate sped, but it wasn't beating nearly as fast as it would have been at the start of this journey.

Nicolas gestured to the group to remain calm, although the fighters still had their hands on the hilts of their various weapons. 'Good evening. Who are you – and what do you want with us?'

'This is the first time I have seen you.' Her water-blue eyes darted right and left, examining their faces, as if she were choosing one. 'My name is Valna. This part of the river belongs to me. You may pay a fee to the Counts and Dukes and cities, but you must never forget me.' She pointed at the Weser. 'You have to give me something living, then you may travel on and stay alive.'

'The Devil take it!' Jäcklein gasped. 'You are a *real* naiad!'

'But no one was ever more beautiful.' The words escaped Moritz, who looked at the young woman as if he had fallen in love with her.

'Or deadlier,' Jäcklein pointed out.

'Utter nonsense!' Moritz got up and bowed awkwardly, his long black curls falling around his head like a curtain.

'What a well-proportioned stature! What a face! What a body . . .'

Nicolas shrugged with regret. 'We don't have anything to spare, I fear. We need the horses and the sailors, and none of us is coming into the water with you. What can I offer you instead, water nymph?'

Valna tiptoed around them on her bare feet, drops of river water still falling from her clothes. 'A life, landsknecht, no more, no less. As you are passing by me for the first time, I will be lenient; I won't drag the chosen victim to the bottom with me at once.' She stopped in front of Moritz and shyly kissed his lips. Then she touched him with her slender fingers, took his hand. 'Could it be that this valiant hero wants to accompany me of his own free will?' She smiled. 'You will not regret it.'

Aenlin saw her sharp white teeth; such a bite might tear deep wounds. 'He surely will, for he cannot breathe on the bottom of the Weser.'

Valna turned to her. 'Let that be the least of your worries, human woman.'

She noticed the glowing symbols on Tahmina's staff. 'I have never met a witch like you.' In a friendly manner she asked, 'Where are you from? Does this mean you are preparing a spell against me?'

'Do we have to? We could also shoot off your head.' Caspar drew his pistols from their sheaths.

'Statius, come on over,' Nicolas called towards the embankment. 'We have a problem with an unwanted visitor.'

'It is you who are unwanted – and impolite,' Valna stated indignantly.

That the naiad remained so calm worried Aenlin. In the meantime, everyone had risen from the deck, all of them touching the hilts of their weapons.

'I'm coming, Captain,' Statius called, running up the plank. 'Don't start without me.'

The sailors noticed the water woman and fled at once – except for one, who shouted curses and threw rocks at her, before following his fellows.

So the rumour from the nearby village was true ...

'Kiss my arse! Who is that?' Statius grabbed his musket with the dagger attached beneath the barrel and stared at the naiad.

'The ruler of this part of the river,' Valna said. 'If you don't give me something that's alive, you will die. It seems to me that this young man would like to come along.'

'Moritz stays,' Nicolas ordered.

'I have a better idea, river cunt.' Statius pointed at some bushes on the riverbank. 'I'll fuck you until you can't walk any more, till you have a sore throat from screaming in ecstasy. That's fee enough – and I'm even willing to squirt it all over you.'

Aenlin sighed. Such a suggestion just had to come from him. *He is simply gross.*

'Or we shoot you, water maid,' Nicolas added. 'Our Caspar is the best shot I know. Tahmina is a mystic who is well versed in the likes of you. What should stop her from killing you if you threaten us?'

Valna took Moritz's hand and clung to him. 'Look.' The water constantly trickling down had painted a dark circle around her bare feet. 'Your young one suits me.' Moritz was gazing enraptured at her. He placed an arm gently around her shoulders. 'I think I've made my decision.'

'Caspar, Tahmina: kill her as soon as she tries to drag our friend down with her,' Nicolas said. 'Leave us be, naiad! That's all we want.'

More symbols on Tahmina's staff came to life, shimmering warnings.

'What's happening here?' Aenlin whispered at her.

'Strong Yatu.' Tahmina peered into the fast-flowing Weser. 'It means nothing good. It originates down there.'

'Do you know the history of the city?' Valna gracefully pointed at Münden with an outstretched arm. 'Tilly's soldiers threw more than two thousand corpses from the bridge over the Werra. The current brought them to me.' Again, she kissed Moritz with her pale greenish lips. 'You see, I have enough dead things in my home. I want to have fun with living things – and keep them afterwards.'

Water roared and numerous pale hands simultaneously grabbed the *Lorelei*'s port side, the barge tilting towards the sudden weight. On both sides of the ship, grey-skinned creatures pulled themselves aboard. Some wore shredded clothing, but some were naked, because years at the bottom of the Weser had destroyed every thread.

'Take no action,' Nicolas said calmly. 'Form a circle.'

They formed up around the enraptured Moritz and Valna, who were making moon eyes at each other. Weapons were drawn, though they looked useless against the superior numbers, roughly three hundred to one.

This was why the naiad had stayed so calm in the face of their threats, Aenlin realised. She had an army.

Hundreds of walking undead had boarded the *Lorelei* and surrounded its passengers. The long-drowned beings stared at their surroundings with lifeless eyes. They wielded rusty weapons, stones and branches.

'I found the corpses,' Valna said, a queen talking to her subjects, 'and I kept them. No one dares deny me my toll any more. Those who laugh at me or make light of me' – she looked at Statius – 'die quicker than they can think of their own end!'

'There are far too many,' Jäcklein muttered. 'If the Lord's angels—'

'Or those from Hell,' Aenlin put in.

'For all I care, the angels of Hell could come to our aid too, and still we'd stand no chance,' said the smallest of the landsknechts, looking disconsolate. 'What shall we do?'

'Mystic, can you do anything?' Nicolas had audibly lost his confidence. 'If you know a spell that would get the undead off our deck, now would be a good time.'

Tahmina shook her head. 'It is just as Jäcklein said: they are far too many.'

'If you attack me, or if I die, they will attack you,' Valna said. 'Let me go and you will leave unscathed. The unpleasantness and impertinence will be forgotten. For you brought me' – again she kissed the young giant, who responded with an appreciative moan – 'something very, very alive. Thank you.'

'Don't. Worry.' Moritz was emphatic. 'I go of my free will.' Again he looked fondly at the naiad. 'Go. Now!' He lifted Valna, who laughed joyfully and put her arms around his strong neck. 'I'll be all right.' Roughly, he elbowed his way between Caspar and Tahmina and jumped over the low side of the *Lorelei*.

As soon he and the beaming water maid disappeared beneath the surface of the Weser, the drowned ones walked back into the river or dropped from the barge into the water, returning to their wet grave.

'To hell with that,' Statius grumbled. He looked into the water, his musket raised and ready for shooting. 'I have half a mind to jump after them and teach this cunt—'

When the water was calm once again, the barge captain stuck his head up from below decks, his face still fearful.

'Captain, cast off,' Nicolas ordered, sheathing his weapons. 'At once! Just as Moritz said.'

The sailor raised his arms. 'But my crew is gone, Captain.'

'Then tell us what to do.' He signalled Statius to harness all the horses to the towlines. 'We can't stay even one heartbeat longer. Caspar, come on, add your Comte to the line, too. We must be quick.'

Now I understand – his gaze! His words! 'Moritz was only

pretending to be in love,' Aenlin said suddenly, as she helped the landsknechts with their preparations. 'What a clever fellow.'

'Are you sure?' Tahmina had started casting off.

'Yes – remember where he put the stresses on his words? I think the brave boy intends to kill the naiad while she's under-water – as long as he has enough air in his lungs. Neither she nor her undead army could harm him.' *The Weser, however, might drown him.*

'But as soon as Valna is dead, her servants will attack us,' Nicolas agreed, 'so let's disappear from the naiad's realm.'

The *Lorelei* had started moving. The nine horses steadily dragged her along, and soon the sail caught the wind, helping her to gain momentum.

'I will try to use the power of Yatu.' Tahmina sat on the deck, her eyes closed, her ebony staff upright in front of her. 'I once faced a Rûd Deva. I think I . . .' Her lips moved, forming mysterious spells and formulae. The sigils in the wood shone brightly, becoming clearly visible in the night, cutting through the darkness like a beam from a lighthouse.

'What is your witch up to?' Nicolas stood at the stern of the barge, a rope in hand, ready to throw to Moritz as soon he appeared. Lanterns shed their light on the foaming, bubbling waters, but so far, the giant was nowhere to be seen.

On the riverbank, the barge captain was goading the horses, but the animals, feeling danger all around them, were already doing their best.

Aenlin, restless, joined Nicolas. 'She's preparing to fend off our doom.' It was going to be an immense effort for her; Aenlin could only hope that Tahmina would be able to hold back the undead long enough. 'I don't see Moritz.'

'But no walking dead, either,' Jäcklein called from the bow, where he was keeping watch.

'All's quiet,' Statius announced tersely from portside. He'd shouldered Moritz's bidenhänder.

'Same here,' Caspar called from starboard. The duellist had readied four pistols; small powder flasks for quick reloading hung from the chest straps of his baldric. He carried musket balls in a separate little pouch. 'I hope the little giant hasn't—'

In an eruption of shimmering droplets, Moritz's body emerged vertically out of the Weser. Jerking up both arms, he shouted, 'Rope!' He started coughing and inadvertently swallowed some water. 'Get me some rope!' With a splash, he sank back into the water up to his neck.

'There he is!' Nicolas threw the rope expertly so the inflated wineskin tied to its end smacked against the water close to the landsknecht. 'Our dance of the dead will be starting any minute. Keep an eye on the Weser!'

Her eyes closed, Tahmina rose in a trance, holding the staff upside down. She moved to the side of the ship, never missing a step, as if she were walking normally with her eyes wide open. 'Aenlin, tell me once the boy is back on board.'

Moritz grabbed the rope and clung to it, crying, 'Quick! They're coming! They—' Abruptly, he sank again.

'Aenlin! Come on, help me!' Nicolas pulled with all his might, but he wasn't able to drag the giant to the surface by himself. His huge muscles bulged under his shirt. 'The rest of you: watch out! Bash in their skulls wherever they appear!'

Aenlin grabbed the rope with both hands and braced herself against the side. 'He's coming up!'

Moritz's head broke the surface, his long black curls hanging down limply. He drew a deep breath, panting so loudly that they heard him on the Lorelei.

Aenlin's heart skipped a beat in dismay: the undead were clinging to him, to the rope – they were everywhere! Some of them were biting the mercenary, but that at least was in vain;

all they succeeded in doing was shattering their teeth against his impenetrable skin. Others were chewing at the rope, trying to separate him from the barge and drag him to the bottom of the river through sheer weight alone.

However, there was no sign of the naiad.

'Your Snootiness,' Nicolas said urgently, 'come over here – shoot the dead off my rope or they'll bite it through.' Hand over hand, he and Aenlin were heaving in the rope. Moritz was getting closer to safety, but now strands of the rope were breaking, weakened by the teeth of the dead.

'Right away.' Turning sidewards, Caspar took up his usual firing position, planting both feet firmly beneath himself, which wasn't easy on the rolling deck of the barge. He took aim.

It really is a gift. Aenlin, who was still tugging on the rope with Nicolas, had no choice but to admire Caspar. Shooting was a notable risk in this bad light and on the ever-shifting surface of the river: an errant musket ball could hit Moritz or the fraying rope, and either could mean his end.

A loud crack made Aenlin flinch, although she had been expecting it.

The skull of the revenant right next to Moritz disintegrated in a cloud of mud and dark liquid. Another crack and another of the undead lost his head. Caspar fired two more successful shots, freeing the rope of their enemies one ball at a time. While he reloaded, they managed to drag Moritz to the stern, but he was too weak to pull himself up.

'Please,' he said as he smashed his elbow against the temple of one of the undead, '*please* get me out of here. I—' Again he sank.

'Let me do that, Captain.' Aenlin dropped the rope, leaving Nicolas, gasping, to bear the weight alone. She leaned over the edge of the barge and grabbed Moritz's long black hair with both hands. 'Got you!'

With all her might, she dropped backwards, levering the

giant landsknecht over the railing. *Lucifer help me!* The effort made her back hurt, but she didn't give up. *I won't let him off the hook!* With a scream, she heaved him onto the deck next to her like a wet sack. 'Out you come!'

Coughing, Moritz doubled over and vomited dirty brown water.

'Now, Tahmina!' Aenlin groaned. 'Save us!'

'Everyone, back away from the river,' the mystic commanded, and she plunged the glowing tip of her staff into the water. As it entered the Weser, it lit it up as if the sun was rising from the bottom of the river.

The magic light made visible what was happening under the surface.

Hundreds of dead people armed to the teeth, some maimed or limbless, some of them bloated and rotting, some skeletal, swam or walked towards the *Lorelei*. Their pale, decaying faces full of hatred and hunger, they fought against the current.

New horrors! As if through glass Aenlin gazed into the illuminated Weser and noticed Valna's mortal remains amid the chaos. 'The water maid is dead!' she cried. Moritz had decapitated her; a clueless revenant was holding her head in his hands. The naiad's body floated in place, ignoring the power of the river, arms slightly spread, still wearing the flowing dress.

'They're coming!' Caspar had reloaded his pistols and now aimed both muzzles at the water. 'I really hope there are some noblemen, officers and council members among them, so I won't die with a list ending at four hundred and one.'

'Can this staff do more than call and illuminate them?' Statius sneered, swinging his bidenhänder. 'Come and taste my blade, Hellspawn!'

The first of the undead reached the surface – and could not break through it.

As if caught under ice, they banged against the lapping water, their mouths wide open, screaming in silent rage – but their anger was to no avail. They had to stay under the surface and watch the *Lorelei* make her escape.

'Fuck my old boots!' Statius brayed with joy. 'You are the best witch I know, Persian lady!'

Nicolas looked relieved. 'This is just the miracle we needed.'

'Look after Moritz, Captain.' Aenlin went over to Tahmina and held her tight to stop her from sliding into the river.

As the light of the staff slowly subsided, the water grew darker and darker. The walking dead turned into blurred silhouettes and finally disappeared under the ripples. The Weser became a flowing black ribbon once again.

'It is over.' Tahmina pulled her staff from the river. Exhausted, she sank into her companion's arms. 'Did I do good?'

'Oh yes.' Aenlin smiled at her and brushed a brown strand of hair from her face. 'Valna will never hurt anybody any more. You have done more than just save us.'

The *Lorelei* reached the outer edge of Münden. The lights of the city promised protection against the water maid's henchmen, but Nicolas was not going to rely on that.

Aenlin was deeply relieved when he ordered the barge captain to keep going and follow the towpath until dawn. Later, once the barge reached Wanfried, they could look for the crew who had fled.

'Sleep. Get some rest,' Aenlin whispered to Tahmina, who nodded and then quickly closed her eyes. 'This time I will guard you.' *With my life.*

Short and true report and terrifying new paper on the six hundred witches, warlocks and devil worshippers; whom the Bishop of Bamberg had burned at the stake after they had confessed in amicable interrogation and under torture. Also, the bishop had more than nine hundred burned at Würtzburg Monastery.

'They have killed several hundred people through their Satanic arts, as well as the good crops, devastated by ripening and frost, amongst them not only common people, but several distinct gentlemen, doctors and wives of doctors, as well as several councillors, who have all been executed and burned: who have confessed such atrocious deeds they have committed with their magic, all of which you will find described herein . . .'

from *New Paper on the Six Hundred Witches*,
Bamberg, 1630

The witches also confessed how three thousand of them had joined the Walpurgis Night dance at the Kreydenberg near Würtzburg ... Amongst those witches were quite some girls of seven, eight, nine and ten years, twenty-two of whom have been executed and burned, at which point they raised a hue and cry about their mothers who had taught them the Satanic arts and in the monastery at Bamberg, more than six hundred witches were burned and to this day, many are being incarcerated and burned.

At Bamberg and Würtzburg, witchcraft has become so rampant that the children in the schools and on the streets taught spells to each other so that several schools were closed completely: At Würtzburg, several monks and priests and many refined gentlemen, mayors and councillors, have been denounced, some of whom have already been burned.

from *Short and True Report*, Bamberg, 1659

CAPITULUM VII

Near Bamberg, May 1629

'Giddyup, the two of you.' Aenlin sat next to Tahmina on the box of the wagon, following the coach that Moritz was driving.

Late afternoon was ending with the loud chittering of crickets and a bird serenade. Summer was coming, even though it still got distinctly colder after sunset.

Aenlin had nothing to do. The horses trotted calmly along the road; they were used to following another vehicle.

'A little faster?' she suggested, to no avail. She found herself talking to the animals to avoid falling asleep, for as soon as she did, the nightmares came, showing her the most atrocious, cruel images of things that had happened during her mission. Tahmina often had to calm her when the tea didn't have the desired results.

Sometimes she dreamed about the inheritance she was waiting for, sometimes about the events of recent days, and the encounter with the naiad – shocking images from the latest part of the journey figured prominently. Before her journey to Hamburg, Aenlin had heard about the religious wars raging in the German lands, but to travel through those regions, to see the destruction, to experience the misery of the people affected, moved and touched her.

It will soon be over. We will reach Bamberg, then we can get back to Hamburg and after that, we can head home.

The *Lorelei* had travelled quickly from Münden to Wanfried on the Werra, past deserted and destroyed villages and farms, the ruins appearing out of the mist as if they were painted-on figments of the imagination. The people had deserted them after Tilly's troops had invaded. Wanfried and its little castle had lost their life and their beauty as well, having been looted and burned.

All the time, corpses and body parts were drifting past them in the river, fresh and old ones alike, caught in the current. Statius commented extensively on the state and degree of decomposition.

They also saw hanged people dangling from bridges and trees, intended as a warning and a deterrent.

Several times, people had shot arrows at the *Lorelei*, but after a few broadsides from the muskets, the footpads had retreated.

At night, Aenlin often heard drums and loud singing, and saw fires burning beyond the reeds. The panicked bleating of animals, probably being sacrificed, reminded her that desperate people would do anything to avoid death and affliction – even dedicating prayers and rituals to heathen deities.

The Dark Lands.

Aenlin remembered Statius' words. She looked up to see rain clouds looming in the distance; the storm would hit them before they reached Bamberg. Since they had taken to the carriages, there had been no more incidents like on the Weser, but . . . *The Dark Lands*. There really was no name more fitting for this realm.

'This is going to be one bad thunderstorm,' Nicolas shouted from the front coach, where he had taken up position. 'We'll take shelter at that place over there. It looks big enough to be a coaching inn – they'll be well used to changing mounts for messengers and post riders, so I'm sure they'll be able to accommodate us.' He pointed to the left. 'I don't want lightning to strike me, so let's get our coaches under cover.'

Moritz drove towards the building, which was intact and undamaged, like a lot of the villages and farms they had passed in the last three days. In the ultra-Catholic Bishopric of Bamberg, no one had to fear the likes of Tilly or the League – and the Prince-Bishop ruled over a vast territory.

A little peace will do us all good. Aenlin stopped the wagon next to the coach and helped Moritz with unhitching the horses. It would have been even better for them to have reached the city, and to be able to leave it the next day.

Caspar, Nicolas, Statius and Jäcklein had gone straight into the inn – to save them some seats, as they said. Their thirst for beer had quickened their pace.

Tahmina looked thoughtfully out of the stable door at the lightning flashing in a black band of clouds in the evening sky. Being cared for and looked after by Aenlin had helped the mystic to recover from her efforts at Münden. 'Bamberg is not a good place for me,' she whispered, stroking Caspar's black stallion, and he snorted, as if to agree. 'There! The Comte thinks the same.'

Moritz led the horses away to the mangers full of hay. 'I won't argue. This is a very bad place.'

Aenlin looked at him in surprise. She had not expected the youngest member of their band to know anything about this place. 'Have you ever been to Bamberg?'

'No, but I have heard that this city shows no mercy for those who are not Catholic. A few years ago, they called in the Jesuits to chase away those Protestants who weren't prepared to give up everything they owned. The Emperor's Edict probably hasn't made things better.' Holding the ebony staff in her left hand, Tahmina looked down at herself and plucked at her midnight blue gown. 'They will not like someone like me.'

'I'll tell them you are . . . from the South Pacific. That you have been converted.' Aenlin smiled and handed over the buckets she'd filled from a hand pump in the yard for the animals. 'I'll also say you were awfully expensive. We'll wrap the staff to hide its symbols.'

'Will you deny your faith, too?' her companion asked softly.

'What faith?' Moritz racked the horses and rubbed them down. 'You're a good Christian woman, aren't you?'

'In a way, yes.' Aenlin grinned. Without Lucifer, there would be no Christendom, so it was no lie. She could say any prayer convincingly, all the while, on the inside, despising them. Aenlin was very skilled at this game: she had to hide her sympathy for the Devil as much as she did her love for a woman. *Maybe Lucifer is a woman – who knows?*

'I don't like the idea of that,' Tahmina said. 'Maybe it is better if I wait outside the gates. Should you need me, I have ways to find you.'

'I see.' Moritz shared the buckets of water between the horses, then climbed onto the roof of the coach and set the bidenhänder beside him. 'You go on inside. I'm not hungry yet, so I'll watch your staff.'

'All right. Thank you!' Aenlin blew him a kiss. 'I'll make sure the captain sends your replacement in good time.'

She and Tahmina left the stable and entered the inn through a side door. Nicolas and his gang had found a table. In front of them they had giant mugs brimming with foam – of course; landsknechts were always thirsty. Caspar was sipping a glass of wine with elegantly exaggerated gestures.

At least, there was no din and no stench. To Aenlin's great joy, the place was not busy. A few bored merchants sat close to the cold fireplace, talking quietly. Two basket-makers sorted their goods and repaired any damage with flexible withies.

Jäcklein waved Aenlin and Tahmina over. Despite their

drinks, the landsknechts were in a foul mood. 'It's getting tricky,' Jäcklein said to the women. 'I've been talking to the merchants over there.'

'Tricky? Why? Are there water nymphs in the river in Bamberg?'

Their faces remained serious as Aenlin took off her hat and smoothed back the ebony strand. 'Moritz is guarding our stuff.'

'I've remembered what I've heard about Bamberg.' Jäcklein pointed to a printed report with one hand, rubbed his unruly blond hair with the other. 'They're hunting witches like rabbits there.'

'They even built a special gaol,' Statius said, 'the so-called House of Malefaction, for witches and warlocks only. There's room enough for thirty.'

'They've already burned a few hundred of them in the city and the monastery – including almost all the members of the Bamberg City Council.' Caspar looked quickly at Tahmina before returning to his wine. 'I assume I don't have to explain what that means to you?'

'I will not set foot within these walls!' The mystic took a seat and grabbed the duellist's goblet. 'I would not make it back out alive.' She drained the mug in one go.

Aenlin raised her eyebrows in warning. It was never a good sign when her companion started drinking.

'This city is a true romping ground for witches,' Jäcklein reported, producing a crumpled broadsheet. 'Here's a list of those who are in prison right now, awaiting their trial – after they have been tried, they will be tortured. This has all the details of the cases – and city's the triumph against evil, of course.'

'And our five targets are on that list?' Aenlin guessed aloud. That explained the worried looks around the table. 'We still need to get them out.'

'Not all of them,' Nicolas said. 'Two have already been executed – for sorcery and witchcraft. Two are in jail in the House of Malefaction: Agatha Mühlbach, also known as Gatchen, and Ursula Garnhuber, known as Ula. They are searching in the monastery and in the city for the last one: Veronica Stadler, or Nica.'

'There is also a reward, but it's too small.' Statius had already emptied his jug and was waving towards the bar for a refill. Cheerfully he twirled the tips of his moustache. 'That's the way to get rich. What do you think? How much has the Prince-Bishop taken from the dead so far? Councillors, witches, Protestants – all their money, all their possessions, it all goes to him.'

'Not so loud,' Nicolas admonished him. 'If somebody should ask, we're witch-hunters, looking for a job.'

'Ho, slow down.' Statius grabbed the jug from the hands of the lad who was working the bar, then chased him away again with a gruff curse and a kick. 'You want to go to the city, Captain?'

'That's our mission, so yes.'

The beefy landsknecht put the jug to his lips, emptied it in two huge gulps, smacked it on the table and belched loudly.

'Don't you think that's a good idea?' asked Aenlin, who saw her inheritance in danger. *If necessary, I'll continue without him. That might even be better.*

'You heard it in my voice, didn't you?' Statius thumped the broadsheet with his fist, as if it were an enemy. 'Our mission is over.'

'Why?' Aenlin asked in a nasty tone. She felt Tahmina secretly touch her thigh.

'Because we can't deliver.' Statius raised his free hand and spread its fingers. 'They are no longer five, and we were supposed to bring five people to Hamburg. And no one ever said we would be freeing witches from a specially built gaol, or that I would have to fuck with the city guard, only to be chased through the Prince-Bishop's entire diocese by his people. In the end, we're going to have the entire Catholic League on our arses.' Ostentatiously, he put his dusty boots on the table. 'We didn't get paid for that, Nicolas. That is not part of our agreement with the moneybags.'

Jäcklein signalled his agreement. 'I don't mind driving them around, but breaking people out of gaol? This is a totally different thing. Bamberg is not a village that our god of war' – he pointed at Statius – 'can defeat single-handedly. As soon as they close the gates, we'll be trapped.'

Nicolas stared at the two men. 'Just so we're clear: we are not voting on this. You're under my command, despite our friendship. Our mission is to get these people to Hamburg. Three of them are left, and we can and will do this.'

Aenlin nodded in agreement, but kept quiet, so as not to stoke the fire.

'Strictly speaking, that was never *our* mission, Captain,' Statius replied haughtily. 'We stole it. No one knows who we are – if we decide to make away with what you still have in your leather bag, the Company won't even notice.'

'Hear, hear,' Caspar said, raising his brows. 'You're all rascals! What a nice surprise.' He called the barman over. 'More wine, please.'

'Why not?' Jäcklein added. 'The de Hertoghe brothers will assume we died on our way here.'

I can't let that happen. 'Don't fool yourselves,' Aenlin said. 'Sooner or later the de Hertoghes will find out what happened in Bamberg – and that three of the women are still alive.'

'Even then, none of the merchants will know who or where we are.' As was his custom, Statius chucked his empty vessel behind the bar and yelled, '*New – full – now!*' across the room.

'And don't forget my wine as well, boy,' Caspar added, 'but please notice that I am asking nicely. Not everyone is as impatient as my friend here.'

'Stop! You can debate all you want with innkeepers and whores, but you will not do so with me.' Nicolas looked at each man in turn, a determined look on his face. 'Remember your honour. We got paid. What are we if we turn cowards now? Also, let's not forget the bounty they still owe us.'

'Ah, never mind,' Jäcklein relented. 'If you insist, Captain, I'm in. But we need a plan, otherwise it'll be the last job we ever do.'

'Not that anyone seems to be interested in what I think, but I agree with my friend.' Caspar nodded at Jäcklein. 'Don't forget that there's a hefty sum to earn if we complete our mission. When we get back, we'll be rich. You will never get as wealthy anywhere else – no battlefield, no looting will bring you that kind of money.'

Aenlin allowed herself to sigh in relief. The voice of reason had spoken.

Nicolas put one hand on Caspar's shoulder and the other on Jäcklein's and gazed at his other companion. 'Stats, I need you, too.'

'What if they are really witches? What if they ensorcel us?' He touched his groin. 'What if they make my cock all small and wrinkly and my balls fall off?'

'Well, be nice to them. Then they'll make all bigger.' Jäcklein grinned. 'I'm not afraid of witches.'

'Oh, don't say that.' The lad working the bar, who couldn't have been older than thirteen, brought the third round of beer and the wine. He didn't dare to make eye contact, but muttered, 'You should be afraid. This could turn out bad. Extraordinarily bad.'

'Hey! Will you stop listening, little monkey,' Statius ordered. 'Get back behind the bar – no, better get to the kitchen! Get us whatever you have – ham, cheese, sausage – and fry us eggs. Two dozen eggs.' He grabbed the boy's earlobe and twisted it around. 'And hurry it up. I'm hungry, butt-face.'

'Wait.' Aenlin freed the wailing boy from the landsknecht's grip and handed him a kreutzer to make up for the abuse. 'What's your name?'

'Franz.'

'Well then, Franz, by God's will and providence,' she said, and she crossed herself quickly and in the wrong direction, 'we are witch-hunters. What do you know about them? What do you mean, extraordinarily bad?'

Franz quickly pocketed the coin. 'Bless your heart!' He didn't look at Aenlin, but kept his gaze fixed on the floor. 'I heard the soldier say the witches were gathering – like at the Kreydenberg on Walpurgis Night, only they're coming here to bring tempests down on the whole diocese. He says they're not going to stop until the prisoners are free and His Eminence has fled.'

There we go: that's the way to do it. Without violence. Aenlin smiled. 'Where do they meet, my dear?'

'At the Devil's Gorge, I assume. In the Hauptsmoorwald.' Franz leaned close to her ear and muttered, 'There are three thousand of them, they say. *Three thousand!* They'll come down on Bamberg like locusts – they'll make it their home, the capital of the witches. It's good that we're a long way away from the city here.' He quickly crossed himself and disappeared through the passage into the kitchen to get the food Statius had demanded.

The roll of thunder came closer, as if to prove the boy's whispered words.

'I know where we'll find our third target,' Aenlin said. 'Veronica Stadler will be at the Devil's Gorge, ready to free her sister witches from that special gaol, using the power of the dark arts.' She wasn't afraid. *That will be easier to stomach than the things we've experienced so far.* She put her hand on Tahmina's forearm. 'Captain, let us deal with that. We're more experienced in these things than you are.'

'Certainly. That's what I wanted to suggest,' Caspar said. 'Also, you are women; you're more likely to win the witches over than the sight of the four of us.' He graciously raised his glass to the others. 'Meanwhile, we'll be busy freeing all the witches from the House of Malefaction so the guard will be just as busy rounding them up again, while we disappear with Gatchen and Ula.'

'Ha! Down the river,' Jäcklein suggested. 'We can be—'

'Never again in or on a river,' said Statius, quick as a shot. 'Without the Persian Pearl, that fucking water maid would have destroyed us.'

Franz, the bar lad, brought their food and another round of beer for all of them. The stew with groats smelled good, and there were also dumplings with the goulash. Statius gave him the evil eye, but the boy had already disappeared.

'In Bamberg, they would surely have caught and burned a naiad long ago. No amount of wetness would have saved her from going up in flame. The Prince-Bishop would've taken care of that.' Nicolas produced his pipe and tobacco from his pockets. 'Well then. We'll look around the city and come up with a plan. If we don't know the lie of the land, we're reduced to guess-work. We need to know the distance between the House of Malefaction and the gates, the number of guards there, things like that.' As he spelled out the list, he stuffed his pipe. 'You know what's important.'

'We'll base ourselves in this inn and start from here, which is safer for what we're intending to do.' Through the window, Aenlin saw rain cut across the land like a grey veil. 'By tomorrow evening, we will have scouted out the Devil's Gorge, then we will report back to each other.'

'Let's not take the coach,' Caspar said, 'so we're more flex-ible. And the Company's crest is emblazoned on the side. Hah! The Catholics would gladly smash the Dutch barouche into its component parts.' He took off his hat and his wig and started eating. 'The brave landsknechts will have to ride or walk.'

Aenlin had had to come to terms with the fact that usually, everybody ate from the same big pot, all sticking their forks in to get a bite. It wasn't her way of enjoying food, but there was no alternative.

'Well, did I already tell you that the Danish King has surrendered?' Jäcklein said. 'They're saying he's signed a peace treaty in Lübeck.'

'Well, shit in my soup,' Statius growled, looking dissatisfied. 'Then this nice war is over. Goodbye, thalers, goodbye, batzes, hellers, guilders and whatever other coins there are. I thought we'd be able to stroll onto the battlefield upon our return and stab us some idiots.'

'Ah, don't worry, my grim companion,' Caspar teased him. 'Seeing how the Protestants are tormented, the Swedes will certainly step into the breach for the Danes. The Emperor's Edict of Restitution will soon give you more work than you have legs to walk to and arms to swing.' He took a bite and raised his goblet of wine again. 'Mark my words.'

Aenlin softly touched Tahmina's knee and gave her a warm look that the mystic reciprocated. Followers of Lucifer could only be looking forward to Devil's Gorge.

Bamberg, May 1629

When they entered the city that the evening, Nicolas, Statius, Moritz, Jäcklein and Caspar took time to admire the wealth and beauty of the place. It stood partly on seven hills and partly on an artificial island in the river Regnitz.

From afar, it looked as if the four gaudily dressed landsknechts were part of the baggage train of the significantly older Caspar, who was on horseback and looked like a nobleman in his own opulent garb. The newest firelock muskets his men were carrying clearly showed that he was well off. No one asked them about their business in Bamberg; no one looked suspiciously at them, since they wore their crosses, visible to all, on their breastplates. They passed through the main gate with a polite 'Good day!'

'This city smells of beer,' Statius said in a satisfied voice. 'They like brewing here. I appreciate that.'

'It is not well fortified.' Jäcklein felt relieved. 'There are lots of escape routes – through the river, for example.'

'No water nymphs,' Moritz muttered. 'Anything but naiads.' He gazed at the Regnitz suspiciously. 'I've had enough of them.'

Nicolas asked the way to the House of Malefaction and took the lead. Over the last few years, on his way from one battle to the next, he had seen a lot of cities and settlements of all sizes. Some resembled each other so much that they became almost interchangeable: they were all built around the church, with the mayor's house usually right next to it and all the other important buildings lining the one road through. Even larger cities rarely had massive protective walls like Hamburg.

But Bamberg was different, and not only because of the island in the middle of the river. The city was made up of half-timbered buildings of all sizes. Cobbled streets and alleys full of twists and turns wound through the hilly city, which allegedly housed twelve thousand inhabitants.

Minus those who have been or are about to be burned as witches and warlocks, Nicolas thought.

The centre of the Bishopric openly displayed its wealth. The house façades featured intricately carved beams, with painted blessings and wisdom to give their admirers food for thought, or to speak of the wealth of the families living there. There was no lack of hostels or inns. Still, all four of them noticed the undercurrent of tension in the streets.

'I would be willing to loot Bamberg any time. What about

you? If the Swedes came to continue what the Danes gave up?'
Statius sniffed loudly. 'Oh, sweet beer, I will enjoy you!'

'Isn't Rome built on seven hills as well?' Caspar, fully aware
of his role, sat grandly on his black stallion, openly displaying
his rich black garb and his weapons. 'Look, my dear Comte –
over there by the gardens, they have tasty carrots and other
delicacies. In the middle of the city! This would be a good place
to live for a horse like you.'

Nicolas had arrived at the same conclusion as Jäcklein: with
a little preparation, it would be easy to escape Bamberg. He'd
quickly grasped the city's street plan. There was the part surrounding the Imperial Cathedral, and the island between the
arms of the Regnitz and the gardeners' city, where they grew
onions, vegetables and liquorice to sell in the surrounding areas
and throughout the land. The cathedral towered over it all,
reminding the residents of the power of the Prince-Bishop. 'We
need a reasonably exact map of this maze, or we'll lose our way
faster than a mole in the sunshine.'

Caspar noticed the House of Malefaction first. 'Now what's
this? Ah – we've found it.' Two men at arms, in breastplates and
helmets, guarded its gate. He stroked his goatee and moustache.
'My dears, how unspectacular. I expected something more . . .
hurly-burly.'

The House of Malefaction looked harmless enough, for all its
inmates were alleged to be highly dangerous. The half-timbered
two-storey building bore a large motto above its entrance:

DISCITE IUSTITIAM MONITI ET NON TEMNERE DIVOS

Statius looked at Caspar. 'How about it, your Aged Snootiness?
As a nobleman you certainly must be able to speak Latin, right?
What does that mean?'

'It means,' one of the guards called out, '"Be warned, learn justice and do not despise the gods." Remember this while you are in our city, soldiers.'

'Shall I go over and make the introductions?' Statius, feeling like he'd been challenged, straightened and took the musket with the dagger attached to the barrel from his shoulder. 'Moritz, what do you think? Shall we give them a proper knock on their helmets?'

'You don't belong to a Swedish army and you're not backed up by twenty thousand men, you fool,' Nicolas said. 'It's just the four of us. So be quiet.' He waved at the guards and thanked them for the explanation.

The tiny windows in the side walls showed where the cells were in the witches' prison. One of them held the two people they had come to free: Ula and Gatchen. On the first-floor wall, there was a little statue of Justitia and another with writing that Nicolas was unable to decipher.

To Nicolas' amazement, Caspar suddenly pulled his black stallion round and rode towards the House of Malefaction. He obviously had a plan.

'What is his Snootiness doing there?' Jäcklein whispered.

Moritz chuckled. 'He'll challenge them to a duel – that would clear the way.'

'Be quiet and let him do his thing.' Nicolas and his men waited at the side of the road, watching anxiously what kind of spectacle the duellist would enact.

'Good men,' Caspar addressed them, his voice dripping with noble haughtiness, 'I am Caspar von und zu dem Dorffe, a witch-hunter, currently free. The talk of various riff-raff waiting to be apprehended has brought me to Bamberg. How may I be of assistance?'

'Good day, dear sir,' replied one of the men at arms politely. 'You should go and see his Eminence.' The guard on the right pointed to the maze of alleys. 'Ask your way to the Residence of Prince-Bishop Johann Georg II, Fuchs Baron of Dornheim. Remember to always use his full name.'

'I shall.' Caspar produced a kreutzer from his pocket and tossed it to him. 'This is for your trouble, my good man.'

'Thank you, Milord.' The guard caught the small coin.

'Oh, lest I forget.' Caspar dismounted and waved his four companions over. 'My men and I, we are looking for a witch who, disguised, struck terror into people's hearts in Wanfried. They say she was also present at the witches' dance on the Kreydenberg.' He threw the long ends of his wig back over his shoulders. 'But I know her real appearance. Could I take a look at your delinquents?'

Under cover of the brim of his hat, Nicolas grinned and leaned on his musket. *Very clever.*

'Why, Milord?'

'To make my witness statement and add to the indictment, should she be among them. That would make a good start for my conversation with His Eminence, as it would guarantee her conviction.' He put a hand on the guard's shoulder. 'Between you and me, if I could talk to her and convict her, Bamberg might even get some information on the army of witches supposedly gathering in the Hauptsmoorwald to call down a tempest upon this city.' Caspar pointed at the motto over the gate. 'The law, my good man: ordained by God.' Then he pressed a guilder into the man's hand.

Watching this, Nicolas could understand why people bought the duellist's role as a nobleman, no matter how silly his made-up title sounded. He never hesitated, never showed any uncertainty. *He is good, both with words and with his pistols.*

The guard looked at the coin. 'You know about the army?'

'But of course, of course! The last witch I burned screamed about it to ease her black soul. She accused that very witch for whom I am searching of connivance. The Devil's leman will surely know exactly where in the woods her sisters will be celebrating their demonic rendezvous with Satan to send this beautiful city to its doom.' He leaned a little closer to the man. 'Provided I can look at her – examine her. What do you think? Do you want to be a hero and save Bamberg? His Eminence might just name a street after you. How would you like that?'

The guard quickly knocked on the heavy door, which opened outwards. 'Sebastian, show the good Count our witches at once! He is looking for one of them – he intends to testify against her.'

'My thanks. This will be for the benefit of all inhabitants of the fair city of Bamberg.' Caspar pointed at Nicolas. 'You come along. The others look out for my Comte.' He followed Sebastian and the captain followed him.

The stench of excrement filled the gloomy house. Soft whimpering and moaning wafted through the rank air. Misery, suffering and pain lived here, gnawing away at those who entered.

'How many are incarcerated here?' Caspar pulled a perfumed kerchief from his sleeve and pressed it against his mouth and nose to stave off the stench.

'Twenty-two,' Sebastian said. 'Two men. The others are women and children.' A clean-shaven man in his twenties, Sebastian wore a large rosary around his neck that rubbed against his breastplate. 'You know about the army, Milord? Then it is true?' He looked at Nicolas encouragingly. 'We have heard so much about it, but—'

'There is no hurry. First, we must find the witch. Then we will soon know more.' Caspar, following Sebastian kept looking around the gaol.

'This is reckless and audacious,' Nicolas whispered, noting the position of the guardrooms and cells. Opposite the entrance was a small chapel, pitting the power of faith against the evils of those incarcerated here. He stood his musket next to the door. It was too long and awkward, and he didn't need it at the moment.

'That's how I am, Captain. And also full of the wisdom of age that you are lacking.' Caspar affectively waved his kerchief. 'Anyone who has four hundred and one on their list can be neither squeamish nor timid.' He pointed at the names written in chalk on the cell doors. Here and there, the shadowy names of former inmates cut through, mixed with those of the current residents, proclaiming nothing but death. 'Let's keep our eyes peeled.'

The eager guard showed Nicolas and Caspar cell after cell, allowing them to investigate the dungeons through the spyholes in the doors. Where the evening light was not sufficient, Sebastian opened the doors to reveal the dirty, tortured faces of the inmates.

Nicolas had seen a lot in his life. He knew well the cruelties of battlefields – the wounds, the stench, the screaming and moaning; people hanging dead on gallows or broken on the wheel didn't shock him, and neither did whipped backs. But when the guard showed him the imprisoned girls, none of them older than ten, bearing the marks of torture after their interrogation as if they were adults, Nicolas choked.

By the grace of God! He knew that evil wore many disguises, but these children didn't feel even remotely like dangerous witches or demons in human guise. *How could anyone do this to them?*

'Did they confess?' Caspar's voice was rough; he, too, was shaken by what he was seeing.

'All of them, Milord – fornicating with the Devil, bewitchment of the inhabitants of Bamberg, damaging curses against fruit-bearing trees.' Sebastian mercilessly closed the spyhole. 'Don't be deceived: these are not merely children. We know what they have been up to. They shamelessly gathered in our city, celebrated orgies, even sacrificed newborn babies.' He crossed himself, kissed the crucifix on his rosary and led them up the stairs to the next cells, which surrounded a larger hall. Here were rooms for the guards too, a confessional chamber and another small chapel. 'I have seen the corpses of the poor folks whose souls they gave to the Devil. Oh, I wish I had not seen that.'

'Oh?' Caspar pointed inconspicuously to the doors past the guardrooms, next to the stairs, to alert Nicolas: the names written on them in chalk were *Agatha Mühlbach* and *Ursula Garnhuber*. They had found the two women they were looking for. 'What was so strange about them?'

'They had skinned a woman alive and wore the strips of her skin as a dress until the skin had dried out,' Sebastian whispered. 'They had torn her face away and they wore it as . . . as if it was a mask.' He produced a dark green sliver of stone from his pocket. 'They did it with this!'

I have never heard of anything like this. Nicolas suddenly realised he was looking at a fragment of a knife blade. 'Obsidian.'

'Exactly.' Sebastian continued the tour of the cells, letting them look inside each chamber in turn. 'They cut the heart from beneath the ribs in several other victims. Then these little witches caught other children and starved them, to gather their desperate tears, from which they brewed potions and elixirs of the Devil.' He crossed himself again and pressed the crucifix against his chapped lips. 'God, protect us from them.'

Nicolas and Caspar exchanged a brief glance. These events sounded unique.

'I have never heard such things reported,' Nicolas remarked. 'You have the worst of the bad in Bamberg, it seems.'

'True enough, true enough. No one knows why this particular plague is haunting us.'

The tour was done. Sebastian stood at the landing. 'Have you seen her, Milord?'

'She could be one of those two.' Caspar pointed at the cells of Gatchen and Ula. 'I would like to examine them further.' He gestured at the guard to open the doors. 'Nicolas, keep an eye on me and this spawn of evil. Should I behave weirdly, shoot them down.' He passed two of his four pistols to the captain, then explained to the guard, 'They fire blessed silver musket balls. They will kill any demon.'

'I cannot do that, Milord! I don't know what Paul promised you, but . . .' Sebastian hemmed and hawed. 'I would prefer if you came back with a writ from the Prince-Bishop to make it official. It would be best if you brought the hangman, or his henchmen or . . .'

Caspar pierced the man with his gaze. 'I cannot. I am wasting time here that Bamberg might not have.'

At his words, thunder shook the sky and loud hail unexpectedly pelted the roof of the House of Malefaction.

Nicolas had to suppress a grin. *As if on command.* At the same time, he couldn't help but feel a certain uneasiness. What if this really was caused by witchcraft?

'The army of witches – do you hear it?' Caspar added. 'I can take my men and disappear, but you and your family, you will feel the hatred of three thousand sorceresses and witches. They are preparing for the attack right now – this hailstorm is just the beginning!'

With a curse, Sebastian unlocked the doors. The two women in simple beige dresses of flax barely moved. Their heads had been shaved and they had not been treated with care.

Nicolas raised both pistols. 'Examine them, Milord – for the city's sake. But be quick about it! I don't want any trouble with those Satanic whores.'

As Caspar entered the cell, a racket sounded suddenly on the ground floor.

'What's going on here?' called an unknown voice, that of a man who was clearly used to being obeyed. 'Where is this mysterious witch-hunter?'

'Upstairs, Milord,' stammered the guard at the entrance. 'He is looking for a witch who knows where in the Hauptsmoorwald they will gather.'

'Why doesn't he tell that to the Prince-Bishop? Why the secrecy?' Heavy steps came quickly up the stairs, but Nicolas didn't hear the clinking and rattling of weapons. 'Hey! Where are you, Count?'

Caspar gestured to Nicolas to stay in his role. 'I am here – and I'm not shagging a witch, believe me.' He left the cell and stepped into the corridor.

Nicolas was expecting a councillor or a magistrate from the city government who had heard about the newcomers. *If he is unarmed, he will pose no danger.*

Instead, a clean-shaven man in his forties wearing the black robe of a cleric reached the landing. Behind him came two strong young men, henchmen of the hangman, according to their badges and their entirely grey garb.

'Ah, the secret power of the Catholic Church arrives.' Caspar waved his hat in greeting. 'Who are you?'

Nicolas held both pistols in his hands, muzzles down, to avoid looking threatening. *A Jesuit. The duellist's razzle-dazzle might not work against the much sharper wits of a cleric.* He prepared to step in, trusting in Jäcklein, Statius and Moritz, waiting outside the House of Malefaction, to let no one escape it.

'Father Hubertus of the Society of Jesus,' said the Jesuit resolutely. 'I have come to lead two delinquents to their interrogation – and I am greatly astonished to find you here. You are a Count?'

'Caspar von und zu dem Dorffe,' he said, and he waved his kerchief. 'I am a witch-hunter. Seems I have come to the right place.' He pointed at the open doors. 'You want those two?'

'Those two, Count.' Father Hubertus scrutinised Nicolas. 'You are a motley crew.'

'Not unlike yours.' Caspar grinned. 'You're busted. I read your order's *Monita Secreta* – your secret instructions. Even a witch might have problems being weirder than a Jesuit.' He shifted one foot in front of him and placed a hand on his hip. 'I hope you are demanding satisfaction for my words, Priest?'

What is he doing? Nicolas had heard about that tract, which had been published ten years ago. It showed the true purpose of the order, most people thought, and the number of friends the Jesuits could count on had fallen dramatically. Caspar was obviously openly hostile to them. *And here I thought Stats would be a problem. But that he should get carried away here . . . ?*

Father Hubertus looked at the duellist with suspicion. 'What strange sort of Count are you?'

'You need me to be more offensive?' Caspar laughed artificially. 'Well, then, let me tell you that the Jesuits are greedy powermongers, and also schemers who conspire against everybody else. You whisper in the ears of those in power and you get your orders from Rome. For you and your ilk, the end justifies any mean. Your morals are those of a goat-fucking sodomite whose pig and sheep have run away. You are cheating on the poor animals with the Devil's beast.' Caspar nodded at the surprised Nicolas. 'Well, that should suffice. Give him a pistol, Captain. The corridor is long enough for a duel of honour.'

'Never in a million years are you a nobleman – or even a witch-hunter. But the truth will out.' Father Hubertus didn't take the weapon Nicolas offered him but instead retreated to the stairs. 'The two of you,' he told the henchmen, 'stop them. You, guardsman, help them. I'll go and g—'

Again, a racket erupted at the entrance below as someone broke open the door.

'Fire! The Hauptsmoorwald is burning!' cried an excited female voice. 'The flames of Hell are blazing skywards! Almighty God, help us! We are in mortal danger!'

'The army of witches,' Sebastian whispered, his face paling. 'What is said is true, Count. They come to free their ilk with sulphur from Hell which not even the rain can extinguish!'

'You fools,' Father Hubertus yelled, 'he is a warlock himself! Kill him and his men!' The Jesuit shoved aside the two henchmen and ran down the stairs, crying, 'Help! Assault! Guards—!'

It had started out so well. 'Stats, silence him,' Nicolas yelled. He raised the pistols and pointed their muzzles at their grey-clad opponents. 'Don't you move a muscle!'

His threat worked. The hangman's helpers didn't budge.

'It's now or never, right, Captain?' Caspar knocked down Sebastian and took from him the keys for the manacles. He hurried into the cells and freed Gatchen and Ula from their chains.

The two women said nothing.

'We won't be coming back to Bamberg,' Caspar said.

'Free all the inmates!' Nicolas ordered, which elicited hoarse screams of joy and cries of relief from throughout the gaol. *We'll be able to disappear while the guards are tied up catching witches and warlocks.*

Caspar dragged the two exhausted women into the corridor, then shoved the three men into the empty cell. Agatha and Ulrika quietly pressed their backs against the wall, holding each other tight. 'Sorry, our attack was bit hasty. But when I see a Jesuit . . .'

'It's too late for remorse. Destiny surely had something in mind for us.' Nicolas helped the duellist free the other prisoners. *We'll have to be quick – quicker than a witch on a broomstick.*

Sufficient Indication of Witchcraft

If someone offers to teach other people witchcraft or threatens to ensorcel someone and the threatened person suffers an appropriate fate soon thereafter, or if a person joins the fellowship of warlocks or witches or associates with suspicious things, gestures, words and ways that imply witchcraft and the fellowship is also otherwise suspicious of this. This is sufficient for a report of witchcraft and is reason enough for an interrogation under torture ... No one shall be interrogated under torture without an honest report ... except under suspicion of witchcraft.

Procedure for the Judgment of Capital Crimes,
Bamberg, 1588

CAPITULUM VIII

Near Bamberg, May 1629

Franz sat on the roof of the landsknechts' coach and looked through the open gates of the barn into the rain. He wore only a shirt, breeches and worn-out shoes, and he'd wrapped himself in a horse rug. The bar lad was enjoying the silence. He had brought half a mug of stale beer and put some leftovers into his worn bag.

Light falling from the windows of the inn pierced the darkness, illuminating the raindrops, turning some of them into shining pearls, others into long silver strings or tiny falling stars.

Aenlin had given him a full guilder as payment for watching their stuff. Unlike that Statius fellow, she had been genuinely nice, so he'd refrained from picking the locks of their bags, chests and boxes and rummaging through their contents for valuables that wouldn't immediately be missed. He would certainly have managed to find something. As a serving lad, he had to look out for himself, but he never stole too much, never raised any suspicion.

Franz spat and sighed contentedly. As compensation for sparing the chests, he would sleep in the comfortable coach. He rarely got such regal opportunities; he had to take them when they arose. The cushions had felt so soft when he brushed them earlier to remove the dust from their long journey.

He didn't recognise the crest on the doors and had never heard of the West India Company – there was neither a sea nor any overseas trading company anywhere in the Bamberg area, or at least none whose employees frequented the coaching inn.

Franz would not have liked that life, not sailing the great, wide ocean in defiance of storms and enemy ships laden with cannon, nor did the work of a witch-hunter, like the landsknechts and the two women did, appeal to him.

He didn't really understand who their leader was. The oldest one, the man in black who was a good shot, was the most pompous of them, but Captain Nicolas, who was more than twenty years his junior, seemed to have the final say. It was a small, special crew with an extraordinary profession.

Franz took a sip of beer and breathed clean air that smelled of horses, leather, straw and rain – no prickling smoke from the fire, no foul-smelling pipe smoke, no chafing heat from the hearth and no stench of frying and stewing food. He liked the silence.

With his right hand, he stroked the roof of the coach. He would enjoy sleeping in it, alone, with no other bodies crowding the bed or throwing him out. He wanted to sleep like a nobleman before arising to collect the guests' chamber pots.

'I need help,' cried a weak voice out in the rain.

Franz blinked and stared into the drizzle. Had the raindrops asked for succour? Or was someone playing tricks on him? A guest? One of his siblings? Or was it a spook, after all?

The darkness spat forth a girl, completely drenched, not much older than Franz himself. Her thin, light dress clung to her; her long hair hung around her heavily. She had wrapped her arms around herself. 'Please help me.'

'Stop!' Wide awake, now, Franz drew his dagger and quickly drank another sip of beer to boost his courage. 'Are you a ghost?'

Clearly exhausted, the girl staggered closer and leaned against the doorframe of the stable. 'I am Osanna,' she stammered, and slid down the wooden frame until she was kneeling in mud at the entrance of the building. 'I am Osanna. Of flesh and blood.'

Franz took the dark-lantern standing behind him and opened two more shutters to get better sight. He shone its light far out into the rainy evening without seeing any threat between the drops.

'Wait, I'll come out.' Nimbly he climbed down and carefully approached her. She looked thin and weak and she was trembling all over. Maybe she was a fugitive from a city or village that had been less lucky in the war. Still, he kept his dagger handy. 'Say the Lord's prayer.'

Weakly, Osanna raised her head. 'You think I'm a demon? Or a witch?'

'They are everywhere, the priest said. I must be careful.'

'Our Father who art in Heaven,' the girl prayed without displaying the slightest sign of disgust or resistance against the holy words of the Lord. 'Hallowed be . . .'

'All right, all right.' Franz helped her up, led her out of the rain, sat her down in the straw and wrapped her in his horse rug. 'You are no witch.' Nonetheless, he cast another glance outside. Nothing. 'What happened to you? Are you alone? Have you been attacked?'

'I have escaped my tormentor. Half a day ago, somewhere in the middle of the woods.' Osanna looked at him with gratitude. 'They call him the Venetian, a man with a silver plague mask, and he is accompanied by a pack of landsknechts who are under his spell. He has provided them with . . . unnatural powers.' Her face was twisted in sheer fear. 'Has he been here already? Has he—?'

'No, no, he hasn't.' A shudder ran down Franz's back, colder than ice. Her fear was clearly real and if what she said was true . . . He suddenly felt very afraid of whatever was approaching the inn. 'Let's go into the tavern. There's a fire and something to eat there and you . . .' Osanna's gaze darted past him to the coach. The look of relief on her face told him that she knew the vehicle. 'Why . . . why is that coach here? The Company has no business in the south.'

'It belongs to a few witch-hunters who—'

She grabbed his arm so hard it hurt and her face brightened. 'Is their captain called Nicolas? His friend's name is Jäcklein and the other one – he is Statius. What was the name of the last one again . . . Moritz! The youngest one is called Moritz.'

'You know them?'

Osanna nodded with relief. 'By Lord God the Almighty! I think they are the arch-enemies of the Venetian.' She turned her head towards the exit, her wet brown hair falling over the horse rug. 'Are they here?'

'No. No, they aren't.' Franz quickly climbed back onto the coach and retrieved his mug and bag so he could offer the girl a few bites and the last sip of beer. He jumped back down to her without spilling anything. 'The landsknechts have gone to Bamberg to look for witches and the two women—'

'Two women?'

'Aenlin and . . . I have forgotten the other one's name.' Franz handed her a piece of bread and let her drink from his tankard. 'She is younger and much more delicate – almost like you. But she's not from around here. Her face is different. Somehow . . . maybe from the Balkan lands. Or from an even more faraway place.'

'They are not here, either?' Suddenly, Osanna sounded disappointed and desperate. 'Oh, Lord of Heavens above, be with us! When the Venetian comes, we will need bold folk like them.'

'They are truly fearless! Despite the dark, they hurried off to the Devil's Gorge – to the Hauptsmoorwald. To look for the army of witches.'

'That is the reason the Venetian has travelled to Bamberg! He wants to join that army of witches!' Osanna stuffed the stale bread into her mouth and devoured the mouldy cheese, then drank the beer greedily. 'Then I cannot stay,' she mumbled. 'This place will fall.'

'But we . . . what use have those evil ones for us?' Her dread had now completely infected Franz, who kept holding up the lantern so he could peer out into rain-soaked darkness for the silhouette of the plague doctor.

The darkness, however, kept its secrets well. The rush of the downpour, the quiet laughter from the inn and the melodious sound of a lute being played within were all he could hear. This night was like any other, in almost every regard.

'Anyone who can be used for evil is of value.' Osanna wrapped the horse rug tighter around herself. 'I'll keep this for my journey. Tell them that a vagrant stole it.' Her gaze met his. 'Or would you like to come along? You might perish otherwise.'

'But my parents and brothers and sisters are here!'

'They will die,' Osanna said insistently. 'The witch-hunters are not here to assist you against the Venetian and his demonic servants. What do you think? How long can you resist him? Everyone unwilling to serve him will perish.'

'But ...' Franz cast a desperate glance into the rain. He couldn't disagree with her prophetic words, for no one in his family knew how to fight, and none were skilled in the art of exorcism. But would they simply believe Osanna's warning? What if they didn't?

Suddenly, Franz had an idea how to save his family. 'I'll hurry to the Devil's Gorge and get the two female hunters – they can help us until the soldiers come back!'

'Yes! Yes, that's a good idea.' Osanna stood and took his hand in her trembling one. 'I'll come with you.'

'Aren't you too weak to—?'

'I'll manage somehow. My words will show them the urgency of the affair.' Her breathing had quickened in fear. 'Also, I'll certainly be safe with them. The Venetian is worse than all witches on this earth!'

Franz retrieved the lantern from the roof of the coach. They had no time to waste.

Briefly he considered going to the inn and telling the people there – but then he would have to talk to the drunken adults and answer dozens of questions and they would certainly want to interrogate Osanna ... Franz decided there was nothing to gain going down that road. First, they needed the witch-hunters, then everything else would fall into place. 'Come on, let's hurry.' He led the way.

Osanna stayed close behind him, her cold, clammy fingers gripping his hand like iron for fear of losing him.

'I am looking for a girl. Her name is Osanna.'

The soft words went unheard inside the inn, drowned out by the music, the singing, the laughter and the clattering of knives and spoons and mugs. The patrons clapped rhythmically, knocking on the benches and tables. That was why no one heard the Venetian, who had crept in like a shadow and now stood next to the door, his case in hand.

In the low-ceilinged room, a smoky warmth had accumulated, heavy with the noise of the patrons. Thanks to the tempest, two more coaches had stopped there, unable to reach Bamberg, which made the innkeeper and his wife happy. Their meagre revenue rose abruptly.

'I am looking for a girl,' the Venetian repeated behind his silver plague mask; the red eye glasses were shimmering. 'Osanna.'

A group of people playing dice were the first to notice the man in the black coat with the gleaming mask. They stopped playing in bewilderment and nudged those sitting next to them, until the whole taproom was looking at the newcomer.

The bard, who had his eyes closed, kept playing, the melody from his lute piercing the silence that was otherwise broken only by the crackling and spitting of the logs on the fire.

No one spoke. The arrival of a plague doctor in full regalia augured ill. The authorities would surely have a reason to send a savant like him – and that made everyone profoundly uneasy.

The bard finally noticed the silence and opened his eyes. When he saw the newcomer, he stopped playing, too.

'A girl,' the Venetian said for the third time. 'Osanna.'

The men and women looked at each other and let their gazes wander throughout the taproom. There was a hesitant shaking of heads, followed by muttering and clearing of throats.

'This Osanna you are looking for does not seem to be among us,' the innkeeper replied with some relief. 'Is she your daughter?'

'Her tracks lead to this inn.' The Venetian turned a little and his highly polished mask flashed in the light, which highlighted its engraved chasings. 'She was not in the stable, and I am therefore looking for her here.'

'Never in the world is she his daughter,' shouted a carter, who looked pretty drunk. 'Do you want to fuck her? With your silver nose? Sniff and poke between her legs?' The man laughed loudly at his own obscene joke.

'Look at me.' The Venetian raised his arms, spreading his gloved fingers. The leather of his brown-black apron creaked quietly. 'What kind of doctor do you think I am?'

The carter licked his lips. 'Stupid question! Anyone can see that you're a plague doctor!'

'Well, well. What a clever man you are. So what might it mean if I am looking for a girl while I am wearing this garb?'

People in the taproom started crossing themselves and praying quietly. Every man and every woman there understood his words. 'Since Osanna's tracks lead to this inn and I was not able to find her in the stable, she might be hiding amongst you secretly.'

People looked around worriedly.

'The poor child is probably hungry. Her clothes are wet. Maybe in her search for food and dry clothes, she has sat down in a corner, behind the stove, in an alcove in the kitchen?' He pointed at the soup tureens. 'Maybe the madness of the plague brought her to you.'

The front door opened and Valentin entered. To protect himself from the rain, the landsknecht wore a colourful cloak from which the hilt of his rapier protruded. He knelt in front of the Venetian, lowered his head and quickly pulled his wet hat from his dark hair. 'Milord, we have found tracks in dry patches under the trees. One set is the girl's, the other is a little bigger. They lead eastwards from the stable.'

Gratefully, the Venetian put his right hand on the landsknecht's shoulder. 'Well done, Ensign.' The plague doctor turned his head left and right, the shattered red glasses resembling dead eyes. 'Who could have accompanied Osanna?'

'That must've been my Franz!' the innkeeper uttered in horror and crossed himself. 'My boy! He is young – he helps us in the tap . . .'

'What was Franz up to in the stable?'

'He . . . was supposed to guard the wagons.'

'Milord, he is talking about the coaches housed there,' Valentin said. He rose. He opened his coat to be able to reach his rapier and his main gauche. His pistol became visible. 'One of them bears the crest of the Company. They are loaded, too, and the chests and crates bear the same crest.'

The plague doctor put his case down beside Valentin and slowly walked through the taproom. 'Innkeeper, what's your name?'

'Martin Huber.'

'Where are the guests travelling in those coaches?'

'They . . .' Huber flinched away from the eerie Venetian. 'They are not here. What about them?'

'That is none of your concern.'

'Are . . . are they suffering from the plague?'

'Answer me!'

'They went to the city,' Huber cried, 'to Bamberg! They are witch-hunters. They went to offer their services to the Prince-Bishop, but the women didn't accompany them. They . . .' His eyes bulged. 'Heaven help us! Franz's and the girl's tracks are leading eastwards?'

Valentin stepped closer. 'No doubt.'

'What is to the east, Innkeeper? It cannot be Bamberg.'

'The Hauptsmoorwald with the . . . with the Devil's Gorge. My Franz thinks that is where the witches are gathering for their attack on the city. The boy thinks the storm is a harbinger of our doom.' Huber paled. 'He told the witch-hunters where to go and . . . and now . . . he is leading the girl right after them! But why?'

'I would be glad to know that, too.' Slowly, the plague doctor sat down in the closest chair, at the table of the people who had been playing dice. They moved away from him, giving him space; the scraping of their chair legs sounded loud in the silence.

'I will need lodging in your inn until tomorrow,' the Venetian announced. 'I'll talk to this band of witch-hunters. Since they have left their belongings and their carriages with you, they will return, and with Osanna – at least, I hope that's the case, for their sakes.' He turned his masked face towards the innkeeper. 'I am travelling with several dozens of faithful souls like my good Valentin here. We will take the best rooms.'

'But dear sir, we . . . we have no vacancies. We are filled up to the last shabby shack,' Huber stammered in reply. 'Sorry, but you cannot stay. I swear that this is no excuse to put you off.'

'I thought so.' The Venetian gestured to Valentin, who opened the door. 'Get the men.'

'But . . . haven't you heard me? The house is packed,' the innkeeper repeated. 'I cannot simply throw out my guests. They have paid and—'

'Don't worry, my dear innkeeper,' the doctor said.

As he spoke, his soldiers crossed the threshold, rapiers drawn, daggers and clubs in hands. The drinkers in the taproom rose.

'We will take care of freeing the beds ourselves. Maybe we will even sleep in them. Then again, maybe not.' The Venetian nodded, and the landsknechts started the slaughter. Not a blow or stab failed to meet its mark.

'There will be no complaints, I promise you.' Droplets of blood spattered the doctor's mask. 'Not a single one.'

Hauptsmoorwald, west of Bamberg, May 1629

Tahmina and Aenlin rode through the pine forest, first following a ridge around the pathless valley of the Regnitz, then turning off it.

The mystic had her staff in her left hand, its shimmering symbols lighting the path they had to take. She had removed her light bonnet and now her midnight-blue gown turned her into a dark silhouette. 'We are on the right track,' she said to her companion. 'I saw a witch's mark on that tall pine over there.'

Aenlin, who hadn't noticed it, was relieved to have Tahmina by her side. She didn't expect trouble when the witches found them, not when they came with good intentions. Their mission was to get Veronica Stadler to Hamburg unharmed – to safety, far away from witch-trials and pyres. 'We will stop this bunch of magic-users from attacking. The inhabitants of the city are not responsible for the Prince-Bishop's delusions.'

'They are not innocent, either. How many people live there? More than twelve thousand? They could take issue with him and send him packing, you know.'

'Don't forget how powerful he is, according to all the reports,' Aenlin replied. 'A violent insurrection would surely provoke a reaction by the Emperor. Then a general like Tilly or Wallenstein would show up and destroy Bamberg, no matter whether the city is Catholic or not. As an example.'

'Speaking of violent death, do you think the witches won't attack us if we explain to them that we're here to save two of them and let the rest of them rot in that House of Malefaction?'

Tahmina guided her horse to the right, avoiding some trees standing closer together. 'The Devil's Gorge must be nearby, so I thought I'd better mention it.'

Sometimes, Aenlin found her companion's habit of second-guessing everything a little devastating. She would have preferred to be going into this encounter unprejudiced.

Sighing, she replied, 'You think we should free all the witches and warlocks.'

'Oh, what a great idea! If I were them, I would demand exactly that.' Tahmina reached out and lovingly touched Aenlin's shoulder. 'Let us be ready for this demand. Nicolas will come up with an appropriate plan.'

The conversation reminded Aenlin of a thought she had had as they left. Something about the gathering-place of the witches didn't really make sense. 'Wait.' She reined in her horse. 'This meeting place at the Devil's Gorge? It appears to be common knowledge, doesn't it?'

'If the bar lad knows it, it certainly is no secret.' Tahmina pulled up her mount, too.

The forest all around them remained black and silent. The dark tree trunks barely reflected the light; within a few feet, it disappeared completely. It felt like they were the only living beings here. No twig cracked; no tree creaked.

Nature holds its breath so they can hear us better. Aenlin's bright garb made her much more clearly visible than Tahmina, sitting beside her. 'If everybody knows, then why don't they send witch-hunters or an army and end this? It would certainly be in the best interest of the Catholic League and they definitely have coin enough to hire some decent landsknechts.' She brushed the ebony strand from her eyes and cast a searching gaze between the pine trunks. *We almost rode into a trap, just like mere beginners.* 'I don't see the slightest sliver of light. The camp must be unlit, if there is one at all.'

'You guessed exactly what I was thinking. According to the witch's rune, we should have been there long ago. Let me check something.' Tahmina made a gesture and said something in the Persian tongue while touching some of the symbols on her staff.

Prompted by her magical command, the symbols created a shimmering green circle which went spreading through the forest like a wave in the water. The moss-coloured light illuminated the pines, their branches and twigs looking like arms and fingers, while holes and cracks gave the trees grotesque faces.

Simpler minds would have fled, but Aenlin remained vigilant. She was not afraid. *As long as the dead do not rise again . . .*

The search spell faded into the distance and elapsed without any resonance. The darkness returned to the forest.

'No camp,' Tahmina declared, 'but someone is here, hidden. A woman. I can feel her aura.'

'Probably a scout observing anyone who approached the Devil's Gorge.' Aenlin made her steed trot on carefully. So it was no trap, but a precaution. 'Hey there! We know you're here and we come in peace. We are looking for Veronica Stadler, also known as Nica, to talk to her and deliver a message. That is all.'

Tahmina spurred her horse on. 'You have seen that we are also skilled at magic and spellcraft, sister. You have nothing to fear from us.'

'Stay right where you are.' The whisper came from all around them, echoing from the branches and in the rustling of the needles. 'Who are you?'

Just as we suspected. A scout.

'My name is Aenlin Kane and this is my friend Tahmina. A friend sent us to talk to Nica.'

'These are not German names,' the forest rustled. 'You have a weird accent.'

'I come from England, Tahmina from Persia. She is a mystic,

sort of related to you. She has mastered the art of Yatu, a special form of magic.' Aenlin dismounted.

'What makes you think I am a witch?' whispered the needles all around them. 'Maybe a demon is speaking to you. Or something worse.'

'Both would have destroyed us at once instead of speaking to us.' Aenlin didn't detect any sounds or light, or any other thing that would give away the witch's position. *Where is she?* 'You wait and watch?'

'Yes. To see who believes the nonsense about an army of witches and warlocks and wishes to send them to Hell. I lead them to the place where we're hiding if they come in peace.' She laughed. It sounded like rustling leaves.

'I see the truth in you. My spell never errs.' A gust of wind swept through the dark forest, stirring up earth, bark and dried needles that kept turning around and around – and finally coalesced into the shape of a woman.

'This is why I show myself to you.' She wore a green-brown cape and a light green bonnet covering her mahogany brown hair. On her right side, she wore a satchel. In her belt she wore a sickle. 'My name is Anna.'

Aenlin quickly bowed. It was hard to guess the witch's age; she might have been in her thirties. 'Thank you for showing yourself to us. Is Veronica with you?'

'Yes.' Anna took the lead. 'Follow me. I'll take you to her.'

They got going just as the tempest approached them from behind, like a defensive wall of rain, lightning and hail to protect the three women.

'So you really do hide in the Hauptsmoorwald.' Aenlin felt as if the ground beneath her feet was growing softer. Her horse continued hesitantly, snorting nervously, until it finally stopped. 'Come on,' she said kindly and stroked its warm nose. 'No one will hurt you. It might get a little strange, though.'

'They don't dare to go any further – neither they, nor the foxes or other inhabitants of the forest will walk the ground. It is a natural obstacle for animals.' Anna pointed at the pine Tahmina had stopped beside. 'Tether them there. We'll pick them up on our way back.' She noticed that her visitors hesitated. 'No one will steal them.' The witch continued, 'We surrounded part of the grove with a spell that makes people give it a wide berth without noticing. This provides us with a safe space.'

Aenlin and Tahmina secured their horses and hurried after Anna. The symbols on the ebony staff remained dark: there was no looming danger from creatures or magic.

Thank you, Lucifer, Aenlin thought. *May it stay that way.*

Soon they reached a more overgrown part of the forest, where some ancient oaks held their ground against the conifers. Branches and twigs interwove above their heads to form a tight canopy. The lightning was barely visible through the green. Suddenly, rain came pounding down, but the water didn't reach the forest floor; it was diverted by the sloping canopy.

Aenlin felt like she was walking through spider webs, but when she tried to brush the gossamer from her face, there were no sticky threads. *What . . . ?*

Some of the carved and etched symbols on her companion's ebony staff had started glowing green and turquoise as it detected magic.

'Black magic,' Tahmina explained softly. 'They're triggered when the staff detects evil intent in the mind of any creature, be it human or animal.'

'Oh, wonderful,' Anna said. 'Your Yatu powers are rather good. Few would have noticed the barrier. It is the perfect protection against those who would be able to pierce our curse of rejection.'

'What does it do?' Aenlin felt an echo of the magic gossamer on her skin. 'Do attackers go up in flames?'

'No,' the witch said, 'the threads cut you to pieces like the sharpest blades imaginable. We want to be surrounded only by those who don't mean us ill. The rest can go to Hell.'

Aenlin had already opened her mouth to stand up for Lucifer; this constant going on and on about Hell was making her sick to the bone. How could the lies of the Bible have such an effect on people?

'Not now,' Tahmina whispered. 'Not here.'

Aenlin felt her companion's hand on her back.

'You will not change her mind anyway,' Tahmina added.

The night became even darker around the trio, until they spotted the light of several lanterns between the trunks and heard scraps of quiet conversation and the melancholy notes of a flute. They had reached the camp.

'Welcome to the witches' grove,' Anna said. She knocked her ring against the blade of her sickle. 'Hey there! Sisters! Look, visitors!'

Calls greeted them: 'New allies?'

'Fugitives from Bamberg?'

'Witches from another part of the empire to help us?' These questions and more, too many for Aenlin to disentangle them all, came from the mouths of a group of women and a few men who were sitting around a fire between some huts.

It reminded Aenlin of outlaw camps in the woods of England, only this one was more beautiful, almost charming to behold. It wasn't thrown together, but built with love and intended for permanent use, for years – and not just since the persecution by the Prince-Bishop and his predecessor. This community had no doubt existed for decades, maybe even centuries.

'Sovereign sister, I bring to you Aenlin Kane and her companion Tahmina, a sister from the Orient.' Anna stepped aside so that everyone gathered was able to see the newcomers. 'They come with peace in their hearts and minds. They are looking for Sister Nica.'

'Welcome. I am Sophia, the sovereign sister of our community – or our coven, whatever you would like to call it.' A tall, sturdy woman had risen from the circle around the fire. Sophia was far past seventy; her garb was simple, her thinning grey hair loose and unkempt. 'What exactly brings you to the Devil's Gorge?'

She took the visitors in a long embrace, filling them with warmth and a slight tickling, as if some secret energy was at work. The smell of moss and gorse flowers surrounded her. 'You are bold, I'll give you that.'

'We have been sent from way up in the north to meet and talk to Veronica Stadler. Men and a coach stand ready to escort her to safety.' Aenlin was being deliberately vague. 'I hope you will understand that I have to tell her everything else in person.'

Sophia clasped her hands in front of her. 'I do. But before we talk about our sister, Have you been to Bamberg?'

'No, we came straight here from the nearby coaching inn.' *That doesn't sound good.* 'Why do you ask?'

'I would have liked to know how the city and our incarcerated sisters and brothers fare.' Sophia led them to the circle and gestured for them to take a seat.

The witches – male and female, busy with dinner, drink and conversation – nodded at them kindly. Not one of them looked dangerous, unnatural, or exceptionally ugly – or pretty – as their enemies claimed. Aenlin had long suspected this would be the case. Tahmina was the best example of a magic-user whose looks differed from what the Church and the fearful ones declared.

Next to the fire, illuminated by several lanterns, stood a model of a city, with markers in some places. Even if there was no army of thousands of witches, at least the rumours about an impending attack appeared to be true. *The coven plans to capture Bamberg.*

'Maybe I can tell you more once our landsknechts are back.' Aenlin sat down on a log and took off her hat, letting her long black hair flow freely.

Tahmina huddled close to her, holding her staff in one hand. The symbols had gone dark. There was nothing to fear.

'Landsknechts?' Sophia handed them wooden cups with red wine that smelled of summer fruit. 'You have brought guards?'

'No,' Aenlin said, 'our employers sent them along. They have decreed safe passage through the Empire to Hamburg for Agatha Mühlbach, Ursula Garnhuber and Veronica Stadler. The landsknechts are exploring Bamberg and the House of Malefaction.'

'Ula and Gatchen, too?' Sophia asked in a surprised voice. She raised her cup. 'Good to know. Landsknechts have a trained eye when it comes to defence mechanisms and guards.' She touched cups with the visitors. 'Who knows what wondrous news you bring to us.'

They drank and Aenlin enjoyed the exceptionally rich flavours of the wine, which tasted like it had been infused with flowers. *Delicious.* Instinctively, she leaned closer to Tahmina. Despite the situation, she felt peaceful and relaxed.

'What about you and this escort?' Sophia realised her mistake at once. 'Ah, right. You cannot tell me.' She smiled. 'These are dangerous times for all sorcerous sisters and brothers in Bamberg.'

'We heard what was happening, and that the pyres are often burning. Now I understand why we are to get those three away from here.' Aenlin looked around. 'What about you? Where are you staying?'

'Fleeing is not a possibility for anyone here. This is our home – some of us are from the city, some from the surrounding region. We fled here to this grove, which has been a place for our coven for centuries, because they are constantly hunting for us.' Sophia breathed deeply. 'This accursed Bishop! He is persecuting us because we do not want to obey him.'

'*Obey?*' Aenlin laughed incredulously. 'He wanted to make a pact with you?'

'No. The Prince-Bishop is a warlock himself, although he

doesn't follow our teachings but his own – demons whisper in his ear. He hunts us because he does not want to share his rule with us. Unfortunately, what he does, he does successfully.'

'You wanted to attack the city.' Tahmina got up and in doing so, touched Aenlin's back tenderly, as if by accident.

Aenlin put the blame for her maudlin mood on the wine. She watched her companion, still as much in love as on their first day together. She felt how much Tahmina meant to her so intensely; she'd do anything to keep her out of harm's way.

Tahmina noticed her gaze and winked at her. Then she looked at the model of Bamberg. 'Is that wise?' she asked, taking a sip of wine for a change. 'Everybody knows that you are coming.'

Sophia snorted. 'It's not wise. It's desperate.'

'Some of us think differently,' Anna said. She was sitting close by, listening to the conversation. 'Me, for example.' She gave Sophia a kind look to show that she meant her no harm. 'We must send the Emperor a petition. Only he can stop the Prince-Bishop. If we use our magic to summon the forces of nature to attack Bamberg, it will be grist for the mill for those who wish to burn the likes of us.'

Sophia waved her words away. 'The Emperor! He doesn't care about what's happening here.'

'Is he also a warlock?' Aenlin would have been very surprised; according to everything she'd heard, Ferdinand II was an ultra-Catholic monarch. *Then again, that's what I thought about the Bishop, too.* 'Is the battle against the Protestants only a pretence?'

'No, I don't think so,' Sophie said, 'but as far as the Bishop is concerned, we are sure. After our last conversation with him, our normal life was over.'

'Yet the attack would still be a mistake,' Anna insisted. 'You know how powerful he is – and which demon he worships. Every soul of a witch he sacrifices to his master will strengthen him. If we attack, that is the excuse he needs to lash out against us with even more force. None of the other rulers, not even the Catholic League or the Emperor, would have reason to stop him.' She looked at the two women. 'You must know that the Bishop himself used a lot of black magic against the inhabitants of Bamberg and the surrounding area to discredit us. But how could we prove that?'

'A priest skilled in the dark arts.' Tahmina stood next to the elaborate model and looked at the wooden replica of the cathedral. 'Have we come this far?'

'It's even worse.' Sophia threw back her grey hair. 'It's good that the war will soon be over – if it went on much longer, even more sinister powers would arise to undermine the Empire – to enforce it with evil and flood it with malice.' She nodded absentmindedly, as if to confirm her own words. 'The despair of the people allows the darkness its biggest land-grab – bigger than through any army.'

'What do you mean by that?' Aenlin was really enjoying the wine, which was warming her stomach and her head. This was a chance to change the topic and talk about Lucifer, her revered master. 'I thought the war raging in the German lands was one of faith. Shouldn't the Lord and all that is good be omnipresent, then? Or am I asking the wrong people?'

'A land of faith? In what?' Anna threw a big log onto the fire, making sparks fly up towards the canopy of branches, but the green needles and leaves were undamaged. 'It is the faith in power. The faith in wealth. In the land of the generals and princes who want to win battles to become richer and richer. Wallenstein, Tilly, the various rulers, even the Emperor . . . this is all they care about. They all fall for this game.'

'But there are powers involved that the naïve do not expect – they don't even realise it. Vast parts of the empire have already fallen into the hands of evil; they have become the Dark Lands.' Sophia cleared her throat. 'Secretly, an even darker fruit is germinating there and it will sprout and bloom to spread itself further.

It emits evil, permeates the air with invisible spores that get into people's heads and clings there.' Absentmindedly, she gazed into the roaring flames. 'Those who want to do wrong crave even more evil. The purest heart turns grey and beats to the rhythm of filthy lucre and greed. Let us look forward to the slaughter's end and hope that humankind will soon find back its way to reason.'

Aenlin shuddered. The sovereign sister was predicting a future that held nothing good for the empire. *If the war continues . . . Didn't Nicolas or Statius say that the Swedes would come? Then what Sophia has seen in the shifting fire will become true.*

'I think sending a petition to the Emperor is a good idea,' Tahmina said into the oppressive silence between them. 'The Bishop cannot resist him, and for now, the secular laws still apply in his bishopric. But if you attack and use nature as your tools so that everyone can see the magic, everything will get considerably worse. Consult the Emperor.'

'What about you?' Anna looked at Aenlin, her eyes full of hope. 'What do you say?'

'I agree with my friend. Don't play into the hands of the sorcerous Bishop. He has prepared for an attack: he has soldiers, weapons, mortars, magic . . . It would be an expensive victory, and it is not even guaranteed. Attacking may give him the pretext he needs to execute all those incarcerated in the House of Malefaction.' Aenlin was getting restless. Her cup was empty and the soothing effect of the wine was fading. She remembered her mission. 'I must ask for Veronica Stadler again.'

'Of course.' Sophia sipped her wine. 'Sister Nica is not here any more.'

'What?' Anna and Aenlin asked in unison.

'She left us straight after nightfall. She wanted to go north, where she has her own people. She wanted to ask for advice.' Sophia looked at Aenlin apologetically. 'You missed her by two or three hours.'

'Oh. I didn't know that,' Anna said to her guests with regret. 'I am sorry. Otherwise I would have told you at once.'

'Damn it!' Aenlin rose. They had to return to the coaching inn at once to let the others know. *And yet, she is beyond reach of the Bishop now. We need only go and get her.* 'Where do we find her?'

'Go to Hanover,' Sophia said. 'There is a hangman there who can help you. Ask him whether the bone turnips grow under the gallows in the moonlight and how to harvest them when the fox barks three times. That's the code phrase that will let him know that a friend sent you. If you don't say those words, he won't speak to you.'

Aenlin could already see the next difficulties: Veronica Stadler led her own coven. It would probably be hard to get her to come along. *We will have to come up with something.*

'She's not from Bamberg?' Aenlin asked.

'No. Sister Nica joined us a few years ago, along with Gatchen and Ula.'

Aenlin assumed she had found the reason the Company wanted those five brought to Hamburg. *They probably belong to the same coven . . .* 'What about the two who have recently been burned? Elfriede Mayer and Hilda Türmer – they were also on our list. Did they belong to Nica's coven too?'

Sophia and Anna looked at each other, as if silently agreeing their answers. 'No. That's the first I have heard of such a thing,' the sovereign sister replied. 'I took those two to be common people from the city who had fallen victim to the duplicitous Bishop's despotism.'

Tahmina had been watching the two witches during the conversation. 'What's wrong with sister Nica?'

'I don't understand.' Sophia sounded surprised.

'When you said she was gone you seemed . . . happy,' Tahmina said. 'Relieved. Liberated. When we said her name, your face hardened. So I assume something about her frightens you.'

Aenlin would have loved to kiss her companion for her keen attention. 'Doesn't she follow your teachings?' she demanded. 'Is there something we should know about Veronica?'

Sophia's expression changed from embarrassed to surprised and ended at alarmed. Abruptly, she looked past Tahmina to the edge of the settlement. 'Who is that? Did he come with you?'

Aenlin turned her head in surprise. *Has Nicolas followed our tracks? In this rain? But how could he and his landsknechts have made it through the spells?*

At the edge of the clearing, in the shadow of the pines, stood a man in a black robe and a thick brown leather apron. On his head, he wore a large, dark hat with circular brim. His face was hidden behind a beautifully crafted silver plague mask. Its glass-covered eye sockets glowed red and incense was curling up from the conspicuous beak nose. He waited there patiently, carrying a worn leather case in his left hand, as if he had come to look after a patient.

'This is the first time I've seen him,' Aenlin said, and grabbed her hat.

'How . . . how did he get through our barriers?' Anna whispered. She was aghast. 'They should have stopped him!'

More and more people had noticed the uninvited guest. There was a commotion that grew into angry shouts when more silhouettes appeared behind the plague doctor. The grove, never before discovered, was being inundated with landsknechts armed to the teeth with muskets and pistols.

'These are not our people,' Aenlin managed to say.

Then the soldiers raised their long firearms. They were strong enough to forgo the Y-shaped supports, which was unusual – and there was a bright red glow in the muzzles, as if they were loaded with burning curses instead of lead balls.

'Fire,' the plague doctor ordered, his voice a dull monotone.

It was known throughout the world and the list of all captives presented should have made it clear how bloodthirstily, ungodly and mercilessly the princely witch-inspectors of Bamberg executed the large number of six hundred people, noble and common, young and old, in such a short period of time, by fire and by sword, confiscating their assets without a proper court of law, as a result of a confused process. The highly oppressed poor people who were currently beseeching Imperial protection were deprived of the sun's light for one, two or three years in these places, in hard, heavy manacles and chains, the innocent incarcerated, and apart from hunger and thirst they waited patiently and steadfastly, in the deepest misery, to prove their innocence.

Up to the hour they would have to – May God have mercy on them! – live miserably without all human comfort or hope for salvation. That is why they are blessed to present to the Emperor, as the Father of all the poor and the head of Christendom, their greatest grievances, their fear and their plight, because in his justice, he will not leave them desolate.

For the sake of the followers of Jesus Christ, they appealed to his Imperial Majesty to order the afore-mentioned witch-inspectors under threat of severe punishment to release those they imprisoned for alleged witchcraft, to be released from that atrocious, vile prison and from the mortal danger from worms and vermin, and to allow them to prove their innocence with the aid of a lawyer in front of an impartial commission.

In the event that, as a result of a lawful investigation of their doings and dealings before and after their grave imprisonment, something significant should be proven against them, they undertake to stand trial, as is fair.

By granting this plea, the Emperor renders a great service to Justice, to the love of God and to Christian love.

However, the poor prisoners would show their gratitude through fervent prayer for his temporal and eternal welfare.

Petition to Emperor Ferdinand II, for the release all prisoners of the city of Bamberg, 1631

CAPITULUM IX

Bamberg, May 1629

The distraction proved to be more than enough. Nicolas, his men and the freed prisoners regrouped on the ground floor of the House of Malefaction. They listened quietly to the ceaseless tolling of the city bells and the excited shouts of 'Fire!' and 'Hauptsmoorwald!' from people crowding the streets and alleys.

Statius had grabbed the Jesuit and now pressed the man against the wall, holding him with one hand by the collar. He easily controlled the man. 'One shout and I'll send you to the Lord,' he said to Father Hubertus, brandishing the dagger in his left hand.

The guards who had been standing outside were lying unconscious in the cells. It had been easy for the landsknechts to subdue the surprised men and drag them into the building.

Nicolas looked at the ragged men, women and children who had been accused of witchcraft, heresy and fornication with the Devil. Many of them had been badly maltreated, their simple flaxen robes marred by stains of diverse colours; they stank of excrement, blood and sweat. The mercenaries took the guards' provisions from the guardrooms and gave them food, bread, meat, cheese and sausage. Most of them cried with gratitude and ate amid their tears.

Still, we can't take them with us. With this baggage train of the damned, they'd catch us before we took our first fifty steps. 'We will tell you when to best make your escape,' Nicolas said. 'Jäcklein!'

'Yes?'

'Wear the priest's robe: you will clear the way for us.' Nicolas grinned. 'It will be easiest if this band of heroic witch-hunters takes a wagon out to the Devil's Gorge, to the witches.'

'With the aid of the Lord. I see.' Jäcklein kicked Father Hubertus. 'Off with the robe. I need it.' He took off his baldric and the puffy shirt and breeches, immediately looking even smaller and thinner than usual.

'Your Haughtiness, go and find us a wagon to get Agatha and Ursula to safety,' Nicolas ordered. 'They're too weak to walk or ride.'

'Consider it done.' Caspar slipped away from the House of Malefaction.

'The punishment of the Almighty will destroy you,' Father Hubertus prophesied, angrily taking off his black robe. He gave it to Jäcklein, leaving him wearing only a thin vest and long underpants.

Jäcklein tore the hat from his blond shock of tousled hair, donned the dark garment and blessed those around him with exaggerated gestures. 'Look how skilled I am at this! As if I had taken lessons!' He laughed and spread his arms, setting his sleeves swinging. 'You evil, evil witches! Truly, I tell you, easier to fit a camel through the eye of a needle than to get Father Hubertus to Heaven.' He also grabbed the man's rosary. 'Goddam! This Jesus has such sad eyes. I'll carve him a smiling face later.'

'You will end up in Hell,' the Jesuit cursed. 'For this, the Devil will throw you in—'

Statius elbowed him in the face. Blood spurted from his nose and dripped from his chin. 'Oops!' Statius said roughly. 'The Devil made me do it. Sorry. I think I'm possessed.'

Some of the tortured prisoners laughed softly.

Nicolas watched Agatha and Ursula. Eyes half closed, they

huddled together against the wall. As if delirious, their lips moved, but no words came forth. *The imprisonment and the interrogations have weakened minds and bodies alike. They'll be useless for now.* 'I hope they won't die on us.'

'I hope so, too. Otherwise, we won't get paid. Or maybe we'll stuff them.' Statius grabbed the priest by the back of his neck. 'Come on, you scoundrel!' He shook him like a ragdoll before dragging him to an empty cell. 'In there.' He slammed the door shut.

At the same time, the main door opened and Caspar came through. His coat was wet and shiny. 'Brace yourselves: it's raining cats and dogs. There's so much water that we might well drown.' He shook the water off his wide hat. 'The wagon is ready.'

'Jäcklein,' Nicolas ordered, 'get yourself up onto the box seat. Moritz, you help me carry those two. Statius, watch out that none of the others flee before we've left.' Apologetically, he turned to the people they had freed. 'We need a little head-start, dear people.' It hurt his soul to leave those weakened folk to their own devices. *I have no choice. Otherwise, they'll catch us before we reach the gate and we'll be hanged.* 'May Destiny be on your side.'

'Please, take me with you,' said a young woman who must have been quite a beauty before her interrogation. Torture, pain and imprisonment had made her face haggard and her blonde hair was shaved to her scalp. There was pure fear in her eyes. 'There's no one who is well-disposed towards me in the whole city any more.'

'I wouldn't mind,' Statius said at once. 'You are mine now, little witch. But don't you dare go putting a spell on me.' Greedily, his gaze roamed her body. 'I'll feed you up and—'

'No. We can only look out for ourselves.' Nicolas stepped aside so Jäcklein could dash out into the bitter weather and climb onto the small wagon, which contained nothing but some straw and some empty sacks. Moritz unceremoniously threw the delirious Ursula over his shoulder.

'Please!' The young woman grabbed Statius' forearm. 'I'm not even a witch—'

'The captain said no,' he answered with regret. He stood in the corridor, one hand on the hilt of his rapier and his legs wide part to stop the prisoners from breaking through. 'What a waste,' he muttered.

Again, he only thinks of himself, not of her misery. As Nicolas lifted the other half-unconscious woman in his arms, she opened her eyes.

'I . . . need my chest,' Agatha whispered through scabbed lips. 'The chest! Here – in the guards' hall. My belongings – everything I own! You will recognise it by the . . . moon. The moon burned into the wood.'

'Stats, you heard the lady. Bring the chest as soon as I call for you.' Bearing Agatha, Nicolas left the House of Malefaction and walked into the rainstorm.

The bells of the city were still tolling, while the inhabitants hid within their homes and gazed into the streets from behind heavy shutters. A grey-white cloud of smoke rose into the dark sky, intertwined with shimmering swathes of purple and yellow that the wind carried towards Bamberg. The stench was awful.

'What's happening in these woods?' Moritz took the unconscious Agatha from Nicolas and laid her down on the bed of straw next to Ursula. Carefully, he covered the unmoving women with the sacks and more straw until they were well hidden. 'Is that Tahmina's and Aenlin's doing?' He packed the muskets beside the women so the rain didn't render them useless.

'As long as it's not them burning, everything's all right.' Caspar sat on his black stallion, water running down his hat and cascading from his cape. 'I saw a contingent of guards running towards the gates, so we don't have much time to use the element of surprise and our Jesuit advantage.'

'Stats! Come on – and don't forget to bring the chest.' Nicolas pulled his hat deeper onto his forehead to stop the water from running into his eyes and jumped onto the bed of the wagon. The cold drops found their way beneath his clothes all the same. *We have to get away, fast.*

The beefy landsknecht still hadn't appeared.

'Stats! Come on!'

Moritz got ready to dismount. 'I can quickly—'

'No. I'll go.' Nicolas jumped down from the wagon and entered the House of Malefaction with a sense of foreboding. Had the Jesuit escaped or—?

He saw at once that something had gone wrong. The witches and warlocks were huddled by the door to the chapel. A large travelling chest bearing the symbol of the moon stood next to the entrance.

In the corridor between the cells, the young woman who had asked them to take her along was lying on the floor. Her dirty sinner's garb had been pushed up, exposing her private parts and the torture wounds on her shanks. Her shorn head was twisted in an unnatural way, her neck broken.

'What the—?' Nicolas listened, touching the hilt of his rapier. 'Stats! Where are you?'

'Here.' Statius stepped from the cell where he had thrown Father Hubertus. His arms were red with fresh blood that also covered the dagger in his left hand. 'I had to silence the priest. With his own tongue.' His evil grin turned the curled tips of his moustache slightly upwards.

'By the fires of Hell, what has happened?'

'He tried calling for help through the open window. I couldn't allow that, right?'

'Right.' Nicolas crouched next to the corpse in the corridor.

He spotted curly black hairs on her face and her upper lip. 'What about her?'

Statius pointed at the huddled prisoners. 'It was them. The beautiful child implored me again, but the others wanted to persuade her to stay. One word led to another.' His face and his voice remained impassive. 'There was a riot: they tore at her, dragging her – they wrung her neck. It was an accident.'

I don't believe a single word you're saying. 'Take the chest and get out.' He rose without looking at his friend. The war awoke the beast in Statius and turned him into a creature without any decency: a shifter, a traducer, a cruel human demon. *What shall I do with you?* But he needed the man for this endeavour and for the escape from Bamberg.

Nicolas looked at the people they had freed. 'I wish you luck, and I truly hope you escape the Prince-Bishop.' *I am so sorry I have to leave them behind. What a mess.* He nodded at them uneasily and turned to go. Statius was just walking out, the chest on his shoulder. The landsknecht was humming a merry tune.

'If you don't kill him,' a girl's voice shouted from the huddled group, 'he will kill you. Very soon.'

Nicolas hesitated for a moment. He would rather not have heard the prophecy – and it was a prophecy; he recognised the truth at its core. He couldn't come up with any reasonable response, so he collected the clothes and weapons Jäcklein had left on the floor and continued on his way.

Standing in the howling wind and the driving rain, Statius washed the Jesuit's blood from his fingers with a grin, letting the storm wash the red from his clothes and skin. He carefully removed all traces of his deed from his dagger.

What shall I do? I cannot let you get away with these things for ever.
None of his landsknechts said a word.

'Let's go,' Nicolas said. He jumped onto the wagon while Moritz picked up the reins and urged the horse forwards.

Jäcklein stood up on the box and blessed everyone and everything they met. 'Beware of the witches and wizards,' he shouted against the tempest, laughing all the time. 'Truly, truly! The blessing of the Lord. Here, some more blessing – here is another one for you, too, sinner.' He roistered cheerfully at the people cowering behind the shutters, 'Make way for the witch-hunters and Father Hubertus! Lift up your heads, ye mighty gates!'

'Faster,' Nicolas commanded. 'Moritz, hie on the horse. Nothing must stop us – otherwise, we'll all hang.'

Moritz cracked the reins, the leather heavy with water, across the back of the horse, goading the animal onwards. Caspar, galloping alongside on his black Comte, grabbed the harness, dragging at the horse to give it some more momentum.

'Make way, ' Jäcklein shouted, 'step back! The witch-hunters and Father Hubertus have come to chase down the witches!' Still he stood and waved his stolen crucifix. 'In the name of the Prince-Bishop, his Excellency and Half-Holiness: *make way!*'

'Don't get carried away,' Nicolas admonished. *No matter how good our disguise might be, we should not ruin it by silliness.*

The wagon carrying the landsknechts and the two prisoners they had freed raced unobstructed through the gate, which was manned by a second guard unit to stop intruders invading the city from outside. Caspar was still galloping alongside on Comte.

People cheered at them, praising their courage, as they raced out of sight.

'We made it!' Jäcklein sent the rosary and the crucifix flying. His robe followed, but it got caught on a branch. He shouted to the wind, raising his fists, 'We've escaped – with our people!'

Moritz patted his shoulder, and Statius and Nicolas did the same as soon as the little mercenary, clad only in his undergarments, sat on the box again.

'Don't slow down.' Nicolas looked at the dark path leading

to the coaching inn. 'Your Haughtiness, take the vanguard and watch for people coming towards us. I'll bring up the rear.'

'Very well.' Caspar rode ahead, and soon his silhouette was lost in the darkness.

The wagon jolted and bounced its passengers through the night. The landsknechts' relief was palpable, but to be on the safe side, they kept the unconscious women they had rescued covered in the straw and sacks.

Nicolas watched Statius covertly. He couldn't forget the witch-child's prophecy – he didn't want to forget it, and neither did he want to forget the atrocities his friend had committed in the past. There would be more crimes, as sure as eggs were eggs; it was as inevitable as a shot on the battlefield.

This is the last time I can be lenient. I swear it, by that poor dead woman in the House of Malefaction. But Nicolas knew that he would never be able to kill Statius – not without a good reason, one that meant more than their fellowship and all that they had experienced and lived through together. *For me to kill him, he would have to attack me directly.*

Hauptsmoorwald, west of Bamberg, May 1629

Aenlin threw herself at Tahmina, forcing her to the ground just as the weapons discharged and sent their glowing musket balls against the assembled witches. Her hat went flying.

Some of the magically altered projectiles streaked above their heads. The heat they radiated felt like a focused ray of sunlight on their skin.

'That's really odd.' Aenlin's heart hammered in her chest as she raised her head and saw the havoc the projectiles were wreaking.

When the musket balls hit something, they exploded with a

loud bang, tearing bodies and trunks alike, shattering smaller trees into kindling. Whenever they hit, the detonations sent glowing shrapnel flying, causing further damage all around. With a hiss, the flaming fragments landed in the needles carpeting the forest floor, dry as tinder, and the first pines caught fire.

'The man wearing the plague doctor's mask. Do you know him?' Aenlin stayed down while half the landsknechts drew their pistols, the muzzles of which also glowed red. The others were reloading their muskets to follow up with a second salvo. They had less than two minutes to get to safety. 'Is he involved with your renegade master?'

'Definitely not.' Tahmina rolled behind an overturned bench. 'Are you all right?'

Aenlin nodded and followed her companion. They quickly embraced, then ducked down before the next salvo.

The men fired the lethal projectiles at the running witches and warlocks, who were trying to protect themselves with spells and curses. The air in the clearing was shimmering and crackling from their efforts to form a shield, but the comet-like projectiles pierced the supernatural barrier, sealing the fate of the desperate people behind it. Burning pieces of bone and lumps of flesh flew through the air. The fires spread.

'Then these mercenaries must've been sent from Bamberg to get rid of the witches.' Aenlin felt guilty. *We should have checked more carefully whether we were being followed.* 'This is all our fault, Tahmina! We must have led them straight to the grove.'

'Maybe – but how did they penetrate the defensive spells unharmed? They should have been cut to pieces.'

Tahmina pulled her ebony staff closer and whispered a Yatu spell. Symbols carved into the wood flared in rapid succession, and a pomegranate-coloured shimmer covered Aenlin and Tahmina like a second skin.

Intrigued, Aenlin extended her fingers. It felt velvety and tough at the same time.

'What is this?'

'I have given us the epidermis of a ruby-fire djinn. We are now protected against the destructive power of the musket balls, although not against the lead itself,' Tahmina explained. 'So keep your head down!'

Aenlin nodded and drew her pistol. *What kind of people are they?* From their hiding place, she watched the battle. She didn't need Nicolas' or Statius' battle experience to tell her this wasn't like any normal fight.

Those witches and warlocks who had not died or been heavily wounded by the evil power of the musket balls defended themselves against the attackers with their magical skills while they encouraged one another.

Some used levitation spells to lift everything that wasn't tied down and sent it as an improvised fusillade of missiles. Others tried to use black magic to cause the men at arms the worst of pain. Still others created greenish or yellowish clouds between their fingers, from which they shot lightning. Meanwhile, two wizards were stoking the fires burning in the grove and throwing gouts of flame against the landsknechts. Ivy and thorny vines snaked towards the enemies like reptiles to entangle them.

But whatever they threw against the mercenaries and their masked commander was stopped by an invisible magical wall between them.

'Do you see that?' These were no witch-hunters, but equal opponents against Sophia and her coven. The fear Aenlin was feeling threatened to overwhelm her; she was even more frightened than she'd been in that alley back in Hamburg. *Maybe demons, summoned by the Prince-Bishop?* 'Nothing is working!'

'That is the boy from the inn over there,' Tahmina said in surprise. 'What can he doing here?'

'Who's that next to him?' Aenlin examined the girl of about fourteen years; she had a horse rug wrapped around her and was holding Franz's hand. She looked terrified, like she wanted to drag him back into the forest.

'Then he is the one who brought the soldiers here?' Tahmina looked around. 'We need to get away from this place.'

I can't succumb to fear. 'We must help the witches!' Aenlin mastered her trembling and aimed her pistol at the man with the silver mask. *My father would have done the same.* 'Otherwise, they'll be destroyed, and the Prince-Bishop will get his way.' She wanted to fire as soon as she detected a weak spot in the plague doctor's defensive spell.

Taking aim, Aenlin focused on the long beak, trying to hit the right eye shimmering bright red – which was when she discovered the mark embedded in the mask's head and cheeks. 'Look! In between all those chasings and patterns? He wears the symbol of Vanth!'

Tahmina cursed in an unknown language. 'Then we were wrong. They are looking for me.'

'Us. They are looking for us.'

'For me.' She slightly raised her staff. 'And for this.'

Aenlin remembered the event in the side alley at the port of Hamburg, when the thieving child had turned into a demon. That meant someone else was behind what was going on here. 'As soon as we have my inheritance, we must find and destroy your master in London.'

The long muskets had been reloaded and now the landsknechts fired the next salvo, and once again, the glowing musket balls raced across the clearing like miniature suns and exploded on impact, sending death into the ranks of the desperate men and women. Less than half of them were repelled magically; loud detonations heralded people and trees being torn apart, sending flaming splinters buzzing through the air.

Total panic was the result. All those still standing took to flight; anyone brave enough to try to help their wounded companions became easier targets for the Reaper.

'We cannot face this plague doctor. Not tonight.' Tahmina was slowly retreating. 'I first have to devise an appropriate spell to counter his magic, otherwise we will share the fate of my brave sisters and brothers.'

Aenlin would have liked to argue, but her friend was right. She couldn't rule out the possibility that this unknown man – or Tahmina's former master – had allied themselves with the Prince-Bishop of Bamberg.

With a heavy heart, she sheathed her weapon. She hadn't fired a single shot. As her tension eased a little, her hands started shaking slightly. *More cruel images of death for me to remember.* She would never be able to drink enough herbal tea to clear her mind.

The cracking and banging stopped. The coven's resistance was broken.

'Hey! There's Aenlin!' Franz's clear treble voice suddenly sounded across the clearing, cutting through the moaning and whimpering of the wounded. 'Aenlin! I beg you: stop the Venetian! He's a beast – *please*, he'll kill us all if you don't stop him—'

What a fool! Why is he shouting at me like this? Aenlin gestured at the boy to disappear back into the forest. '*Go!*' she replied. '*Don't let him—!*'

But it was too late. The plague doctor had turned his head and now the eyes under the red glass focused on Tahmina and Aenlin. Even from that distance, Aenlin could see them light up in silent joy.

Two of his landsknechts immediately brought the muzzles of their muskets around and fired, sending the glowing musket balls streaking towards the women.

The ruby-fire djinn spell responded instantly, forming a rosy sphere around them. The projectiles lost their devastating glow as they passed through the Yatu magic and hit an oak, as harmless lead musket balls once again.

'No – bring them to me. *Alive*, Captain.' The Venetian spoke in a muffled voice, thick smoke rising from his silver beak, as if he was breathing some sort of dragon's breath. 'Where they are, you will also find the mercenaries you are looking for. Kill the rest.'

'Understood.' One of the landsknechts aimed his pistol at Franz and fired.

The glowing projectile hit the boy's abdomen and he cried out as it exploded. The girl ran away screaming, covered head to toe in Franz's blood.

'*Run!*' Aenlin grabbed Tahmina's hand and ran from the Venetian and his deadly henchmen. The protective spheres coalesced, forming a pomegranate-coloured gleam around them, as if they were spirits.

Suddenly, Sophia rose from the sea of dead and wounded. Her grey hair was streaked red with blood, her whole body covered in countless wounds caused by lead splinters and shards. She swayed, but she stood firm. 'Whoever you are,' she shouted at the plague doctor, 'simmer in your own sweat and cook until the flesh falls from your bones!' With a tremendous cry, she commanded the raging fire to attack her enemies.

'Tahmina, wait.' Aenlin had to stop and watch how the witch fared against her opponents. *I really hope they burn!*

The flames came together, forming a surge of fire that hit the Venetian's spell and broke over it, as if it were a real wave washing over the obstacle. It engulfed the spell from all sides like magma, and the enemies were both protected, but also trapped under their magical bowl.

The landsknechts retreated to the centre of the dome as if in a tercio and raised their hands to protected their eyes against the heat that was obviously filling their protected area. Only the Venetian remained impassive and stiff as a statue.

Then shattered pines and broken branches crashed down from all sides on the transparent magical shield, hiding what was happening beneath the hemisphere.

'Go!' Tahmina dragged Aenlin along.

'But I—'

'It is too dangerous to stay – we have no idea what will happen.'

They left the clearing at a run, and after giving the combat zone a wide berth, they finally reached their horses. The beasts were soaking wet, thanks to the rain drenching the land, but waiting patiently right where they had left them.

The women mounted quickly and pounded away through the fire-lit Hauptsmoorwald towards the inn, to meet Nicolas.

Tahmina and Aenlin didn't exchange a single word, even when they looked back to see the inferno raging amidst the pines and oaks. The billowing smoke kept changing colour, clouds forming into a new tempest rising from the woods.

The rain can't extinguish the flames. Aenlin's disappointment grew. *The grove is lost. And so is Sophia.*

From afar, they saw the flames of another fire. They slowed a little, approaching the conflagration carefully.

Where once the coaching inn had stood, was now just a smoking wooden framework, mostly collapsed, although some parts of what had once been the stable and the main building were still standing defiantly. The driving rain was choking off the flames, but it was too late for the inn. The building was lost.

Lucifer, what are you up to? Why are you testing me so hard? 'Is *everyone* conspiring against us?' With difficulty, Aenlin managed to calm her spooked horse. 'Do you see any corpses?'

'No, but there might be some in the wreckage of the buildings.'

Tahmina gazed into the remains of the stable. 'Our wagons are gone.'

'Nicolas wouldn't have left them behind.' In the soaked ground, Aenlin could see wheel tracks, surrounded by footprints. A great many footprints. 'I know who has them: the Venetian and his mercenaries.'

'May the djinni of Shiraz turn him to dust!' Tahmina guided her horse under a leafy walnut tree, trying to shelter from the rain. 'This means he has our money and all the Company's articles, warrants, writs and charters.'

We're doomed. Aenlin followed her under the branches. Hidden by the heavy branches thick with dripping leaves, she kissed her companion deeply. 'I'm so glad you're safe and sound.' Her relief was heartfelt.

'You protected me against that first salvo.'

'You protected me against the second one.' Aenlin took her hand and squeezed it.

'Your fingers are trembling,' the mystic pointed out.

As soon as Aenlin took a deep breath, she felt her stomach roiling. Excitement, fear, battle-fever, all the enormous new experiences, the magic and death – you didn't go through something like this without consequences. It was just one more lesson on her way to becoming an adventurer.

She suppressed the nausea as best as she could. 'I would really like one of your infusions right now,' she whispered. She was soaked and the warmth was leaching out of her. She knew she'd soon be shivering in earnest, this time from the cold.

The crackling and rustling of the dying fire mingled with the rushing, pattering drops on their massive umbrella.

Tahmina dismounted. 'How long do we wait for Nicolas?' She added quickly, 'I mean, because of our pursuers.'

'As long as we have to.' *As long as we can.* Aenlin jumped from the saddle and carefully gathered some of the smouldering from the ruins of the inn and built up a smaller fire under the shelter of the walnut tree to warm them. 'I know what you mean, though. I don't like it either.' She really hoped that Sophia had roasted the landsknechts and their leader in their magical global protection like they were in an oven. *Lucifer, if you must keep throwing obstacles in our way, at least grant her success.*

'Who knows what's happening in Bamberg as we speak?'

'Maybe it will give Nicolas an unexpected opportunity to free those last two prisoners.' Tahmina stepped closer to the flames and held out her hands as her midnight-blue gown started drying slowly. Her brown hair was curling in the warm, damp air. 'After this, there will surely be too much upheaval to successfully free them.'

Aenlin took off her sodden baldric and tied back her hair. She moved close to the fire, so close it was almost painful, in a bid to dry her clothes; it was worth putting up with the discomfort, otherwise they'd never be dry. In her mind's eye, she saw the silver mask with the long beak. 'The Venetian, he's a plague doctor by his garb, but in truth, he's an extremely dangerous wizard.' *Or a demon?*

'There does not have to be a human behind this mask,' Tahmina pointed out. 'It is cleverly chosen: it makes people keep their distance. But he is only one of Vanth's henchmen, sent to get me.'

'Is this about you or the staff?'

'It is always about the staff. I am irrelevant.' Tahmina looked at her companion, hesitating to say the next words. 'You do not know all of its powers, Aenlin, nor mine. The artefact can do more than—'

Aenlin broke in, 'Shush—' She had heard something. 'As curious as I am, we'll have to talk about this another time. Someone is coming – let's pray it's not the Venetian.' She grabbed her baldric and quickly pulled herself into the lowest branches of the walnut tree. 'Hide!' she hissed, drawing her pistol.

Suddenly, waiting felt like foolish. *If the witches and warlocks have lost the battle against this man, what can I do?* But by then it was too late.

In the dying light of the flames, she saw a single rider on a black horse, approaching the remains of the inn.

The Comte – and Caspar!

'I hope you're not the sole survivor,' Aenlin called from the tree, feeling a sudden spurt of hope.

The duellist stopped. 'Have the two of you set the forest *and* the inn on fire? The food wasn't that bad.' He pointed backwards. 'The others are on their way. We got the two women who were imprisoned, but I'll tell you the rest when we're all a bit more comfortable. It's too wet for my taste – and for the Comte's.'

Aenlin climbed down to the next branch, feeling more confident now. *At least you granted them success, Lucifer.* 'That's what we will do, then. Alas, the person we're looking for is over the hills and far away and—'

'—the henchmen of the Prince-Bishop have attacked us,' Tahmina interjected.

Aenlin could see she was obviously trying to avoid any mention of the Venetian, Vanth or the foreign mercenaries.

'Landsknechts appeared – they fought against the witches. And us.'

'Bless my soul! How very unpleasant – and this Veronica Stadler has already left?'

'Yes, before we arrived. She was heading to Hanover.' Aenlin saw the silhouette of a wagon appear in the distance, backlit by the fire: Nicolas and his men were approaching. 'When we arrived, the fires were still burning. I guess the mercenaries were looking for a bit of extra income, so they attacked the coaching inn.'

'A profitable idea,' Caspar agreed. 'If they stole our coaches, they'll have quite a sum in their pockets.' He guided the stallion beneath the walnut tree, where the animal shook the water from his coat with a snort.

Tahmina raised a hand in a vain attempt to protect herself from the flying droplets. 'He feels like us.'

'Well, I guess no one but fish like this kind of weather.' Caspar slid from the saddle. 'Although there's rather more than enough fire round here for my taste.'

'What the sodding Hell happened here?' Statius called from afar. 'Fuck my old boots – *everything* burned down?'

'Everything burned down.' Aenlin jumped from the tree as the wagon arrived and briefly reported what had happened. 'I can't exclude the possibility of the mercenaries following us,' she added, after a brief look at Tahmina. *I'll keep your secret for now.* 'They might assume we're witches, too.'

'Would one of you like to ride my broom?' Statius offered, with a filthy laugh. 'It's smooth and it'll fit you nicely, that I guarantee—'

'Stats, will you for once and for all *shut it*?' Nicolas looked at the smouldering, charred remains of the inn as the last standing bits collapsed one by one. 'Let's move.' He pointed along the road to the north. 'At least for as far as our horse can manage, until we find lodging somewhere. Our two guests are in desperate need of medical attention and care. They'll need a place to gather a little strength for the long journey. Otherwise we'll have very few saved people to present to the Company, I'm afraid.'

'All right.' Aenlin mounted her horse and Tahmina and Caspar did the same. 'Let's go.'

Tahmina nodded gratefully.

Near Wanfried, May 1629

'I'll check on our scout.' Aenlin looked out towards the beech tree, where Jäcklein was hiding with a musket, keeping watch. No one would be approaching the deserted logging camp unnoticed. She waved at him and he touched the brim of his hat. 'Everything quiet, Captain,' she relayed.

'That's the way I want it to stay.' Nicolas tucked his long ash-blond hair behind his ears and stirred the soup. Moritz had bought the ingredients from a small settlement downstream. Their temporary home was a two-roomed cottage made of roughly hewn timbers; one room had a stone fireplace for cooking and heating. They'd filled the equally roughly hewn cots around the sides of the back room with leaves and moss to make them more comfortable. It wasn't grand, but it was a roof over their heads and offered a little comfort and privacy.

'How are they?' Aenlin's gaze wandered from the shuttered window to where Tahmina was taking care of the two women the landsknechts had saved. Agatha and Ursula lay covered with thin blankets on two benches against the wall. They'd been sleeping almost all the time, thanks to the soothing potion the mystic had given them; she said it would help heal the wounds they'd suffered during the interrogation, the torture and the imprisonment a little faster.

Aenlin wanted to talk with them about Veronica, the woman who got away, and Nicolas had some questions about her and her coven too, but neither was able to say more than 'thanks' or 'please' at the moment. The request that Nicolas save the chest was the longest sentence anyone had heard from them since they were freed.

Tahmina touched their foreheads. She had asked that the witches stay close to her in the common room during the day so she could react quickly to any changes. 'For both, the fever is down,' she announced. 'In a day or two, we will be able to travel on.'

'Perfect. I would rather be half a world away already.' Statius cut smoked ham and put it into the pot.

To Aenlin's surprise, Statius had deigned to wash the group's dirty clothes with soap they had found in the cottage. The sweat of the last days and the resultant rank odour were now thankfully gone, washed downstream in the nearby river. He'd pounded the cloth with a lump of wood as if it was bodies and heads, but everything was clean in the end.

'That's true for all of us.' Nicolas tasted and smacked his lips. 'It's pretty tasty. A little more salt and it's ready.'

Moritz and Caspar sat at the rough table, playing cards for money.

Aenlin's gaze wandered back and forth between the giant's long black curls and the duellist's magnificent head of hair; they both looked as if they were wearing wigs. Yet again, Caspar beat Moritz at Supérieur, a game he'd learned in France. It had originally ended once the ace of spades was drawn, but the men had decided to ignore this rule. Laughing, Caspar pocketed the coins he had won, while Moritz applauded.

They drank water, or infusions made of the greenery Tahmina gathered: another first for the landsknechts.

'This logging camp is a real blessing,' Caspar said, counting his winnings. 'We couldn't have gone to Wanfried – they'd have hanged us, or at the very least, chased us away with a sound beating.'

'Well, they would have tried,' Statius corrected, baring his teeth.

'We have done exactly the right thing.' Nicolas kept stirring so the barley wouldn't burn. 'At least we know that no one from

Bamberg is following us. We've seen neither the henchmen of the Prince-Bishop nor any paid mercenaries.'

'Or angry witches and warlocks,' Caspar added, looking at Statius. 'That wouldn't have surprised me.'

'I don't care who or what follows us. I'll confront anyone and anything.' The beefy landsknecht chewed on a stringy piece of meat, then spat the gristle into the fire underneath the cauldron.

Aenlin didn't doubt his words.

After their escape from Bamberg, they had taken the wagon south, stealing a larger one and some provisions on their way. Agatha and Ursula had been feverish the whole time. Their wounds were worse than their rescuers had thought, so Tahmina had insisted on stopping so the weakened women had peace to heal and rally their strength.

They had found the logging camp and the remote cottage just in time; no one would be hewing trees in the spring and first months of summer.

Aenlin joined her companion to help her apply the fomentations and poultices she'd prepared for Agatha and Ursula. 'Did they talk in that strange language again?'

Tahmina nodded. 'I do not recognise it. It is nothing spoken in this part of the world. Also, not Persian, not Arabic, nor is it an Indian dialect.'

'Maybe . . . a magic language?' Caspar asked.

'Or something made up?' Moritz suggested.

'Or maybe it just doesn't make any sense,' Statius muttered. 'Maybe it's just feverish nonsense. Like drunkards slurring away.'

Nicolas handed Statius the spoon. 'Keep stirring.' He rose and called from the door, 'Come and eat, Jäcklein!'

'No change of guard?' the landsknecht replied from the lookout.

'No.'

'What if somebody comes?'

'Then I'll cut them into the soup,' Statius muttered and started ladling the food into the bowls they had found in the room. 'Some more meat would be good.'

'Come on down – before Stats finishes the bacon all by himself.' Nicolas turned to ferry the full bowls to the table, where Moritz was packing away the playing cards.

Statius broke the loaf of bread into chunks and passed them around. The noisy slurping and belching that always accompanied the landsknechts' eating filled Aenlin and Tahmina with horror, while to the mercenaries' amusement, Caspar ate with exaggerated punctilio.

'What shall we do if we don't find this woman?' Statius asked between mouthfuls. 'What was her name again?'

'Veronica Stadler, also known as Nica.' Jäcklein chewed on a hard bread crust. 'I've thought about that, too.'

'We simply claim she's dead. Like the other ones on the list.' Statius produced a scrap of paper from beneath his shirt and threw it on the table.

'But Agatha and Ursula will know the truth,' Aenlin pointed out, worrying for her inheritance. *We've come too far to start playing games now.* 'Besides, she has gone to Hanover – that's not far from Hamburg.'

'How would they know? They were incarcerated in the House of Malefaction.' Statius kept eating. 'They know nothing – look at them lying there all the time. Like dolls.'

'Here, here. Stats' idea would save us work.' Jäcklein knocked on the edge of his bowl. 'Let's declare them dead and return to the city.'

'And what if Veronica Stadler shows up in Hamburg?' Aenlin had several reasons not to lie to their employers, other than the need to retrieve her inheritance: her reputation was on the line.

'I agree with Aenlin,' said Caspar, and Moritz nodded decidedly. 'This could go wrong – like one of my musket balls.'

'You're wanted anyway, your Haughtiness,' Statius retorted and swept his neck-length brown hair from his face. 'This serves to increase the bounty on your head – that's all you would risk.'

'I'll tell you again and keep telling you until you listen to me: it is not a clever idea to get in trouble with the Company,' Aenlin said, thinking, *If you don't want to come, I will travel to Hanover alone to find Nica.*

'Ah, they won't notice a thing.' Jäcklein pointed at the sleeping women. 'The de Hertoghes will be overjoyed if we bring in at least two of them intact.'

'We've already wasted far too much effort, in my opinion.' Statius looked at Nicolas, who had been listening quietly while eating his food. 'So, Captain. What do you think about my suggestion?'

Nicolas scooped up the last of the barley and meat with his piece of bread. 'We were not paid enough for what we had to do and whom we had to confront. Also, we're not yet in Hamburg – or in Hanover, where this Stadler woman is supposed to be. I think we should get a nice bit extra for our efforts, on top of what was agreed.'

'Then we'll negotiate again,' Aenlin said angrily. She felt Tahmina secretly touching her leg under the table, both supporting her, and reminding her to keep calm. *The decision will go in my favour, if I keep pushing.* 'That would be more honest than falsely claiming she's dead.'

'What if the Company won't meet our demands?' Statius deliberately licked his bowl clean, and in a particularly lewd manner, all the while keeping his eyes on Tahmina.

'Dear people, I could be your father, which applies to everyone here, although I certainly wouldn't like all of you to be my off-spring! This debate is all very pleasant, but it is our captain who has the final say.' Caspar finished his drink, the steam curling around his little black beard. 'Before we keep wasting the air that we breathe, Nicolas, I beg you, let us know what you prefer.'

As Nicolas chewed, he looked in turn at those seated around the table.

He was not yet decided, still weighing the advantages and disadvantages, Aenlin could see it in his face.

'We cannot be certain that the women we saved know nothing,' she said. 'They are witches – they could communicate mentally and thus—'

'We'll get them drunk,' Statius said, interrupting her. 'Before the handover. Wine, brandy, a little fly agaric, or whatever we can find to addle their senses. We'll hand them over in that state in Hamburg. That should suffice.' He cast Nicolas a triumphant look. 'What do you think, Captain?'

Aenlin would have loved to slap the mercenary, because he wouldn't stop contradicting her. *Lucifer, why don't you just stop his heart? I really would appreciate it.*

Nicolas kept chewing. He wiped his bowl with his bread before replying, 'I'm thinking.'

'Oh-oh. That'll take some time.' Jäcklein feigned boredom. He picked up the cards and dealt hands to Moritz, Caspar, Statius and himself. 'Well, let's do something entertaining while we wait for wisdom to strike our captain.'

'Don't bother me with your cards. You'd cheat anyway.' Statius got up in a sour mood. He thought he'd won this debate.

Tahmina slowly lifted her hand from Aenlin's thigh so he wouldn't notice the intimacy between the two women. 'You have two more days to think,' she told Nicolas, 'then Agatha and Ursula should be fit to travel.'

Outside, a horse whinnied.

A visitor? Aenlin listened up. 'Was that your Comte?'

Caspar got up and straightened his wig. 'I thought so too.' He went to the window and looked outside, one hand at the butt of his pistol. 'I can't see anything. He's probably just bored. I guess I should gallop my good stallion across the field so he can use up some of that energy—'

A loud wooden crash from the wall nearest the table made everyone whirl around.

Statius was squatting in front of Agatha's chest. He had smashed the lock with a heavy kick.

'What the fuck are you up to?' Jäcklein threw the playing cards at him. 'Are you nosing around in our guests' belongings? Stop that!'

The pieces of painted cardboard rained down on the soldier. 'I'm just curious about what they carry around. I've never seen real witches' utensils.' He quickly opened the lid and took out the layer of straw and padded sacks that was protecting the cargo.

Aenlin knew he was lying – just like so many things the landsknecht said. It was a great pity there was no protective spell on Agatha's belongings that might have gone right through him, marrow and bone. She had heard of the events in the House of Malefaction; Moritz had told her and Tahmina what had happened. *He's brutal. He enjoys the suffering of others. He humiliates the weak. He's ruthless to the core.* But once the time for negotiations was done, you could win battles with men like him.

Statius stopped digging around and took something out of the chest. He held up it reverently. 'An archangel lick my arse!' he called out in surprise. 'By all Satanic cunts, what is that?'

In his hand, he held a waist-high wooden staff as thick as his forearm. It had a leather-wrapped hilt and a leather loop. Pieces of stone the length of a finger were set into the upper half. They shimmered greenish-black.

The band rose from their footstools and benches to have a closer look.

Aenlin noticed symbols engraved in between the stones. They

didn't look anything like those on Tahmina's staff. 'What could that be?' she whispered to her companion.

'I have never seen anything like that.' Tahmina took a step towards the weapon that Statius was swinging to try it out. The staff whirred quietly; the stones left greenish traces of their movement in the air. 'That is obsidian!'

'Like the stone they supposedly used to skin their victims in Bamberg,' Jäcklein reminded them. 'What is that?'

'It is not good for fighting: the stone blades are sharp, but they will shatter against any steel, any breastplate.' Statius carelessly threw the wooden staff aside and started digging through the chest again; the weapon rolled across the floor without any of the obsidian falling off. 'A knife made from the same crap,' he commented, putting it on the floor. 'Another staff and . . .' There was a rustling sound as he pulled out a cape made of gorgeous feathers in bright colours. 'Women's crap.' It, too, landed on the floor next to him. 'They're not rich, then.'

'There are no such birds in these climes,' Caspar said in surprise. 'I did once see such poultry, in the aviary of a nobleman I duelled.'

'Neither are there such . . . kittens in these climes – they come straight from Hell!' Statius had dragged from the chest a black skin bearing a spotted tabby pattern, followed by another with black, white and brown spots. The heads of the cat-like predators were still attached so they could be worn like cowls. 'Fuck me to death – what are these? Look at those teeth and claws!' Statius examined them. 'They're also made from this obsidian stuff.'

Tahmina took a deep breath. 'Jaguar skins. The black one once belonged to a panther – it is the same animal, but of another colour.'

'What about the feathers?' Jäcklein knelt next to the chest and put his hand inside. 'Oh, there's more. I know this one: these are an eagle's claws.' He held his find high.

'Where on earth did they get those things?' Moritz was completely fascinated with the strangeness of the objects they had found.

'Trade. They exist only in the New World,' Tahmina said. Sometimes, living animals were transported across the sea for a lot of money and ended up in the kennels of the rich and the noble, who considered it fashionable to keep exotic creatures. Others settled for trophies.

That can't be the witches' intention. This must have something to do with magic. 'I don't understand what need Agatha could have for these,' Aenlin said.

'These skins,' Nicolas said, 'they ... they could be slipped on. It looks to me as if these two witches wanted to turn into animals – into eagles and ...' He looked at Tahmina. 'What did you call it?'

'Jaguar,' she said. 'Jaguar and panther.'

'That must be it, Captain!' Jäcklein caressed the panther's head. 'Like wolfbänner – you know, those who can change themselves into wolves with a spell! They want to turn into these beasts to hunt humans.'

'What about the eagle?' Moritz came closer and reverently touched the feathers. 'How beautiful they are to the touch – they feel warm, almost alive.'

Aenlin looked at the things the landsknechts had taken out of the chest. *We should put them back. This is wrong. Their belongings are not our business.*

'I know: for scouting! The eagle tells the hellcats where they can find prey.' Jäcklein sounded completely convinced his theory was right. 'Good kitty. Very good kitty.' He caressed the panther's chin. 'You're not eating anyone any more.'

'I would love to be a predator – to hunt and tear,' Statius whispered in awe. He put on the spotted skin of the jaguar, shoving his arms into the forelegs, which ended in clawed gloves. With a loud hiss, he jumped onto the table, his mouth opened wide, his teeth bared.

Caspar, Moritz and Jäcklein laughed and retreated from him, shaking with fear like bad actors. Statius jumped down again, playing the jaguar, hunting them, and they fled, screaming like little children.

'Tahmina, what do you think? What is that staff for?' Nicolas pointed at the club-like weapon. 'It's not made for fighting.'

'Maybe for sacrificing something? For smashing skulls and opening veins?' Her tone of voice made it obvious that she disliked the items they had found. 'Didn't the bar-lad, Franz, say something about such atrocities being committed in Bamberg?'

Nicolas frowned. 'Yes, he did: he talked about extraordinary cruelties, not the sort that are commonly associated with witches.'

Do we have any helpful clues? Aenlin could not suppress her curiosity, as wrong as it felt. She leaned over the chest herself and found more robes, pendants, tablets, clasps and golden wrist bands, all carefully wrapped up. Statius had missed the engraved and jewel-inlaid pieces of jewellery. *This . . . this is worth a fortune!* She briefly held up a necklace to show it to the captain and Tahmina. 'Agatha and Ursula are definitely no common witches!' She remembered the stories about skinned people, masks made of cut-off faces, elixirs from the tears of desperate children, hearts cut out from beneath the ribs.

'I agree.' Tahmina looked at the jewellery and then abruptly turned her gaze to the staff. 'Put the jewellery back – everything – quickly!' She grabbed her own black staff, which was leaning against the wall. 'Something bad is happening!'

Several of the sigils had started glowing, and other symbols flashed as if there were a miniature thunderstorm raging within the wood.

Statius, Caspar and Moritz were still capering about the room.

Jäcklein had donned the feathered cape and followed the others, hopping and cawing loudly, although he looked more like a chicken than like an eagle.

'Look at these children!' Nicolas was laughing until he cried at the sight of his men behaving like idiots, but now he shouted, 'Sit back down!' They couldn't hear him because of the din they were making, so he threw spoons at them to get their attention. 'Enough – enough now, you silly fools!'

Aenlin suddenly felt a warning pain in her temples. She stopped in the act of putting the jewellery back. *What . . . what is happening to me?* In her head, a dark female voice was whispering in a foreign language. No, not completely foreign. She recognised some words that Agatha and Ursula had used in their fever dreams.

Aenlin's vision was becoming hazy, and she felt sick. 'I think I . . . I . . . cannot. I cannot . . . put it down.'

Statius' hissing and snarling suddenly sounded like a real predator – and the scream of an eagle pierced the animal noises. Drumming and chanting rose, sounding fascinating – frightening – powerful . . . and with a pull that Aenlin could not resist.

'Aenlin!' Tahmina's worried voice sounded through the darkness full of strange sounds – the darkness that grabbed Aenlin and devoured the barren room. 'Put it down!' she begged. *'Please!'*

She couldn't feel the necklace between her fingers any more. Neither could she feel her legs, nor the rest of her body, not even her breath. The only thing she could hear clearly was her heart, beating in unison with the drums, until the two became one.

Here lay arms shot off, on which the fingers still moved, as if they would yet be fighting; and elsewhere rascals were in full flight that had shed no drop of blood: there lay severed legs, which though delivered from the burden of the body, yet were far heavier than they had been before: there could one see crippled soldiers begging for death, and on the contrary others beseeching quarter and the sparing of their lives.

Simplicius Simplicissimus (1668)
by Hans Jakob Christoffel von Grimmelshausen

CAPITULUM X

Near Wanfried, May 1629

Osanna carefully entered the devastated logging camp. The wagon and horse tracks had led them straight to this deserted place in the woods where the landsknechts had found shelter. She had long since exchanged the saddlecloth and her camisole for a coat and a farmer's dress she had stolen on her way; drawstring shoes protected her feet.

The hut was a ruin, with fire still smouldering under the rafters. Grey smoke billowed skywards. The nearby trees showed traces of fire, and of claw and teeth marks; the gouges were deep and fresh.

Osanna walked slowly through the chaos and looked around.

The wounds on the tree trunks indicated missed blows from blades, the imprints on the ground, of a fight; it smelled of churned forest soil. She found several pools of blood and a lot of blood splatter, but no corpses.

She looked at the collapsed cottage. Maybe the dead were lying underneath the wreckage.

On the ground she found three feathers from a bird she didn't know. The bright colours shimmered impressively in the sunlight filtering through the firs.

Carefully, Osanna picked them up and brushed her dirty fingertips over them. *Soft and delicate.*

'They're not here any more,' she said loudly, standing in the middle of the devastated camp.

Branches crackled and broke in the underbrush. The masked Venetian in his black garb and leather apron stepped forth, followed by his landsknechts.

At his order and directed by Barthel and Valentin, the mercenaries started clearing away the debris to find out if anyone was buried beneath it.

Osanna knelt submissively in front of the Venetian and presented the feathers to him. 'I found these, Master.'

The plague doctor approached her and caressed her brown hair, then he took the three feathers from her hand. 'Gorgeous,' came his muffled voice from behind the silver mask. 'Not from the Old World.'

Valentin, who was digging in the churned-up dirt, yelled, 'Master! I found something.' He picked up his find and came running. 'Is that glass?'

The Venetian took it and held it up to the light of the sun. The piercing rays made the green material shimmer, without actually shining through it. 'Obsidian,' he said, sounding astonished. 'Polished like a blade and broken off, by the looks of it.' He rubbed the barely visible symbols on it. 'Interesting find, Ensign.'

'Feathers from an unknown bird, obsidian bearing strange sigils – and all of that in a deserted logging camp,' Osanna said. 'What does it mean?'

'These must have belonged to the two witches they freed in Bamberg.' The Venetian turned his head, lowering his beak. 'Those women may look as if they belonged here, but they have learned a very different art, not common witchcraft.' With a few long strides, he walked over to one of the damaged trees and touched the irregular cuts. 'Claws and talons. More than unusual.'

'They could be wolfbänner,' Valentin said. 'They might have changed and attacked them.'

'Who?' The Venetian looked over to the landsknechts digging

in the debris and the rubble. 'At this time of the year, there should have been no loggers here – and why would the witches attack their liberators?'

'There was an argument – maybe about the payment?' Valentin thought like a mercenary. 'Or amongst the landsknechts themselves, about the women? Or Nicolas and his men wanted to leave, but the witches didn't want to let them?'

Osanna slowly shook her head. Tucking her long hair under her headscarf, she said, 'There's something else behind this.' She pointed at the feathers and the obsidian. 'For what kind of spell would someone use those, Master? You certainly know.'

The Venetian didn't answer. Thanks to his mask, neither Osanna nor Valentin could see what he might be thinking – or whether he was a mortal at all. This remained a secret.

'Master,' Barthel called from a few feet away, 'here, Master – we got one!'

The three of them climbed over the smouldering debris and the charred timber shingles to where Barthel was standing next to the collapsed fireplace. Two of their men lifted up the sooty boards so the newcomers could look inside the fireplace.

Osanna recognised the wounded man at once. 'That is their leader. They called him Nicolas.'

She saw plenty of wounds on his body, every one of them enough to kill a man.

The plague doctor crouched next to the man and put down his case, which opened by itself, releasing a small cloud of black spores into the air. It hovered over the striking landsknecht until it finally covered his bloody, beaten face.

Osanna, Valentin and Barthel watched in excitement.

They were extremely disappointed when Nicolas didn't stir. The spores covered his face like black crumbs without sinking in.

'It is too late.' The Venetian rose and his case closed. Nothing in his voice betrayed his feelings. 'He is dead. This man is for the birds.'

'One less bastard,' Barthel said with a satisfied snarl, and spat on the corpse. 'We'll get the others as well.'

'They killed their own leader?' Valentin looked incredulously at the body, then bent and pulled open the dead man's mouth. Inside, there was a playing card: the ace of spades. 'What happened here?'

'I cannot question him. The dead do not talk to me.' Suddenly, the Venetian shouted, the silver mask dampening his roar in a weird way, 'I had *plans* for him! Grand designs! And now – *this*!' Angrily, he threw the feathers and the chunk of obsidian down on the corpse. 'These wretched witches have ruined everything! I'll hold them accountable.' He turned, picked up his case and crossed the field of rubble, sending ash and dust rising around his boots. 'They will regret the day they set foot on this land.'

'What shall we do, Master?' Barthel put one hand on the hilt of his rapier. 'Put him into the embers to—?'

'No. Weigh the body down with some rocks and throw him into the river so the fish can devour him. Leave the card where it is. May his soul stay here for ever and haunt the loggers. We will spend the night in Wanfried. The fact that we have new enemies now thwarts my plans. I didn't see this coming. I must . . . prepare.'

'Understood, Master. Consider it done.'

Barthel gave the necessary orders and two of the landsknechts grabbed the feet and dragged the corpse to the river, followed by two others who lugged a rock and a hefty coil of rope.

'What about me, Master?' Osanna picked up a feather and wove it into her dress as a keepsake. She liked to adorn herself with pretty things.

'You go ahead and check Wanfried. Should the witches and their followers have been there, we will spend the night in the same inn. I need something of them, even the shortest piece of hair or fingernail – anything they might have lost.' Again, the Venetian uttered a muffled cry. 'How could *dare* they? How *could* they?'

With a loud splash, Nicolas' corpse entered the Werra, the rocks pushing the body beneath the surface of the water, sinking it at the spot where the rafts usually crossed. Small bubbles of air rose from his clothes as the rival landsknecht captain disappeared into the deep.

Osanna nodded at Barthel and Valentin, who touched their hats, then trotted off along the overgrown path towards Wanfried. They'd get to the small settlement faster by using this footpath rather than the one along the river.

She liked her new role, which had turned a simple serving wench into a spy and a fighter for a cause bigger than anything she had ever known.

She would never have dreamed of this back in her impoverished home town of Altona. All those times of humiliation, of being beaten by her father and abused the guests, of nights forced into the beds of strangers who took her for a few kreutzers were over. Forever.

Near Wanfried, May 1629

Tahmina raced through the dark forest, her staff tilted in her left hand. The glowing symbols were holding back the darkness of night, while at the same time showing her a way to Aenlin.

Her detection spell, intended to find a beloved person, appeared to be suffering from the effects of recent events, however. The symbols were flickering erratically, as if they were uncertain of the way, and other magical powers were also failing the mystic. She was beginning to feel as if she had overused her skills and needed to rest them – no real surprise, considering what had happened in the hut after Statius had forced open and looted Agatha's chest.

The joking landsknechts and Caspar had got all worked up about their game – and suddenly, they couldn't stop. Ignoring their captain's reproving comments, they chased each other around and over the table, stools and benches. Statius' roars had become increasingly savage, the look in his dark eyes and on his face turning feral until he had lost any semblance of humanity.

Tahmina, watching them, had despaired. They were behaving as if they were afflicted by St Vitus' dance, the illness that made people dance and jump and twitch until they collapsed from exhaustion – but the flickering symbols on her staff told her that there was a magical cause to the men's behaviour. The skins had ensorcelled them!

Tahmina had started to prepare a Yatu spell to forcibly calm down the over-excited men when Nicolas started shouting at his men, 'Sit back down! Come to your senses! Enough now, you silly fools!'

He'd grabbed Jäcklein, who shook him off violently and went back to jumping around the room, all the while making loud croaking noises, in a bad imitation of an eagle.

'What is happening to you?' Nicolas demanded.

'Aenlin, stay close to me. Put the jewellery back in that chest – it is cursed,' Tahmina had commanded, but when her companion had not answered, Tahmina had interrupted her Yatu spell and turned around. 'Do you hear me? Put it down! Otherwise . . .' Her voice had faltered, for Aenlin had looked almost delirious, her gaze empty, as if she were staring inwards.

No – not her, too!

'Örmozd, holiest of ghosts! Omniscient one, friend and keeper of the good,' Tahmina had started another spell, grabbing her staff with both hands while all its symbols had glowed milk-white. 'I summon—'

But Agatha had risen on her cot. Her weakness had completely gone; she'd shown no traces of her suffering or the stupor that had enveloped her since her rescue. Her eyes were glowing with an obsidian light as she pointed her crooked fingers at the frolicking landsknechts. 'From now on, you will obey me!' she said menacingly. 'Be my arms, my swords, my companions: unto your death, if I demand it!'

Dark green beams of energy shot from her fingertips towards everyone present.

'*Stop that!*' Tahmina smashed the end of her staff down on the cottage floor, triggering a counter-spell and deflecting the glowing green spell with a silvery flitter. Terrified, she watched the strange magic form loops around the landsknechts, Caspar and Aenlin. The victims of the spell stood rigid, bowing their heads, and the noisy hubbub stopped abruptly. Jäcklein dropped the talon, Aenlin let go of the jewellery.

She has possessed them!

'You won't get me that easily, witch,' Nicolas shouted, and he tore himself free, breaking his loop. The spell dispersed without penetrating his skin.

He . . . he resists magic? For a heartbeat, Tahmina lost her focus. *That is the reason I cannot fathom him.* She turned her attention back to Agatha, who had also noticed this miracle.

'How could you?' Nicolas shouted angrily. 'We have helped you and Ursula!'

Tahmina whirled her staff around and an orange bolt of fire shot from its tip towards the witch. *All these days, she was only pretending to be helpless.*

Agatha raised her hand into the magic ray of fire, absorbing it, and the fading flames turned greenish before dying. 'If I understand correctly, you do only what you have been paid for. I don't have to be grateful.' She leaped off the cot. 'And I never will be!'

Tahmina looked at her staff, which had become unusually hot in her hands, and saw its magical engravings losing their power. *She has damaged it? How . . . how can that be?*

'Let my people go,' Nicolas demanded. 'You don't have to force them to help you. We will escort you to Hamburg.' He joined Tahmina. 'Is she out of her mind?' he whispered to her. 'Is this the after-effects of the interrogation, or the potions and fomentations you gave her to heal her?'

'No. She is in her right senses.' Tahmina realised that what they were facing was not Western magic. *Was she inventing a new form of witchcraft? That was what made it hard to counter the attacks adequately. Ōrmozd, please, listen to my voice . . .* In her mind, she repeated formulae to bolster her own powers.

'I do not want to go to Hamburg, mercenary,' Agatha said. 'Ursula and I, we have our own plans. The two of you will join us.' She raised her arms, pointing her crooked fingers at them. 'Or you will die.'

Tahmina looked at Ursula, who was still lying on her cot, her eyes closed. 'Captain, attack Ula,' she whispered. 'If Agatha—'

'Kill Nicolas,' the witch commanded, and the landsknechts, Caspar and Aenlin awoke from their torpor. They drew their rapiers, swords and daggers and went for their leader, who started dodging and parrying.

'Stop them, mystic,' Nicolas yelled – and at once found himself in dire straits as his own friends, the duellist and Aenlin quickly and mercilessly attacked him, while he strived not to hurt them with his own defensive moves.

That will not work. Again, Tahmina summoned a bolt of flame to throw at Agatha – as at that very moment, Statius stabbed the captain's belly and followed through with a blow from his obsidian claw. When Nicolas doubled over in pain, Jäcklein hacked at his right flank, and he fell to the floor. At once, they all went for the screaming man with blades and talons and claws – then Caspar fired at the prostrate man, filling the room with gun smoke.

I must destroy that witch! 'Perish!' Tahmina kept up the red-hot stream of flame and twisted her staff around. She didn't have time to raise a protective spell of her own. 'You will not harm Aenlin!'

'Well, you failed the first time, and you'll fail again,' Agatha replied, sending dark green and black lightning from her fingertips at the mystic. The energies surrounded the orange flames and pushed them back towards the end of the staff until they hit the wood with a loud hiss. 'You will die!'

The ebony became searingly hot and there was a deafening detonation. The blast hit Tahmina, but she didn't drop her staff, repeating to herself, *I must not lose it.* She spiralled through the air, surrounded by the debris of the destroyed cottage, hit something – and lost consciousness.

Tahmina had awakened to find herself hanging between two low branches of a fir tree, dazed, covered in cuts and bruises and hurting all over. Her midnight-blue robe was torn and riddled with holes. She had climbed down and using her detection spell to give chase, started running through the dense forest. Ever since then, she'd been pushing through thickets, forcing her way through brambles and vines, occasionally walking over soft moss, until, finally, darkness surrounded her.

Wheezing, she stopped. Focusing on the symbols and the intensity of their light, she moved the flickering staff around her, checking for the right direction.

'Damn!' The artefact had changed its mind again, so she would have to correct her course. She hoped it was not leading her completely astray, or in the wrong direction, away from Aenlin and the others. *Can I still trust it?*

Again, the symbols flickered, looking as indecisive and clueless as the mystic herself.

'Ōrmozd, you have left me.' Panting, Tahmina leaned back against a tree.

She could not go on any more. Her legs were on fire and she was incredibly thirsty, to say nothing of her hunger. She had only her satchel with her herbs, tinctures and ointments, the same things she had used to heal the wounded witches. The handful of mushrooms she had picked here and there hadn't filled her stomach.

Worried as she was, when Tahmina had started following, she had thought she would quickly catch up with Aenlin and the landsknechts. Instead, she stood in the middle of nowhere, surrounded by a night-dark forest full of eerie sounds.

Even the staff is failing me. Tahmina had tears in her eyes as despair raged in her. *Aenlin . . . Oh Aenlin, where are you?* She slid down the rough tree trunk, sank to her knees between the roots of the tree and cried. She felt lost and alone, separated from her beloved, who was in mortal danger and under another's control. 'By the djinni of Shiraz, what a terrible country . . .'

After a while, she recovered herself and got up, sniffing. *My heart-sickness does Aenlin no good.* She needed a place to stay for the night, preferably high up in the branches of a tree, to avoid being attacked in her sleep, whether by human or animal, or something worse.

Tahmina was not sure what the witches intended to do. They would surely be going to Hanover, where Veronica, the third of them, had already travelled. But what if that had been a lie, a distraction for potential pursuers? If that was the case, going there would be a useless waste of time.

'So only you can show me the right direction,' Tahmina said to her staff, 'even if you are not serving me so well right now.'

With the glowing of the symbols lighting her way, she started looking for a suitable conifer in which to sleep.

She heard running water and followed the soft gurgling until she reached a rivulet. It was clear and smelled clean. *Also, it is too shallow for naiads.* She cupped her hand, scooped up some water and washed her arms and neck, then her face, and finally, she drank deeply. *How refreshing!*

But when Tahmina dipped her hands in the water for the fifth time, she noticed another smell. 'Blood,' she whispered. She let the water trickle back into the rivulet. *Where did that smell come from?*

She moved her light over the rivulet and saw that it was turning red a little way upstream, as if someone had emptied barrels of blood into the water.

Was this the witches' work? Tahmina dimmed the light of her staff and followed the stream to discover the source of the blood.

She was hoping to find Nicolas and the landsknechts. Or Aenlin. *Maybe they butchered a deer . . . ?*

Soon, she heard muffled gasping and panting coming from behind two rocky, oblong-shaped hills in the middle of the forest. Someone there was suffering.

Carefully she approached the sound – and quickly realised her mistake.

These were no hills: two giants were lying in front of Tahmina, one at least ten feet tall, the other, the smaller, stood around seven feet. The tallest one had been dismembered: his head decapitated, his arms hacked off and blood was spurting from the stumps into the stream. His clothing, leather and furs, had been slashed in several places and strips of his skin had been peeled off.

'Örmozd, great Creator,' gasped Tahmina with a start.

'Who . . . are you?' The smaller giant, younger and more slender, rolled onto his back to get a better view of her. Leaves, twigs and dirt were stuck in his brown beard and curls; no wonder Tahmina had mistaken him for dead. He looked at the carved, glowing staff. 'Ah, another Hagzussa. Kill me, then, wretched woman. Finish what your friends began!'

'I know them, but they are no friends of mine.' Tahmina had to force herself to approach the giant, her heart beating fast. She had heard about those creatures; they were supposed to be wild, evil man-eaters who destroyed villages and farms by throwing rocks and stones at them. The giants hailed from the north, and hated Christians for outlawing their old gods. *But maybe I can use him.* 'If you promise not to hurt me, I will help you. Then we can talk.'

The giant stifled a laugh that turned into coughing. 'How could I hurt you? These fucking soldiers cut almost all of my tendons!'

'Promise. Swear by your life.'

'I swear, Hagzussa, by Odin and Thor.' The giant looked around pleadingly. 'My name is Tännel. If you save me from death, you shall get more than my thanks.'

Tahmina climbed the decapitated giant lying next to him to look down on the wounded Tännel. She made the light of the staff glow more brightly so she was able to examine his wounds. *Bad.* 'You have been stabbed several times,' she said. 'Also, there are cuts that—'

'Stop, stop! I don't care.' Tännel groaned. 'I am dying just from listening to you. I am getting weaker.'

Tahmina quickly considered her options. When studying the art of Yatu, she had put her focus on demonology, not on alleviating and healing magic. Her spells might just be enough to mend the severed sinews so Tännel would be able to move, but he would never be as nimble as before. The gaping cuts she would have to stitch up by hand; treating his many wounds would use up the last of her ointments, tinctures and herbs.

'Needle and thread,' she announced. 'Do you have those?'

'You want to stitch me up? You are a Hagzussa!'

'Not one of those who can magically seal wounds.' Tahmina explained what she intended to do. 'I will stitch up your cuts so they can heal on their own. After a few days, you will have to remove the stitches, Tännel.'

'All right. Agreed.' The giant nodded at his dead friend. 'You might find what you need in his satchel. The mercenaries didn't take it.'

Tahmina started searching. 'I hope your skin is not too thick,' she murmured. Stitching him up would be arduous work. No matter how much she dug around in the satchel, there was neither needle nor thread. 'No, I am afraid you are wrong,' she said at last.

'So what now?'

'Now I come up with something else.' She took some dried beef from her own bag and quickly ate some, conscious that she needed to regain a bit of strength. It did not taste too bad; it was probably smoked boar. As she ate, she examined the corpse. *His clothes!* she thought suddenly. *They have probably been sewn together with thread of some sort.*

She used her dagger to unpick some of the seams in the dead giant's jerkin and cut the thread into usable lengths. *It's coarse, but it will suffice.* She had found a corked jug of what she guessed must be brandy in his bag, which must have contained as much as ten human carafes. *I can use this to clean the wounds,* she thought, dragging it over to the wounded giant.

'Here we go,' Tahmina warned him. She jabbed her glowing staff into the wound to reconnect the severed sinews. As its light hit the cut edges, she said, 'Tell me about yourself. What has happened?'

'You're rummaging around inside me and you want me to—?'

'It will distract you, and keep you awake,' she explained. 'Also, the pain will be easier to bear.' She was also afraid that Tännel would die from his massive blood loss before her battlefield repairs could kick in. *So it is better if you do not lose consciousness. I need your knowledge about the witches, the landsknechts and especially Aenlin.* 'Well? I am listening?'

'You said you are no friend of theirs?'

'No.'

'But why are you following them? You were following them, right?'

'I am afraid they have ensorcelled my friend, just like they did the soldiers.'

Tännel moaned when the spell took hold. There was a crackling and cracking noise as the severed sinews crawled towards each other and knitted themselves together. 'Ah, that's why. I didn't know how to explain it.'

'That they attacked you?'

'That one of our own – just a boy! – attacked us and beat my friend to a pulp.' Tännel tentatively moved his knee, which worked at once. 'Thank you!' he called. 'This is a miracle . . .'

'Hold still,' she snapped at him. 'You are pumping blood out of your wounds.' She started tending to the deepest cuts. The giant's blood smelled human and was just as red. She could not detect anything different about it. 'You mean the youngest landsknecht? Moritz?' *That explains his physique, and how he has the strength of a hundred men.*

'Yes, I know him. But he is not called Moritz. At least that's not the name my parents gave him.' Tännel clenched his teeth as Tahmina rummaged around in the gaping hole to remove dirt, then washed out the wound with brandy, then pierced his skin with her dagger to thread through the yarn that she had doused in alcohol. Finally, she applied some ointment to the whole area. 'He was baptised Holder, to honour the goddess Hulda.'

'Forgive him. He is probably not in control of himself any longer.'

'But he was well in control of his blade. We knew that Holder would be a great fighter one day, but ...' Tännel clung to two trees with his giant hands. The wood creaked under the pressure of his fingers. 'Triple spit, that hurts like Hell. I also feel sick!' Bark and wood chips went flying. 'What are you doing, Hagzussa?'

'I had to go down to the bone.' Tahmina was covered in blood, because in one spot, a huge artery had been cut open. 'Be quiet and keep still.' She knew she had to take care of it at once. 'I will not let you die.'

She cast the Yatu spell to create a flame, but she restricted it to a flamelet just a finger-length long, jutting from the tip of her staff. The blood vessel, as thick as her forearm, shuddered as it kept pumping with Tännel's heartbeat. *If red-hot iron works, this will, too*, she told herself. Carefully, she held the puncture closed and sealed it with the focused flamelet.

Tännel suppressed a cry. Smoke and vapour rose in the air, acrid in Tahmina's nostrils. *It worked!*

'You thought the soldiers had caught Holder,' she said, to distract the giant.

'Yes – and when we stopped them to talk to him, they attacked us.'

Tahmina moved carefully; she didn't want to scorch the impressive muscles laid bare. 'How did they manage to subdue the two of you? They are just common landsknechts – except for Moritz, of course.'

'Oh, Odin and Loki help us! No, they were not common, not by far.' Tännel groaned, his body flopping. 'I ... I feel dizzy, Hagzussa. All my strength is gone – but there is no pain any more. Is that good?'

Tahmina considered it not good at all. *These are the effects of the blood loss.* 'It's the herbs,' she said. 'They are sedating you.'

'Didn't you say I should stay awake?' Tännel was not really speaking any more but mumbling; still, his voice carried far in the quiet forest.

'It would be better.' Tahmina's fingers, her arms, shoulders – everything felt exhausted. This effort was almost more than she could endure. 'Did they say where they were going?'

Tännel didn't answer, but he let go of the crushed tree trunks. The firs, broken, crashed to the ground.

'Do not fall asleep,' Tahmina commanded. She rushed to the giant's head to see his eyelids were closed, the eyes underneath moving rapidly left and right. 'Hey! Hey, Tännel!' she shouted into his ear as she pulled his thick beard. 'We have an agreement! Come on, do your part!'

'I am awake, I am awake, Hagzussa,' he whispered.

'Where did they want to go?'

'I'll tell you as soon as I can think straight,' he slurred. 'Everything is black, black and . . . cold. I'll sleep a while.'

'By the djinni of Yazd!' Tahmina cursed and touching the artery in his neck, felt for his heartbeat. It was weak and irregular – then his heart skipped a beat and returned to a steadier rhythm that was three times as fast.

He will not be able to resist death on his own for very much longer. Quickly she combined the remains of her elixirs into a strengthening potion that could have turned a herd of horses ready for the slaughterhouse into the world's fastest steeds. He *had* to stay awake. *Otherwise, all my efforts are in vain.* She climbed the giant's chest and cried, 'Tännel! Tännel, open your mouth!'

The giant didn't react.

He is drifting off. 'This will burn,' she said, more to herself than to him, and poured the potion into his vast right nostril.

The liquid seeped into his nose, through the bristly hair and reached his throat to work its magic.

Abruptly, Tännel opened his eyes and uttered a cry that almost deafened the mystic. His torso jerked upright – and with a scream, Tahmina went flying.

Wanfried, May 1629

'Hey! You lousy piece of soldier shit. Open up your eyes now!'

It took Nicolas a while to understand that the man shouting into his ear was talking to him, for he had his eyes closed. He didn't move in any case, trying to hide the fact that he was awake so he could work out where he was and what was happening from the sounds he could hear. He knew this voice – but from where?

'There,' said a woman who was standing on his other side. 'He twitched.'

'He didn't,' said the known unknown man.

According to the echoes, he was in a large room. He could smell a mixture of many different things, like a trading station where a variety of goods were stored. He also felt something in his mouth. *Wadded paper?*

The woman grumbled, 'Are you sure he's not dead as a doornail?'

'As certain as the screams in Hell. This bastard can survive everything – at least, that's what I think.'

Cramm – *Joss von Cramm!* Finally, Nicolas could put a name to the voice. Cramm was a mercenary crimper, someone who wandered about, ruthlessly collecting everyone who had a sword in his hand and a cock between his legs. He also talked the clueless, the malcontents and the daring into going to war by promising good pay and even better loot as soon as the pillaging began.

How and when did he come into play? Nicolas' last memory was the attack by his own people. It was as if they'd gone mad, mercilessly hitting, stabbing and shooting – and they had been moving much too quickly for him to be able to parry all the attacks, despite all the fighting tricks and ruses he knew. There was no cure for treason. But what had happened afterwards?

Nicolas decided that he had to open his eyes. He spat out the soggy paper. 'I am awake,' he said weakly, lifting his eyelids.

'See? What did I tell you?' Joss von Cramm's face was hovering above him. The forty-year-old man laughed happily.

Nicolas took note of the jacket with a flat lace collar, a wig that was obviously made of horsehair, his goatee and moustache. Nothing about him looked elegant; everything spoke of fake wealth. There was nothing of real splendour here, unlike Caspar von und zu dem Dorffe.

'Tell me, where did they send your soul back from? From Heaven or from Hell, you son of a bitch?'

Nicolas straightened, and realised that he was naked and covered with a sheet – a shroud. 'I was dead and gone?'

He looked around, his long ash-blond hair falling to his naked shoulders. His nose had not deceived him. There were shelves stacked with crates and sacks, and piles of barrels lined the walls; next to them were flagons of wine, loaves of cheese and filled sacks on which the word *overseas* was stamped. He thought he could make out the scents of coffee, sugar, oil, spices, tobacco, wool, wine, honey and fish.

A woman in a shift, wearing a floppy hat on her light-coloured hair, walked to a table and poured something into a wooden cup that she gave to Nicolas. He quickly downed it – it was watered-down wine – and, with a pleading look, asked for more.

'Pretty dead and gone,' Cramm declared. 'The fishermen who dragged you from the Werra said so – they wanted to sell your corpse to the hangman so he could extract your fat. Man, did they run when they found out that you had met the Grim Reaper with a beating heart.'

Nicolas looked down at himself, at the fresh scars where the blades and balls had hit him; they merged with the patchwork of old long-healed wounds. There was a misshapen playing card next to his cot, barely recognisable as the ace of spades. *The card of death. A gleeful last salute.* 'The hangman bandaged me up?'

'No. He wanted to burn you as undead demon spawn.' Cramm grinned sleazily. 'But as Destiny would have it, I was the friendly executioner's guest that day, and I bought you, body and soul. You, completely.' He pointed at the fresher scars. 'I didn't bandage you up. You heal very quickly, Nicolas, which is why you're the perfect choice for what I have to offer.'

This was all going a bit too fast for Nicolas. Seconds ago, he had been dead at the bottom of the Werra; now a crimper wanted Nicolas to do something for him. He emptied his cup again, but he was still thirsty. 'What day is it?'

'They dragged you from the river four days ago. You'd been weighed down with rocks. Someone really wanted to feed you to the fishes.'

'The date, Cramm!'

'May twenty-eighth.' He looked at the woman. 'Sounds like he's been down with the fishes for a while. The water's washed the memories right out of his ears.'

This revelation came as a shock: he'd spent three days in the river, four more in a state between life and death. Another miracle, like the ones that had happened in battle, when he stopped thinking and consisted only of sheer resolve and the will to kill.

Three days underwater. 'My stuff?'

'Those stinking, hacked-up rags full of holes? I threw them away and got you new clothes. I'll set them against your pay.' Cramm nodded like a father. 'Listen up now, for I won't tell you twice: *you owe me*. Without me, the hangman would have taken you apart and melted out your fat, and not even you would have survived that.'

Nicolas didn't doubt the crimper's words. Judging by his surroundings, he guessed he was in one of the warehouses on the

Schlagd, where goods were transferred and then shipped down the Werra and the Weser by barge, or transported by wagon overland towards Nuremberg and Leipzig. 'Have you seen my landsknechts, Cramm?'

Cramm laughed. 'Ah, did they do this to you?'

'I didn't say that.'

'Not with words, maybe, but with your face.' Cramm sat down on a bench beside the table and threw Nicolas undergarments and new clothes. 'No, none of yours have passed through.'

'This time I'm reading your face: so there were others.'

'No,' he lied.

'A plague doctor and his troops,' said the woman. 'They said they were here on behalf of the Sovereign to check Wanfried for the Black Death – but they travelled on after only two days, and they hadn't visited a single household here.'

'Will you shut up?' Cramm threatened her. 'After all, the captain was in the doctor's services.'

The woman curtsied awkwardly. 'I am Brigitta, this man's wife – and no, I don't know why. Ah, yes, I do. Because of his promises that he didn't keep after being inside me for the first time.'

'So he doesn't only betray those he enlists, but also his women.' Nicolas grinned. 'But no, I have no truck with this company. I had other commitments.' He got dressed in front of the couple without caring about his nakedness. *Let her see what she cannot have – and I don't mind if he is annoyed.* 'Cramm, what did you spend on my behalf? I'll pay you back as soon as I—'

Cramm laughed aloud. 'Forget it! You can't buy your freedom. You're working for me, my friend.'

'But I am currently in someone else's service.' The clothes fitted well: flared, colourfully striped breeches, stockings, tall boots, a red shirt with white puffy sleeves and a green jerkin. He had worn worse.

'You were dead, Nicolas – that ends any contract, right?' He winked. 'I've thought it through. Legally, you're free.'

'How much, Cramm?'

'You don't have any money. Your pockets were empty and you've already signed a promissory note.' He produced a folded piece of paper with Nicolas' signature. 'In your sleep.'

Nicolas was fully dressed, but missing a baldric. Obviously, the crimper didn't want to give him his rapier and dagger before they'd come to an agreement. *He knows why*. Nicolas would not dream of going to war for the man. He had to follow his people and save them from Agatha's and Ursula's claws. 'What do you want?'

Making Cramm believe he was considering his offer would buy Nicolas time to come up with a plan for escaping Wanfried. The city had only a rampart and palisades, not much to stop him.

Casually, Cramm put a hand on the butt of the pistol that he carried in his belt. 'There is always a war somewhere, Nicolas. That's how people like us make a living.'

'Not right now.'

'Oh, yes – not in the Holy Roman Empire, maybe, but in Poland, where they're fighting against the Swedes. Gustavus Adolphus and his faithful are on a final campaign to end the war on this front. The German Emperor has sent some auxiliaries to the Poles to destroy the Swedes.' Cramm poured himself some wine. 'I can understand: if they arrest the Swedish King there, the Emperor doesn't have to worry about Gustavus Adolphus intervening in the conflicts between the German Catholics and Protestants any more.'

'What's any of that to me?' Nicolas tucked his hair under the black velvet hat to keep it from falling into his face all the time.

'I promised the Poles, the Swedes and the Imperial troops I'd muster some more men for them. When I crimp, I always let the new men choose which side they want to join. Am I not truly fair?'

'Sure, as long as you get your money.' Nicolas looked around again. This time he noticed that they were not alone. Four landsknechts wearing armbands with the initials *JvC* to show who they fought for were standing next to the large honey barrels. If he declined to oblige Cramm, they'd give him a thorough beating. *I need to avoid that.* 'Who did you promise me to? The Swedes, the Imperial troops, or the Poles?'

'I'll let you choose.'

'Can you recommend a side? Who will win?'

'If I heard right, the Emperor has sent five thousand infantry and cavalry troops to Poland, led by Hans Georg von Arnim. However, the Swedish King has recently crossed over, allegedly with four thousand riders and five thousand footmen. Only the Almighty knows how many the Poles have.' Cramm crossed himself several times in a row. 'If we only knew in advance whose side God is on, right?'

'When will the slaughter begin?'

'It already has, it already has. That's why you must leave quickly, my good, my best, my absolute best. There's been a skirmish here, a scuffle there – but the great hewing and stabbing is soon to come. The powder and the cannonballs are already sailing there from Hamburg. The war cannot stagnate for ever. Somebody must win. There will surely be a lot to loot.'

'I don't care what you call me as long as I'm not your arse.' Nicolas wandered about the warehouse, examining the goods, the crates and barrels. *I need a way out, now.* 'Sounds as if the Poles and the Imperial troops are at a disadvantage.'

'So you will fight for Sweden?'

'I didn't say that.' Nicolas saw a small window above a stack of crates. Cramm's landsknechts guarded the two doors, but it didn't look like they had noticed this bolthole. 'I assume there'll be a peace treaty with the Poles once the Swedish King is bested.'

'So do I. Anyway, there'll be a German attack on the Baltic coast – Gustavus Adolphus is not going to let the German

Protestants starve.' Cramm squinted. 'Unless you could get your hands on the Swedish King and arrest him. What do you think – how much would the Emperor and the Poles pay you for him? You'll be rich for the rest of your life.'

'What about you? What you want from me?'

The crimper spread his arms. 'Among us pious children of God, let us say thirty per cent of your income, whether you get pay and a commendation or if you loot and seize some land. Or collar the King of Sweden.'

'You trust me to pay you your share?' *Up the crates, through the window and away.* He didn't want to risk a fight, not while he was unarmed and still ailing from that last battle.

'Oh, certainly, certainly. I'll even come along, so you won't have to carry it too far. I'll take the men I've enlisted and distribute them among the various camps on the way, depending on their preferences and what they've signed.' Cramm pretended to be juggling. 'Travelling with me is fun. I can do a lot of tricks. If you want, you can even have my wife. For another ten per cent.'

'I would be willing to pay money myself for such a handsome man. I am sure *you* can do' – Brigitta shifted her gaze from Nicolas to Cramm – 'what *you* cannot.'

Cramm became impatient. 'So?'

'No. I am still in service.' *Up and away.* Nicolas ran through the warehouse and quickly climbed the crates. 'In my own service!'

'Don't shoot, you fools,' Cramm commanded as his landsknechts drew their pistols. 'Two of you follow him, you others, get out and catch him outside!'

Nicolas climbed the windowsill and with a kick, sent the stack of crates below him flying. The mercenaries came crashing down with the wooden crates, cursing.

'See you, Cramm. I always pay my debts – but when I want to.'

With that, he jumped to freedom – and landed right in front of some very surprised landsknechts.

They don't spare anybody, regardless of their estate or office.

No places are too free or too sacred for them. Neither the churches not the altar nor the graves, not even the dead bodies are safe from their thieving and predatory acts of violence.

Apologia on Landsknechts (1622)
by Ernst von Mansfeld

CAPITULUM XI

Near Wanfried, May 1629

With aching limbs, Tahmina pushed herself up and found her staff. *I had to fly again.* Her landing had at least been light; she had flown past trees and landed on the soft forest floor, which had cushioned her impact. She hurt all over and her clothes, already damp and bloodstained, were now stiff with hardened mud and dirt.

Straightening her robe, she turned to look for Tännel, and saw him no more than ten paces away.

'Blessed be Ōrmozd!' she whispered. 'I could have been dead.' She returned to the giant, who lay stretched out on the forest floor.

He was snoring.

Quickly, she checked the wound and the repaired vein for damage, but his heart was beating steadier than before, thanks to the potion she had poured into his nose.

Tahmina returned to tending to his other wounds by the light of her staff. Periodically she washed her forearms and hands, and paused to eat and drink from the dismembered giant's provisions. She had to keep stopping to relax her aching shoulders, arms and fingers, too. The work was arduous, but in the end she was successful.

This giant is fascinating. Tahmina knew of no such creatures in her homeland, and in the German realms and lands, giants were believed to be extinct. However, the fact that some of them still existed in secret, did not surprise the mystic, for they represented elemental forces, the old Norse gods and goddesses whom the Christians had suppressed. If Tännel and his ilk ever dared visit a town, they would probably be burned like the witches were, or forced into some army to die among a barrage of cannonballs.

Moritz is just a boisterous giant child, she had realised. For him, the journey with the landsknechts had been a fascinating adventure, just like for any little boy. He didn't know yet what being in a real battle meant – and now he was under Agatha's control.

Tännel moved just as the sun announced her presence by sending warm light shimmering between the firs and pine trees.

'Thank you, Hagzussa,' he said weakly, sitting up carefully. With a groan, he leaned against the tree behind him. It creaked, and some of its roots were pulled from the ground, but the tree just about withstood the giant's weight. 'You shall be rewarded.'

'I do not care for rewards, but you can tell me where the foreign witches went with the landsknechts and Moritz ... I mean, Holder.' She sat down on an uprooted tree next to him. 'I will lift the curse that binds him. Forgive him what he did, because he did not act of his own free will. He will be eternally sorry once he learns what he has done.'

'I know, Hagzussa. We are few and far apart now. This is why a young giant is so valuable to us.'

'Are you not already considered extinct?'

'We didn't contradict him when Emperor Maximilian claimed to have killed the last of us a hundred years ago in Worms.' Tännel looked at the stitched-up wounds in his flesh through the gashes in his leather clothing. 'But we – the children of the legendary giant Ecke, who fought Dietrich von Bern of Bruns and his family, who protected his grove against the priests – are not fully extinct. Our time will come, when the old gods return and send the Christians to the Hell they invented. Until then, we live in hiding, as hard as that is.' He took a deep breath, which sounded as if somebody had opened a giant bellows and filled it with air. 'When the witches thought I was dying, I heard them say they wanted to go to Heiligenstadt to meet a third one. They called her Nica.'

The clue I was hoping for! Despite her exhaustion, Tahmina suddenly felt more alive, more cheerful. 'To do what?'

'To make plans to further evil, to strengthen it so it may grow and spread, until the Old World descends into one great slaughter. That's what they said. Their voices were dripping with hatred and thirst for revenge.' Tännel sounded worried. 'Free Holder from their magical bonds, Hagzussa. Kill them, if you want to do your world a favour.' He smiled at her grimly. 'What is your name, Hagzussa?'

'Tahmina.'

'Well then, Tahmina. If you need help, call my name to the wind three times. I will come and aid you – but I'll not be coming alone. There won't be a second defeat like the last one.'

So, to Heiligenstadt. 'Thank you, Tännel.' Simply knowing the name of the place didn't help; she didn't know her way around the Empire and had no map. *I don't even know where I am right now.* 'How do I get there?'

'Go straight on towards the sunrise. By noon, you will come to a gorge. Follow it northwards and you will reach a town where you can get anything you need for the rest of your journey.'

'Good. Thank you.' Tahmina smiled up at him. 'Go easy on yourself for the next few days. Remove the stitches in a week from now, and keep the wounds clean so they will not get infected.' She rose. 'I will save my friend and Holder. I promise you this.'

Tännel gratefully bowed his giant head; his thick, deep-brown beard and long curls swinging. 'Odin and Thor go with you.' He rose carefully, to avoid tearing open his wounds. As he limped away in the opposite direction, he turned to call, 'I will take care of my friend's funeral. Do not forget to call on me when you need help, Hagzussa.' He disappeared between the firs. For a giant, he walked quietly; only the rustling and crackling of branches and twigs told her which way he was going.

Tahmina filled her bag with provisions from the dead giant's store and set off at a brisk pace, due east, where the sun was just rising, to find the town Tännel had talked about. She would have to find out its name, as he had not mentioned that.

On her way, she drove away tiredness by thinking about the events at the logging camp. The feathers, the weapons, the jaguar skins from the witch's chest – they had come from the New World. The witches' intention to plunge the Old World into chaos, or even to its doom, didn't sound like the machinations of evil Tahmina had read about when studying the mystical texts.

Evil was most comfortable when it could cause damage secretly, corrupting everything that was good and turning an idyllic world into its opposite. It thrived in such misery. However, it could not cause too much damage, for in the worst, the greatest terror, humans tended to seek the good. *What do Agatha and her friends intend to do?* What Tännel had heard didn't sound like secrecy and subversion at all.

Still lost in thought, Tahmina reached the gorge and, following the giant's instructions, turned north towards the town. She stopped at a small waterfall to wash off the worst of the dirt. She could do nothing about the gashes and holes in her robe, but at least she was able to get much of the blood out of the fabric, and the ice-cold water on her skin, massaging it in to her shoulders, her back and her arms, revived her.

This war between Catholics and Protestants is especially perfidious, she thought. Just as in the Islamic world, different sects were always fighting, which made it easy for evil to show up, well disguised and camouflaged and whisper the worst deeds in the ears of the noblest people.

Every human being with a modicum of education knew that the war was not about the interpretation of Faith alone, but mostly about power and domains, which no one represented as honestly and as openly as the mercenaries. Today they fought for one side, tomorrow for the other, changing as quickly as their banners.

Tahmina's renegade master had recognised the signs of evil that had become visible in Europe; he had turned his back on the mystic school to broaden his influence through his knowledge of devas and evil djinni. Before his journey, he had killed everyone at home he considered capable of stopping him – but in his arrogance, he had spared Tahmina. *He will see that he has under-estimated me.* Tahmina was angry that the episode in Hamburg had turned into such a time-consuming adventure. The tracks of her old master turned cold, so she would have to start looking for them once again, with great difficulty, in England.

At least she would gain some knowledge of Western demon-ology, as well as information about Agatha and Ursula, the two foreign witches who used such a strange form of magic, in which panther and jaguar skins, obsidian weapons and the feathers of unknown birds played so great a role.

By noon, Tahmina's robe had dried and she had reached a rocky road leading to some settlement. Was that really Heiligenstadt? She walked along the winding road through flat valleys and past low hills. On her way, she passed a place where a stake stuck up, surrounded by the charred remains of a pyre. The town clearly indulged in the widespread practice of burning convicted witches and warlocks.

Tahmina slowed her steps and looked down at herself. With her exotic looks, she was obviously a suspicious character to superstitious, fearful people. Without Aenlin, she could not pose as an exotic maid. *But what else can I do?*

A rumbling and rattling warned her of an approaching cart. Tahmina quickly disappeared into the undergrowth to await whatever was approaching.

A carter, singing quietly to himself, drove a team of two horses along the road to the town. His cart was packed with medium-sized barrels.

Tahmina studied it briefly, then decided, *I am slim enough.* She waited until the cart had passed, then left the thicket and quickly, silently, climbed aboard. She wedged herself into a small gap between two casks and covered herself with a coiled rope to hide herself from being seen from above.

She would get an impression of the town unnoticed before moving through it openly.

The wagon moved on. From time to time, the carter stood up to piss from the box seat, wetting the casks with his urine and singing loudly before sitting down again and singing even louder to announce his approach to guards at a gate.

Tahmina heard an amused voice say, 'Stop. What's your load?'

'Sounded to me like a dozen notes out of tune,' said another man.

The cart jolted to a stop.

'Good day to you, esteemed guards,' replied the carter. 'I carry wine from Nuremberg. No one there wants to drink the dry stuff, so I'll sell it in the north. I advise you not to taste it, though. You'll only upset your stomachs.' There followed the rustling of paper and the clinking of coins. 'The papers, and the fee for my stay.'

'God – it smells like horse piss,' one of the guards confirmed. 'You may pass. Get rid of it!'

'Thanks. Don't buy any wine from Nuremberg – stick with your beer.' Singing loudly, the carter clicked his tongue and continued his journey.

Clever fellow. This way, they keep their hands off his cargo. Tahmina gazed through a gap between the rumbling casks. To her, it looked a town like any other. Some of the half-timbered buildings they passed bore scorch marks. The war had not spared those homes, no matter whose soldiers had passed through here.

The cart turned off the main road and entered a warren of alleys. Here, numerous craftsmen had their workshops, as she saw from the battered guild signs over the doors. The scents of freshly baked bread and smoked meat hung in the air. The carter's loud singing echoed from the walls, where laundry pegged to taut clotheslines flew in the spring wind.

Looks quite peaceful. The place appeared to have survived a looting in the past, and looked like it was thriving now, as far as such a thing was possible in these times.

The wagon turned another corner, drove past several inns, some small and others bigger, with sweeping upper levels that formed a sort of roof across the alley.

A bad European habit, Tahmina thought. It made it easier for fires to jump from building to building and burn down an entire city in one night. Firewalls made of brick would have helped . . .

Her right leg had gone to sleep and the smell of urine was gradually becoming too much for her to bear. She toyed with the idea of leaving right then, but she had not yet come up with a good lie to explain her exotic looks. *In Hamburg, I would cause less of a sensation, but here?* Tahmina looked up at the clotheslines. *That is it!* She would exchange her robe for something in the current fashion and wrap the staff in rags. That way, she could pose as a travelling handmaid looking for a job as a sutler.

At that moment a feather floated past the cart, swept around playfully by a breeze.

Tahmina recognised it at once: it had once been part of the feather jacket from Agatha's chest. *Aenlin is here!*

But before she could jump from her hiding place between

the barrels to grab the drifting feather, a group of children appeared. One girl noticed the extraordinary colours and picked it up at once. There was a brawl, but in the end the finder ran away with her treasure, laughing loudly, followed by the others, noisily whooping with joy.

Tahmina scanned the partially open shutters of the taverns and inns as the cart passed. She thought perhaps that her companion and the landsknechts had taken up residence in one of them.

Without the carter noticing, Tahmina took up her staff, left her hiding place and leapt down to the empty street. It was time to use the full power of the ebony staff. *For Aenlin.*

Wanfried, May 1629

The five of Joss von Cramm's mercenaries who had gathered outside for a smoke had no time to react before Nicolas floored three of them with heavy blows of his fists. Their clay pipes shattered, the glowing tobacco falling into their beards and on the clothing of the downed men.

'Here,' called one landsknecht, who jumped back from Nicolas to draw his rapier. 'We have him!'

'You have me?' Laughing, Nicolas grabbed a dagger from one of the men at his feet and a sword from another. 'Then come and take me.'

'You'll see where your big mouth gets you!' The fifth landsknecht swept a sword from his sheath and raced forward, aiming its tip at Nicolas' heart.

The landsknecht captain deflected the slender blade with his dagger and smashed the basket hilt into the attacker's face, dropping the man to the ground, nursing a bleeding nose and a split lip. 'Oops,' Nicolas said, laughing. 'Was there something down there that made you trip?'

'Pig-licker!' The fallen man stabbed at Nicolas again, this time aiming for his shin. 'I'll soon cut you down to size!'

Nicolas raised his foot and stepped down on the blade, pressing it against the ground and trapping his opponent's hand so the man couldn't free himself from the weapon's pinned basket. 'Rather not, right?'

The last of the landsknechts tried to use his inattention to attack with his rapier, crying, 'You'll soon be whining!' but Nicolas parried the man's blow with his longer blade, then threw his newly acquired dagger.

'I fear you'll be the first to whine!'

It struck the man's right shoulder, his weapons arm, and the landsknecht dropped his rapier with a scream.

'Told you so! Have someone burn out the wound with brandy. This rapier is covered in old blood and the rust of centuries, if I'm not mistaken – that could lead to a bad infection if you're not careful.'

Joss von Cramm and four more of his landsknechts had come running around the corner of the warehouse, blades drawn and ready to join the fight.

'Nicolas, come to your senses – what's the use of this silly rebellion? Do you want to follow your people to Heiligenstadt so they can kill you again and cut you into little pieces?'

Mentally, Nicolas rejoiced. *So that's my destination!* But first, he had to rid himself of his own chains, which were tightening by the second. 'How can we come to an agreement?'

'Agreement?' Cramm ordered two of his mercenaries to get a net. 'We already have one: you owe me and you will work off your debts by going to Poland and fighting. I'll come with you wherever you go to enjoy your fighting skills and get half of your pay, until your debts are paid in full.'

'*Half?*'

'Yes, half!'

'Didn't you say thirty per cent?'

'That was before you damaged my men.' Cramm pointed at the wounded mercenaries with the tip of his rapier. 'Look what you've done to them! They'll be missing the next battles, just like they're now missing the teeth they lost by your hand.'

What am I going to do now? Nicolas looked around quickly. Dock workers had stopped their loading and unloading to watch the events from a safe distance. The number of onlookers was growing quickly, and he could see several were grabbing a variety of makeshift weapons, including stones and clubs, in case the dispute wandered in their direction. Landsknechts were not exceedingly popular in Wanfried, not since Wallenstein's men had burned down the place.

'You simply can't escape,' Cramm was boasting. 'Don't be a fool, Nicolas. After all, I saved your life.' He nodded towards their audience. 'Or do you want me to tell them that you survived several days underwater? That you should be *very* dead, considering your wounds? What do you think they'll do to you if they consider you a warlock or a wizard, or something evil?'

'Would you really do that?'

The crimper left him in no doubt. 'Instead of burning to ash on a pyre, you have only to go to war. Don't be so stupid!'

Nicolas saw the two landsknechts had returned with the net Cramm had called for. *Now I really do need an idea.* 'Do you think you can drag me to battle in that?'

'I will do exactly that if necessary.' With his free hand, Cramm waved the signed contract around. 'I won't hesitate to put a bounty on your head, either, if you run away. I like you and the way you are, Nicolas. We had a lot of fun after the battles looting towns and cities together. But I will not let you defraud me of my money!'

'You will never have to pay that bounty.'

'That's the best thing about it,' Cramm laughed. ' I know that you can best most of those who'd try to catch you – but you'll not have a second of peace any more, no matter what principality or county of the Empire you end up in. Swashbuckler after swashbuckler will show up, every one of them believing they can best you. Huzzah! That will be a life – *not*.'

Nicolas was counting on Cramm not taking this business that far – he was counting on his avarice. Just in case, he would have to pay that bounty one day.

'Here's my offer once again, Joss. Let me go and put my affairs in order, and once that's done, I will return, and I will bring you the money. I will stick to that contract, even if you did guide my hand to sign it while I slept.'

'I did not! You signed it of your own free will. My Brigitta is my witness, willing to swear to it in any court.' He gestured at the two mercenaries with the net to step closer, while two more lowered their pikes at Nicolas to drive him back. *Right towards the audience.*

'I will ask you nicely one last time – otherwise, there will be a bounty on your head.'

The landsknechts he had floored were rising slowly, groaning, holding their cheeks and spitting blood. The number of opponents was growing and the same was true for the audience of onlookers, who had begun betting on the outcome of the confrontation.

I need an idea. Nicolas backed away slowly, using the warehouse wall to his right as cover. 'Joss, you have to know: I used to like you.'

'I liked you, too. Once.'

'Will we still be good friends after this?'

'It depends on you whether we're going to be friends, acquaintances or enemies.' More quickly, Cramm added, 'I don't want to tempt Providence, but you're not going easy on our friendship, my dear.'

'Didn't you call me your best earlier?'

'See? You're rapidly losing my affection.'

'Then let's just wait and see how you will call me when next we meet. Until then, I'll take my leave. Adieu!' Nicolas ran and the tips of the pikes just missed him. With giant leaps, he ran up a stack of huge logs, pushed off them and jumped to the roof of the next warehouse.

Shots were fired, until, amidst the deafening noise, Cramm shouted that no one should shoot the fucking bastard. He yelled, 'I need him alive; do you understand? Alive and kicking, he's worth a lot of coin. Dead, he's worth nothing.'

Nicolas could feel that his wounds had not completely healed. The effort was making him cough, and he could taste river water in his mouth.

The landsknechts down on the ground were following him, urged on by the yelling crimper.

If I can't return to ground level, I'll have to go up. He jumped from the roof to the jib of a cargo crane and pulled himself onto it so he could continue to run above his pursuers.

The mercenaries were poking at his feet and legs with the curved tips of their long pikes, forcing Nicolas to leap over them until he was above the Werra, where a barge was just putting out to sail downstream. *Ah – there's my route to freedom.*

'Don't you dare,' Cramm called, raising his rapier. 'I know what you're up to – remember the bounty, Nicolas!'

'I think everything is said and done between us.' Nicolas raised his hat. 'You will get your money, Cramm, and in the meantime, find others to send to the butcher's block. The battlefield craves fresh meat to shoot and hack to pieces.'

He estimated the distance and jumped down onto a stack of grain sacks. The landing proved to be harder than he'd anticipated, but at least he had escaped the crimper. *For now.*

'Hey, friend!' A sailor was standing less than three feet away, pointing a musket with a glowing fuse at him. A large, snarling dog stood next to the man. 'If you should be thinking of trying to steal my barge—'

'No, no,' Nicolas said at once, raising his arms in surrender. 'Never! Just take me with you for a few miles and then you'll be rid of me. That's all I ask. In the meantime, I'll scrub your deck and give you a helping hand. You have nothing to fear from me.'

'Good. Good, good.' The mariner extinguished the fuse with a well-aimed spurt of spit. 'I can come up with plenty of work for you.'

'Go to Hell, Nicolas!' Cramm was shouting after him from the quay. He laughed loudly. 'I *will* see you again – and then you will be giving me *sixty* per cent of your pay.'

'Agreed – and I'll shove the thalers up your arse one by one so you can keep count of the coins.' Nicolas waved his black velvet hat. 'Until then, buy plenty of grease, Merchant of Death!'

'I will get my way.' Cramm turned his back on the barge and called back his landsknechts. They quickly disappeared between the warehouses.

Nicolas sat down on the pile of sacks as the Werra carried him away from Wanfried. His new destination was Heiligenstadt, where he hoped to find his men – or at least find out where they had gone.

He would never have imagined that his mission for the Company would have turned out like this. It was no longer about getting Agatha and Ursula to Hamburg. He had to free his friends before they died under the influence of the spell the witch had put on them. *They have mutinied for the witch and now they would die for her.*

Then there was the plague doctor, who was playing his own little game – he was probably following the witches too.

'Well, landsknecht,' the sailor called him over, 'grab the scrubbing brush and clean the deck.'

'Of course.' Nicolas went to work earning his passage. It was enough for him to be indebted to Joss von Cramm.

Heiligenstadt, May 1629

'Can you hear me?' Tahmina whispered to Aenlin. 'Are you there, darling?'

When Aenlin heard the familiar voice, her sight clarified, as if a veil had been pulled from her eyes. She blinked, having no idea where she was – she'd just been in the hut, rummaging around in Agatha's chest, and now she was sitting on a foot-stool in a spacious room lined with cots and hammocks. The landsknechts and Caspar were lying in them, fully dressed, with their eyes wide open. Their breathing was soft and regular, so they were not dead.

She could see some of their equipment stacked in a corner, and guessed the other weapons and provisions had been stored in the chests and boxes piled up against the wall. A permeating stench of sweat emanated from her and the men; the food in the half-empty bowls on the tables buzzed with flies. There was also a faint odour of blood.

Nicolas and Tahmina were missing. *By Lucifer! I . . . I just heard her, though?* Fear gripped Aenlin as quickly as her thinking and her sight had returned. *I must have imagined that . . .* She didn't know how much time had passed, nor where she was. *Aid me, Bringer of Light!* she pleaded, slowly rising from the stool. Her limbs felt rusty, unused, and obeyed her only reluctantly.

'Aenlin! Can you hear me? Please, say something.'

Although Aenlin was terrified, she was so happy to hear the voice of her beloved again. 'Yes – where are you? Are you invisible?'

'No. I am using a spell to speak into your mind.'

The mystic had mentioned this skill once, but she'd never used it before. She had said it was exhausting and dangerous, like most of the advanced arts. *If she is risking using it, we must be in real trouble.* 'Where are we? What—?'

Tahmina interrupted her. 'I do not know, but you are under the spell of the women we freed in Bamberg. Agatha and Ursula are more than witches. I have broken the spell, but I cannot completely remove it from you. It is very . . . strong and alien. I need to study it further to completely dispel it. I can only give you a few moments, so you must use them well.'

'Will the spell be broken once the enchantresses are dead?' If that was the case, Aenlin would know what to do.

'Maybe. Maybe not.'

'Then I'll find out what you have to do – or if I can, I will free myself and the landsknechts on my own.' Aenlin now understood why her body felt so sluggish and rebellious; it must be the effect of the spell. Her clothes were dirty and torn – it looked like they hadn't gone easy on her during the journey to wherever they were. She quickly tied back her long hair, except for the one night-black strand that fell into her face. 'I don't see Nicolas. Except for him, everyone is here . . .'

'He is dead.'

Aenlin felt sick. The bad news just kept coming. 'How?'

'His own men killed him – they were under the effects of the witches' spell.' Tahmina quickly summarised what she had heard from Tännel. 'He also said that Agatha, Ursula and Nica want to keep strengthening evil until the Old World can never be freed from the clutches of war and wickedness.'

That didn't sound like the usual accusations against witches and warlocks, Aenlin thought. There was obviously something bigger going on here. But what would the enchantresses get out of it? 'I'm looking around this room – I think this might be an inn. Where are we?'

'Heiligenstadt.'

'What about you?'

'Me too, but ... I would rather not tell you where exactly I am hiding. Just in case Agatha forces you to repeat our conversation to her.' Tahmina sounded depressed. 'I will not be able to suppress the spell for very much longer, darling. Hurry, look around and tell me where you are.'

Aenlin gazed at the unmoving mercenaries on their cots and hammocks, then looked out through the window. Two storeys below was a narrow alley. She pushed a shutter aside and leaned out. 'It is an inn,' she said, 'and the sign says "The Drunkard". We're on the first floor.' Aenlin looked down at herself. She was thinner now, and she could feel a heavy scratch marring her right cheek. *I should eat more.*

She found a dagger and a pistol in a chest holding their weapons and, for want of for a baldric, shoved them under her loose-fitting belt. Slowly she approached the door. 'It's all quiet.' *Very quiet.*

'Be careful! They will act as soon as they notice that you have evaded their spell.' Tahmina's worry was clearly audible in her voice. 'I ... I don't want to lose you.'

Aenlin smiled. Her relationship with Tahmina empowered her. 'I will return to you: I swear this by the Bringer of Light.'

Her legs were still unusually stiff, feeling as if they'd been wrapped in thick bandages. She approached the door, opened it cautiously and listened. Everything was still quiet. *As a grave.* Then an overwhelming stench of blood almost made her step back into the room. *A stench like that stinks like a slaughterfest!*

She stepped onto a gallery overlooking the entrance and looked down into the empty taproom. Neither patrons nor serving staff were visible. The Drunkard must be closed. Carefully, she approached the rail to get a better view, flinching as the floorboards creaked treacherously under her boots.

Aenlin soon saw where the stench of blood was coming from. Naked corpses, of men and women both, were lying next to each other on the bar, each painted grey with ash. They all had been decapitated and had large holes in their torsos. Most of their blood had been gathered in buckets that were standing in front of the bar.

Their hearts have been cut out . . .

Looking around, Aenlin spotted several flayed corpses hanging upside down, tied to the heavy rafters. Below them, red puddles and lines had been formed by their slow swinging backwards and forwards. Their faces, too, had been flayed.

Aenlin was feeling horribly sick; it was taking all her will-power to stop herself from vomiting. Agatha and Ursula had wasted no time in committing new atrocities. 'I think they must have performed a ritual, or they sacrificed to a dark power, or to some demon,' she whispered to Tahmina, describing what she saw. Meanwhile, she cocked her pistol.

Agatha stepped into the taproom from a side door, naked except for a loincloth and the feather cloak. She was in the process of donning a malevolent mask. In her right hand she carried a mace with an obsidian blade. It was wet with fresh blood.

Aenlin ducked behind the rail. 'They are continuing what they have started,' she whispered.

The enchantress put the weapon on the bar and used the blood from one of the buckets to paint on the floor a symbol that vaguely resembled a sun surrounded by a halo. As she worked, Aenlin could just make out something that sounded like muffled incantations or prayers in an unintelligible language issuing from behind the mask of wood and obsidian.

Almost at once, Ursula came in, wearing a wet red cape made from flayed skin; she too wore a dripping mask that had once been the face of another human being. She picked the hacked-out hearts of the decapitated people from the buckets and placed them carefully in the middle of the sun sigil.

Aenlin had never seen such cruelty, nor had she ever read of anything like it in any treatise on magic or worship. 'They are performing an invocation,' she whispered, and she described to Tahmina what she was watching with increasing terror.

When the preparations were finished, Agatha and Ursula stepped into the middle of the blood sun and sat down facing each other. They held hands, raised their arms and started chanting a simple, monotonous melody.

Breathlessly Tahmina asked, 'What are they doing?'

Aenlin described what she saw as exactly and as quietly as she could. With one hand, she clutched the butt of the cocked pistol; it might be useless, but it gave her some security in the middle of this madness. *As if a musket ball could stop this insanity.* She had to forcibly keep down the contents of her stomach.

All at once, the sun symbol glowed as if the day star itself was rising. The hearts smouldered and burned, even with no flames beneath them, while the women's chant increased in volume and pace. The organs finally fell to ash, leaving flickering fire and black smoke rising to the ceiling.

Ursula produced a stoppered bottle containing a clear liquid. She removed the cork and poured the contents on the flames. There was a hiss and a new smell, the odour of salt, permeated the ubiquitous stench of blood.

'I think they must be extinguishing the fire with the tears they collected,' Aenlin whispered, remembering the descriptions of the atrocities they had been accused of committing: *tears of innocent, tortured children.*

Then the shimmer of the blood sun vanished.

Breathing hard, looking exhausted, Agatha and Ursula sank to the floor. Their limbs twitching as if they were possessed, the women rolled about, squirming.

The building trembled slightly, making the hanging bodies sway and the decapitated corpses fall from the bar.

'What was that?' Tahmina asked angrily.

'Did ... did you notice that, too?' Aenlin's finger almost slipped from the trigger guard. As a precaution, she uncocked the pistol.

'It ... must have been noticeable all over Heiligenstadt. What is happening?'

Aenlin looked back between the wooden struts. After the tremor, the Drunkard was quiet again, the only sound the gasping of the witches, who were slowly calming down, recovering from their exhaustion, the twitching stilling. Sweat ran down their bodies and mingled with the blood of their victims.

Nothing else? Aenlin had expected a more spectacular outcome. In fact, she had been expecting the worst. 'There is no demon nor any other dread thing rising from the deep – but maybe they have planted the seed of evil the giant was talking about.'

'So it may arise and pollute the earth and its inhabitants,' Tahmina continued.

Aenlin looked at the dazed women. *A shot to the head, a blade to the heart.* 'It would be easy for me to kill them.' Or to club them to death with their own obsidian weapon.

'No. No, do not kill them just yet. Not before we know how to break their spell. Otherwise, you might die with them.' Tahmina let out a laboured groan. 'I feel that this strange spell is getting stronger again. We will soon lose our connection.'

'Then I will return to the room.' With enormous uneasiness, Aenlin watched Agatha and Ursula getting to their feet and taking off the masks to embrace each other with relief. Obviously, their ritual had been a success.

Aenlin didn't want to be a mindless slave again. She was very tempted to run down the stairs to the taproom and kill the witches. *For the massacre of all these people, and for what they did secretly. For what they have done to me and the landsknechts. For the murder of Nicolas.* Aenlin touched her pistol. 'It would be so easy to destroy them,' she whispered.

'No. Not now. If their death does not break the curse, the third enchantress would always have power over you,' Tahmina said. 'Trust me: I will gather my strength and soon I will be able to free you from your magical chains once again, at least for a while. Let me find a way to completely break the spell. Please! We have no idea how powerful they really are.'

'I am at your mercy.' Still crouching, Aenlin reluctantly returned to the room. It took even more effort to put the pistol and the dagger back into the chest, but her beloved was right. There were too many riddles to solve: who were they, and what were they up to? And they shouldn't forget: they were wanted in Hamburg – why?

'Take care of me, love.'

'I will.'

Tahmina's voice in her head faded, the rest of her loving words blown away as if by a gathering storm.

CAPITULUM XII

Heiligenstadt, June 1629

Another town, like so many others. Nicolas Rourke had walked through the Geisler Gate wearing clothes that wouldn't advertise the fact that he was a landsknecht. On his way there, he had exchanged the distinctive garb that Joss von Cramm had given him for drab, nondescript clothing. The broad brim of his stolen hat ensured more than half his face was in shadow. Only the stolen rapier and pistols would suggest his ability to defend himself. After some pickpocketing at an inn, he also had a few coins.

There was a good reason for his change of clothes, for Catholic Heiligenstadt was another of those places that had once been visited by landsknechts and, ever since, did not care for soldiers, especially not lone mercenaries who could be denied entry or beaten up and thrown bleeding into the bushes.

Or hanged right there from the bridge. Nicolas dared to take a deep breath only once the gate was a few feet behind him and no one had summoned him back.

Bamberg, Hamburg and one or two other cities had impressed him because they were not the usual mix of half-timbered and brick buildings. The façades of Heiligenstadt, however, looked just like everywhere else. *Or maybe I just can't tell the differences.*

He put his hands into his pockets and continued to look around the town, as he had been doing for the last few days, searching for Statius, Jäcklein, Caspar and the enchantresses. He never stayed in the same place twice, sleeping in secret in stables to save what little money he had. Some houses sported repaired beams and walls, the damage probably the result of the soldiers' visit, who had doubtless used every opportunity to grab provisions, to pillage and to loot.

Nicolas was not surprised to find that there was a Jesuit college here. Ever since the Imperial Edict of Restitution, the Counter-Reformation had been picking up pace. Apart from that, he saw the usual: a town hall, granary, a monastery, a wine cellar, a brewery, a general store, various mills sited along the river and watercourses of the city, a priory and some handsome buildings of unknown purpose.

He took note of the location of the most important so he could get his bearings; he had to know how to become invisible quickly, should the city watch come after him. *They have a nice wall. It won't be easy to get through.*

Nicolas considered the behaviour of the inhabitants a good omen: the people on the streets looked neither stressed nor fearful; they were just going about their business.

So far, he had found no hint of those he sought, and the same was true for the plague doctor Cramm – or rather, Cramm's wife – had told him about. *I have never heard of a medico travelling with landsknechts*, he thought.

Tahmina and Aenlin had told him about the mercenaries who had invaded the Hauptsmoorwald and destroyed the witches' grove, so he assumed that the man with the beaked mask was a mercenary leader sent by the Prince-Bishop of Bamberg to get them. Maybe his disguise as a plague doctor helped him to travel unmolested. It didn't, however, make him inconspicuous. *If my investigations in Heiligenstadt continue to be unsuccessful, I can try to track him down instead.*

After turning random corners, Nicolas reached a small market close to St Nikolaus Chapel, where wooden stalls were stacked with bread, sausages and cheese and knife-grinders offered their services, and a newspaper vendor peddled papers, most of which were already many days old.

Nicolas sat down at a small fountain to eat his sweet pastries; he could listen to what people were discussing; it was a safer way to gather information than making enquiries, which often raised suspicion.

Nicolas enjoyed the honeyed pastries, but in the two hours he spent there, he heard only the usual worries about the war, the plague, the soldiers, the exiled Danes, the Swedish threat and the Protestant neighbours. Not a single syllable did he catch referring to his landsknechts, the enchantresses or the plague doctor. Still, he did learn the best of the city's gossip, and there was a lot of excitement about the theft of some relics, for which the Protestants and the Jews were blamed in turn.

What a pity. Nicolas rose and used the water pump next to the washing trough, catching the clear water in his cupped hands to drink, then splashing his neck to cool himself down before rising and turning towards the alley he had come from.

That was when he noticed a girl of maybe fourteen years in a light yellow headscarf, standing at a baker's stall. She was putting several loaves of bread into a big satchel. Her profile looked familiar . . .

That's impossible—! Nicolas stayed close to the cutler's grinding wheel, pulling the brim of his hat down further so she would not recognise him. When the girl turned towards him while she was paying, he no longer had any doubts.

It is . . . ! That's Osanna! What is the serving wench from Altona doing in Heiligenstadt? He couldn't rule out the possibility of her visiting relatives there, but it really was a weird coincidence. *And what if I'm wrong?*

When she had finished packing away the numerous loaves

of bread and started moving quickly across the marketplace, Nicolas followed her.

Osanna went through the narrow streets without ever stopping until she entered an inn through a side door.

It was called Handsome Hans, although both the sign and the building were looking distinctly weather-beaten. The walls sported old scorch marks and holes from musket balls. It surely wasn't the best inn in Heiligenstadt.

Using cracks in the brickwork and wooden rafters, Nicolas climbed a house on the other side of the street until he could look through the window of the inn Osanna had entered. He was in time to see the girl hurrying up the stairs to the first floor, where she entered a room.

It didn't look to Nicholas like a family visit, more like someone had sent her out to get provisions. Inconspicuously.

To find out who was in that guest room, he would have to change position, which meant he'd run the risk of being seen by passers-by on the street, or by patrons of the Handsome Hans. *I'll risk it anyway.*

With a bold leap, he jumped over to the inn.

His boots hit the slate roof with a crash, sending some of the shingles sliding away noisily before shattering down in the alley. Cursing under his breath, he climbed the sloping roof so he could duck down behind the weathered chimney.

No sound came from the derelict-looking inn; it looked like nobody cared about what might be happening on the ramshackle roof.

Next to the chimney was a gaping hole in the beaver-tail tiling; the owner of the house either badly neglected his property – or more likely, had long since fled, maybe because of his unwelcome religion. Nicolas pushed himself through to land in the attic.

Swiftly, Nicolas descended rotting stairs and reached the first floor, where he thought Osanna was. He took off his hat and walked past the closed doors, listening closely, but heard no noise behind any of them – until he reached a room from which Osanna's voice was clearly audible. Instantly, he stopped and pressed his ear against the wood.

'. . . we should wait until the Venetian is back,' she was saying. 'We cannot simply decide to attack the mystic. That is for him to decide!'

'No, Ensign Valentin is right,' a man's voice replied. 'I won't sit on my hands any longer. She knows where to find the witches. What do you think, Barthel?'

At the mention of this name, Nicolas started. If he really had just found the landsknechts whose mission he'd stolen, this series of events was becoming too much of a coincidence. *Was Captain Barthel Hofmeister so angry about this theft that he had followed him here? But how do the serving wench and the plague doctor fit in this picture?*

'I think the Venetian would be happy if we present the Persian Princess to him, nicely bound and gagged, when he arrives in Heiligenstadt,' Barthel answered.

'But she is a magic-user,' Osanna said, 'and you are not. Remember what she did in that clearing. Without me, you would not even know where she is. *I* found her! Valentin, tell—'

'We just have to be quick enough,' said another man, dismissing her objection. 'She doesn't know we're coming.'

'You don't understand how dangerous—'

'Make us some food, girl and then get back to the street,' Barthel said. 'Keep your eyes and ears open – try to find out if anybody has seen those accursed witches and the landsknechts, if anyone knows where they went.'

'You heard the man,' the other one – probably this Ensign Valentin – agreed. 'Coats on as soon as the sun sinks. Ten of you will come with me. Let's go and get this mystic.' He called out the names of those who were to join him on this endeavour. 'Load your pistols with salt – whatever happens, you cannot kill them, or the Venetian will dismember us with his own hands.'

From this, Nicolas concluded, Tahmina was not with Jäcklein and Aenlin, and just as importantly, it sounded like she was free of the spell!

Even as he crouched here, the mystic must be looking for a way to remove the curse from her friend and the mercenaries. But if the Venetian and Barthel's landsknechts should get her, things would become complicated.

Everything will be lost if that happens. Nicolas looked around for an empty, unlocked room on the same floor and found one next to the stairs, into which he retreated. He left the door slightly ajar, so he would be able to watch the landsknechts' room. They would not leave without him noticing.

Nicolas thought about ways to stop Tahmina's abduction, although he didn't really have a lot of options apart from confronting his opponents and eliminating them. He would have to let one of them live so Nicolas could interrogate him. The ensign would have been his first choice.

'"The Venetian",' Nicolas muttered under his breath. Aenlin had told him that was what Franz, the bar lad, had called the plague doctor in the forest. Certainly, he was a man skilled in using and deflecting magic – and somehow, he had met Barthel Hofmeister and his men.

There was a soft, rushing sound above his head as heavy rain started to fall upon Heiligenstadt. The sounds of water gurgling and splashing arose all about the dilapidated building, followed by the smell of rain.

Whistling, a boy carrying two buckets appeared on the stairs. He put one in the corridor, where water was already leaking through the roof and stoically sat down next to it. In just a few minutes the pail was full; he exchanged it for the empty one and poured the collected water out of the nearest window.

Nicolas assumed it was cheaper to give the boy a few kreutzers for his services than to have the roof repaired.

The rain clouds had quickly darkened the sky.

He heard someone say, 'Let's go!' and a dark-haired man, probably the ensign, left the group's barracks. 'You know what to do.'

The men adjusted their big floppy hats and pulled on waxed coachman's coats against the rain. They passed the lad with a friendly word or two, some tousling his hair. One of them gave him a piece of bread, another one a coin.

After they had vanished down the stairs, Nicolas stepped from his hiding place and followed them. *All right, then. Lead me to Tahmina, you thatchgallows.*

Ensign Valentin led them through the evening city, using the narrowest alleys to get to the northern part of the town.

The weather had driven the inhabitants of Heiligenstadt indoors, so there was almost no one on the streets; those few they did meet, the men greeted politely and with friendly smiles, staggering slightly to give the impression of a merry band who had been drinking, but they gave up the mimicry as soon as they thought themselves unobserved.

Nicolas kept his distance. He wasn't wearing a coat and his hat offered extremely limited protection, so he was quickly drenched to the skin after just a minute or two outside.

This is going to be some dance. He'd have to come up with a good strategy if he was going to prevail against eleven experienced fighters, especially since the last man was turning around every few paces to check for pursuers. This was clearly not their first clandestine endeavour.

An especially narrow passage a little way ahead of the group offered the best opportunity Nicolas thought he'd find for an attack. The landsknechts would have to go in single file, as there wasn't room for them to walk side by side.

All right, here we go. Nicolas ran up, drawing his pistol, then took it by the barrel to use as a club. The heavy rain swallowed the noise of his soles on the cobblestones.

He reached the rearmost mercenary without the man noticing him. When the metal-sheathed butt of the pistol hit the man's neck, he collapsed with a *huff*.

Good start.

Nicolas stepped over him and readied himself for the next blow. It connected, too; the landsknecht fell and landed on the hard ground. Nicolas felled the third and fourth men as easily. Like human breadcrumbs, they formed an obvious trail for the night-watchman of the city guard. He imagined they'd be quite surprised.

Nicolas took aim at the fifth man, but the landsknecht must have heard the one behind him fall, because he'd started to turn. He couldn't dodge the pistol butt rushing towards his head, but he was able to shout out a warning before he was clouted and collapsed.

The remaining mercenaries turned to face their attacker.

'God bless you.' Nicolas kicked the man in front of him in the chest with all his might, launching him backwards into his companions. All handicapped by their heavy coats, three other men went down with him as he sagged to the ground.

'I was told you're up to no good.' He ran across the men on the ground, kicking their heads as he went to knock them all senseless. 'I'm afraid I will have to object.'

The last three landsknechts retreated until the alley broadened enough for them to be able to use their weapons. Because of the rain and the relatively harmless salt that had replaced the normal load of lead in their barrels, they didn't resort to their firearms.

Nicolas drew his blade, but didn't sheath his own pistol, instead holding it straight out in front of him. 'Which one of you is Valentin?'

'You know my name, yet you don't know who I am. Strange.' The ensign took half a step towards him and looked him up and down. With his hat and his tight-laced leather collar, his face was barely visible. 'What kind of a jerk are you to mess with us?'

'My name is Nicolas. You witch-hunters from Bamberg will

not be hurting my friend Tahmina.' The tip of his rapier moved across the trio, searching for a target, parting the droplets that fell onto the blade's razor-sharp edge. 'Who wants to give it a try?'

'What kind of bird are you? I didn't see you in the clearing.' Valentin was trying to understand who his opponent was. 'What's your business with the mystic?'

'What's it to you?'

'You've only attacked us because of her – that's reason enough to ask.' Valentin's two men had spread out to the left and to the right of him, ready to attack the stranger from three sides.

'Why is Osanna with you?'

Now Valentin really was baffled. 'You know the serving wench?' He took a closer look under the broad rim of his opponent's hat – and understood. 'By the Almighty! You're the dead mercenary! But we threw you into the river – weighted down with rocks!' He took a step backwards and crossed himself, quickly followed by the other two. 'May all the saints help us: you must come right out of Hell!'

Nicolas tried to hide his surprise. *So they really have followed us – and they found me. And they wanted to drown me.* 'I'll be sending you all there if you don't tell me where I can find Tahmina.'

Valentin looked deeply terrified. 'How is that even possible? You had no heartbeat – you weren't breathing – and we spent at least another half an hour on the banks of the Werra without—'

'*Where* is Tahmina?' Nicolas asked sharply. He aimed his pistol at the leader's head. 'Unlike yours, this pistol does not contain salt.'

'My, my! He has been paying attention. You must have followed Osanna.' Valentin whistled to call his men back. When they joined him again, he asked, 'Why did you steal the Company mission from us in Altona?'

'Why do you travel with the Venetian?'

'Because he pays well.'

'Yes, but why are you travelling across the Empire? To find

us?' Saying the words aloud, it made very little sense to Nicolas. 'For your employer, this is about Aenlin and Tahmina, yes?'

'That doesn't matter. For me and Barthel, this about you and yours. Of course, we were lucky to meet the Venetian.' Valentin's eyes rolled back in his head so that their whites were clearly visible, and his two companions did the same. In a different, ghostly voice, he said, 'His pay is worth so much more than gold.'

Their faces suddenly turned grey, while the bones of their cheeks, foreheads, noses and chins turned black, becoming visible under their skin, making their heads look positively skull-like. Small, slit pupils became visible in the white of their eyes. Each of the mercenaries appeared to be inhabited by a second being, a demonic creature that was now showing its true colours. At the same time, the blades of their rapiers and swords started glowing, vaporising drops of water with a hiss. A little mist formed on the blades' gleaming surfaces.

Real demon warriors! Nicolas had no intention of fleeing, but he inwardly congratulated himself on having felled the other opponents before the demons took over. As humans, they were much more easily subdued.

'You picked the wrong man for your tricks!' Nicolas cried as he fired, really hoping that the powder on the priming pan had not got too wet.

Sparks flew, smoke rose and a ball hit the mercenary who had quickly stepped in front of his leader.

The ball tore a hole in his body and coughing hoarsely, the man collapsed to the wet cobblestones between Valentin and Nicolas. At the same instant, everything unearthly about him disappeared, until his normal eyes were staring sightlessly into the evening sky. Hissing angrily, his glowing rapier was extinguished in the cooling rain.

'What . . . what have you done?' Valentin cried out.

'I shot him. What would you call it?' Nicolas retorted.

'But you should not ... Ah! You too have been ensorcelled! Was it the Passau Art? Or was that an infernal musket ball?' Valentin stabbed at him with his glowing blade, shouting, 'Die!'

What does he mean by that? Nicolas wanted to deflect the glowing rapier with the barrel of his pistol, to duck underneath the blow and stab his own blade into Valentin's heart, but when the rapier and pistol clashed, there was a shrill shriek – and the front part of the firearm clattered to the cobblestones, neatly sheared off.

The glowing blade advanced unopposed and pierced Nicolas' right side.

At once, searing pain flooded him. The wound wasn't lethal – the blade hadn't penetrated his side, just caught a glancing blow, but the added pain from the searingly hot metal threatened to bring him to his knees. With a loud cry, Nicolas dodged the next attack and staggered backwards into the narrow alley.

Valentin and his remaining mercenary pursued him, their slit-pupilled eyes shimmering faintly. Their blades, still with that reddish shine, sliced through almost everything they touched; even on metal and stone, they left a deep notch.

Nicolas tripped over the unconscious landsknechts, which gave him an idea. He quickly dropped the useless rapier, bent down and took two of the defeated men's pistols. *Better than nothing.* He fired at Valentin and his companion.

They could not escape the stinging hail of salt, which tore holes in their skin and eyes. The wounds might not have been lethal, but it was enough to blind his opponents.

'Goat-fucker!' Valentin poked for him blindly.

Nicolas focused on the ensign's arm and kicked at it from below, making Valentin's hand jerk to the side and stab the lethal weapon through the throat and shoulder of the landsknecht next to him. The glowing blade went through flesh and bone like a warm knife through butter and Nicolas' next opponent dropped dead, killed by his own leader.

'If you kill me, you will never know where this mystic is,' Valentin shouted, pointing the glowing blade forward. It was hissing, the blood and water on it boiling away. He rubbed his wide eyes, which were leaking pink fluid from where the salt had damaged them. 'Let me go.'

'I will find her without you.' Nicolas threw away the pistols and took loaded ones from the holsters of the next two men on the ground. 'What did this Venetian turn you into?' He quickly pushed ball from his ammunition pouch into both muzzles and shot the ensign in the thigh.

The waxed cloth of his coat and his puffy breeches couldn't stop the mixture of lead and salt. With a scream, Valentin buckled. 'How the fuck did you do that?'

'The next ball will hit your groin if you don't—'

'Go to Hell!' Jerking up his left hand, Valentin raised a pistol that he had taken from the holster of one of the unconscious landsknechts without Nicolas noticing. He dropped, shot in the middle of his movement, but at the same time stretched out his arm, pointing the glowing blade at Nicolas' chest.

Bastard! The grains hit Nicolas, most of them striking his face. He barely managed to close his eyes in time, but he couldn't dodge the steel. The glowing rapier pierced Nicolas just below his sternum.

This kind of pain was new to him, for all he had suffered half a dozen bad wounds on the battlefield.

Is this my death, finally? Nicolas fell to his knees, bringing his face to the same height as that of his opponent, who was staring at him, blinking. Nicolas could not speak.

'Don't tell me you are unkillable!' The angry words escaped from Valentin' mouth. 'We sacrificed a lot for our gifts! How about you?' He tore out his blade and stabbed Nicolas a second time. 'What did *you* sacrifice?'

The glowing rapier pierced Nicolas' heart and again, the pain was indescribable. The muscle had stopped moving. His body was petrified, but he continued thinking, *I must fight back.*

'No! No, that . . .' Valentin tore out the blade and saw the blood on it vaporising. 'Who do you serve? Who do you serve, fucking dog? What did you swear, to get such immortality?'

Immortality? The burning metal had barely left his heart when Nicolas felt a tickle and a tug. The small wound within him healed and his heart started beating again. The holes in his chest and back had closed, too.

Nicolas sank against the wall, breathing hectically. *How does this work?* Everything tasted and smelled of blood. Even if he had narrowly escaped the Grim Reaper, he felt unable to fight back.

Meanwhile, Valentin had managed to get up, and stood unsteadily in front of him, cursing. 'Well then: I will slice you apart and burn every single shred of you! Then I'll go to the Dovecote and grab that Persian bint – and the Venetian will be proud of me.'

The glowing tip of his blade approached Nicolas' right eye. 'I might just pierce this one for now and see what happens. I'll shove my blade up into your brain to incinerate it, so I can watch the smoke pouring out of your ears and nose!' Valentin laughed grimly. 'You should not have stolen our mission.'

Must. Fight. Back! With an extreme effort, Nicolas raised his second pistol as high as he could in his weakened state and shot the salt load into Valentin's groin.

Including the lead ball.

Heiligenstadt, June 1629

'Can you hear me? Are you there, my love?'

Aenlin felt huge relief as the terrible curse lifted from her will and she heard Tahmina's soft voice in her mind again. The same words as before. She sighed.

She was lying on a cot inside the same room of the inn where she had awakened the first time. So the group hadn't left the city, although she had no idea how much time had passed since her last lucid moments, or what had happened in the meantime.

'I praise you, Lucifer,' Aenlin whispered. She had to use every minute free of the *geas* to collect knowledge about her enemies. 'Thank you, beloved!'

'Sorry it took me so long.'

Aenlin could hear her contrition and exhaustion.

'This curse is keeping me enormously occupied. It is like nothing I have ever seen, not in what I have read, nor in my studies. We know almost nothing about the magic of the New World, but I think that is what this is.'

Aenlin thought about what she was saying. 'Good. I can try to reach the chest and—'

'What is it you keep mumbling to yourself?' Statius' voice said, right next to her. 'This doesn't feel like a dream to me.'

Startled, Aenlin turned to face the landsknecht, who was sitting on a chair, naked to the waist, his booted feet propped up. He was carving a small bone that looked like it had come from a human skeleton. He had slicked back his hair with scented oil; only at the back of his neck were some curls still visible. Tahmina had not mentioned that she had freed anyone else from the spell – but even if she had, she would not have chosen this man of all the potential candidates.

'No, Statius,' Aenlin replied, hoping Tahmina would understand what was happening. 'I am not dreaming, and neither are you.' *Has his mind broken free on its own? Or is he a guard, set on us by the witches?*

Jäcklein, Caspar and Moritz were lying fully dressed on their beds, their eyes wide open, gazing into space, obviously still under Agatha's control.

The heavyset man was still whittling away at the bone. 'Well, shit in my boots! They've chosen you, too? If I'd had to bet, my money would be gone by now.' Statius looked out of the window, where it was raining cats and dogs. 'This is what they call spring here. It's supposed to become an ocean, or maybe a deluge, washing evil away into the rivers.'

Chosen? Aenlin straightened and took a seat. The smell of sweat told her the witches didn't bother to make those they'd bewitched wash themselves or change their clothes, but Statius was wearing clean clothes and he'd washed and trimmed his beard, and washed his shirts too, which she could see were all hanging up to dry.

'Aenlin,' Tahmina asked, 'what is happening there? Is this creature not under their spell any more?'

'No,' she answered, looking at the landsknecht.

'You don't think so?' Statius took her word as an answer to what he had said. 'Well, I don't give a flying fuck. We won't be stuck in this fucking city for very much longer.' He regarded her, twirling the tips of his moustache. 'Why did they choose you? Because you're Solomon Kane's daughter?'

'Probably.'

'Is it true what they say about your father? That he's been to Africa to kill blood-drinkers, demons and other creatures of evil?' Statius blew on his creation, then dropped it to the floor and smashed it under his boot heel. The scars on his chest and shoulders twitched as his muscles stretched. 'Shit! I am just not good at this. Moritz makes it look so easy. Well, my profession will always be killing.'

'Just like mine.' Aenlin nodded, trying to smile grimly while also trying to understand exactly what had happened. *Statius is not under any spell. He must have joined Agatha and Ursula of his own free will, lured by the atrocities the enchantresses are committing.* 'The killing of demons,' she concluded.

'I assumed that's why they chose you. The Persian wouldn't have been suitable, even if she can do some nice tricks. Good thing we're rid of her.' Statius rose, took a shirt from the back of a chair and put it on. 'Come. Let's go down and ask—'

'I still feel nauseous. Maybe I haven't eaten enough. I really wouldn't want to look weak and powerless in front of the mistresses.' Pretending to be dizzy, she sank back to the bed. 'Distract me a little, Statius, until I'm feeling a bit better. What do you think of their plans?'

'I like them – otherwise, I would long since have killed and flayed them, just like they do their victims.' Statius laughed darkly and adjusted his shirt, pulling up the wide sleeves. 'For me, there can't be enough war, in Europe and all over the world! I'll go from battle to battle, killing and amassing riches.' He produced his knife and cleaned his fingernails, sending flecks of dried blood drifting to the floorboards. 'If this works out, I'll soon have my own little realm – and I will rule by the grace of Tzontemoc! Oh, that will be fun! Bloody fun!' He paused. 'Tell me, has your father ever been there?'

Tzontemoc? Who is that? A man? A demon? A prince – but from where? And how did he come to be in the Empire? 'Where?'

'In the land of the Aztecs, of course.'

Of course – the New World! Aenlin tried not to show her excitement. 'No, he has never been there, I don't think. I never met my father, so everything I know about him I had to read or to hear from my mother. But she didn't talk much about him. Aztecs are foreign to me.'

'Same here. I didn't even know they existed. Them and their gods ... Thrice-whisked pigshit, I can't pronounce or even remember their damned names! I sound even more like a village idiot whenever I try.' Statius balanced his knife on his freshly cleaned finger. 'But no matter if it's Tzontemoc or Tlaloc or whatever they are called – do you know what I like best?'

'Hmmm?'

'That they demand cruel sacrifices – that they scream for blood. For lives. They want skulls and garbs made of human skin and the tears of the innocent.' Statius whispered all of this in clear admiration. 'Now these are gods! Think about their rituals, the suffering of the victims – not like Jesus, who meekly let himself be nailed to the cross like a stupid lamb. Not like this toothless Christian God from the New Testament, nor like the old Germanic deities. No, Aenlin, these are gods after my fashion!' He raised his strong, callused hands. There was dried blood deeply embedded in some of the lines and crevices. 'They are so simple. They fill me to the bottom of my rotten soul. I am an Aztec, through and through.'

'Well, killing will remain your job, Statius. I come into play when the demons show up, like that naiad, or anything else that wants to stop us.' Aenlin played calm while her mind whirled. *I hope Tahmina is getting the gist of my words.*

Statius rubbed his hands together, making little red flakes rain down on the floor. 'That's good. We'll need clever people like you, what with everything that's going on around here.'

'Why do you say that?' Aenlin hoped that her enquiries didn't sound too dumb. 'I thought . . .'

'I didn't completely get it myself, but as far as I understand, these are good times for idolaters, dark cults and monstrous creatures, witches being the most harmless amongst them. Our home-grown witches at least. Not Gatchen and Ula.' Statius wiped his fingers clean. 'The country is crawling with them, and they're gathering their followers. For now, they're living amongst us undetected, but soon they'll rise and create even more chaos in Europe.' He took a deep breath and howled with joy. It sounded completely inhuman. 'This is my time, Aenlin! *Mine!*' The enormous muscles of his arms and chest bulged under his shirt. 'Let the Aztecs have their revenge, planting the seeds of evil and resentment in our soil – and I will gladly help them.'

Aenlin was frantically trying to work out how to ask further questions without Statius realising that she wasn't on his side. How much did he truly know about the witches' plans? Had Agatha and Ursula completely disclosed the truth to him? 'I really understand this thirst for revenge,' she said.

'Who of sound mind wouldn't? We conquered and destroyed their home, stole their treasures, defiled their temples and took away their gods. We turned them from a proud people to a broken one and in return, they are now bringing us destruction and suffering. In the end, I will feel like a saint, helping the oppressed.' Again he laughed out loud, as if he were intoxicated. 'Saint Stats! Pray to him, or sacrifice yourself to him!'

So this is what they are up to! The Aztecs want to weaken Europe and cause its downfall. As much as Aenlin understood the rage and the hatred that the inhabitants of the New World must have felt for their tormentors, she could not let a whole continent fall into utter ruin. 'That's how they convinced me, too,' she agreed for the sake of appearances. 'How long will we stay in Heiligenstadt?'

'Only until the last sacrifices are made. Then Heiligenstadt will bear another seed for the eternal war.' Statius sounded overjoyed. 'They should be done by this evening, so tomorrow we'll be setting off again.'

Aenlin tried a wild guess. 'I always wanted to go to Hanover.'

'Did they tell you that's where we are going?'

'I ...' *Fuck. I was wrong.* She pressed her hand against her forehead. 'Oh dear, I think I mixed that up.'

'Ah, good. For a moment there I was afraid I had a memory like a sieve.' Statius looked at the wet shutters, watched the raindrops running down. 'This weather is shittier than a cow's arse. Unsuitable for comfy travelling.'

'Where are we travelling?'

'Wernigerode.'

'Ah, yes, to meet the third witch,' Aenlin guessed again. 'Nica, who fled from the Hauptsmoorwald by her own efforts.'

This time, Statius frowned. 'No, Nica has her own plans.' He turned to her. 'You know what I've noticed? You're asking an awful lot of questions, Aenlin Kane, particularly for a chosen one who should know what's coming.'

'I know, I know. I'm sorry. My head is really suffering from the after-effects of the spell they put on us,' she said contritely. *I must be more careful.* 'Help me out here so I won't disgrace myself before the mistresses.' She pushed the rebellious strand of midnight-black hair behind her ear and smiled.

Statius took a seat again and started moving his chair towards her. The wood creaked under his weight. 'Let's try it the other way around, shall we? Do you remember that we killed Nicolas? All together?'

'No! Me, too?' Aenlin was shocked. *I have already aided them?*

'When Agatha put her spell on us. All right, something different, then. What do you remember about the things they have revealed to you?'

'That we . . . must plant more seeds in the Old World.'

'Where are the other disguised Aztecs?'

'What do you mean by—?'

'In which countries?'

'Ah. Well, in . . . France. Sweden and . . .' Aenlin touched her temple. *He knows I'm trying to fool him.* The group's weapons were lined up in an open crate behind the mercenary. To reach a pistol, she'd have to get past him. 'It's hazy.'

Statius didn't tell her whether she had answered correctly. 'Who wanted them brought to Hamburg? Do you remember that?'

Aenlin was afraid to drift into a completely wrong direction with her answers and give away that she knew nothing. 'I think . . . I think . . .'

'Don't over-exert yourself. Another simple one: Why is their skin the same colour as ours, although they are Aztecs?' Statius dug deeper. 'Do you remember this secret?'

'Oh dear, oh dear.' Aenlin laughed anxiously. *I must stop answering him.* 'Good that we have spoken, Stats. I think I'll lie down again and hope that sleep will bring everything back. Please don't tell the mistresses that I'm so confused.'

Statius nodded understandingly. 'I'd better not talk about any of this, then?'

'That would be best.'

'Well then, I won't.' Statius rose from his chair and sat down on the bed next to her. 'What's in it for me, though?' He put his hand on her thigh. 'I mean, what if they doubt you and sacrifice you? Your life would certainly appease the gods. And it's a privilege to be sacrificed to them.'

'Let's leave it at my gratefulness for now. My body is not to your taste.' Aenlin squinted at the weapons chest. *If I jumped up very quickly, I might just make it. He mustn't grab me.*

'I'm a mercenary and I want my pay – I get paid for *everything* I do for others. Or don't do.' One hand was moving upwards over her breeches; with the other, he forcefully spread her legs. 'Since I can't fuck your little Persian, you'll do. Don't you worry about my taste. You'll be just as good as any other woman.'

Aenlin wanted to answer him, but the Aztec spell was getting stronger again. She could no longer move her lips. *O Lucifer, no!*

'I will be tender; I won't overwork your cunny with my thick cock – and once you've got used to it, you'll be wanting it all the time.'

Aenlin lost control of her body and mind. *No! No, not now! Bringer of Light, I implore thee—!*

In her panic, she felt Statius opening her laced-up shirt.

'Good, you're not rejecting me. Wise of you. Otherwise, I would have just taken what you owe me.'

Then Aenlin's world was extinguished.

To Dierdorf, June 12.

A bad country full of words and wilderness. Here we got rations not even the dogs wanted to eat.

Here I drank a little in the evening and was a stone's throw behind the regiment the next morning.

There were three farmers in the hedgerow who gave me a sound beating and took my coat, my backpack, everything.

So I reached the regiment all battered, but they only laughed at me.

from the diary of the mercenary Peter Hagendorf, entry from 1642

'The villages were burned down, demolished and brought to the camp, for [the soldiers] had to bake and brew with the wood. In Stausebach, forty-one buildings were demolished. Twenty-seven remained standing. Not a single farm remained intact. They demolished the roofs everywhere and inside, they smashed and devastated everything in a way that no one was able to live there any more. Three of my buildings were demolished as well.'

Notes by the farmer Caspar Preis, 1673

CAPITULUM XIII

Heiligenstadt, June 1629

Tahmina ran through the city as fast as she could. She had lost the connection to her beloved, and if she had understood the conversation with Statius correctly, Aenlin was in terrible danger. Tahmina might have heard only her beloved's side of the conversation, but that was enough to connect the dots. *I must act – in this magical stasis, she has no will of her own.*

She had left the Dovecot, the inn where she'd been staying, and now ran towards the Drunkard to intervene, no matter what the New World enchantresses might throw against her.

She had mended her robe and cleaned off most of the stains, with only some slight shadows remaining as memories of the giant's blood, but her robe and hood were no protection against the rain. Tahmina held her staff tightly; its sigils were glowing softly in preparation for what was to come. She didn't feel adequately prepared: in this plan, there were no djinni she could ask for help, and she knew of none comparable in the Empire. She could rely only on herself, her staff and her Yatu magic.

First, Tahmina intended to break the spell that the landsknechts were under so they could help her. She could only hope that afterwards, her powers would be enough to prevail against Agatha and Ursula.

The rain scourged her face and her robe grew heavy and wet, entangling her legs, but Tahmina would not be stopped.

Aenlin must not be harmed, especially not by Statius, who had obviously sided with the strange witches. *Small wonder, for he is a creature of cruelty.*

She reached the inn. Its shutters were closed and the plague mark was displayed on the main door, which would keep people from entering against the owners' will. But she could see candles burning in some of the windows, light falling through the cracks between the shutters. No other inhabitant of Heiligenstadt was aware of what happened behind those shutters.

As Tahmina carefully approached the inn, she started looking for a way to get inside. The room where Aenlin had had her conflict with Stats was on the first floor. *But where exactly?* she thought desperately. She considered using her detection spell, but that would run the risk of Agatha and Ursula noticing her too soon and she would lose the element of surprise.

Tahmina's imagination persisted in showing her the most atrocious images of things the brutal landsknecht would be doing to her defenceless beloved. Without the curse, Aenlin would have been able to defend herself, but under the spell, she was just a plaything for that terrible man.

Tahmina felt the intense magical aura surrounding the inn: Agatha and Ursula had performed rituals and sacrifices to plant something poisonous in the soil and in the minds of the people of Heiligenstadt: hatred, evil, malice.

Did they do something else, as well? Many centuries ago, this settlement had been called Zuenchen, an old word for a grove. In an ancient century – older than the Christian God, dating from before the so-called demon had been exorcised – churches and religious symbols had been erected and the city had been renamed. Holy relics of several saints had been brought here to fend off evil.

Tahmina prepared to climb the outside of the inn so she could get in through the first open window. She shoved her staff into her belt so it rested against her back, leaving both hands free. The climb through the wind and pounding rain was exhausting, but at last she managed to climb inside. She was standing in an empty room, her staff in her right hand, when a loud rumbling arose behind her. *By the djinni, what—?*

A wet hand touched her shoulder and another one covered her mouth to stop her from crying out or casting a spell.

'It's me: Nicolas,' a man whispered behind her. 'You were just too quick on the streets for me to catch you up.' He took away his fingers and stepped into the faint light filtering in through the windows. 'See?'

Tahmina fought down her surprise. 'It is . . . it is really you!' She had no doubt whatsoever, for she recognised the mysterious, unreadable aura surrounding him. *A miracle!* She saw the fresh slashes in his clothes, and the blood. 'How did you—?'

'I found the Venetian and sent eleven of his people to Hell,' he whispered. 'Let's do the same to the enchantresses. We can discuss the rest later.'

'Don't be surprised if your own men don't recognise you, or even attack you. They are under Agatha's spell.' Tahmina was happy to have the captain back, no matter how he had pulled off his return from the dead. That could wait. 'This way.'

She opened the door and walked out, trying to ignore her soaking wet robe, even though it was hampering her movements.

The stench of decay and blood took her breath away. Choking, she had to force herself not to vomit as Nicolas coughed softly.

Through the rails, they could see traces of the massacres and sacrifices: the flayed bodies hanging; bashed-in skulls strung up over the rafters. This taproom had been the stage for an orgy of violence beyond anything Tahmina could ever have imagined.

In the middle of the room was a large cauldron that the enchantresses appeared to be using as a brazier. Even from up here, they could see it held charred human remains.

'There.' Nicolas pointed at something next to the cauldron. 'What's that?'

Tahmina didn't want to explore this place of bestial cruelties any further. She had to save Aenlin from Statius. But at Nicolas' words, she looked down. The shattered, empty containers next to the brazier bore Christian symbols.

'They burned the relics,' she whispered in a terrified voice. They had robbed the city of their most valuable patron saints. Sergius and Bacchus, Aureus and Justinus had been destroyed. 'Hurry up – we must leave here as quickly as possible!'

'Not without my men.' Nicolas raised his head and listened. 'Can you hear that?' Drawing his rapier, he pushed Tahmina aside and approached a door, from beyond which came a soft male voice. 'That's Stats!' With that, he opened the door and hurried into the room.

Tahmina was on his heels, her head full of Yatu spells ready to use at in an instant.

Statius was lying halfway over Aenlin; her top was open and he was grabbing her breasts roughly. Her soft white skin was covered in bite marks. His breeches were open and pushed down to his knees, but he had not yet gone any further. He was so drunk, he didn't notice the mystic and the captain.

'Stats! Get your hands off her!' Nicolas ran to the man and grabbed him by his shirt collar to drag him off his helpless victim.

With a thud, the surprised mercenary landed on the rough floorboards. He stared up at his commanding officer in horror. '*Nicolas?*'

Tahmina was unutterably relieved that they had arrived in time. She would have dearly loved to beat the rapist to death with her staff, but first, she had to check on Aenlin.

Statius was staring incredulously at his captain. 'Fuck my arse with a carrot! You . . . you did it again! You escaped the reaper!'

With a fake laugh, he pretended to be shocked when he looked at Aenlin. 'What have I done? They . . . they made me do it. The enchantresses!' He rose, pretending to be furious. 'You know how they try to control our minds. Otherwise, we would have never attacked you in that hut and—'

'He lies! He has switched sides.' Tahmina knelt on the floor next to her friend and concentrated on lacing up her top. She hated Statius with all her heart. Never before had she felt such disgust for a human being, not even for her former master. 'Aenlin told me so before he attacked her. He is in league with the witches.'

Once Aenlin was dressed, she turned her attention to the resting landsknechts and her beloved, trusting in the captain to have her back while she tried to lift the spell.

Nicolas aimed the tip of his rapier at Statius' throat. A drop of water fell from the handguard, ran along the blade to drip onto the man's skin. 'Is she telling the truth?'

'You believe this nonentity more than me?' The mercenary rose, pulled up his breeches and started lacing them closed. 'We've fought in so many—'

'Then why are you not under their spell?'

'When you dragged me off Aenlin, it grew weaker. Agatha's getting sloppy.' Statius' lie was audible. 'They've their hands full with their fucking rituals.' He pulled out his rapier and slicked back his oiled hair. 'Come on! Let's bring them down – once they're dead, the spell our friends are under will be broken.' He went past Nicolas and opened the door. 'What are you waiting for?'

'Do not go,' Tahmina said, pressing the tip of her staff against Aenlin's forehead. 'He will try to kill you again.'

Nicolas watched his companion, trying to look him in the eye. Without a word, the two strong men faced each other.

Ōrmozd, help me. When Tahmina started the counter-spell

for demonic possession, the symbols began glowing, hissing as she repeated her invocation. Aenlin's expression changed; her open eyes focused, turning towards the mystic. The symbols were quickly changing colour as the counter-spell broke the foreign enchantresses' curse.

'Ōrmozd, I call on thee and charge thee: restore the light within her.' Tahmina let power from her body and her mind flow into the magic staff to help it work.

It is going to be a challenge freeing the other landsknechts. It will take a lot of time and patience and we have neither . . .

'Darling,' Aenlin's voice was weak. 'You found me.'

Tahmina's throat constricted; tears of joy welling in her eyes. 'Yes. I have found you.' She removed the tip of her staff from Aenlin's forehead and carefully kissed her.

Neither Statius nor Nicolas saw the intimate display of affection, for they were still facing each other, locked in a staring contest.

'Nicolas is alive? But Statius said we'd killed him.' Aenlin straightened and noticed her loosely laced blouse and the bite marks on her skin. She looked at Statius in horrified anger, then jumped off the cot and grabbed her blade from the weapons chest. *'You traitor!'* she cried. 'You've joined them so you can indulge in your own cruelty! You wanted to—'

Statius gave up on his bad acting, turned and fled out of the room, shouting, 'She's here! The Persian bint is here!' He jumped over the railing and fell to the ground floor with a loud crash. He hit a table, which collapsed noisily under him. 'We're under attack!' he yelled.

'Tahmina, free my men,' Nicolas shouted, taking the pistols from the chest and examining them. *'Now!'*

'Meanwhile, we will take care of the enchantresses.' Aenlin found her baldric and fastened the straps. She kissed Tahmina again, touching her cheek. 'Let's conquer evil: here and now!'

Without warning, a violent impact shook the inn, making the

rafters tremble; dust and chips of wood rained down from every crack, while outside, roof tiles were falling past the window and shattering noisily on the wet cobblestones.

There was a dark moaning and rumbling, followed by a continuous trembling, shaking the building to its core, as if a monster was rattling its foundation.

They heard wooden floorboards bursting apart in the tap-room.

'Your men will have to wait.' Resolutely, Tahmina raised her staff and followed Aenlin and Nicolas, who were looking down into the room below them.

Ōrmozd, grant me your *succour*.

Where the sacrificial cauldron had stood there was now a gaping hole, from which purple and dark blue light issued, with plumes of white, grey and brown billowing forth; the stench reminded Tahmina of festering wounds. The soil around the edges of this abyss was steadily trickling down, so the hole was growing steadily larger.

'Agatha and Ursula have destroyed the protection of the saints and summoned a creature from the New World,' Tahmina said, terrified. 'If I don't stop this, the whole city will be wiped out!'

Nicolas raised his pistol and fired at Statius. He ducked behind the bar, which was piled high with carcasses. 'How could you, Stats?' His ball hit a corpse, tearing a hole in the rotting flesh. 'You will not escape me!'

'It's you who's on the wrong side,' Statius replied from his noxious cover. 'You're like me, Captain: you can't exist without war and battles. You *are* war. I saw it with my own two eyes. Join us and ride with us from battle to battle. Who could hurt you? Who could kill you?'

'I'll see what's waiting for us.' Aenlin hurried down the stairs.

'Death. Nothing else.' One of the witches appeared from a side door, wearing a dress made of stiff, dried-out flayed skin.

The jacket made of feathers was draped around her shoulders and a giant confection of exotic feathers graced her head. A mask, also made of human skin, didn't quite cover the eye area; it revealed that her opponent was Agatha. She was wearing the crudely fashioned golden and bejewelled clasps and bracelets.

'You will go down together with Heiligenstadt, and horror will thrive. We will soon be wreaking our revenge against our oppressors!' In her right hand, she held the paddle-like club with the obsidian blades; in her left was the obsidian knife.

Statius joined her, levelling his rapier at Nicolas. 'My offer to you won't be open for very much longer, Captain. They would love you to join them, God of War.' He pointed at the hole in the floor with the tip of his blade. 'Otherwise, that's where you'll be going.'

'Where's Ursula?' Aenlin looked around in alarm. 'Has she fled? Or is she preparing an ambush?'

What are they summoning? Tahmina could feel the malice crawling up through this maw of Hell – and she could see the magical bond forming between the foreign enchantress and the approaching demon; it would be there until the creature was fully summoned; only then would Agatha be able to use her powers for more black magic. *All her power is channelled into the invocation – for now.*

'Attack the enchantress!' she ordered, '*quickly!*'

'My true name is Simia and I am a priestess,' Agatha shouted at her. 'I am the chosen priestess of my people, empowered to see to it that there will be no rest in Europe for ever more.' She raised her arms, showing off her bloodied weapons. 'No mercy! No quarter! There will be no peace for you!'

The shaking became more intense, the rumbling turned into a thundering snort and greenish-black flames shot forth from the abyss. A paw-like hand appeared, long claws piercing the boards and the soil beneath.

'Hurry!' Tahmina raised her staff above her head and closed her eyes. Using a Yatu formula, she created a spell to exorcise evil djinni and devas. She would soon find out if it was of any use against a demon from the New World. What an irony that it was not the Christian God who came to the rescue in Heiligenstadt's hour of need, but one of a completely different faith.

Ōrmozd, bring the light!

'Take care,' yelled Nicolas, who moved swiftly to stand behind Tahmina. Weapons rang as he started fighting.

Although Tahmina's eyes were closed, she had an idea of what was happening: the priestess had woken Jäcklein, Moritz and Caspar and was making them attack their captain – again.

'Hurry up, mystic!' Nicolas huffed. 'I'm not sure how much longer I can keep them at bay.'

Tahmina intensified her formulae, repeating them over and over, her voice getting louder with every repetition: Ōrmozd, friend and protector of good, enemy of lies and avenger of injustice. She raised her staff above her head like a beacon; its engravings and ornaments blazing brightly in the murky light of the taproom. *Do not let darkness triumph!*

Suddenly, there was a crack behind her.

A glowing pain went straight through Tahmina's torso, but she kept up her spell, even as she tasted blood in her mouth.

Her heart beating fast, Aenlin ran towards Agatha, who stood ready with her obsidian weapons drawn. She was hell-bent on defeating her dangerous enemy, but Statius stood in her way, as solid as a wall.

She ignored the fact that she didn't have much experience, relying instead on her countless hours of training, and hoping that her father's talents would manifest themselves when she needed them most. There was no way back, in any case.

Statius raised his rapier and his dagger. 'I will not kill you, but I will strike you down,' he hissed, his eyes full of desire and malice, 'then I will take what you denied me earlier.'

'That won't be possible without your dick!' Aenlin didn't know if her pistols were loaded, so she drew one of her stilettos from the wide baldric covering her chest, reaching for the second even as she threw the first at her opponent.

Statius dodged the first blade, but the second one found his left shoulder. He cried out, 'I will fuck you to death, you frigging harlot!' He tore the blood-drenched stiletto from his flesh. 'And afterwards, I will sacrifice your heart to my new gods!'

From the abyss next to him, a second monstrous hand appeared. The rumbling and snarling of a gargantuan angry cat came from the Hell-maw as the ground shook once more, even worse this time – then everything went suddenly still.

'What in Lucifer's name—?'

Aenlin dodged to one side as the tips of a vast feather head-piece in various shades of green appeared above the edge of the abyss. What followed from the hole were several long horns, until finally what appeared was a horned jaguar's head, thrice the size of a horse skull, its ears laid back, its fangs bared threateningly.

The massive creature, a hybrid of man and animal, heaved itself energetically from the deep until its head touched the ceiling. A shield magically appeared in its left hand, while its right hand suddenly wielded a club-like staff studded with obsidian blades, like the one Agatha held. Its muscles were thick as interwoven ropes.

A demon from the New World! Instead of feet, it had cloven hooves, and bat-like, leathery wings unfolded on its back. The giant jaguar demon first snarled at Statius, then at Tahmina, as it beat its wings, raising a powerful blast.

'Tahmina! Now!'

The windstorm forced Agatha, Statius and Aenlin backwards as it sent dust and everything not fastened down flying about the room.

The jaguar demon's roar was so loud that it must have been audible throughout the city. It looked first at the Aztec, who prostrated herself before it and spoke to it in a foreign language.

Statius, using this moment of distraction, attacked Aenlin. 'Now I got you, you—'

But the demon misinterpreted the mercenary's attack and hit him with the flat of its shield, propelling Statius across the room to smash through the massive rail of the balcony. He crashed to the floor, where he lay unmoving, like a fat beetle.

Rumbling, the giant demon turned to Aenlin, stamped the ground with its goat foot and shook its staff at her as if challenging her.

David against Goliath – only I don't even have a sling. 'Lucifer aid me,' Aenlin yelled, grabbing her rapier. She was a Kane, daughter of Solomon Kane, conqueror of beasts and darkness. Within her, the fear faded as she looked at the fiend. 'Let me come into my inheritance,' she prayed. 'Don't let me die, Bringer of Light. You know I still have much to do.'

The jaguar demon used its blade-studded club like a scythe, swinging the heavy top with the obsidian blades in a semicircle.

Aenlin didn't even try to block the weapon but instead jumped backwards. The club hissed past her, pulling at her clothes, her dark hair.

The giant creature spread its wings again, creating another wave of wind and blowing Aenlin away like a wad of cotton. She landed beside the entrance, beneath the balcony, surrounded by the bodies of sacrificed victims, by skulls, ash and bones.

The creature came running, holding its shield diagonally in front of its body and raising its staff again; its towering headpiece made the huge demon look even taller. Where its horned head smashed against the rafters, the flayed corpses fell to the floor.

Damn. Aenlin grabbed her two stilettos, which had landed next to her, then struggled to her feet. *He doesn't even have to use a weapon against me, just bats me away like an obnoxious fly.*

Tahmina jumped down from the upper floor to land on their giant opponent's shield. Though struggling to keep her balance, she reached over the upper edge of the shield to attack the beast's head. 'Kill the priestess,' she shouted at Aenlin. Blood was visible on her lips and her chin. 'She is summoning another one of these demons!'

'But . . .' *She's hurt!* Aenlin picked up the rapier. She would have preferred to fight alongside her beloved.

'*Do it!*' The gleaming end of Tahmina's staff hit the demon's leathery snout, producing a flash of light, and at once the creature snarled in agony. A stench of burnt skin filled the air. 'Your blade is useless against this enemy.'

Aenlin ran past their gigantic opponent towards Agatha, who was kneeling beside the abyss, chanting a second invocation. 'Agatha!' Aenlin screamed. The faster this fight was over, the sooner she could check on her beloved's injury. 'Stop—!'

Agatha paused and took off her mask, revealing her face, which was caked with dried blood and painted with unknown characters. She didn't look at all like an Aztec, or anyone else from the New World. 'Your heart will serve us as a sacrifice, Aenlin Kane: the heart of a warrior to raise another demon of war.' She brandished her obsidian war club and her blade and proclaimed, 'My name is Simia!'

'Lucifer is on my side!' Aenlin cried, bravely attacking the enchantress. 'You can't make a whole continent bleed for your suffering!'

'I would not try to if I didn't think it possible,' Simia retorted. She was terrifying to behold, and her parries with the dangerous weapon were quick and assertive. 'Conquistadores raped our mothers and grandmothers and left them to die. When we were born, looking like their oppressors, they knew that we would be the vehicle of their vengeance.'

Aenlin blocked her blow, but the obsidian withstood the steel. The Aztec magic had somehow changed it, made it more resilient. She had the presence of mind to dodge the priestess' knife and instead, kicked her in the stomach. 'What do you want to achieve by that? Isn't it bad enough that—?'

'No, it is not,' Simia spat. 'For you, it can *never* be bad enough! You slaughtered us – and now we will make you kill each other.' Aenlin couldn't let up, even once, for the Aztec enchantress was much too quick, attacking repeatedly without giving Aenlin the chance for a counter-offensive. 'What happy chance that other powers are raging in these Dark Lands, too. What we cannot achieve, they will. Even Kemet's divine power is here to find vengeance for the Europeans' deeds. Darkness shall reign!'

'Not if I can help it.' Aenlin kicked a severed head towards Simia, trying to distract her. 'You cannot pay back injustice with injustice.'

The priestess dodged the skull. 'That is what your father thought, too, Aenlin Kane, but it did him no good.'

In that same instant, Aenlin threw one of her stilettos. *Got you!* The tip cut through the air and buried itself into the side of Simia's neck. A little blood trickled from the wound. The enchantress staggered, but didn't remove the slender knife. She raised the obsidian staff again. 'You have come too late – much too late.'

As the priestess brought down her staff, Aenlin dropped backwards to the floor and held her rapier steady, her arm outstretched. 'Die, in the name of the Bringer of Light!'

Simia had already launched herself at Aenlin. She impaled herself on the slender blade, which pierced her chest. With a cough, she dropped her obsidian weapons. 'Nothing can stop Itochu. She will reach Doom's Peak. But I' – she tore the knife from her neck and blood immediately spurted from the wound – 'shall call another Xolotl. Your friend cannot destroy two of them.'

Bleeding profusely, Simia tried to throw herself into the abyss – but Aenlin shouted, 'No!' as she raised her foot and kicked Simia's right leg.

Simia lost her balance and crashed to the ground at the edge of the gaping hole. Still bleeding freely, she crawled forwards, preparing to throw herself into the hollow darkness.

'No! You will stay – and waste your life.' Aenlin grabbed Simia's calf and dragged her back from the abyss. 'Your time has come,' she said, throwing herself atop the thrashing priestess. Even though she was dying, she remained incredibly strong.

Panting, the two women struggled, but Simia's resistance suddenly ended as she slumped beneath Aenlin.

Now Aenlin could hear the badly damaged inn was creaking and groaning. More rafters broke away from the walls and braces broke; roof tiles were falling into the room and tumbling into the abyss. Fires were burning here and there, ignited by falling candles and smashed oil lamps.

'Tahmina!' Aenlin looked around, to where her beloved had been fighting the great jaguar demon Agatha – Simia – had called a Xolotl. 'Tahmina?'

The giant beast was lying in its own seething blood, flowing from the gaping holes in its skull where its horns had been torn off. Like lava, the blood spread through the house, seeping into the floorboards, causing yet more fires. Where its right leg was twitching, the goat hoof at its end was making long furrows in the wood. The creature's claws still gripped the shield and the staff.

Nicolas stood next to it, lifting the comatose mystic over his shoulder as if she weighed nothing. 'Let's get out of here!' He threw the mystic's staff at Aenlin, who caught it. 'Everything's collapsing. Let's hope the debris will seal this abyss so nothing else can crawl out of it.'

'What about Tahmina?' Aenlin picked up one of her stilettos and ran towards the captain, who was kicking open the Drunkard's door. *Dearest, no!* As her hands held Tahmina's head, she noticed the massive amount of blood running from her mouth and from a wound on her back. *She's dying!* 'By Lucifer! No – no, not her!'

'She's still alive,' Nicolas said, ushering Aenlin through the door. 'She was shot, but she kept fighting this demon until it finally died.' He followed Aenlin ran outside.

'Where are your men – and Caspar?'

'Fled, I'm afraid. The spell wasn't broken. They followed the other witch, to protect her.'

'Statius?' At least he should be dead!

'Lost somewhere under the balcony, may Hell take him!'

A heartbeat later, the building collapsed. Smoke and clouds of dust rose in a filthy mist that enveloped the surrounding streets.

They could hear people shouting for help from the nearby houses, and the sound of bells ringing came from all directions as Heiligenstadt put its citizens on alert to stop the flames from spreading. Of course, no one had any idea what had really been going on inside the inn.

'We need a decent doctor.' Nicolas cradled Tahmina in his arms as they raced through the clouds of smoke and ash that were hiding them from curious gazes. 'I noticed one while I was exploring the city. Come!'

Aenlin felt like crying. They had won the fight, defeated a New World priestess and her demon creature, but they had paid a high price – a price that could not, under any circumstances, be allowed to rise any further.

'I will give you my soul, Lucifer, if you let her survive,' she promised.

There was soft laughter in the alley they were running through. Laughter that was not of this world.

Heiligenstadt, June 1629

Osanna had stretched out her hand as if to protect herself from the heat of the burning building.

She was the only one not joining in the firefighting operations. She stood there, watching the flames devour the Drunkard, even as, all around her, everyone else was shouting, running and passing on leather buckets to cast ridiculously tiny amounts of water into the conflagration. Her master's leather case rested on the ground next to her.

Now carts carrying barrels of water, water hoses and pumps came rumbling up the street, ready to pour water into the flames, which now were blazing in unnatural colours above the structure.

Osanna had felt the quake, the vibrations deep below the ground, and when Valentin and his men had not returned, Captain Barthel had ordered the others to spread out and search the city for them, while she stayed in their lodging, waiting for someone to return – Valentin, Barthel or the Venetian.

'Careful, mate,' cried a man. 'Make way! Make way!' As he spoke, another wall came tumbling down, projecting crackling sparks into the night sky, as if they were happy to break free of the flames. Children were sent chasing after the burning dots being carried on the wind through the city, to spot and report new fires.

There was another quake, followed by the collapse of a sizable part of the ruin. The burning debris filled the abyss that had for some reason opened beneath the house.

'Go on, go on!' someone shouted, and the chain of buckets, the water hoses and the pumps started their tedious work anew.

But the quaking of the earth and the shaking of the buildings were not the only things that had been observed in Heiligenstadt.

All around Osanna, the toiling people talked about the loud rumbling and roaring that had come from the plague-stricken tavern. Some thought it was a hallucination, others a thunder-storm; some even claimed to have seen witches fly out of the chimney and lights flickering behind the closed shutters. People were saying a doorway to Hell had opened in there. Forces of darkness, so they whispered, had stolen the relics of the saints.

'Enough of this,' shouted a sweating, soot-covered man. 'Empty the barrels into the ruin and let it go at that for now. Then damp down the neighbouring roofs and walls. We need to keep the next-door houses from being destroyed. Come on, spread out.'

'Why are you just standing there, girl?' barked an older woman, who'd just spotted Osanna. 'Hurry up, get onto the roof.'

Osanna had no intention of obeying, but neither did she object. Instead, still staring at the inferno, she picked up her master's leather case and moved away.

She did have good reason – and at last she saw movement within the raging flames. A silhouette with a circular hat, a pointy-beaked plague mask, a black robe and a brown leather apron stepped calmly from the inferno.

My Venetian! Osanna's heart leapt with joy. She felt so much for him; she had adored and followed him ever since he had rescued her from her miserable life. Barthel and the mercenaries might be happy about Vanth's gifts, but Osanna felt she had received a far higher blessing from this man – the highest of all.

As soon as he arrived at the Handsome Hans, she had led him to the fire, which he had calmly entered, out of view of the firefighters, the way other people would have entered some harmless mist.

In his arms, the alleged plague doctor carried a charred figure. He stepped unharmed from the blaze: his hat hadn't caught fire, his leather apron wasn't smoking; even the fabric of his black robe remained completely untouched by the heat.

Fascinated, Osanna watched the mirror images of the flames

in the broken glass eyepieces of the silver mask. 'Master, whom do you have there?'

The Venetian placed the man, burned beyond recognition, on the ground, but no one around them seemed to care. The inhabitants of Heiligenstadt were too busy saving their town.

The man's fingers had shrivelled; heat had shortened their sinews and turned his hands into bony claws. His skin was black charcoal and ash, with only an occasional pink shimmer wherever pieces of it flaked away. The smell of roasted flesh pervaded the air. But the man still lived.

With unblinking, wide-open eyes, the fellow the Venetian had saved was staring out at the world.

Osanna realised that his eyelids had burned away. Shrivelled lips bared his teeth. It was a miracle he was not dead. The man had to have the constitution of a bull.

'My bag,' the Venetian demanded, and Osanna passed it to him immediately. She shuddered as she gazed at the injured man. 'Who is this, Master? What do we want with him?'

'You will see.' He opened the clasp, took a handful of spores from his suitcase and sprinkled them on the man lying on the ground. 'Listen. You are mine now,' he told the burnt man. 'I will save your life, and for this, I demand your service until I release you.'

The spores formed a grey layer on the man's charred skin that turned into a covering of mould. The burly fellow lay there coated as if in thick spiderwebs – until he suddenly awoke from his torpor and jumped up with a scream, frantically brushing away the gossamer. Underneath was unscathed skin – and he even had facial hair, a well-trimmed moustache with horizontal tips, and a goatee.

'That ... that is Statius!' Osanna recognised him at once. Her memories of the landsknecht and his crude behaviour in Altona were everything but fond. *He was pushy, crude, obnoxious.* 'Master, he is one of—'

'Not any more. He is mine now.' The Venetian rose, a full head smaller than the mercenary who was standing naked before him. 'Welcome to my ranks, Statius.'

Osanna inspected the warrior's body.

The new skin was streaked with black lines, which continued over his face too. The bones of his forehead, cheeks, chin and nose had turned dark, making him look like Death's cousin. His brown curls retained the gossamer's translucent quality, which made him look completely ghostly.

Statius raised his arms to gaze at them. 'What . . . what have you done?' No word of thanks, of praise or of humility. Osanna didn't like that. 'I look like a . . . like a—'

'Do you not you like it?'

'No!' Statius raised his fingers accusingly. 'Look!'

The Venetian grabbed Statius by the balls. 'Would you prefer me to drag you by your bollocks back into the Hell from which I saved you?'

Statius whined, but didn't attempt to strike his saviour.

Osanna basked in his pain.

'No. No, I will stay with you, Master. Thank you! Thank you a thousand times for not letting me die.'

'It is a little late for your friendly words.' The plague doctor still held his balls. 'You are the only one of your band to have escaped those foreign witches.'

'Yes,' Statius spluttered. 'Yes, Master. She put a spell on us, but my strong mind refused to obey her orders. Then she left me to die.'

'They killed good people,' said the Venetian, '*my* people. Eleven of them. They must be held accountable for those deaths.'

'Yes, Master! I am completely with you, Master.' Statius looked at Osanna, only now realising who was standing in front of him. 'You? The barmaid? May a giant piss all over me! How did you make it all the way here from Altona – and why?'

'Like her, you will be of use to me. You will tell me all you know about the witches – what they did in that house, what they talked about, where they wanted to go – and what they were intending to do.'

'Of course, Master,' Statius said excitedly. 'I want revenge for what they did to my companions – I want to free my friends.' He touched the skin of his arms, legs and shoulders. He also examined his cock and sighed deeply. 'These priestesses will die.'

'Priestesses? Not witches? Do you know where they wanted to go?' The masked one picked up a blanket that had slipped from a clothesline and threw it to Statius.

'Yes, Master.' Statius draped the blanket around his shoulders. 'It will be my pleasure to guide you.'

The Venetian turned, closed his case and picked it up before stepping into the billowing smoke. 'Come. I will introduce you to the others. Forgive them if they hate you. You and Nicolas, you stole their company's mission in Altona. But someday they will praise you, because, in the end, they met me because of you.' The smoke obscured his silhouette.

Wrapped in his blanket, Statius walked next to Osanna. 'The little serving wench,' he repeated, watching her. 'You look good. Better. That I should see you again . . .'

'I didn't ask for it.'

'Oh, listen, the little whore is rebellious.' Statius leaned closer to her so that one tip of his moustache touched Osanna's cheek. 'It won't help you. I will take you whenever I want to. Surely the other landsknechts have all been between your legs – one more cock won't matter.'

Osanna knew better than to answer, but the times when she would have given herself to someone like Statius were over. The landsknecht would learn that the hard way, should he try to make good on his promise. The Venetian had not torn off his balls. Osanna planned to rectify this omission as soon as Statius misbehaved.

On July 4, we reached the French border and passed a castle. Inside, there were seven farmers who tried to resist the whole army. So we burned down the castle, including the farmers.

from the diary of the mercenary Peter Hagendorf, entry made in the year 1636

CAPITULUM XIV

Heiligenstadt, June 1629

Aenlin sat on a footstool next to Tahmina's bed and held her hand. *Stay by me. You will recover, from the wound and the terror.*

Looking pale and fragile, almost corpse-like, the mystic lay with her long chestnut-brown hair surrounding her head like a corona. Her heart beat faintly.

It's as if Tahmina is afraid of waking up, Aenlin thought.

'I have seen this before,' Nicolas said from the doorway, 'in wounded men on the battlefield. They fell into torpor because their bodies needed all their strength to regenerate.' He had brought food and drink, hoping the scent would put revive Tahmina.

'When will she wake up?'

Nicolas put down the tray with the roasted chicken. He didn't bother lying. 'Some never do. Others wake up after several weeks, although that doesn't guarantee their survival.' He closed the door onto the corridor. 'But your friend will pull through. Anyone who's defeated an Aztec demon is hard to kill.'

'Thank you.' She respected him enormously for carrying the unconscious woman out of the collapsing building, and for comforting them both.

They'd changed their first plan and instead, found quarters in the small inn next to the brewery. They'd taken Tahmina there under cover of dark, in utmost secrecy, where they'd washed her and tended to her wounds. To avoid attracting attention, they'd not sent for a doctor but instead relied on their own experience; the captain had treated the gun wound very well, and Aenlin had used her own training to bandage Tahmina's injuries.

After the fire, the disappearance of the relics and the mysterious earthquake, the mood in Heiligenstadt was extremely tense. Everyone agreed all of these events just had to have supernatural causes, so the search for witches and warlocks had begun and the first suspects had been arrested.

'Any news?' Aenlin asked. It was the captain's job to keep his eyes and ears open; He was wearing patched and darned clothes so no one would know his profession; he certainly didn't look like a landsknecht captain right now.

'There is now a crater at the site of the Drunkard, which they found when clearing away the debris. All that remains of the house are smashed tiles and broken bricks, some ash and half-melted nails and brackets. The bones of the victims have been burned completely to ash in this inferno, or they fell down into the hole and were smashed to pieces by the falling tiles.'

'So there is no proof of the Aztecs' atrocities.'

'Nor of the demon we saw and defeated.' Nicolas sat on the edge of the bed, using his hat to fan the scent of roast chicken towards Tahmina. 'The hole is only two feet deep now. The tunnel through which the fiend rose into the world has disappeared.'

'A Xolotl: that's what Agatha called it.' Aenlin had at first imagined another world, far beneath the surface of the earth, ruled by monsters and fiends who broke through to the surface from time to time to attack people. 'I think there never was a tunnel. Only a manifestation in that spot.'

'I have no clue about magic,' Nicolas admitted.

Aenlin smiled at him. 'Doesn't matter.' If he didn't understand the magical things that happened on earth, she would use another language to explain it to him. *Or is this an act?*

'If you say so.' Nicolas could not resist the smell and ripped off a leg of the chicken. 'The Venetian and his men have gone, I heard. Two days ago. I'm sure he's pursuing the priestess who escaped.'

'This plague doctor is a follower of the demon called Vanth. I saw its symbol on his mask.'

'Good. Let him kill them.' Nicolas chewed, then wiped the fat from the corners of his mouth. 'Vanth tolerates no other cults beside his own. Is that the reason?'

'Before her death, Agatha told me that they are not the only ones by a long shot who have come to the German lands to spread darkness and to rule from within. Their focus is the Holy Roman Empire, with its abundance of violence, hatred and war. To keep it that way, they intend to plant the seeds of evil into the soil.'

'Just like they have done in Heiligenstadt, after they destroyed the relics.' Nicolas wiped his greasy hand on his boot. 'Did you or Tahmina find out where the third priestess has gone? This Veronica? Or did you, on your journey with Agatha—?'

'No.' Aenlin remembered nothing of the time when she had been under the Aztec's spell. The only things clear in her mind were the few minutes that Tahmina had given her, when her mind was her own again. She also remembered how Statius had fondled her. *Dirty pig! Death by fire was too good for you.* She shivered and lowered her forehead to Tahmina's fingers. 'Don't leave me,' she whispered to her beloved. *What should I do without you?*

'What do we do now?' Nicolas wondered aloud.

'We wait.'

'For her to come to her senses?'

'Yes.'

'Until then, Ursula and Veronica will be abroad, and who knows what they will do to my men and Caspar? They sacrifice human beings in their dreadful rituals to honour their Aztec deities.' Nicolas' voice told Aenlin that he was desperate to get going. 'You saw this Xolotl she called forth from the earth. Imagine such a . . .'

Aenlin raised her eyes. 'I cannot stop you.'

'But . . . you are Solomon Kane's daughter! You defeated the first Aztec – the first of three. It is your job, your inheritance! Isn't this what destiny and God chose you for?'

'God didn't show up to help us,' Aenlin pointed out. 'Without you, she and I would both be dead.' *Don't talk to me about God.* She preferred to put her trust in Lucifer, whom the Almighty had betrayed. *And Lucifer sent me Nicolas.* 'We cannot go to war against two of them. How many demons will they summon – and how many can we stop without Tahmina?'

'But—'

'I can tell you the answer to that: *not a single one.*' Aenlin saw no reason to sugar-coat their circumstances. 'Then there's the Venetian: he's a follower of Vanth! You described to me what his followers are capable of, acting as if they are possessed, making their blades and balls glow red-hot. They shot the witches in the grove to pieces before my eyes – witches who used the strongest of magic and sorcery, yet still perished! What could I do against him?'

Nicolas pointed vaguely towards the mystic's ebony staff.

You cannot be serious! 'Untrained? I might destroy it because I don't know how to use it.' Aenlin was getting angry. 'Who's going to stay here to protect Tahmina if we both go chasing after the plague doctor and the priestesses? How safe is it to be in Heiligenstadt after they've sown their seeds of evil into the town's soil?'

'The innkeepers here are nice people – they'll watch over your friend—'

'*Nice people?* Being nice will neither save her from a treacherous blade nor from a freshly hatched demon!' Aenlin refused to leave her companion behind; she wasn't responsible for what had happened, or what would happen. Lucifer knew that she had tried hard, and she'd already paid a high price. 'There will be others who will stop the Aztecs. The Venetian, for example.'

'Well then. What will you do instead?'

'As soon Tahmina is better, I'll go to Hamburg and talk to the Company, ask them to give me my inheritance. They'll understand once they know the whole story. After that, it's back to England as fast as possible.'

'Where evil already lurks – that's what Agatha told you, yes? Why would they spare that island? After all, the English trading ships also make their profit from the misery of the New World.'

Aenlin didn't want to think about this; she'd blocked it out, just as she had the fact that Tahmina's former master was in London, and that an unknown somebody urgently wanted to talk to the mystic. *A secret society knows about my beloved.* She leaned forwards and kissed Tahmina's brow tenderly. The midnight-black strand of hair that fell onto the sleeping woman's face made it look as if there was a crack in her countenance.

Quickly, Aenlin pulled back her hair. 'I cannot leave her.'

Nicolas sighed. 'Then I will have to go alone.' He reached for the magic staff.

'Stop! What do you think you are doing?' Aenlin immediately snatched the carved staff from him. 'You know even less about using it than me.'

'I have to try. If I knock, bump and rub it the right way once I meet the Aztecs and a Xolotl, something is bound to happen.' Nicolas looked completely determined. 'If the two of you – or at least you – won't come along, I have no other choice.'

'Against my will?'

'I *must* do this, Aenlin. You're denying your father's blood in your veins. Solomon Kane would've come with me at once to stop this manifold evil.'

His words struck her like blows, but she saw no way to fulfil his wishes. 'Go without the staff. You will manage without it. You're immortal, after all.'

This time, his expression changed. 'Yes, what a misery.'

'You call that a misery?' She felt a twinge of guilt for having been an accomplice in his murder.

'Because I don't know where it comes from,' Nicolas replied sharply. 'It may seem like an advantage to you, but I consider it a curse.'

Aenlin leaned towards the unconscious woman. 'You told me you were dead, at the bottom of the Werra – wounded many times over and weighed down with rocks. Tahmina felt at once that . . .' She bit her tongue.

Nicolas raised his head, the ash-blond hair flying around his face. 'She knew it?'

'She . . . felt that you . . . are different.'

'The Devil take it! Why didn't you tell me before?' He stood up, looking excited. 'What is it about me? Am I possessed? Is there a demon living within me? Or an angel? Did my parents drink a serum that changed me? Have they been bewitched or . . . ?' He rubbed the back of his neck and started to pace around the room. 'By God – Tahmina could have helped me to find out more!'

'What do you know about your parents?' Aenlin was glad of the new topic. 'Were they alchemists?'

Nicolas, who was still standing, slumped slightly. 'Nothing,' he answered softly. He went to the bunk bed and poured himself some of the wine waiting there. 'I know nothing of them.'

'So you lived in an orphanage?'

'I know absolutely *nothing* about my childhood, my youth or my life as an adult before 1618.' Nicolas' voice now sounded raw. 'Statius found me on the battlefield, covered in blood and without any memory. I had stab wounds, holes from musket balls, blows to the head, and no one was betting that I would draw even one more breath.'

Aenlin said nothing, not wanting to interrupt him. *Tahmina's intuition was dead right: a man full of secrets!*

'He brought me to the field-hospital, where we met Jäcklein. Because we liked each other, we travelled together from battle to battle. We helped each other out countless times.' Nicolas looked out through the shutters at the crowded plaza and the street outside. 'Ah, my sodding head! My lost memories never returned. I don't know if I have a home, a wife, children – or if so, where they might be. Siblings, parents, a village, friends – everything that makes a man a man has been cut from my mind. All that remained was a man of war.'

'I'm sorry,' Aenlin said sadly. *What a fate! What burden he must carry!*

'Ever since 1618, I have been wading through carnage, through battle after battle.' Nicolas emptied his cup in one gulp. 'We became like brothers, Jäcklein, Statius and me.' His hand gripped the cup tightly until his knuckles stood out white. 'But for Stats to meet such a fate ... ! What a pig he had become. Those fucking priestesses from the New World, with their evil spells! I *will* make them pay.'

Aenlin didn't mention that Agatha's spell had not been the reason for Statius' behaviour, for Nicolas would stick to his version of the truth to honour his friend. The cruel landsknecht was dead, burned to ashes. It was better that way.

'I will take the staff.' Gruffly, Nicolas put down his cup. 'You can give it to me of your own accord ... '

'Or what, Nicolas?' Slowly, Aenlin let go of her beloved's hand, rose and walked towards her baldric to get her rapier. Her stilettos she had handy, tucked into her belt and nestled at the small of her back, as always. 'It does not belong to you, and it will be of more harm than good to you. Not to mention the fact that it would be theft.'

'Or robbery. That depends.' Nicolas turned around, his right hand at the basket of his rapier. The determination in his eyes had turned to wrath.

At that moment they heard solid, heavy footsteps beyond the door, accompanied by the clinking of a baldric and the sound of metal scraping against metal. An armoured person was moving along the corridor – and stopped outside their room.

Nicolas and Aenlin drew their blades and took up defensive stance. Their disagreement over the staff would have to wait.

Someone knocked on the door politely.

'Don't shoot,' said a man's voice from the corridor. 'I will enter now, if you don't mind.'

'Do we mind?' Aenlin grabbed her firearm. 'Did you recognise his voice?'

'No.' Nicolas also raised his cocked pistol. 'Who is there?'

'A friend. Can we talk inside? The walls out here could have ears I don't wish to share my news with.' Slowly, the unknown man pushed down the handle and opened the door. 'Keep calm. Please.'

'What—?' Nicolas exclaimed as he saw the dark-haired man, who was wearing a leather coat and a broad-brimmed hat sporting a feather. He appeared to be about Nicolas' age.

'You know him?' The visitor's face looked very pale to Aenlin, as if he were suffering from anaemia.

'This . . . this is Valentin. One of the mercenaries following the Venetian, Barthel's ensign!' He jerked his pistol up and aimed at the man's head. 'But what's more peculiar is that I shot him.'

'A revenant!' Aenlin cursed. 'Now the plague doctor's started sending his dead after us—'

Valentin raised his arms to prove that he meant no harm, showing them his empty hands. 'Look, I don't want to hurt you.'

Slowly he crossed the threshold and pushed the door closed with the heel of his boot.

'Why not?' Nicolas quickly looked out the window while Aenlin watched the entrance to see whether any further surprises approached. 'Are you alone?'

'Yes. I can control only one corpse.' Valentin pointed at the resting Tahmina. 'I deliberately put myself into a trance. For my body, time passes more slowly when I send my mind into a corpse to control it.'

'Thousands of howling Hellhounds!' Nicolas still didn't lower his pistol. 'What are you talking about? What kind of a fucking ruse is that supposed to b—?'

'Stop! Stop, wait! Maybe it's true!' Aenlin was watching her companion in bewilderment. Nothing showed that suggested Tahmina's mind was outside her body, but she was able to communicate telepathically, so perhaps this was true. 'She did tell me she could do that.'

'Necromancy!' Nicolas didn't sound convinced. 'That is the darkest of arts.'

'No,' Valentin said, smiling in a weirdly familiar way, 'for then I would be giving unholy life to a dead man. Instead, I am using a corpse to be able to move around. To talk to you. I am Tahmina. Ask me what we have been through together.'

'He doesn't have to. I know it's you.' Quickly, Aenlin sat down next to the unmoving mystic. 'Since you've found yourself a body, I assume you want to pursue the Aztecs and the Venetian.'

Valentin nodded. 'We will leave my body here. Let us tell the innkeepers I am your maid, that I have fallen ill and am too weak to travel on, which is why you will pick me up in a few days' time.' The ensign produced a full purse from the pocket of his coat. 'This should be enough to pay our bill here, and for our journey.'

'What a crazy miracle.' Nicolas put away his pistol and his rapier. He walked around Valentin's body, watching him. He touched the dead man's throat, feeling the blood vessels with his middle and index fingers. 'Nothing. Nothing – and cool.' He sniffed loudly. 'Is that the stench of decay?'

'Yes, that is unavoidable,' Tahmina explained through the dead man's mouth. 'The man is dead. His corpse is decaying, even if my spell has slowed the process considerably. During our journey, I will probably have to look for a new body. But he still has a little of the demonic power the Venetian imbued him with, which might be an advantage.'

You are incredibly brave, my darling, and a role model for me. Aenlin caressed the sleeping woman's face. 'How long can you do this?'

'A day outside my mortal shell is like an hour for my body. After several weeks, I will die of thirst, unless someone gives me water. But I cannot chew in this state.'

Aenlin felt reassured. 'What if your heart stops? Your real heart within your own body?'

'Then my mind will dissolve within seconds.'

'A dangerous thing.' Nicolas drew his dagger and slightly pricked Valentin's side. 'Does that hurt?'

'No – but if this borrowed body is destroyed, I will have to look for new one. Therefore, I must take good care of my temporary home.' The ensign clucked his tongue disapprovingly. 'It is detrimental to its durability if you poke holes in it.'

'Food? Drink?' Nicolas enquired.

'No – what for? The mercenary is dead.'

Aenlin couldn't argue with her companion; she was risking her own life, too. But she didn't like the idea of leaving Tahmina's body behind. 'How about we take you along? Your own body?'

'You would have to keep an eye on it constantly. Remember: if it dies, I die.' Valentin shook his head. 'No, we leave me here. That is the simplest solution.' She cleared her throat, and touched the flesh, as if she wanted to feel her voice. 'It is unfamiliar, to experience myself like this.'

'Wait until you have to pee,' Nicolas replied with a grin.

'As a corpse, I will not have to.'

Aenlin took a deep breath. 'Can you read the mercenary's memories?'

'I tried. He suffered some brain damage, but a little piece of it is unscathed.' Valentin crossed his arms in front of his armoured chest. 'The Venetian wants to kill the priestesses because they could thwart his plans. Apart from my own powers, Valentin can do this.' The landsknecht's eyes rolled back in his head until only their whites were visible and shadows turned his pale face into a skull. 'That is the tinge of demonic power still inhabiting this decaying flesh.' He drew his rapier and less than four heartbeats later, the blade glowed red. 'With this, I can cut to pieces any Xolotl trying to stop us.'

Nicolas clapped his hands. 'Let the merry chase begin! You must defeat two more, Aenlin Kane – like your father would have done.'

Looks like I'll be coming into my inheritance in an unusual way. Aenlin took the mystic's staff and tenderly kissed the sleeping woman's lips, caressed her cheek and touched her forehead. 'I am looking forward to seeing you again,' she whispered.

It felt like goodbye.

This frightened Aenlin enormously.

Free Imperial city of Mühlhausen, July 1629

Osanna followed Statius at a distance, quite a challenge to do so unnoticed, for many inhabitants had left the walls of the city to move to another dominion – one that was not Protestant. They had had to pay enormous levies to save the city from the Imperial troops, and these levies were collected in the form of taxes.

Mühlhausen had a massive rampart, but it was hard to tell how long it would withstand the Union, which was why the city preferred to pay to save its citizens, its beautiful houses and its considerable number of churches from being burnt down.

Osanna preferred Mühlhausen to Heiligenstadt. She had liked the city's skyline with its countless spires on first sight. After walking past meadows and fields of wheat and barley, they had entered the city through the Erfurt Gate. No one had stopped the plague doctor and his protectors, for as usual, he had claimed to have come for the wellbeing of the inhabitants.

Within the walls, Mühlhausen was just like any other city of that size: half-timbered buildings, alleys and lanes, wealth here, labourers' houses there, signs above doors advertising trades and inns, everyone busy – and over it all, the omnipresent bells ringing from church towers to announce the hour or call the faithful to prayer. Osanna never wanted to return to miserable, piss-poor Altona.

The Venetian and the landsknechts had found a place to stay, an empty house in Unterer Steinweg, and they mostly stayed there, but not a day went by when Statius did not leave to roam the streets of Mühlhausen. He had told the master another priestess from the New World was hiding in the town and he would look for her – he alone, because otherwise, she would smell a rat.

Osanna straightened her shift and adjusted her headscarf, which was sliding on her dark blonde hair. She didn't believe that Statius was telling the truth, and one of the reasons she was suspicious was his behaviour back in Altona. There were other things too, including the way he had talked about the atrocities the priestesses committed, for no one had heard about anything like that in Mühlhausen.

Over the last few days, she had talked to some residents about Mühlhausen's past. A few witch trials had been held there; the first investigations had begun five years ago, and ever since, the city had filled its witches' tower with suspects. The interrogations, the executions and the burnings happened on the Galgenberg, right under the city gallows; witches and warlocks were rarely exiled. Recently there had been an accusation of scrying, which Osanna considered harmless, and the earlier denunciations sounded more like envy and jealousy than like terrible discoveries of true evil. No one had mentioned decapitations, cut-out hearts, flayed people, dead children, or anything like that. No, she simply didn't trust Statius, no matter what he said.

Osanna had told the Venetian of her suspicions, and he had given her permission to tail the landsknecht. Unlike her, the Venetian wasn't worried, because he had imbued the man with the breath of Vanth. Furthermore, he was occupying himself every free minute with the contents of his case, readying himself for a potential fight in Mühlhausen. No one knew what spells their opponents from the New World used, but the destruction in Heiligenstadt and the violent deaths of Valentin and his men had impressed him.

Statius, singing off-key, left a hedge-tavern. Judging by the lyrics, it must be a landsknecht song. His skin still bore the lines that had appeared during his resurrection; he tried to cover them with make-up, and told everybody he had once been the victim of a witch; he had killed her afterwards, single-handedly, for her black magic. In times like these, no one doubted his story – in fact, quite the contrary; the story brought him sympathy and sometimes admiration for his courage in facing the witch. He was especially boastful in front of women he wanted to lie with.

Quietly Osanna followed him, pondering his actions when he entered a basement tavern. The man was pretty drunk, even considering his habits. *Could it be that the priestess he is looking for is down there?*

'If she exists at all,' Osanna whispered. In her opinion, the mercenary was trying to keep them in Mühlhausen longer than necessary. *But why?*

Osanna followed him down into a vaulted cellar, using the alcoves in the walls and hiding behind people to continue shadowing him without being noticed. He disappeared through a door into an adjacent room, from where she heard a single loud voice speaking. Thick tobacco smoke billowed out

Osanna paused. *What's happening?*

When an armoured man wearing a long cape walked straight towards the door, his helmet under his arm, Osanna quietly followed. The room was lit by candles and oil lamps, so she hid immediately, ducking down behind a bench right next to the door. She breathed shallowly, trying to slow her beating heart, and listened. The walls smelled of moisture, saltpetre and pipe smoke, which tickled her throat. It might be summer outside, but this vault was chilly.

'Ah, you found the way,' said the speaker to the newcomer. His audience laughed quietly, some banging mugs and tankards on the table. 'You missed the first part.'

'That's why I'm late,' the man replied. His answer was met with more laughter. 'I only want to know what to tell my men.'

'Then you have arrived just in time, Captain,' Statius answered. 'It's time.'

Soldiers? Osanna poked her head around the corner of the bench to get a better view of the room, which was an impressive groined vault. Wheel-like chandeliers hung from the ceiling and there were lamp-holders on the walls, giving out a lot of light. Small statues stood in the alcoves, but Osanna couldn't decipher the writing on the signs in front of them. The walls were whitewashed, marred by patches of saltpetre and mould.

Two dozen men were standing around a large oak table spread with papers, drawings, maps and documents. The men were smoking pipes and drinking beer as they plotted. Judging by their robes and expensive garb, all but the captain must be councillors or guild members.

Statius stood amongst them, deciphering a broadsheet. 'This says it all: a little over a week ago, the Swedes lost the battle against Polish and Imperial troops at Stuhm. Gustavus Adolphus just managed to escape his pursuers and returned to his kingdom.' He threw the paper back on the table. 'I was part of an Imperial military contingent aiding the Poles, just like the mercenaries now travelling with the plague doctor. It was our disguise, so no one would smell a rat.'

'You said there are two hundred landsknechts stationed close to our city, ready to attack?' a councillor asked. 'When I heard this news for the first time, I really didn't want to believe it.'

'Soldiers always think of themselves first. Until we're hired again, we have to make a living somehow.' Statius stood out among the assembled crowd in his baggy, brightly coloured mercenary garb and large floppy hat on his oiled hair. 'The fake doctor and his men have not come at the behest of the Elector and because of the plague, as you were told. They don't care about the health of your citizens. They only use this as a pretence to scout your city and your defences. Tonight, they'll open the gates.' He looked around, twirling his moustache. 'Believe me, we are well trained. Mühlhausen will fall.'

'But we pay taxes so the Imperial troops will leave us in peace,' one man protested.

'That may be. But that doesn't include us. We're not Imperial troops.' Statius grabbed a tankard full of beer and drained it. 'See? I took it, and you couldn't stop me. I would have subdued any of you who might have tried.' With a belch, he threw the empty tankard on the table, its noisy clatter making the gathering jump. 'This night's attack is a certainty, as is the pillaging – unless you kill the Venetian and his men beforehand.

Right now. If the gates are not opened, the rest of the troops can't get in. We are not equipped for sieges.'

What a bastard! Osanna was seething with rage. In return for saving his life, Statius was betraying his benefactor, demanding his death. *I knew it.*

'Shocking!' Another councillor rose in outrage.

'No, it isn't. Sit back down. The Emperor doesn't care if a Protestant city is attacked – sure, he'll complain loudly, but deep inside, he'll be happy.' Statius put his hands on his hips. 'All over the country, everyone's full of it.'

'What about you? You claim to be an honest mercenary?' The speaker of the gathering gave him a meaningful gaze.

'Honest enough to get my pay from you and be on my way, Master Tailor. I don't want to be involved in the downfall of Mühlhausen.' Statius extended his hand. 'What are five hundred ducats, compared to a burned-down city?'

Tailor leaned to one side and picked up a bag, which he threw at Statius' feet. His voice filled with contempt, he said, 'Fifty is enough. For now. You'll get the rest after letting us into the house where this gang of killers is holed up. Then we'll see how honest you really are.'

Statius took the clinking pouch. 'That is not what we agreed upon, Master Tailor, but I don't care. Your city is at stake and I don't want to waste any precious time.' He looked at the captain. 'Where are your men?'

'Behind the Church of All Saints.'

'How many?'

'A hundred soldiers and some volunteers who know how to fight. That should be enough against two dozen who won't be expecting our attack. Once their leader is dead, they'll fall to pieces anyway.'

'The best way to strike panic in a man is with a blade, preferably to his head. Believe me, I'm good at these things.' Before he left, Statius looked at everyone present in turn. 'Listen out for my signal.'

'Is it still the same?'

'Yes.' Statius walked towards the door. 'And hurry up. Expect the worst with this bunch. I discovered them carrying unholy symbols – maybe they follow the Devil, or even more evil powers. But I have heard that the people of Mühlhausen are experienced in these matters.' He looked around condescendingly. 'Oh, and I'll order more beer for you gentlemen. This round is on me. Take it off the rest of my pay.' Then he was gone, without noticing Osanna in her cranny.

The captain of the guard left soon afterwards.

Osanna cowered behind the small bench, petrified. *Betrayal – of the worst kind!* So now she knew what Statius really did when he was out on his scouting missions. The priestess he was looking for had probably never even been in Mühlhausen. Or if she had, she'd long since fled to safety.

That meant that Vanth's powers of possession had failed. The Venetian was so sure of Vanth's infallibility that he had never even considered such a possibility.

Statius had defied the exaltation and the revival – so obviously he was still controlled by beings whose power was greater than that of the demon Vanth. In her shock, Osanna had almost forgotten that a hundred soldiers armed to the teeth were waiting to attack the Venetian and his band of protectors.

Statius wants to have the master and all of us killed! Osanna seized the moment when the waiter brought the beer to scuttle out of the room and run back outside. *I can't let this happen!*

She sped through the evening streets of the town as fast as she could, desperate to reach their lodgings before the traitorous landsknecht. Statius was incredibly strong, but he wasn't quick.

Such infamy, Osanna thought angrily. *The master saved this arsehole's life!* What's more, he'd made Statius his confidant, often talking to him to learn more about the priestesses. He'd divulged plans even she and Barthel didn't know about.

His trust was going to have dire consequences in Mühlhausen.

Sweating profusely, Osanna reached Unterer Steinweg and their lodgings, right next to the Church of All Saints. Light shone from inside and she could hear laughter and soft clinking through the open windows. The landsknechts were completely oblivious to what was going on.

Thank Vanth! They haven't yet attacked. She walked towards their lodgings with a profound feeling of relief. *I can—*

A strong hand grabbed her throat and jerked her to the side, into the shadows of a passageway, and a fist punched her temple. The blow made Osanna dizzy, but she didn't lose consciousness, although thanks to the steely grip around her throat, she could barely breathe. Screaming was impossible.

'You little spy,' Statius whispered in her ear. He pressed her face into the wall, his strong hand shifting to the back of her neck. 'Do you think I didn't notice you in the cellar? That I hadn't seen you following me earlier?'

'Traitor,' she gasped.

'You can't betray what you never believed in,' he retorted with an evil laugh. 'This masked fool is an idiot. He thinks he controls my mind like that of Barthel and his men – but how could I betray my priestesses from the New World? Their plans are much more promising than yours.'

'He saved your life!'

'Because he wanted something from me.' Statius' sour breath reeked of beer as he whispered in her ear, 'You lot, on the other hand, want nothing that suits me. Me, a servant of demons? Ha! Never. There is only one cause I serve: my own.' He dragged Osanna deeper into the alley, into the darkness where no one without a lantern would see them from the street. 'Did you hear what we discussed in the basement?'

Osanna's daze lessened. *I must warn the others.* To do so, she had to escape her tormentor.

'Answer me!'

'Yes,' she spat, 'every treacherous word!' She kicked back at the mercenary's groin with her heel, but Statius blocked her attack with his knee.

'Forget it, girlie.'

When she tried to kick his instep, he smashed her forehead into the wall until warm blood was trickling down between her eyes and along her nose from the cut on her forehead and all she could see were fiery wheels and stars. She went slack in his grip; her headscarf fell to the ground.

'So now you know that I will kill your master and tear the mask off his face myself.'

Osanna wanted to push herself off the wall to make the man stagger, but she was too weak. 'You will fail.'

'Have you never wondered what he looks like?'

'No.'

'What if he's a demon? Or a rotting skeleton?' Statius dragged her along by the neck up some steps to a dark inner courtyard on the first floor of some abandoned buildings. 'A ghost, even? Don't you want to know?'

'He is a servant of Vanth. I don't care what he looks like. He gave me a new life, an existence with meaning and purpose.'

Statius kicked in a door, went through the empty room to the windows and opened a shutter.

From there, they had a clear view of the gang's house and the church right next to it, where a hundred attackers were now lurking.

The landsknechts were in their quarters, completely unsuspecting as they laughed, played cards and drank. The silhouette of the plague doctor was visible on the topmost floor, clearly recognisable by his circular hat and the long beak. He sat at a desk, writing.

'There they are, the meek little lambs. And soon, they will be slaughtered lambs. The butchers are already waiting.' Statius changed his grip and started throttling her to keep her from screaming a warning.

Osanna spat blood. When the landsknecht had bashed her head against the bricks, he had not only hurt her forehead, but also loosened two or three teeth. 'We have Vanth's blessing,' she croaked. 'They will tear the hundred men to pieces and then take their revenge on the city.'

'Let Mühlhausen burn.' Statius laughed grimly. 'There can never be enough blood and thunder for me: these are the things I love about war. Moreover, I will kill the Venetian. The time for his humbug act is over.'

'He will see through you!' she managed, trying to hit his nose with her elbow. 'You are a dead man!'

Deflecting her blow was almost too easy for Statius. 'Not if I come to his aid in the moment of his greatest peril, in the middle of the fight against the city guard. He trusts me – he'll be *so* happy to see me.' He pushed Osanna's legs apart with his foot, while tearing at her shift with his free hand until it was hanging off her. 'Well, until the moment I pierce his heart with my rapier and fire a ball through his mask. I will grab that thing by the beak, tear it off his face and piss on him.'

Osanna, knowing all too well what was about to happen to her, tried again to break his grip. 'You foul pig—!'

Statius pressed against her from behind, making her feel his arousal. 'I really wanted to do this in Altona, but now your time has come,' he whispered in a voice that was hoarse with lust. More fabric tore until nothing impeded him any more.

Osanna went slack again in his grip, unable to avoid the inevitable. The landsknecht was just too strong for her.

But when Statius let go of her throat to grab her hair and bend her forwards, she let out a long, piercing scream that echoed from the neighbouring houses and the nearby church. It was shrill as a swift's cry, as panic-filled as a cornered animal. She shrieked until her voice broke, begging, *Vanth, please!* She hoped her master had heard her – that Barthel would hear her.

That *someone* from the band would hear her and do *something*.

But there was no reaction from within the house: the drinking, chatting and laughing continued unabated. Her last warning went unheard.

Statius dragged her head back by her hair and laughed. 'That was plenty loud enough. Thank you.'

She heard quick steps down below, and the rattling and clattering of metal echoing outside. The soldiers appeared from behind the church and approached the doors of the Venetian's accommodation. Lightning-quick, they opened the doors and entered the building, while reinforcements surrounded the house.

No! Osanna finally understood that it was she who had given the signal they had been waiting for: Statius had been planning all along to take her against her will.

She screamed again.

Towers are on fire, churches turned upside down,

The town hall is in ruins, the strong cut down, destroyed.

Young girls are raped, wherever we turn our gaze,

Fire, plague and death pierce heart and spirit through.

Andreas Gryphius, *Tears of the Fatherland* (1636)

CAPITULUM XV

North of Heiligenstadt, July 1629

Aenlin drew her horse aside to make way for the coach coming towards them on the rocky road. 'Take care!' she called. 'Someone's in a hurry.'

Nicolas rode behind her with Valentin, still possessed by Tahmina's spirit. Aenlin and Tahmina had forced the reluctant captain to try riding, because it was the fastest way to travel; carts and coaches would be far too slow to catch up with the priestesses. To their surprise, he was managing quite well this time, as if he were using knowledge acquired long before.

The approaching coach, bearing what looked like a noble family, had luggage piled high on its roof. On the back stood two servants in long leather coats, heavily armed and wearing scarves to protect their mouths and noses. On the box, a guard holding a musket sat next to the coachman.

'Looks like an escape to me,' Valentin shouted from behind.

'I thought so too,' Nicolas replied. 'Have the priestesses been wreaking havoc again?'

'And if so, where?' Aenlin would have loved an answer, but the coach had long since passed them by and would certainly not have stopped for the likes of them. However, there was a coaching inn on the horizon, where tired steeds could be exchanged for fresh ones. 'Let's ask over there. I'm sure they'll have heard the latest news.'

'My arse would certainly appreciate that,' Nicolas shouted, making Valentin laugh.

Even in the man's laughter, Aenlin could hear Tahmina's own special way of expressing her amusement. *It's very strange.*

The three of them approached the coaching inn. Horses were whinnying in the stables, while others grazed in the paddock, relaxing from their arduous duties.

The Elector's coat of arms was painted on the side of the inn to show who protected these premises. Five men-at-arms, in breastplates and carrying halberds, underlined the point.

'There's a wonderful smell of cabbage and meat.' Nicolas drew up his horse and stiffly dismounted before rubbing his aching buttocks. 'At least I'm not blistered yet. But every muscle in my body is aching.' He nodded at the guards, who returned his greeting. Like Valentin, he was wearing plain clothing, to avoid being recognised as a landsknecht.

Aenlin too now wore boots and breeches, with her baldric fastened over shirt and jerkin. She had deliberately avoided the expensive clothes she had worn at the beginning of their journey, to attract as little attention as possible. The fabric just had to be light – *bright as the light, like Lucifer.*

'Next time grease your breeches,' Valentin's corpse recommended. 'Inside.' He dismounted like a normal person. The man moved like Tahmina and talked with the same accent, although her body was recovering in a bed now many miles back the way they'd come.

Oriental mystics really can do some special miracles. 'We're only resting here briefly, just to ask around,' Aenlin declared. 'The horses are still fresh, so we'll be on our way quickly enough.'

'Sounds like we have a female captain now.' But Nicolas grinned and led his horse to the stables. A groom appeared at the entrance and offered help with rubbing down and caring for the animals.

'Just water and feed them,' Aenlin shouted across the yard as she too dismounted. 'We won't be staying long.

The groom bowed and took the reins. The guards looked at them appraisingly, but didn't approach. They obviously didn't consider the newcomers dangerous.

Aenlin, Valentin and Nicolas went over to the small inn, which sounded quiet. It was late afternoon, so the regular messengers and post-riders would have already been and gone on their way.

Upon entering, Aenlin saw two men and two women, all elderly and in plain clothes, speaking quietly to each other as they tucked into a hearty meal of the cabbage and meat Nicolas had smelled. They looked up from their food to examine the newcomers. A boy of maybe eight years sat next to the bar, plucking at an out-of-tune lute; perhaps a guest had forgotten it. The instrument looked pretty battered.

'Two plates and beer, lad,' Nicolas ordered loudly. 'Please.'

'Three,' Valentin corrected.

'I thought you didn't eat,' Aenlin said, puzzled.

'We should keep up appearances.' Valentin looked pale, but otherwise, there was no hint of anything odd. The strong odour of the mint leaves he had rubbed himself down with that morning was masking the slightly sweet scent of decay.

They sat down in the far corner of the room, so they'd have a good view of their surroundings.

The boy had exchanged the lute for three mugs and led them to their table, when the side door opened to admit a man in his forties with a cheap-looking wig and well-trimmed goatee and moustache, wearing clothes that had once been expensive. He was fidgeting with his breeches as he walked to the bar.

'Damn,' Nicolas exclaimed, trying to duck behind Valentin and hiding his face with the brim of his hat. But he'd moved too late: the man had seen him and stopped.

'Who's that?' Aenlin was wary. They really didn't need any

trouble now, and with the Elector's guards right in front of the door, any problem could quickly become more official than they wanted. *I really don't want to see my face on a warrant.*

'Joss von Cramm. A crimper – that's a recruiter – looking for landsknechts for armies. Any army, no matter what side or country, as long as they'll pay.' Nicolas spoke quickly as the older man approached their table. 'He wanted to recruit me in Wanfried, because he had saved my life.'

'Is he alone?'

'He rarely is. Usually, he travels in the company of some ruffians in case the crimping gets mediaeval—'

'Good afternoon.' Cramm made a formal, if inelegant, bow. 'Now this is what I call a reunion.' He looked at Nicolas. 'You and Valentin – so what's happened that has suddenly made you best of friends? Is it this pretty young lady who's tamed you?' Without asking for permission, he sat down and grabbed a mug. 'I'll drink to that.' He emptied the vessel in one gulp and gestured for a new one.

The boy stopped playing with the lute and went to work.

Aenlin was slightly shocked. Obviously, a man like Cramm would know almost every decent mercenary romping about the Empire, and he'd certainly know about any rivalries between the various landsknecht outfits. *We might as well expect the worst.*

Cramm hadn't waited for an answer, but carried on, 'I assume this lady is the obligation you ditched me for.' He leaned back in his chair, looking at Aenlin. He'd masked the smell of sweat and dust with the overpowering scent of lavender water. 'How much?'

Aenlin played dumb. 'I don't understand.'

'How much will it cost to ransom the immortal Nicolas from your services? His services I will get for free because he owes me his life. Don't you, my dear?' Cramm grinned at Nicolas, but his eyes remained cold. 'But of course, I respect the fact that I will have to ransom him first. Business is business, after all.'

'How was the last battle?' Nicolas asked, trying to change the topic.

Valentin sat up straight and looked around the room.

Aenlin tried to understand why this man was being so civil. Maybe the crimper was looking for an amicable arrangement because he was travelling without his thugs.

The boy was still carrying the lute in his left hand when he brought Cramm's tankard.

'Oh, the Swedes don't like me at all. I promised Gustavus Adolphus' captains I'd send you to defeat the Imperial troops and the Poles. Without you, the Swedes had to beat a hasty retreat and almost lost their monarch.' Cramm took the lute from the boy and absentmindedly tuned it, then played a few notes.

The boy put down the mug and returned to the bar. He was looking anxious.

'I think he has signed a truce now, so the war with the Poles is over.'

'Bad for business,' Valentin said, without looking at the crimper. He kept his eyes focused on the taproom.

'Depends. I think the Swedish King will land in the Empire early next year, once winter's over. Stralsund has been a Swedish garrison town since last year, and his bulwark against Wallenstein, who wasn't able to take it.'

'I know.' Valentin's face was dark. 'I was standing next to him when he swore to conquer the city, even if it was chained to the sky.'

Aenlin didn't know whether Tahmina had made that up or if she'd taken it from the dead landsknecht's memories, but she knew she was doing this to avoid raising any suspicion that there might be something wrong with Valentin.

'Suddenly, a ball hit his glass of wine – it had been fired by one of the defending gunmen,' the ensign went on, gesturing grandly. 'A little more to the left and the leader of the Imperial troops would have been dead. Afterwards, they killed twelve hundred of his men, musket ball by musket ball.'

Cramm played more slowly, a catchy tune. He wasn't bad. 'Ah, if you had only been on their side, Nicolas, my god of war. Now the Protestants everywhere are complaining; they all want Swedish assistance.' He slowed the tune to accompany his tale. 'I don't have to be a prophet to see the next war on the horizon. The next big war.' Again he looked at Aenlin. 'How much?'

'You cannot ransom him – not for a thousand thalers, batzes or guilders.' She put a hand on Nicolas' forearm. 'An immortal god of war is worth more than his weight in gold.' As a peace offering, she pushed Valentin's plate towards the crimper. 'Let me invite you to join us. Eat, drink and enjoy.'

'How generous.' Cramm tossed the lute at the boy, but his little fingers fumbled the catch and the instrument landed behind the bar with a crash, the strings ringing. Cramm tucked into the cabbage hungrily, then bit into the bulging sausage; fat splattered his beard and moustache. 'How long will he be in your service?'

He doesn't give up, does he? Aenlin shook her head as if thinking about his question, brushing away the strand of hair falling forward as usual. 'That depends. Hopefully, Nicolas will be free before the next war.' She wished the man would just disappear. *But maybe he has heard news from somewhere?*

As if reading her thoughts, Tahmina asked, 'Any news, Cramm?' Valentin put his arms on the table, leaned forward and looked straight at the crimper. 'Any profitable battle fronts we should know about?'

'If you were in northern Africa,' he said as he chewed, 'you could pick up some sailors from Lübeck. The Hanseatic city has set up an institution to buy the freedom of its sailors captured by pirates – that's pretty profitable. We don't bother with small jobs for little money.'

'How about France?' Cramm picked up his leather satchel,

opened it and took out a pack of wrinkled documents that he picked through quickly. He picked out one letter. 'There you go! A few days ago, Richelieu issued a new Edict against the Huguenots. They have to disband their armies and their fortresses will be razed. That would certainly be profitable.' He passed Valentin the paper. 'Ah, I almost forgot – you can't read. Or can you?' He pocketed it again. 'Anyway, Richelieu will surely start exiling Protestants again. Or the armoured Cardinal will come to the Empire to join the fight against the Swedes. Wouldn't that be great?'

He told them that in faraway Japan, they were searching for secret Christians amidst the populace. Suspects had to publicly step on paintings of Jesus to prove that they had not converted illicitly. According to this particular journal, the culprits were immediately sentenced to death.

Japan, Aenlin thought in wonder. *The world keeps getting smaller.*

'By then, I will certainly have released Nicolas from my service,' she said calmly, and continued eating.

'Have you heard anything about the Venetian?' Nicolas asked.

Cramm pointed at Valentin. 'Ask him. He was part of his outfit, wreaking havoc alongside him.'

Aenlin listened attentively but kept quiet, letting the mercenaries and Tahmina carry the conversation. After all, someone had to remember what they had said.

'That was ages ago,' Valentin replied. 'We had a dispute; I left – for good reasons. What's the fellow done this time?'

Cramm chewed silently, examining the trio, then he took a long sip of beer. 'He's being hunted, in a town not far from here. They suspected him and his men to be Catholic spies planning to secretly open the gates for some soldiers to come pillaging.' He laughed. 'As is quite the vogue right now.'

Aenlin felt quiet anticipation. *Are we rid of the Venetian and his demonic servants?* 'How did that turn out?' she asked.

Cramm shrugged. 'Don't know.'

'Ho,' Nicolas exclaimed. 'That was a lie. I can see through you, old man. You're wanting money for your information.'

The crimper blinked, chewing his sausage with his mouth wide open. 'Clever fellow.'

'Do not pay him,' Valentin recommended, moving his head in a way that Aenlin knew only too well. 'We can find out without him.'

The door opened and the groom popped his head inside. 'Herr Cramm! Your horse is ready. You can continue your journey.'

Cramm rose, grabbing the rest of the sausage. 'A good day to you. Wars demand fresh meat for the carnage and I must procure it – like a butcher, but without getting my hands dirty.'

'It's still a bloody business,' Aenlin remarked.

'I'll wash my hands with the coin they pay me. Coins are good for cleaning your hands, remember that.' Cramm went to the door. 'Thanks for the meal. If you want to know where this little story happened, ask around for the events in Mühlhausen. I will take my leave.' He took his hat from a hook. 'Nicolas, remember: you won't get rid of me that easily. You are deep in debt with me – deeper than the Werra.'

With that, he left.

Mühlhausen! Aenlin looked at Valentin and then at Nicolas. 'Finish your meal. Quickly.'

Free Imperial city of Mühlhausen, July 1629

Statius ran across the roofs and protruding dormers of the houses of Unterer Steinweg to finally leap through the closed window into the topmost floor of their lodgings, shattering it. *The Venetian is not getting away!*

He landed in the empty room amid a rain of shards, rolled

and came to his feet. Without stopping, he opened the door and ran charging down the corridor until he reached the doctor's room. 'Master! Master, we—!'

The room was empty.

'The Almighty sweep my arse with his beard!' From the floors beneath him, Statius could hear angry shouting and clamouring, pistols firing and the sound of clashing blades. Louder still were the death cries of the city guards, who were falling victim by the dozens to the glowing blades, while the exploding musket balls tore cruel wounds in tender flesh.

Statius didn't care about those losses. There was only one thing that counted. 'Master?'

He quickly checked the other rooms, but there was no sign of the Venetian, so he hurried down the stairs, approaching the battle he had started with the signal they had agreed upon. *Music to my ears.* He had planned to take Osanna in her room and make her scream so loudly that it would be audible behind the Church of All Saints. Well, things had happened differently, but he'd still got his piercing scream.

Statius reached the landing, where some of the landsknechts were busy reloading pistols and handing them down to their comrades, in whose hands they spat glowing death and burning doom.

'That's it – let's kill those bastards,' Statius shouted as he ran by. 'Where's the master?'

'Down the stairs to the right,' someone answered. 'He's planning on attacking those idiots from behind.'

'Good. I have news for him.' Statius reached a small chamber, where he found Barthel preparing to climb out through the window. The only other person there was the plague doctor; the rest of the mercenaries taking part in the sortie had already climbed down the outer wall to attack the city guards from behind.

Great. 'Master! I bring urgent news!'

Barthel, who was clinging to the windowsill outside, paused. 'Statius! Where in the Devil's name have you been?' His unshaved face showed anger and surprise. 'I was looking for you—'

'I was in Osanna's room. She betrayed us,' Statius said, feigning outrage. 'She was giving signals from her room!'

'How strange,' said the Venetian. 'I thought I heard her scream – just before the city guard attacked from the house across the street.' The silver mask turned towards Statius, its red glass eyes glowing. 'Imagine: Osanna told me *you* were planning something. Where is she so we can interrogate her once we have defeated those idiots?'

'I had to kill her – she intended lighting up a powder keg of powder – to destroy the top floor, with you inside, Master.' Statius knew the end of this little charade had come. 'Wait, Captain. I'll climb down with you.' As he spoke, he drew his pistol and shot the surprised Barthel in the face. 'In the name of Tzontemoc: off to the realm of the dead with you!'

While Vanth's demonic powers granted the mercenaries special abilities, Statius' new god had blessed him as well: the captain was not immortal any more. The lead ball crashed through his forehead, shattering his skull. Barthel let go of the windowsill, fell backwards and a moment later Statius heard his impact on the ground, followed by the frightened cries of the landsknechts who'd already escaped the house.

The grey cloud of gunpowder smoke slowly drifted out of the window.

One down. Statius dropped his weapon and drew the other, at the same time pulling his sword from its scabbard. 'Die, idolater!' he shouted. The muzzle swivelled through the smoke, looking for a target.

The silhouette of the plague doctor became visible. He was holding a pistol in each gloved hand. 'How about a shoot-out?

If we survive, we go at each other with blades. What do you think, Statius?'

The barrels of both the Venetian's pistols were glowing from within.

'You will not survive.' Statius fired and quickly ducked. 'For Tzontemoc!' he shouted again.

The ball hit the silver mask with a clang, denting it but not piercing it, although the impact threw his opponent's head back. The doctor slightly raised his arms – and both shots missed.

Fuck! The damned mask saved him. The glowing musket balls whistled above Statius' head and hit the wall, where they exploded on impact, tearing fist-sized holes in the wood and stone.

'What did I tell you?' Laughing, the Venetian dropped his firearms to draw a rapier and an axe. 'This is where the real fun begins!'

'Miserable coward. You cheated!' Statius drew his own rapier. 'If you didn't wear this mask, your face would be gone by now!'

The Venetian attacked with skill and prowess, driving attack after attack, and in between, trying to hit Statius with his sharpened metal beak.

Statius, sweating profusely, was using all his considerable ability just to avoid being hit. Using his sword in his right hand, his rapier in his left, his flashing bladework saved his life more than once. 'Where did you learn to fight like this, you fucking bastard?' he screamed in anger.

'You betrayed me, Statius.' The Venetian stabbed at him and followed up with a feint of his axe and a kick that surprised the landsknecht, catching him in the side and throwing him against the windowsill. 'Is this how you thank me for saving your life?'

'This is my proof that Vanth has no power over me – and never did.' He extended both rapier and sword in a bid to block his enemy. 'I don't serve your fucking demon. Tzontemoc is the better god.'

'These ridiculous monstrosities from the New World send their priestesses to thwart my plans! Who do they think they are?'

'They came for vengeance: to plant the seeds of war so Europe will drown in its own blood.' Statius heard the noise of battle in the house dying down. 'You won't stop them! They will have their way.'

'What did they give you for your loyalty?' The Venetian's blade had started to glow red. 'What can *you* do to stop me?' He had barely spoken the words when his blades stopped glowing, turning back into regular cold steel.

Tzontemoc is with me! A closer look at his enemy told Statius that the ball that had hit the mask hadn't completely obliterated the symbol of Vanth, but it had deformed it; there was a finger-length crack in the silver. *Is that it? Is the mask the source of all his power?*

'My turn.' In a flurry of lunges and feints, Statius forced the now anxious Venetian backwards. The man's parries became slower, and the first sword-cuts appeared in his leather apron and his coat.

'Fucking little masked man,' Statius yelled, feeling the rising flush of victory. 'I will sacrifice you to Tzontemoc!' He turned to use the momentum for a forceful stab with his rapier – at least that was what he wanted his enemy to believe.

The plague doctor obliged, moving to block the blade by crossing his axe and his rapier. 'You will never—'

Statius went under his own armpit to stab the Venetian in the chest – the masked man had not seen that move coming. Statius quickly released the sword hilt and stepped away. 'Well, how does it feel?'

Gasping, the plague doctor staggered backwards, his glass eyes glowing bright red. A scream sounded from beneath the mask as he dropped his axe and his rapier. He pulled Statius' sword from his body, then dropped it, while blood gushed from the wound.

The symbols and sigils on the battered silver mask were glowing, as if trying to strengthen its wounded wearer.

'So it is this that gives you your power,' Statius whispered. He hit the Venetian again, this time with the flat of his rapier blade. 'Let's see what's hidden beneath!'

The blade smashed down on the silver with a loud, ringing clatter. The steel broke with a whirring sound and the Venetian's head jerked sideways. The mask flew off his face, turning and spiralling through the air and finally clattering to the floorboards. The sharpened tip of the beak-like nose drove into the wood.

'Turn around, you scoundrel,' Statius shouted. He dropped the shattered rapier and pointed his dagger at his enemy, who had turned his face slightly away. 'I want to see your face.'

Very slowly, the Venetian straightened, showing Statius his face, a harmless, normal face of a man in his fifties, a little pudgy, with light blue eyes and a trimmed, grey-streaked beard. When he took off the hat, Statius saw cropped salt-and-pepper hair. Small scars spoke of battles and other altercations he had survived in the past.

'Go fuck an ox! You're just a man of flesh and blood.' With one quick step, Statius moved between him and his mask. 'Without this thing, you are nothing – a dotard, too old to fight me.' Quickly, he picked up the Venetian's rapier. 'Who are you?'

'Melchior Pieck – that is my name.' Although he still wore the black clothes, the gloves and the leather apron, he no longer looked in the least bit creepy.

'The one they call Bracke? After the scent hound?' Statius aimed the steel tip of his dagger at Pieck's throat. There was nothing at all terrifying in his opponent any more.

'So this is how your legend ends.' *For I need this mask.* Statius had managed to do what few others could have done and he knew to whom he owed this: *Blessed be Tzontemoc.*

'Where is Osanna?'

'Why do you care? That's what you want to hear from me while you take your dying breath?' Statius roared with triumphant laughter. 'The whereabouts of that whore?'

'What did you do to her?'

'I took her and I threw her away. That's how I behave when I'm at war.' Statius smiled coldly. 'And I am *always* at war, Bracke.'

'She was carrying my child,' Bracke said, his voice broken. 'She had received Vanth's greatest blessing.'

Statius laughed aloud again. 'So that's what pinched my cock when I rammed it into her? Your child is as now well as its mother.'

'Get away from the master,' a warning voice yelled as a landsknecht entered the room, his pistol drawn. 'You piece of shit, you *will* lower your blade! One wrong move, one blink of your eye and I will shoot your head to pieces.'

'I wouldn't dream of it.' With the tip of his boot, Statius indicated the mask. 'Without the mask, Bracke will be hurt – and if he dies, your blessings might vanish – so no more demonic powers, no exploding balls, no glowing blades. You—'

Suddenly, the mask was glowing bright silver, blazing like the midday sun.

'You bastard!' Blinded by the light, Statius closed his eyes and quickly stabbed at Bracke, but he met with no resistance – obviously, his rapier had missed his opponent.

The landsknecht's pistol rang out.

Heat rushed past Statius, taking with it the tip of his nose.

Screaming in pain, he bent and covered the bleeding wound with his hands. He lost his balance and, still blinded from the glare, he tripped over the backrest of a chair and fell—

—and fell and fell.

Statius' fall took longer than expected, then he hit something that was soft and hard at the same time. The impact drove the breath from his lungs; he heard bones and ribs crack. The air was cool, but full of shouting and screaming. He was on Unterer Steinweg, right next to the house, and it was Barthel's dead body which had cushioned his impact.

If I'd hit the cobblestones, I'd have shattered my skull. Statius rose with a moan, pressed one hand against his truncated nose and used the other to pick up the dead captain's pistol.

When he looked up at the window he had fallen from, he saw Bracke there, once again wearing the mask and the black hat. He had turned into the Venetian once again, and his glass eyes were glowing red.

Quickly, Statius raised the firearm and shot, but he missed his target; instead, the ball tore a long splinter of wood from the window frame. 'I *will* get you,' he promised. 'I have already killed your beloved and your child, but you, I will sacrifice to Tzontemoc!'

He dropped the smoking pistol and limped away, just as two more landsknechts appeared next to their leader. *I must find my priestesses and warn them.*

Mühlhausen was in turmoil: armed men had gathered at the house next to the Church of All Saints, while others were employed in carrying wounded city guards out of the danger zone.

'Quickly,' Statius called at them, holding his nose, which was dripping red; much of the blood was already congealing in his moustache. He picked up an abandoned musket dropped by a city guard and cried, 'Hurry up – kill the Catholic spies! Wipe them out before they can open the gates—'

He staggered past Osanna's naked corpse, which he had thrown from the house, through the ranks of volunteers, until two caring women accosted him, offering to tend to his wounds.

Statius followed them, thanking them profusely. *Let them patch me up.* Then he'd see what he could do to them. He always was at war.

Elend Farm and Mill, near the Brocken, July 1629

'Are you awake?'

Jäcklein heard the begging voice of a child and opened his eyes.

'Please – please, let us go!'

He had to blink several times to see clearly. He was lying on a dirty floor. Somewhere close he could hear something continuously rattling – like in a sawmill.

He had an awful taste in his bone-dry mouth. With a moan, he sat up and looked around to find himself in a simple wooden room – but how had he ended up here? And where was *here*? His last memory was of the logging camp, where they'd been fooling about with the stuff in Agatha's chest.

The gigantic boy Moritz was lying slumped on a bench, breathing deeply and slowly. Next to him was Caspar, his mouth wide open, snoring inelegantly. Their clothes were dirty, as was their skin, and not even the duellist's expensive wardrobe was worth anything any more. His wig had vanished too.

'The hangman and the Devil take it,' Jäcklein muttered, running his hands through his greasy blond hair, which felt like it hadn't seen water, let alone soap, for ages.

He felt eyes on him and finally spotted four poorly dressed children of various ages, bound with ropes to an iron stove. They were watching him. No parents or other adults were anywhere to be seen and the only sound was that continuous, aggravating rattling.

Jäcklein rose slowly, smelling the stench of his own body

and his completely filthy clothes. His breeches and sleeves had lost all puffiness, all the colours had faded. The fabrics were covered in a thick crust of dirt, piss and blood. He couldn't even remember the last time he had washed his hands. *What the fuck has happened? Where are Nicolas, Stats, Aenlin and Tahmina?*

'Hey, sleepyheads,' he shouted at Moritz and Caspar, 'rise and shine. Do any of you know what's happened?' Jäcklein looked at the children. 'Where am I?'

The youngest ones, cowering, retreated as far as the ropes allowed, but one of them stayed where he was, staring silently at the floor. Their torn, patched clothes and the bruises he could see on their limbs suggested that they had to work hard for little or no pay. At last the oldest boy stretched out his hands with a pleading look. 'Spare us!'

Caspar and Moritz were coming to at last, rubbing their eyes and yawning. They looked first at the squalid Jäcklein, then at each other, disgusted by their sickening stench and filthy clothes.

'Get up ...' the giant began, pushing his hand through his sticky black curls.

'I just said so,' Jäcklein replied. 'What's up? Are either of you clever enough to remember what happened? Where's the captain? And the others?'

Caspar was the first to spot the jug of water. He got up and hurriedly poured himself a cup. 'Thirsty,' he said, refilling the vessel, 'as thirsty as the Comte after a hundred miles.' He touched his face. 'I have a beard? How long have we been on the road?'

'Who are they?' Moritz pointed at the children.

'We live here,' the boy answered. 'In Elend. That's the name of our village. Elend.' The boy looked at the landsknechts in confusion. 'Why do you suddenly speak differently?'

'Did I speak French before?' Jäcklein's head was empty. He

had no memory of *anything* that had happened after the logging camp. He used his dagger to cut the children's bonds, noticing how much blood covered the blade. *Old blood and new blood, and some long hairs, too.* 'By the Devil's grandmother, that must've been some slaughter-fest . . .'

'I don't know anything.' Moritz rubbed his dirty forehead, then sat up suddenly. 'Oh! I do!' He frowned slightly. 'Statius put this skin around his shoulders – the patterned one from the big cat of the New World, remember?'

'Yes! We were hopping around the room . . . maybe the others are outside?' Caspar went to the door to open it and look outside. 'Oh my! What's this?'

Jäcklein managed to free the last of the children, who ran to join the little ones huddling in a corner to avoid getting too close to the stinking, terrifying men.

'What's up?' he asked now. 'Did your stallion give birth to a filly?'

Moritz had pulled himself up and made his way to the water jug too. 'I feel completely parched,' he said.

'There's a wagon there – it's . . . full of people.' Excitedly, Caspar waved them over. 'Look!'

What deviltry has been done to us? Jäcklein glanced outside. 'What about the captain and the others? Are they anywhere to be seen?'

The little house was in a clearing, surrounded by forest. A sawmill stood opposite, with a hay wagon standing next to it. The wagon was piled with men, women and children, young and old, all bound and gagged and stacked like herrings in barrels. A great cloud of flies were buzzing around them, turning them into food for maggots. Some of them were clearly dead, but at a second look, some were moving weakly.

The horse hitched to the wagon and pawing at the ground was the Comte. He snorted when he saw his master. The formerly splendid stallion had lost weight; welts on his back and rump showed that he had been beaten mercilessly.

'Odin, I pray that this is not our own work,' whispered Moritz. He started looking among those bound people for anyone still alive. 'We have to help them before they die!'

'You go ahead – I'll give you a hand in just a minute.' Jäcklein turned back to the children and raised his empty, dirty hands. 'Look, we'll not hurt you. But something's happened to us – we think a demon or a witch must have ensorcelled our minds. When did we arrive here?'

'Yesterday,' the eldest boy answered. He introduced himself as David. 'With the wagon. There was also a woman, but she left shortly after you had arrived. She looked ill.'

'A woman? Was she called Aenlin?'

'No.'

'Tahmina?'

'No. You called her Ula. I think' – David lowered his voice – 'I think she's the witch who put a spell on you. She ordered you to tie up our parents and us and bring us along.'

Ula – that was Ursula. She and Agatha are witches of the worst kind, as guilty as anything of true evil.

'But?' Jäcklein knew from David's tone of voice that something unforeseen had happened.

'You suddenly . . . fell asleep. Right where you stood. You just keeled over.' David's eyes suddenly opened wide at the sight of a man and a woman entering the room. 'Mummy! Papa!' He and the other children ran to embrace their parents, sobbing in relief.

'What have we done?' Moritz asked bitterly, carrying three people into the room and laying them carefully on the floor. They looked half-dead. He found some more cups, filled them with water and handed them out to the emaciated figures.

'The witches we freed in Bamberg? Guess that was a mistake.'

Caspar brought in more survivors. 'This is Maria – she's from a village many miles away. She says we collected everyone on the wagon on our way here. *All of them.*'

Jäcklein scratched his head, hating the feel of his sticky blond hair. For the first time, it wasn't sticking out in all directions. 'Why?'

'You were supposed to bring them to the Brocken,' said the children's mother; her simple shift was stained with blood and other less identifiable fluids. 'We were to be sacrifices – that's what she told you. I am Katharina, the children's mother. This is my husband, Peter.'

Her husband dropped heavily onto the bench. His hands were dark blue from the tightness of his bonds; at his request, his children started massaging his fingers to help get the circulation going.

'Heaven, death and the Devil!' Jäcklein shouted angrily, then he begged, '*Please*, forgive what we have done to you, Katharina. However, we weren't acting of our own free will. David will explain. The witch will pay for this. To use us for—'

'The others aren't here,' said Moritz, who was carrying in more survivors, 'and they're not on the wagon, either. There's no trace of the captain, or our friends.'

'We'll look after these people.' Katharina sent two of the children outside to get more water from the well. 'Go and kill the witch before she wreaks even more havoc, or summons a killer storm.'

'Agreed,' Jäcklein said. They'd have to go to the Brocken and find out from Ula where their friends were. *If she's done them any harm, she'll die very painfully.* He checked own his weapons before telling the others, 'Grab your muskets and whatever ammunition you can find.'

'Musket balls against an enchantress who can bewitch our mind?' Nonetheless, Caspar was checking his pistols. 'I trust my steady hand, but if someone puts a spell on me, all my skill will be in vain.'

'Don't despair, your Snootiness,' Jäcklein said. 'There must be a reason she's not keeping up her spell any more – we'll just have to grasp this opportunity. Who knows how long she'll be distracted?'

'Maybe your friends are on the wagon?' David suggested, but Caspar was shaking his head.

'No.' He was loading pistol after pistol with a speed that made Jäcklein envious. 'Moritz checked. They're not there.'

'No, I meant the other wagon full of people – the one the witch drove away.' The boy pointed to the southwest.

'Heavens above!' Caspar started loading even faster. 'Ula must have begun her sacrifices.'

'Whatever that means.' Jäcklein downed another mug of water. 'How far is it to the Brocken?' he asked.

'Three hours by foot, then up the mountain,' Katharina answered. 'You'll make it before nightfall.'

Moritz and Caspar hurried outside. There was no time for washing; they had to prevent the worst from happening, even if they did stink like polecats.

'The witch is the only one who knows the truth.' Jäcklein mounted behind Caspar, but Moritz spared the snorting stallion his weight by jogging alongside them. 'Let's catch them and save our friends!'

The chase was on.

The Little Book of War, being a thorough manual of warcraft: namely, how to erect a fortress including its inner and outer works, how to furnish it with all necessary paraphernalia and how to keep it up: as well as how any war official, high or low, shall ask during a campaign and during a training exercise of the armed formations of the array, on horseback or on foot, in skirmishes, attacks, frays and assaults according to their estate and oath: with an added translation and explication of foreign terms and names of warfare common at this time and how to understand them, in drawings and writing/partly quoted from established authors, but mostly portrayed from personal experience and duly dedicated for edification to those who are under weapons to act as their dear Fatherland's protectors in need and make more easily accessible through educational copperplates by Capt Hans Conrad Lavater, citizen of Zurich.

Hans Conrad Lavater,
Introduction to *Little Book of War*, 1644

CAPITULUM XVI

The Brocken, July 1629

Statius left the last drifting patches of fog behind as he reached the crest of the Brocken. It had been known as a place for witches and all sorts of spirits to romp and dance for centuries. The priestesses called it Doom's Peak.

The knapsack with his meagre belongings was heavy, but as a landsknecht, he was used to that. In his left hand was the musket he'd stolen; as he'd done while on board the *Lorelei*, he'd attached a dagger beneath its barrel to use it in a mêlée once its gunpowder load had been discharged.

His injured nose was making breathing difficult: the tip had been ripped off completely and the rest of it was bandaged up so it could heal. After his generous helpers had mended the wound as best they could, he had left Mühlhausen without further ado. He was dressed in clean, inconspicuous clothes, carrying only his stolen weapons, the knapsack and some provisions so that he could help Ula – whose real name was Itochu, as befitted an Aztec. She needed him; he could feel it very strongly.

Where are you? Statius looked around.

He caught sight of several bodies lying on the ground, a little way back from the top. It was too far for him to see if Itochu was among them, or whether they were resting or dead. He cocked his loaded musket and approached.

Statius was still congratulating himself on his ruse, having set half the citizens of Mühlhausen on the Venetian, who'd proved to be a man of flesh and blood, even though he wielded supernatural powers.

That was what Statius would demand from the Aztecs: more power, more strength and invincibility, just like Moritz. They had to make him frozen, even if it cost a hundred lives.

I won't hesitate to get these things, and the wars in which I shall rage will last for ever. I will have a life full of atrocities, blood, gold and lust.

He hurried onwards carefully, his injured nose throbbing painfully.

Three children, two men and four women lay bound on the ground. When they heard his footsteps, the soft scraping of his soles, they looked up. As they caught sight of Statius, he saw the hope dawn in their eyes.

Itochu was crouching on the flat crest, her body tilted to one side, her left hand holding the obsidian knife. She was wheezing now, and coughing weakly. Her gaze looked feverish, sweat prickled her temples and her shorn scalp, and her dress was soaked. For the sacrificial ceremony, she had to wear the traditional garb: the black animal's skin lay at her feet, but she looked too weak to shape-change.

This is bad – unbelievably bad. 'Mistress!' He walked past the prisoners begging him for help, ignoring them completely, and knelt beside her. 'How can I be of service?' he asked, helping her to sit up.

It took Itochu a few seconds to recognise him. 'Stats?'

'Yes, Mistress.'

She touched his bearded face. 'Where is Simia?'

'Dead, Mistress.'

'Then you have to' – she searched the folds of her dress – 'take this to Mano.' She produced a long, slender knife made from a piece of obsidian. It shimmered black; something green was embedded in the blade.

'What is that?'

'The claw of Itzli. Take it to Mano. She knows what to do.'

'But why don't you?'

'I am too weak.' Itochu coughed again. 'This cursed Old World with its afflictions – they have killed thousands of us, and now one of them is killing me.' She coughed hoarsely, the pain making her shudder. 'Take her the claw,' she managed. 'She will reward you immensely.'

She's dying! No, I – I . . . 'I want to be a demon!' he said quickly. 'A demon like those from your world of the dead. Like . . . a Xolotl in human guise – and more!' Statius removed his hat from his brown curls. 'Can Mano do this for me?'

Suddenly he saw the dark patches under Itochu's arms and at last he noticed the gangrenous smell she exuded. The priestess was suffering from the Black Death; those were ulcers in her armpits. *She will not be able to fulfil Tzontemoc's will any longer.*

'She can,' she answered, coughing again. 'She is the strongest of us all.'

'Where do I find her, Mistress?'

'Go to Hamburg. She is there, in the—' Itochu gasped, spitting red gobbets to clear her mouth after another fit of coughing.

Statius was beginning to worry that she might die before telling him more. 'Mistress! Please tell me—'

'The skin,' she said, 'wear it, and you will travel more quickly. I wanted to use it, but first . . . first see to it that their blood . . .' Itochu opened her feverish eyes wide, then all life drained out of them in an instant.

Angrily, Statius jumped to his feet. The dead woman collapsed and rolled onto her belly. 'You fucking stupid piece of pigshit,' he shouted, kicking the corpse, breaking several bones in the process. 'You should have told me *exactly* where to find Mano!' In his anger, he kept kicking at the Aztec until he had pulverised her head, staining his high leather boots with her blood.

He pocketed the obsidian blade and looked at the black panther skin. *How the Hell can that thing help me travel faster?* But she had sounded sincere.

He threw his knapsack and his hat to the rocky ground next to the musket before picking up the skin and draping it around his shoulders, as he had done before. Then, slowly, he pulled the panther skull onto his own head.

Nothing happened.

'That can't be all,' he whispered to himself. He pulled out the obsidian knife and weighed it in his right hand, then cast a look at the prisoners. *Blood. Didn't Itochu start to say something about blood?*

'Well, then. Change me, you sheep!' Statius bent over a woman to slice open her throat. 'Let's start with you.'

She sighed briefly, then the warm blood was flowing so freely from the cut that he had to catch it with both hands. He started smearing all over his body, ignoring the screaming of the terrified prisoners.

I must become a predator. When he still felt no change, he drank deeply from the blood. *So I shall behave like one.*

Now the blood was coating his mouth and running down his throat, he thought he felt a twinge running through his body from the tips of his hair to his toes. With a soft smacking and crackling, the panther hide sank through his clothing and blended with him.

Statius twisted in pain. In his mind, he heard the snarl of the feline predator entering him. The spell of the skin was turning him into something new. His hands became claws, his fingernails dark green talons. He was becoming a werebeast, like the creature people called a *werewolf*. His sense of smell was much improved; his eyes and ears had become sharper – and he felt so much stronger.

Laughing loudly, he picked up the dead woman with one hand and tore off a piece of her shoulder with his teeth. The taste was exquisite, and increasingly aromatic the longer he chewed it. It would have been such a waste for Itochu to have this gift!

Snarling softly, he looked around the Brocken.

The wind, the scents, the magnificent view across the forests, covered in mist that looked like cotton wool. *Known, new, overwhelming.* He had become a *special* sort of ruler. *A king among beasts and hunters.*

Statius felt it: in this form and with these skills, he was able to run like the wind, almost without resting. A large bite of human meat had given him such strength. He would be able to find more than enough prey in the fields and the villages as he journeyed.

The claw of Itzli. Statius drew the knife and looked at it. It was the first time he had heard this god's name. *What will Mano do with it?* he thought. Then, *Why don't I use it myself?*

Instead of taking it to the Aztec in Hamburg, he could try to find its secret and summon a demon himself.

No, Statius scolded himself, *it's too early for that.* He knew nothing about the language or the correct invocations. In the end, it was nothing but a gewgaw in his ignorant hands, useful only for slitting throats or skinning apples. *But it's far too good for that.*

'You will serve me,' Statius promised the weapon, pocketing it. Itochu had promised him an immense reward. The enchanted panther skin and these new powers were a promising start for a prospective demon.

'Stats? By all the saints of Cologne: *Stats!*'

The shout of joy sounding nearby made him turn slowly. The beast within snarled in anticipation, but it retreated, lurking, until only the crooked hands with the glass talons remained.

Jäcklein, Moritz and Caspar had appeared at the other end of the crest of the Brocken. Caspar and Jäcklein were riding the black stallion, while the young giant was walking alongside.

Fresh meat, his stomach growled, and Statius called happily, 'Ho!' He started waving, while in the other hand he clutched the obsidian knife in his pocket.

He would take Mano the artefact. *But before that, I want to see what happens when I kill with it.* Surely the act of murder would imbue him with even more strength and power. *The gods of the New World take pleasure in atrocities and rivers of blood, just like me.* With regret, he looked at the living prisoners and the approaching landsknechts, but he knew it was only a pleasure deferred.

'You've got here just in time, old friends. I've been waiting for you.' Statius trotted towards the three sheep.

'Wait,' Jäcklein said softly, dismounting the black stallion. 'Am I the only one who thinks Stats looks kind of weird?'

'There are two corpses,' Moritz pointed at the bodies, 'and more prisoners, too.'

'There's blood on his face and around his mouth. Actually . . .' Caspar dropped the Comte's reins. 'Actually, it's all over him. Has he been rolling around in it?'

Jäcklein caught sight of the dagger-like item in his friend's hand. 'This is more than his usual berserker rage.'

They had needed no directions; they'd just followed the wheel tracks and the trail of corpses that had fallen from the wagon's bed to get to the top of the mountain. When they'd found the wagon, half a dozen women and children had still been alive. The landsknechts had freed them and after telling them how to find the mill, they left the survivors to help each other get to Elend, where their wounds and other needs could be properly tended to.

'What if he's still under the influence of the Aztec?' Caspar pulled a spyglass from his dirty saddlebag and looked at the two female corpses. 'Stone the crows!' He briefly described what the corpses looked like. 'The trampled one could be Ula. Her skull's been smashed flat as a pancake, but she's wearing that flashy Aztec jewellery.'

It was him. Stats killed the priestess and tore the other one to pieces. Jäcklein watched his blood-spattered friend approach. His grin didn't bode well. It was evil, and full of anticipation. 'Stop right there, Stats,' he called. 'Are you all right?'

'Oh, I couldn't be better,' the landsknecht called back. 'There was a fight, but I defeated Itochu. Now only Nica is left.'

'Why's he calling her Itochu?' Moritz whispered. 'Can her spirit have possessed him?'

'Why not? I think these witches are capable of doing any-thing.' Caspar put away his spyglass, took his duelling pistols from their sheaths and primed them, cocking them audibly. 'I think something fishy is going on here.'

'So do I.' Jäcklein drew his rapier and a pistol. 'I told you to stop were you were, Stats.'

Statius slowed his steps. 'Well, fuck a dwarf in the ear! What's wrong with you lot?' He laughed throatily. 'Shouldn't you be happy about our reunion?' Then he turned full circle, looking around. 'Where are Nicolas and Aenlin? Where's Tahmina? Come out, come out, wherever you are! Come on, you three! You're just trying to tease me, aren't you?'

Jäcklein motioned for Moritz to approach Stats, knowing Stats couldn't hurt him. 'I'll send the boy to you, Stats. Don't take this the wrong way, old friend, but I want him to inspect you. You look a little odd to me. Bit like a wolf after visiting the chicken coop.'

'What's that knife in your hand?' Caspar demanded.

'No knife – an artefact. The claw of Itzli, or at least, that's what Itochu called it before she died.' Statius stopped. His boots were shimmering, wet with blood, and he was covered up to his knees and beyond. He'd wiped the gore from his mouth, but it still clung to his goatee and his twisted moustache. 'All right, then. Come on over and see if I still have my mind. I won't bite you.'

He's already bitten someone else. Jäcklein's tension rose.

'Moritz.'

'Yes?'

'Look at him closely,' Jäcklein ordered. 'Look into his eyes, and if you think he's no longer in control of himself, knock him to the ground. I'm afraid there's something very wrong going on here.'

'He can't hurt me,' Moritz said carelessly. 'My skin is hard as a breastplate. There's no water around here he could drown me in.'

Caspar slowly stepped aside to be able to aim past the giant at Stats. 'I may be wrong, but did I hear some sort of . . . admiration when Stats said her name?'

'Whose name? The witch's?'

'Yes.'

'But he stamped on her skull until it was flatter than an empty tick. That's not exactly a sign of admiration.' Jäcklein had not the foggiest idea what might have happened here. The bound people were crying inarticulately. *Are they trying to warn us?* he wondered. *About him?*

Caspar raised his right arm and aimed a pistol at Statius. 'Why do you call her by that name, Stats?'

Moritz was still walking unwaveringly towards him; he was now little more than ten feet away from the beefy landsknecht.

'Why do you ask?' Statius raised his arms. 'Is that forbidden?'

'No swearing, no hatred, no foul invective,' the duellist said carefully. 'Why's this, I wonder?'

'Has it been like that?' Statius asked in amazement. 'I didn't realise. Well, it doesn't matter.'

Moritz reached him and the men shook hands.

'Can you see it, too?' Caspar whispered to Jäcklein. 'Stats has grown.'

'Fuck me! You're right.' The mercenary was now half a head taller than their most impressive member, and he'd also put on some muscle. 'It's as if somebody's blown him up.'

'Should we call the boy back?' Caspar's arm was completely still, although he'd stood there unmoving for quite a while.

Jäcklein was undecided. *There's definitely something odd going on here.* 'How're you doing, Stats?'

'Can't complain.' He let Moritz walk around him, inspecting him, then the boy stood in front of him so the tips of their noses almost touched. 'Ask him how I am.'

'It is him,' Moritz said, and he laughed. 'He's grown – judging by his size, we could almost be brothers now. Only his nose has suffered.' He would have continued, but Statius moved like lightning, stabbing him with his Aztec knife, which was now giving off an unholy light.

Instead of sliding off, bending, or breaking like every other weapons had done when touching the giant's skin, the blade penetrated it – but Moritz had had the presence of mind to twist his head, so it pierced his jaw instead of his throat and got stuck in the bone. The blade flashed as soon as it pierced Moritz's flesh.

'I knew it!' Caspar fired, his pistol spitting a musket ball at Statius with a loud bang. 'There is devilment against us!'

The projectile hit the strapping mercenary's right shoulder and emerged the other side in a small red fountain – and an instant later, the wound had closed.

Statius screamed and laughed at the same time, but he didn't move an inch. 'You can't hurt me with that, you fucking *squib*!' He tore the strange knife from Moritz's jaw and prepared to strike again.

'Tzontemoc! I send you the soul of a great warrior!'

Caspar took aim with his second firearm. 'Then let's try this!' There was another loud bang, the ball buzzed towards its target and hit Statius' skull.

The skin burst open and blood flowed freely – but the lead did not penetrate the bone.

With an exclamation of surprise, Statius took a step backwards, wiping the blood from his eyes. 'Your souls will all belong to Tzontemoc, and each death will make me stronger!' This wound, too, sealed itself magically.

'By all Saints!' Caspar dropped the fired pistols and drew a loaded one from his custom-made sheaths. Quickly, he took the silver ball from his pouch of ammunition and loaded the third firearm with it. 'I'll crack you all right.'

'Wake up, Stats!' Moritz had drawn his heavy sword. The bidenhänder whistled through the air now as he hit the mercenary with the flat of the blade. 'I don't want to hurt you—'

'Don't you get it? I want to hurt *you*!' Statius dodged the massive sword and hit the giant in the stomach with his fist.

The blow made Moritz rise on the tips of his toes before falling to his knees, retching and vomiting. The bidenhänder clattered against the rock. 'You are nothing but a sacrificial lamb.'

He really is still under the witches' spell! 'Stats, *fight it*,' Jäcklein screamed, running to the young mercenary's aid.

'Fight what? The blessings of my new god?' Statius grabbed the giant's black curls and yanked up his head, then he hit Moritz with the back of his right hand. The boy dropped to the ground, unconscious. 'You'll all die for him, and through your blood and the life you give, I will rise in his favour.' With his long glassy index claw, he plucked the deformed ball from his forehead and dropped the lead to the rocks beneath his feet.

'Your feeble weapons cannot kill me any more.' He stepped over Moritz. 'The way I see it, my gods have even found a way to make our frozen one vulnerable. Isn't that great?'

Jäcklein raised his pistol, but it seemed useless. Regular lead would never stop his former companion. *He's talking as if he is acting of own free will . . .* 'What did they do to you?'

'Nothing. Well, nothing that I don't want.'

'You're possessed!'

'I am *free*! I am *chosen! I am all I ever wanted to be!*' Statius hurried towards Jäcklein, raising the strange dagger. 'Call it whatever you like, but know that I have left you behind, you who wanted to tame me, who wanted to keep me from what is within my soul – from what runs through my veins.'

His face was changing, looking more feline every moment. His teeth turned to sharp, pointed fangs. 'I am a *predator*, Jäcklein! I thirst for blood and I crave human meat!' He began running.

'Caspar,' Jäcklein screamed, more afraid than he'd ever been, in any battle he had fought. Amid the tercio, under attack by cuirassiers, through the carnage, surrounded by stabbing pikes and rushed by enemies – never had he felt such fear, not even when they'd been fighting the undead or other instruments of evil.

Statius – his *friend* – had become a demon incarnate: he was showing his true colours.

Jäcklein heard two bangs in rapid succession.

The landsknecht rushing towards him didn't try to dodge the balls. The silver shattered against his cheek and forehead, bursting open the skin – which healed right away.

'Did you think I was a common werewolf, that you could kill with silver through the brain?' Statius impaled himself on Jäcklein's outstretched rapier, which pierced his right side. 'You see? I am more than human now!'

By all the saints in Heaven! Jäcklein released the hilt of his weapon and staggered backwards. 'Stats,' he stammered, 'no! I can't believe it – and I don't want to! Please! Wake up—!'

'I am wide awake, old friend.' Statius tore the rapier from his body and threw it away, and with his other hand, he punched at Jäcklein. '*Wide* awake!'

Jäcklein, dodging the blow, jumped to Caspar's side. 'Any more ideas, your Snootiness?'

'Yes.' The duellist raised his pistols. 'Get down.'

Statius opened his mouth and laughed loudly, ridiculing this pathetic attempt to kill him with balls yet again.

But this time, two jets of flame as long as a man's arm burst from the muzzles, engulfing Statius' head in a cloud of fire. His oily brown curls, his eyebrows and his beard vanished in smoke and the skin of his face was burned crisp and blistered. Screaming with rage and pain, Statius retreated half a step.

The weapons had been loaded with black powder only.

'Now!' Caspar dropped his pistols and drew his daggers, crossing the blades to shear off Statius' head in a scissor-like move. 'Come on, do something, or we're all dead!' Jäcklein was more than willing to act – but before he could draw his dagger, someone had grabbed him by the back of his neck and jerked him backwards so that his arse hit the ground, hard. Next to him, Caspar landed in the same way.

'Stay down,' he heard Nicolas say, and something glowing streaked over his head.

Valentin's remaining demonic powers heated up the blade of his rapier as the searing tip pierced Statius' right arm. Smoke rose up, flesh burned – and this time, it didn't regenerate.

'You filthy sons of bitches!' the injured mercenary shouted, clutching his wound. He looked at it for a heartbeat in bewilderment, unable to comprehend what had happened – then he stared at the trio who had stepped out of the roiling mist. 'I will *devour* you, head and gizzard!'

Nicolas and Aenlin were guarding Valentin, who was standing protectively over Jäcklein and Caspar, his rapier glowing. The hot, shimmering blade was keeping Statius at a distance.

'I never thought that one day, we would meet as enemies,' Nicolas said sadly. 'After all the battles in which we helped each other, closer than brothers.'

He . . . he has grown! Aenlin kept her eyes on their hulking opponent, who was waiting for a mistake, for a second of inattention to attack. *Forget it.*

'Surrender. Tahmina will find a way to rid you of the influence of the priestess.'

Statius laughed bitterly. 'You weren't listening when you crept up on me through the mist. I don't *want* her influence to end.' He pointed at his altered clawed hands; his talons shimmered like obsidian. 'I have become *more* – more than human, created for a time of war, the eternal war that is going to rage for ever in Europe.' He raised the obsidian artefact, sticky with Moritz's blood. 'I am really looking forward to sacrificing you!'

Valentin kept his searing blade directed at Statius while raising the hand that held a pistol whose muzzle was glowing like a furnace. 'I will kill you if you don't surrender. You are a beast and you always have been. This curse of the New World has only brought to light your true colours.'

Statius nodded. 'This *is* what I wanted: what I always wanted to be.'

'And yet I ask you, for the last time, Stats: surrender.' Nicolas extended his hand. 'Tahmina will find a—'

'The next time I get my hands on that little Persian I will push my cock into her pussy so hard it gushes!' Statius looked at Aenlin. 'You'll be experiencing this yourself within the next few minutes, you stupid mare. And afterwards, she will—'

'I am Tahmina,' Valentin said, 'but I doubt that I will make you happy.' He fired.

The red-hot ball burst from the barrel and hit Statius square in the chest, where it exploded with a loud bang. The explosion threw the mercenary backwards, somersaulting arse over tit several times before he ended up lying next to the unconscious Moritz.

Statius' clothes and skin were torn; blood streamed from his belly. But he was still not dead. 'Oh, you just wait – wait till I get you.' He pushed himself into a sitting position.

He must not get up, not under any circumstances! Aenlin ran towards Statius, Valentin and Nicolas flanking her, shouting, 'Quickly, before he gets up!'

'Kill him,' Jäcklein called after them. 'Don't believe his protestations if he tries to weasel out.'

'The old Stats doesn't exist any more,' Nicolas agreed.

'I disliked the old Stats, and nor do I like this one. We—' Abruptly, before reaching their opponent, Valentin began to stumble. 'Damn.'

'What is it?' Aenlin took his arm, supporting him. 'Tahmina? Can you hear me? What is happening to you? We need you and the ensign's power!'

'The corpse's flesh is failing me. His muscles.' Valentin's movements became more and more grotesque as if his body was guided by a drunken puppeteer. 'By the djinni of Yadz I . . . I am losing him! The dying demon seed within the corpse is revolting against me.'

'You come to me – how nice of you all.' Statius rose with a roar and in plain view of his former friends, turned into a hybrid of man and panther, taller than Moritz and utterly terrifying. The beastman had the face of a human predator, with long fangs in its maw.

'Be my sacrifices to Tzontemoc!' The obsidian blade flashed ominously in his clawed hand. With long strides, he came running towards them, the words he threw contemptuously their way turning into meaningless jabber.

Valentin's legs gave way and he fell. 'I . . .'

Nicolas stepped in front of the two of them, brandishing his two-handed sword. 'Help him up,' he told Aenlin. 'We need Vanth's power against Stats!'

Lucifer, lend him strength. Aenlin tried to pull the fallen man to his feet, but Tahmina was unable to move the corpse any longer. The ensign lay on the rocky ground as if he weighed several tons. 'You must try,' she implored her companion. 'I cannot lift the body to guide his hand with the glowing blade.'

'Perish in the name of Tzontemoc!' Statius hissed, his words barely intelligible. He dodged the captain's brutal blow.

The bidenhänder missed its mark. At the same moment, Statius drove the strange obsidian knife through Nicolas' clothes, deep into his bowels and dragged it upwards to make the wound bigger.

Instead of giving up the fight, Nicolas embraced his former companion with both arms and dropped to the ground, dragging Statius along. 'It is not over yet.'

Taken by surprise, Statius fell, caught face-down in the dying man's grip.

Nicolas is sacrificing himself!

'Hang on!' Aenlin grabbed Valentin's arm and bent it unnaturally far to the side. The limb snapped from its joint and the tip of Valentin's blade, still imbued with demonic powers, pierced Statius' back. She drove it into his heart. 'Tahmina! Now!'

The rapier blazed brightly as the mystic channelled the unholy power through the metal and into the body of the beast.

Statius howled and screamed at the same time, thrashing and kicking. In his agony, he tore into Nicolas' throat and face, ripping away chunks of flesh while his heart burned within his body until greenish-black flames licked from the stab wound, engulfing him.

'Nicolas!' Aenlin dived towards them and grabbed the strap of his baldric. *Aid me, Lucifer!* With all her might, she dragged the captain away from Statius' burning body.

A final scream, and the beastman lay still.

The obsidian fire danced across the blade of the rapier towards Valentin, engulfing him. The long-dead mercenary, once a servant of the Venetian, perished in the unnatural flames alongside Statius, until both bodies had disintegrated into a fine ash that rose into the misty-grey sky and disappeared. Within seconds, nothing was left of the two men except the stolen knife, lying harmlessly on the ground.

Nicolas! Aenlin turned to the grievously wounded man, who was pouring blood from where the blade had slit open his abdominal wall. Bite marks on his neck, shoulders and face completed the picture of a fatally wounded man who was only heartbeats away from entering the Afterlife. 'But not him,' she whispered. *He is immortal, after all. He must be.*

'Captain!' Jäcklein approached.

Caspar ran past them to check on Moritz. 'Oh Jesus, Joseph and Mary! What a mess!'

He'll need our help until his gift kicks in and starts healing him. 'Give me a hand in closing the gaping wounds,' Aenlin ordered. She was familiar with human anatomy and had practised this procedure in her training – but mostly on dead pigs.

She ran quickly to the edge of the plateau, where she had dropped her gear. Rummaging through her knapsack and her bags, she finally found her sewing kit. She took out Nicolas' bottle of liquor as well. *Finally, I can put the foul stuff to good use.*

'Let's patch him up so his bowels and intestines won't fall out and he won't lose any more blood. He'll have to manage the rest himself.' *May whatever god protects him lend him aid.*

Jäcklein looked at the young woman appreciatively. 'I have watched soldiers lose their minds or consciousness on the battlefield when they saw such wounds, and you're just talking pragmatically about how you'll go about patching him up.'

'Maybe I'll do the rest afterwards.' Aenlin was ignoring the stench and pretending the blood was nothing more than sticky red water. 'How's Moritz?' she shouted at Caspar.

'A deep stab wound, but it's not too bad,' the duellist replied. 'I will take care of it.'

'How did Valentin come to join you?' Jäcklein started tending to Nicolas' face, which was covered in scratches and bite marks.

'That wasn't Valentin but Tahmina.' Quickly, Aenlin summed up recent events, using the story to distract herself while she stitched up the captain's dreadful wounds. She told the landsknecht how they had been looking for the Venetian when they had heard of the strange band led by a priestess and decided to follow that lead. 'It was the right decision – otherwise this would have ended very badly indeed.' She pointed at Valentin's corpse. 'Tahmina's mind seems to be reverting to her own body as we speak.'

'What shall we do after we've managed to keep our wounded friends from dying?' Jäcklein pointed to the sacrificial knife lying on the ground. 'Stats called that thing "the claw of Itzli" – whoever or whatever Itzli might be. He got it from the witch over there.' He gazed at the corpse with the trampled face. 'Two of them are dead. But where is Veronica? What are her plans?'

He was asking the right questions, but Aenlin had no answers for him, not without her companion, who was recovering in Heiligenstadt, waiting for the group to return. Without her help, they would have died battling Statius. She sewed quickly, pulling the wounds together tightly and dowsing the injuries in alcohol. Nicolas didn't move, not when she stitched him together, nor when the burning alcohol touched his skin.

'We'll go to Heiligenstadt,' she declared. 'There, we'll regroup and consider our options. Only Tahmina's gifts can help us from now on.'

'True enough. Travelling the land in search of a woman none of us has seen before is not the best method to find her.' Jäcklein finished his work. 'Oh my. I might have stitched the captain a perpetual grin.'

'He can take it,' Caspar commented, as he and Moritz joined them. 'It'll lighten the mood.' The young man had a bloody throat and a hugely swollen lower jaw. 'Here, I picked this up.' He showed them the sacrificial knife. 'Do you want me to destroy it? It's made of obsidian, so a ball or a hefty kick will be enough to shatter it.'

'No, wait.' Aenlin looked at the artefact. *We need a trap: something that will force Nica to come to us.* 'This will be our bait.'

'You think she'll come to get it?' Jäcklein's narrow face was a mixture of doubt and a little fear.

'Yes. It belonged to the Aztecs – it even has a name, so it's unique. Whatever Nica has in mind, she will surely need it. So she will come looking for us.'

'But what if she has another knife?' Moritz asked.

Aenlin had to admit that possibility. 'Tahmina will take a look at it. She knows more about this kind of thing.'

'I only hope this Nica won't send her demons to eliminate us.' Caspar was reloading his pistols. He put silver balls into four of them. 'I am afraid I won't be much help against them.'

'None of us was.' Jäcklein pointed at Moritz. 'Not even you, giant lad.' Then they embraced. 'Shit, I'm so happy that you only got a scratch, my boy.'

'So am I, my friend.' With a grin, Moritz raised the obsidian knife. 'This will help us.'

Aenlin looked at the three battered men surrounding her and then at the unconscious captain. This time, it really wasn't clear if he would survive his wounds.

The Swedes have come
They took all the plunder
They smashed the windows
And carried away the lead
To run balls
And shoot everyone.

Swedish song from the Thirty Years' War

CAPITULUM XVII

Free Imperial City of Mühlhausen, September 1629

'They've reoccupied the house.' Aenlin stood before the building in which, little more than a month earlier, the city guard had struggled desperately against the Venetian and Barthel's landsknechts. She had dispensed with her usual martial garb as part of her disguise and was currently wearing a simple but elegant white dress with a black shawl of Norfolk lace around her shoulders. A fashionable hat covered her shining dark locks.

Caspar and Moritz stood next to her, leaving Jäcklein in their billet to guard Nicolas. The captain was still recovering from his wounds, but they had to force him to stay in bed. Tahmina, however, was in the best of health and making plans to find the last of the Aztec priestesses.

'Mühlhausen has neither space nor time to waste.' Caspar wore his four pistols very visibly over the stately black clothes tailor-made for him. The two mercenaries had chosen simpler garb, as befitted servants; no one would take them for landsknechts now.

They were posing as foreign nobles with a German retinue, a story that Aenlin skilfully dropped into every conversation, and no one who saw her strolling about would have doubted that. The residents were no longer afraid of Catholic spies or soldiers within their walls, so the group was able to make the rounds of the city without being looked at askance.

By now, they knew every detail of the night of the attack on the Venetian and his men. They knew the spot where they'd found the naked corpse of a young woman, pregnant, raped and pushed to her death. Judging by the description and the drawing in the newspaper, it had been Osanna.

'If I heard right, it's Huguenots. They fled from Richelieu.' Moritz carried the giant baskets with their groceries. After Statius' attack, he had become more taciturn and cautious. He'd lost much of his insouciance, having been shown by Statius that he could die, frozen or not. Lately he was more often silent than not, and when he did speak, it was to offer suggestions, but never anecdotes or banter.

Aenlin missed his laughter. She pushed the midnight-black strand of hair from her left eye. 'Let's go back with the food – otherwise Jäcklein will be so hungry that he'll start eating the furniture.'

Caspar, in his elegant outfit playing the role of an elder nobleman accompanied by his daughter, started walking. 'Has Tahmina made any progress finding the Aztec?'

'No.' Aenlin forgave him for asking the same thing ten times a day; they all felt the same. The band was ready and waiting for action. 'I'd rather have her taken today than tomorrow.'

'Taken,' Moritz said seriously. 'You mean kill her.'

'We should capture and interrogate Nica, then give her to the authorities, together with our report,' Caspar objected. 'Who knows how many more of them there are, living undetected amongst us?'

'Instigating official action against the native witches of the Empire is their work,' Aenlin agreed. *I would bet my soul on it.*

'It's no coincidence that pyres are burning everywhere,' the duellist said, stroking his moustache. 'As if they were just waiting to be ignited. Maybe the witches are simply waiting for the right occasion.'

'It's also their fault that the Horseman of War is galloping through the lands, waving his bloody red flag.' Moritz sounded more adult than ever. 'This priestess must die. She has brought enough evil on our homeland.'

'After the conquistadores looted, raped and ruined her own homeland,' Caspar pointed out. 'I can understand her.'

'Would you like to change sides like Statius did?' Moritz sounded irritable.

'Now hold on a minute,' Aenlin said. 'Caspar is certainly right: while we don't endorse it, their thirst for revenge is understandable. We agree on that.'

Secretly, she made a gesture of blessing in Lucifer's name at the spot where Osanna's body had been found in Unterer Steinweg near the Church of All Saints. *Bearer of Light, be gracious. If God doesn't take them in, have mercy upon them.*

Caspar, however, crossed himself.

Moritz mixed up the gesture, showing that he was not too familiar with Christianity. Aenlin assumed that he secretly followed the Old Faith.

'I'm pretty sure Statius did that to her,' Moritz said. 'He was already lusting after her back in Altona. They say the rape was absolutely brutal . . .'

'May her soul rest in peace.' The death of the heavy-handed landsknecht was the first thing in a long time that brought Aenlin a real sense of relief. The New World magic had turned him into a beast, one they had barely managed to vanquish. Without Tahmina's power over Valentin's corpse, they would all be dead by now. And beating Nica was going to be even harder.

'I wonder if she followed the Venetian of her own free will, or if he had given her a gift, like Valentin and Barthel,' Caspar mused. 'These exploding balls and the searing blades that cut through everything they touch can be a great advantage in times like these.'

'We'll never find out.' Aenlin pitied Osanna, no matter why she had followed the fake plague doctor. It had caused her death. *Far too early, and pointlessly.* 'Have you heard anything in your travels about what happened to the Venetian?'

The two men shook their heads.

Aenlin didn't really care to know his whereabouts; their main concern had to be the whereabouts of the third priestess. 'If I were Nica, I would start something unbelievably bad after my sisters' deaths. Something cruel and terrifying, shaking the whole continent.'

'Exactly.' Caspar took a handful of plums from the basket and ate one, spitting the stone into the gutter.

'But what could be worse?' Moritz carried the two huge wicker baskets containing bread, fruit, vegetables, cheese, sausage and fresh meat as if they weighed nothing at all.

'More war,' Caspar suggested. 'More nations becoming involved.'

'Diseases,' Moritz added. 'Did you see that Ula was afflicted by the plague?'

Aenlin shuddered. 'What are you saying?'

'When we burned the corpses of the woman and the Aztec, I noticed the smell,' Moritz explained. 'Also, there were ulcers under her arms. She must have been dying already when Statius killed her. Don't worry, I didn't touch her. I pushed her into the flames with a branch.'

'The miasma! We all have breathed it in!' Caspar shouted and threw a plum at the giant. 'Because of you, we're all going to die of the plague!'

Moritz caught the fruit between his teeth and chewed it, crunching the pit with his teeth. 'No, I don't think so. We would have felt it by now – or do you have an itch under your noble arms?'

'How does the lad do this?' Caspar laughed. 'You just can't be angry with him.'

Aenlin knocked on the door and entered the house they had rented. If more fleeing German, French and other Protestants, Mennonites and Jews arrived, Mühlhausen would soon be over-crowded, for the city's strong walls promised protection and safety.

'We're back!' she called.

To their surprise, Jäcklein, Tahmina and Nicolas had gathered in the large room. The captain wore only plain breeches, but Tahmina had donned her new robe, the dark blue perfectly matching her eyes; around her waist, she wore a belt with a number of small pouches attached. Jäcklein, however, was skulking around in his nightshirt like a layabout.

There was a fire blazing in the hearth and the cauldron stood ready for their meal.

At the back of the room, the floorboards were covered in chalked sigils and symbols. The mystic was obviously preparing a new ritual to find the Aztec.

'Don't give me that look,' Jäcklein said defensively, rubbing his shock of tousled hair. 'How could I have stopped her when she didn't want to stay put?'

'You could have subdued her,' Moritz commented laconically, putting the groceries down next to the fire.

'But with lots of love.' Caspar followed the giant and together they started preparing the meal, chopping the ingredients, putting them into the pot, adding water, stirring everything together and leaving it to simmer nicely.

'Any news?' Nicolas said. He was pale, but he looked healthy. His bare torso was still bandaged, but there was neither blood nor pus seeping through the fabric. They had long since removed the stitches and he had healed well. He had even shaved, which accentuated his strong features, and cut his ash-blond hair.

Aenlin hung her hat on a hook. Shaking her head, she sat down next to them. 'Everything's quiet. No one's heard anything, either about an especially powerful witch or about the Venetian.' She hung her black lace shawl over her chair and smoothed down her light dress. *It feels so unfamiliar.*

'But I have news.' Tahmina pointed at the obsidian blade on the table in front of her. 'For a short while, I was able to glimpse the presence of the Aztec.'

Aenlin took her hands, immediately worried because she didn't know how dangerous these magical investigations might be. The more harmless Tahmina made them sound, the less Aenlin believed her. Despite all its power, the art of Yatu could be enormously risky. 'Where did you find her?'

'Why didn't you tell me?' Nicolas looked at her reproachfully.

'Now hold on, Captain,' Tahmina replied, her voice friendly. 'Nica is too far away for us to grab a sword, run over and hack her to pieces right away. I wished to wait until we were all gathered here together.'

'Well then, where is this bitch?' Jäcklein poured himself some wine and gulped it loudly. 'I'll drink to your discovery.'

'I cannot tell for sure. What I felt is more like . . . an impression of her surroundings,' Tahmina said apologetically. 'I told you, it was only a brief contact, an idea of the environment, more than anything.'

'Then keep searching!' Nicolas demanded. 'We can—'

'She will, as soon she considers it safe,' Aenlin said. 'Let us hear her out, Captain.'

'She's close to water,' Tahmina said, her blue eyes gazing lovingly at Aenlin. 'The vibrations were clear: water from the sea, but a river that—'

'Hamburg,' Nicolas broke in. 'She is in Hamburg! A thousand curses upon her! She is getting away – she's sailing back to the New World, having done the last of her dirty deeds.' He smashed a fist against the table.

'Tell me again why we made you captain in the first place?'

Jäcklein pushed the wine towards him. 'Can't have been because of your prudence. Here, drink this and cool your hot head.'

'There may be many such places, so I will try again.' Tahmina rose and went to the corner of the room she had prepared for the ritual. 'Keep an eye on me – wake me from my trance when I start screaming.'

Screaming? Aenlin followed her at once and sat on a footstool next to the chalk symbols. She had often seen her beloved perform rituals, mostly for self-purification, to gain power and calm, and to bolster her mind. 'How dangerous is it really?' she whispered. 'Please don't lie to me.'

'There should not be any problem.' Tahmina sat at the centre of the ritual area, lit the braziers she had set on the floor and took little pearls of scented incense from the pouch at her waist. She closed her eyes and fell into a trance, mumbling undecipherable sounds.

'Did she just say "should"?' Nicolas joined them, crossing his muscular arms in front of his chest. 'Can Nica and Tahmina . . . fight in this state?' He lacked the appropriate word.

'Magically,' added Jäcklein, standing there in his nightshirt, wine in hand. 'Oh holy shit of all saints: does that mean we're in danger, too? Or is there something we can do?'

Aenlin didn't know the answer. She and Tahmina had always talked and laughed a lot together, and they had undertaken many things together, but she had never shared the secrets of the Yatu magic with her. 'She's a true mystic,' she whispered unhappily. Aloud she said, 'No, Jäcklein, we can only wait. You could pray if you feel like it.'

Anxiously, Moritz and Caspar joined them, too.

All eyes were on Tahmina, who was surrounded and shielded by the wisps of incense wafting away as if in a latticework.

Tahmina's mind flew over the land, which she vaguely perceived as a multicoloured tapestry. Mountains, cities, forests, fields, people, animals – none of these things existed below her; there was only energy, impressions, vibrations and the emanations of special places of faith or magic.

Her senses were geared towards the unknown, the alien being that she had felt within the sacrificial obsidian dagger known as the claw of Itzli.

In this state, time passed very differently, and without Tahmina being aware of it.

She reached the spot where in her probing concentric circles above the Empire she had touched the unknown.

It was impossible to explain to outsiders who had no connection to her style of mysticism what she did. The ritual took place far beyond the earthly realm, way beyond reason. To discern and correlate the tiny differences in everything, training and good intuition were necessary—

Djinni of Shiraz! This was the spot . . .

'Oh . . . you are back,' said a voice abruptly within her mind. 'I expected as much. My name is Nica. But you already know that.'

Tahmina stopped probing and paused. There was a glittering ribbon far below her. She carefully floated down and focused on the earthly realm within which most people lived. The Aztec had found Tahmina first. *So I am not the only one skilled at exploring.*

With every step she floated downwards, her surroundings became clearer: a large city, crossed by more than one river, from which the vibrations of many people came rushing towards her. There was also magic, sometimes in whole areas, sometimes in discrete spots, which was making her probing harder. The Aztec was using the other auras as cover. *I will never find her like that.*

'Have you been waiting for me?'

'Yes. I wanted to talk to you.'

'About what?'

'About everything.' Nica talked calmly and fearlessly, like a ruler meeting another to prevent a war.

'Don't you rather need the dagger? The claw of Itzli?'

The priestess laughed. 'You cut quickly to the heart of the matter, Tahmina.'

'Time is of the essence for all of us, for we cannot stop it, not even with the strongest of curses.' The unknown city below her was gradually taking shape. She could make out the outlines of buildings, squares, streets and alleys. 'You will make me an offer to get it back.'

'What kind of offer would this be? What could you, a mystic from the East, possibly be interested in?'

'You could offer to take me along to the New World. Or to teach me your art. Or ask me to adopt your deities and join your fight.'

'None of these things to be dismissed out of hand. And what would be your response?' Nica was toying with her, her voice still relaxed.

'Refusal, of course.' *I must draw her out.* 'Although the New World suffered terribly under the conquistadores, you cannot simply—'

'I can do anything. Anything I want. Nothing will be forgiven or forgotten. The Christians, with all their love of charity, came to our country without being asked. They plundered, they murdered, they raped. They mocked our faith and brought diseases that killed thousands.'

'But—'

'Do you think they will spare your home, Tahmina? Or any country where they think they might find riches? If they decide to conquer the Orient tomorrow, they will come with their ships and their cannons and their muskets, just like the Crusaders of old. Greed motivates them – nothing but greed. The sweet words are just for show, to make them look more noble.'

'You and your friends were sent here to bring back to Europe the war it brought to you. That is even less noble!'

'Why would we act nobly towards such people?' Nica's voice suddenly turned so cold that Tahmina felt afraid. 'We are far from done with this continent. Its wealth is growing from the bones of conquered nations. The whole foundation is rotten to the core. One day it will be so decayed it will tumble, and guilt will descend upon the Empire.'

Tahmina risked another attempt to interrupt her. 'You wish to speed this decay.'

'As long as Europe wears itself down, the people of the rest of the world are safe from its insatiable hunger for gold, for power.' Nica spoke emphatically. 'We can chase the conquistadores from our country. Be free.'

'Free? The Aztecs killed their own kind long before—'

'That has nothing to do with you!' the priestess interrupted her. 'Do you not see that we are only defending ourselves? Defending ourselves against imminent extinction at the hands of all those strangers?'

Tahmina floated even lower and finally recognised the city. She had seen its outline on a map and on various engravings before. Nicolas' first assumption had been correct. *It seems it will all end where it started. In Hamburg.* 'I must confess that your words have moved me,' she said softly.

'I'm glad to hear this, Tahmina.'

'However, it is not my decision alone whether to give you back the dagger. We are many and I will not act against the will of my friends.' Nica would never have believed her if she had given in completely.

'Then come to Hamburg,' the Aztec suggested. 'I will wait for you here, to explain to you why we did what we did. Surely the daughter of the great Solomon Kane will understand that our deeds were justified, that my people are in the right.'

'You will have to explain to Aenlin why you wanted to kill us. Do you think you can do that?'

'I won't presume to, but I hope that she will understand my deeds are justified. After our encounter, you will be free to do what you see fit with the claw of Itzli: keep it, destroy it, or maybe hand it over to me.' Nica spoke calmly. 'How about a peace treaty for as long as we are in Hamburg? Afterwards, you may try to catch me – depending on how our encounter goes.'

Tahmina heard no deceitfulness in her voice whatsoever. 'You will not try to attack us? Neither with landsknechts nor with demons?' As hard as she was trying, she could not detect Nica in the city. Her aura was hidden amongst the thousands of inhabitants from all over the world, under cover of all the magical places and creatures of Hamburg. *I must seal this pact. It is the best you will offer us.*

'This I swear upon my life, Tahmina. I am more honest than any European you know.'

Tahmina took her time answering because she didn't want to sound too relieved. 'Agreed.'

'So be it. How soon can you reach Hamburg?'

Tahmina calculated the distance that they could cover either by coach or travelling on the Elbe via Magdeburg, if she remembered the map correctly. 'I think it will take us a fortnight. Are you in a hurry? Remember, you might not get the dagger at all. That decision is not yet made.'

'I don't care about the dagger.' Nica's voice died away, fading like that of someone shouting in a storm. 'We should meet at the Lower Port. Do you have any suggestions or should we—?'

'The Thirsty Roper. Let us meet there,' Tahmina said. That was the right place, if this thing was supposed to end where it had started.

'I will wait for you there. Don't worry. I will keep my word.'

And with that, Nica was gone.

Tahmina returned to her body at once, to tell Aenlin, Nicolas and the others about her encounter and plan their next steps.

One thing was giving the mystic quite a headache: no one knew what the Aztec looked like. If she looked European, like Ursula and Agatha had, she would be just another face in the crowd.

Magdeburg, September 1629

'Do you think that will work?' Moritz looked at the thick lead sheeting with which he and Jäcklein had lined the inside of the keg. Both had taken off their jerkins; their baldrics and weapons were hanging from a wooden beam. They had worked up quite a sweat toiling in the barn.

'Of course! I've pulled the edges up over the battens so the wood won't be damaged. Consider this my contribution to the upcoming war against the Swedes: the keg-mine: a portable fougasse.' Jäcklein caressed the iron bands around the outside of the keg with satisfaction; they made it easy to distinguish the vessel from the other barrels. 'I've been toying with this idea for a long time. The thing will be filled with black powder and scraps of iron and propped up against the interior wall of a city. Then you put a wedge underneath so the opening is tilted slightly upwards and – *click!*' – he pulled the string that triggered a snap-lock set in the bottom of the keg – 'and the attackers all get hit by flying metal.' He knocked on the outer wall of the keg. 'Not as heavy as a cannon, easier to carry, excellent as a trap in the streets. Incredibly dangerous in close combat.'

Moritz looked at the line of five kegs they had finished. 'But you haven't actually tested it yet.'

'How could I? In the middle of Magdeburg?' Jäcklein laughed and wiped chips of wood from his shirt. They fell to the floor

with a soft rustle. 'It will work. It really is remarkably like a fougasse, just without the hole in the ground. You rarely find holes
in cities – well, unless a demon has come creeping out of one.'

Moritz scratched his black curls. 'You want to sell this to
merchants?'

'As soon as we're in Hamburg, yes. I will be a rich man.'

'But how do you stop them from just copying them and
stealing your idea?' Moritz kicked one of the kegs. 'If I were a
merchant, I'd buy one, dismantle it, figure out the construction
and start building them myself. I can make them cheaper and
quicker.'

Jäcklein's face fell as he realised that his idea might soon
be available in every city in the Empire without him earning a
single kreutzer. 'The Devil's grandmother take it! My beautiful
work – those who are already fat will just grow even fatter on
my brainpower.'

'What would you think if you invade the city with Nicolas and
me, and in every house you want to loot, such a keg of death is
waiting for you?' Moritz grinned. 'I mean, you can build really
tiny ones, too, right?'

Jäcklein's expression turned reproachful. 'Why didn't you tell
me this earlier, Moritz Giantshanks?'

'You were having so much fun and I was glad I could help.
It was a nice distraction.'

'But you didn't think to mention that I was building my own
death? It's all very well for you to laugh – the scrap metal will
just bounce off of you.'

'I told you just in time, right?' The young mercenary was
leaning against the supporting beam of the barn they had been
working in for two days, at a safe distance from the black
powder. Several lamps shed enough light for them to work in
the building, which was attached to the inn where the alleged
foreign nobles and their entourage had taken up residence. 'I

thought he might be able to use it when we get to Hamburg to face the Aztec, or a new Xolotl or whatever she's going to conjure.'

'She promised not to harm us.'

'Do you believe that?'

'Nah, none of us do,' Jäcklein replied. He laughed in spite of himself. 'All right, let's fill these things. We'll tell the guards we are delivering powder; no one will know what it really is. Let her hire landsknechts and conjure beasts from the hells of the New World – we have Jäcklein's keg-mine!' He wiped some sawdust from the top of the barrel. '"Keg of death" is not a bad name. I will use it.'

Through the wooden wall of the barn, they could hear the evening hustle and bustle of a city that rarely slept. Magdeburg was part of the Hansa, the sole trade centre for crops for a large area, shipping coveted grain through half of Europe by water and by land, catering to regions as far away as northern France, Poland, Russia, even Norway and Sweden.

The fact that Magdeburg was a staunch supporter of the Reformation against the Emperor also made the city a point of interest for the oppressed and refugees. The Protestant bastion stood strong here. The city still printed leaflets against Catholicism, proudly bearing the sobriquet 'our Lord's Chancery', although the Emperor and his Catholic league obviously begged to differ. Its ramparts and staunch walls and its economic importance allowed Magdeburg to adopt this tone.

The group had not yet decided what to do when they got to Hamburg. The quick journey from Mühlhausen to Magdeburg had not been long enough to reach a decision, for Nicolas had different goals from Aenlin and Tahmina, and Caspar nursed yet another plan, while Moritz and Jäcklein preferred to go straight to the West India Company to grill the de Hertoghe brothers about who was behind the original mission – for that person surely had to know about the true nature and origin of the Aztecs.

'Let's see what kind of passage the captain manages to book for us.' Jäcklein knew they'd been working on their own account for quite a while. They had to stop Nica, no matter how justified her deeds might be. It wasn't right to plunge a whole continent into permanent misery, burning the Old World in the eternal fires of war.

'What do you think will happen?' Moritz asked as they prepared the first keg, compacted the black powder, covered it and tamped it again. 'In Hamburg.'

'I think it's pretty obvious what we'll do.'

'Kill the priestess?'

Jäcklein nodded slightly. 'In the end, Tahmina will feel the same. She considers those New World witches too dangerous. After all, just remember what they did to us.' He had been carefully pouring black powder into the keg, but he stopped, sending black dust swirling up. 'I keep asking myself how many good people we killed under their spell.'

'I don't remember a thing,' Moritz confessed. 'Not even the rituals Aenlin described in the inn. When we attacked and tried to kill her.'

'Exactly! I attacked my own captain – my friend! I tried to slit his throat! The man I entrusted with my life, and would do so again any second! Who's like a brother to me.' He poured every last grain of the dangerous powder from the small bucket into the keg. 'We shouldn't even dream of Nica staying true to her word.'

'Didn't one of the witches say that there were more than three of them originally?'

'I guess so.'

'Shouldn't we try to find out where the others are? Wouldn't this Nica woman know that? She appears to be their leader.'

Jäcklein put down the bucket. 'I quite agree. When we meet her, Tahmina will have to decide whether she can chance it, if she can try and keep the Aztec powers at bay.'

'And if not?'

'If not, the priestess is dead.' Jäcklein was feeling thirsty, the fine black powder dust clogging his throat. 'I'll get us some beer – otherwise, I might start clearing my throat, and that might strike a spark that could cause our keg-mine to explode accidentally.'

'Good idea. A large one for me. What are we going to do after we've defeated the priestess?'

Jäcklein went to the door leading to the taproom, leaving behind his weapons and jerkin. 'What could we do? We are landsknechts, my giant friend. It is always on to the next battlefield, the next pay.'

'I don't know.' Moritz sighed.

'You don't know what?'

'Whether this is the right thing for me. I have had a first taste of it now, but ... this hewing and stabbing and dying, it hurts my soul.'

'Didn't I tell you from the start you were too good for our craft?' Jäcklein put a hand on the door handle. 'Would you like my advice?'

'Yes.'

'It hurts my soul, too. But mine is used to it. Callused. Scarred.' He pushed open the door and entered the corridor to the taproom, which was filled with loud laughter and music. 'Keep your soul in one piece, Moritz. Turn your back on our profession as soon as possible. The craft of death is not for you.' He disappeared from the barn with a sympathetic smile.

Moritz sighed. Jäcklein's words had only confirmed what he really wanted to do. But first, he would go with his friends to finish their mission, which had become so much more important – for the Empire and for Europe. For all creatures living in Europe, whether in the open or hidden.

He appreciated Jäcklein's bluntness. Nicolas would surely want to keep him in his service, if only for his fighting prowess and his uniqueness.

No, I have seen enough. Enough death and doom to realise that this was no adventure, no game, no fun. The few thalers, guilders, batzes, or whatever coins the respective regions paid were not worth this – the bleeding and the screaming, the noises and stench of battle, the brutalisation that Statius had gone through long before his final change – Moritz would never forget any of that. Hopefully, his family would be waiting for him; they would surely forgive him for running away, violating their community rules.

It was then that Moritz recognised an emotion he had been pushing aside for weeks, even months: homesickness. He longed for his parents, his siblings, his few friends.

He had agreed to set foot on a ship, to sail on a river again, only to speed up the whole affair. What he really wanted was to return to the deep woods and mountains whose quiet and desolation he had once fled. *Now I am looking forward to returning there.*

Quietly, the small door leading from the street into the barn fell shut. The door was like a sallyport, saving people the trouble of opening the big gate every time a person on foot wanted to enter the barn, which was filled with wagons, luggage and goods.

Moritz raised his head but saw no one. It couldn't have been the breeze; it was too light for that. *And we locked it, I'm sure of that.*

The events of the last weeks had taught him not to take such things like a door blowing shut lightly. He quietly drew his two-handed sword from the hanging baldric and turned up the wick of one of the lamps hanging a safe distance from the keg-mine.

He heard shuffling steps: more than one intruder was moving alongside the wagons and crates, trying to approach him without being seen.

The Venetian and his men! Quietly, Moritz clambered on top of the nearest wagon and looked around. *How have they found us in Magdeburg?* He looked around attentively, on high alert. Magic could hurt him, even kill him, as Statius and the naiad had proved; when the water maiden almost drowned him, he had learned that some things were fatal, even for frozen ones. 'Come out and face me in a fight,' he demanded. 'I can hear you. You botched your surprise entrance, you cowards!'

Silhouettes slowly rose from their cover, but stayed in the shadows. The young giant could make out half a dozen opponents, all wielding strangely shaped swords with jagged blades.

'There you are, demon servants.' Moritz was not afraid of their superior numbers; a giant like him could easily vanquish Vanth's servants, as long as he wasn't hit by their glowing balls and searing blades. 'Where is the Venetian? Is he too much of a coward to confront us personally?'

'You won't stop us,' one of the intruders replied in a husky voice, stepping into the lamplight.

Moritz, shocked by what he saw, immediately steadied himself on the wagon. 'By all the giants of the Kyffhäuser!'

His opponent had a human-sized eagle's head on his human neck. His muscular, tattoo-covered torso was partly hidden by a wrap made of colourful feathers and some sort of leather armour festooned with the sun symbol. The being wore a long, ornate loincloth. 'You will die, human, by order of our mistress. Not one of you will reach Hamburg.'

The hybrid creature ran towards Moritz, using the wagons, crates and boxes stacked in the barn like a stair. In its right hand, it carried a mace sparkling with polished obsidian. A hit by this weapon would inflict grievous wounds, even on the young giant.

The attack was the signal for the other creatures to start moving as well.

Odin aid me! Moritz did the unexpected and leaped at his first opponent, who was just in the process of taking a big swing at him. With both feet, he kicked the eagle warrior in the chest and the face, throwing him backwards. The monster crashed into the crates and ended up lying on the floor, his neck bent in an unnatural angle.

'Learn what it means to attack somebody like me!' Moritz skilfully landed behind a second eagle-headed attacker, hitting him in the side at navel height with a horizontal blow of his sword. The feather trimming and the leather offered no protection against the bidenhänder's razor-sharp edge and Moritz's strength. He cut his enemy in half; the legs made two more steps as the torso slid down, spraying blood across the barn.

'You're a nice bunch of demon warriors,' Moritz sneered. He parried a blow with his bidenhänder, cutting the wooden mace in half. *Thor, guide my hand.* His next stab drove his blade to the hilt through an enemy's neck, then the giant jerked his sword upwards and split the eagle head in half, from top to beak. In a fountain of red, the dead creature fell back against a wagon and slid to the ground. 'You are inept!'

With a low, buzzing sound, something flew out of the darkness of the barn and hit his thigh.

Moritz had not even seen the thrown weapon coming and its lethally sharp obsidian blades tore a sizable chunk out of his leg. Screaming in pain, he staggered sidewards, bracing himself against a wagon that would shield his back against sneak attacks. 'That won't suffice!' His gaze went to the side door, through which Jäcklein would hopefully return soon. *I could use some help here.* He didn't show his discomfiture to his enemies, though. 'Come on, then, give me your best effort! My sword—'

The wagon swayed slightly, then a shadow fell on him from above.

Moritz had the presence of mind to raise his massive sword above his head horizontally, blocking the eagle warrior's vertical blow, which would otherwise have split his skull. The gleaming obsidian shards stopped right in front of his eyes, quietly crackling like embers in anticipation of turning to flames.

Odin and Hulda, that was close! But before Moritz could topple the enemy above him, the eagle warrior kicked him in the back of his head, throwing him forward – right into the attacks of the two foes who remained.

One blade rushed towards his chest; the other one was aimed at his abdomen.

Staggering forward, Moritz tried to block and was able to divert the obsidian sword that would have split open his ribs otherwise.

The second blade pierced his belly, though, and the enemy jerked it sideward, howling in triumph.

Never in his life had Moritz felt such pain. Skin and flesh gave way before the obsidian pieces, which bit deeper, entangling themselves in his guts, ready to tear them from his body.

He fell backwards to the floor of the barn, blood gushing from his mouth.

The three remaining eagle warriors approached him warily, raising their swords threateningly. Their pointed beaks were slightly open, their black eyes were watchful.

They will kill me. Then they would only have to wait for Jäcklein – who had no idea what was happening in the barn in his absence. How could they have known that Nica would send her demonic servants from the New World against them? So she clearly intended to do her best to stop them from reaching Hamburg, where she would be bound by her word. *What a clever, insidious woman.*

These thoughts and others raced through his mind, overlaid with intense pain and homesickness, an irrepressible desire to be with his family, so strong that it brought tears to his eyes.

'You are only the first,' one of the eagle warriors croaked. 'Your friends will be easy to kill. You will not be able to warn them.'

Moritz propped himself up on his elbows and looked at the terrible wound that would soon kill him.

And he realised that there was something more between his fingers than rustling straw: a thin cord.

'Yes, I will,' he said weakly, toppling the keg next to him. 'They will understand my signal.' Moritz pulled at the cord. 'You won't be killing anyone else!'

Hulda, Goddess of Death, here I come!

From the inside of the keg-mine, he heard the soft clicking of the spark that would ignite the black powder.

At the same moment, the side door opened and Jäcklein entered the barn.

On June 10th /the King of Denmark sent/500 soldiers/to the inhabitants of Stralsund/and the King of Sweden sent 100 living oxen/100 tons of black powder/and 6 cannon/along with their paraphernalia/ to them too/to lend them any possible assistance/as they were to be besieged. After noon, Colonel Hulcky used a stratagem/he had several empty barrels filled with lead/and brought to 3 spots in town/secretly put the inhabitants to the walls and parapets/to light the barrels/and make a great hue and cry/when the city started burning in 3 places/which led to the field marshal inciting an attack/in which/the hidden ambush was sprung/there was a mighty resistance/ and the attack was repelled/whereupon Stralsund/lost 200 men/but the field marshal/a multiple of this/and many were wounded.

Anonymous, Description of the siege of Stralsund by Imperial troops led by Hans Georg von Arnim, 1628

CAPITULUM XVIII

Magdeburg, September 1629

Caspar examined the lead balls in a carved ivory box that the merchant was furtively showing him. The shop advertised curios, exotica and exquisite goods. He'd gone in just before closing time and asked for special projectiles. 'Are these magic balls?'

'Of course, Count von und zu dem Dorffe.'

'How can I be sure of that?'

The merchant, who was dressed in a jerkin, expensive shirt, silk breeches, silk stockings and buckled shoes, blinked and kept an eye on the entrance. 'The hangman swore it to me.'

'Then he must have told you how he made them?'

'No, Count. He told me he got them from a friend. From Passau. You know the art coming from there, yes?'

Caspar grinned. The new wig clinched his appearance. The merchant had fallen for his fictitious family name and attitude and believed him to be of noble descent. *It can be so simple.* He had refrained from duelling during their mission, but with their job soon ending, he had to consider what happened next. He had always been fascinated by magical projectiles, although he didn't need them; the aura of infallibility in conjunction with the myth of the seventh ball had its own special allure for any duellist.

'Who doesn't? But how do I know they are the real thing?'

Caspar picked up one of the balls between his thumb and index finger. 'Should I try it on you? Then it would be worthless if I reloaded my pistol with it.'

'Give it back!' The merchant quickly took it from his hand and put it back into the box, which he locked into a drawer. 'No one is forcing you to buy them from me,' he said huffily. 'Fare thee well, Count. I am sure you are deadly enough without them.'

'I am, my friend. I am.' Caspar didn't intend leaving the shop. He had donned his lavish garb and carried four pistols, although only one of them was visible. The others, and four throwing daggers, were hidden beneath his coat. His wide sleeves concealed two more blades. As long as they were on their mission, he was always ready for combat. His gaze drifted through the shop – and came to an abrupt halt. *Well I never . . . !*

'I just had an idea.'

'Have the goodness to take your idea and leave my shop.'

'Now, now . . . is that what passes for the proverbial Protestant business acumen?' Caspar strolled into a small room, where he had spotted a long peacock feather. 'What's in here?'

He stepped into the middle of a collection of masks from the New World. Some of them resembled the ones the priestesses had worn; others looked quite different. Stone reliefs hung from the walls and lay on the floor, probably chiselled from the pyramids and buildings of those native to the Americas. Primitive weapons were on display, too – amongst them one of the mace-like wooden clubs with obsidian shards he'd come to know so well.

'This is not for you, Count.' The merchant scurried after him. 'Unless you intend to establish an exotic room at your estate – then I am your man.'

Caspar pointed at a weapon made of obsidian and dark wood and resembling the ones their enemies had used. 'What can you tell me about this thing?'

'Two gold coins, no matter what currency, but the weight—'

'I don't care about the price. I wonder what was it used for.'

'Whatever you can imagine. Cruel sacrifices, wars; they even killed children with it.' He pointed at the dried blood between the chunks of stone. 'Look: it's from over there. Isn't that dreadful?'

'From over there?'

'From the New World – but not from the Mayans, from the Aztecs. They're extinct now, but they were hated for their bloodthirstiness and cruelty,' babbled the merchant, back in his element. 'Here! This would be an excellent match.' He half-lifted a relief, obviously struggling with its weight, to show it to Caspar. 'So what do you think? Five thalers for both. I will also deliver within four miles.'

Their art is completely different from ours. It took Caspar a few seconds to realise that the interconnected, entwined lines formed the silhouette of a woman striking a weird pose; the subject was pulling a thorn-studded cord through her own tongue. *More angular, less realistic and more abstract than the images I'm familiar with.* The lower end of the cord rested in a basket, while her blood dripped down to soak some sort of sacrificial cloth. Servants standing next to the woman kept more cloths in readiness. 'What is that? A sacrifice?'

'A self-mortification. Their rulers did that to propitiate the gods. They fertilised their fields with the blood of enemies they had sacrificed and—' The merchant's arms started to tremble. He put down the relief and chose another one. 'Would this be more to your taste, Count?'

Caspar looked at the new lump of masonry, which was just as unusual and alien. It took some attention to recognise the subject amidst all the strange design elements, but once found, it jumped out at him: a man in a cape made from a great cat, wearing a headdress and jewellery on his arms and legs, was stabbing some kind of stick into his manhood.

'Is he poking around in his cock with a needle?'

'Yes, I do believe so.'

'Why?'

'To draw some blood.' The merchant pointed at the relief and explained, 'Here, you see? His servants must prop up the King, otherwise he would collapse from pain. First, they all drank a concoction of poisonous toad slime so they could withstand the ordeal—'

Caspar took the relief from him and put it down. 'I could only use this for firing practice. I will not so mistreat and pierce my penis. And I don't want to have to stare at something like that all the time. Neither will my guests.'

'Then how about something with ball games? I must have this chiselled stone relief somewhere . . .' He looked around as if searching for something. 'You know, the losers were sacrificed afterwards.'

'The losers? I would have sacrificed the winners. They had worked harder.' Caspar pointed at the obsidian weapon again. 'Do you have a tale about this, too? What can these stone blades do? Are they magical or—?'

'No. But I can tell you they are popular.'

'In Magdeburg?' The man's words were giving Caspar a bad feeling.

'Just two days ago, I sold all I had.' He pointed at the last one. 'I got this one only today.'

'How many were there?'

'More than a dozen.'

'Who bought them?'

'A Duchess who happened to be passing through the city.'

'What did she look like?'

'Young and pretty, I daresay. Black hair, dark eyes and an . . . unusual face.'

'What does that mean?'

'Peculiar cheekbones. And her skin was incredibly clear. She had a natural colour, you know, like Spaniards or Italians . . .'

Or someone who is the offspring of an Aztec and conquistador. 'Any distinctive characteristics?'

'No, nothing. Oh, yes! One eyebrow was higher than the other. But why do you care? Are you looking for a paramour? Or a bride? I have a daughter who—' The merchant looked puzzled, for the duellist had turned around and was leaving his shop. 'A good evening to you, Count. May your life—'

But Caspar was already out on the street and running towards their lodgings.

It might be a coincidence that an unknown, darkish-looking female bought almost a dozen of the weapons that the Aztec priestesses used. But he didn't believe in coincidence. He had to get back to his friends. Something is going on here.

He took a shortcut down a back alley and noticed three men in plain dark clothes loitering there. They looked at him with piercing glances, as if they knew him or had been waiting for him. But he decided he'd just go his merry way, unless they tried to rob him.

When a fourth man joined them, stepping out of a courtyard, Caspar stopped dead. The stranger wore a silver face mask with a long beak oozing smoke.

The Venetian! He drew two of his pistols and cocked them in a fluid motion. *So he is following us after all. This encounter will be his downfall.*

Caspar aimed and shot a ball through the masked man's chest, then another through his right eye before the quartet even realised what was happening. He knew how dangerous the servants of Vanth were. *I don't like to face glowing blades and exploding balls.*

The Venetian collapsed with a death rattle and hit the cobblestones; his long silver nose pointed skywards like a mast from which to fly the white flag.

Caspar had immediately exchanged his used pistols for the loaded ones and now ducked beneath the fading cloud of smoke to take new aim. 'What now? Chance it!'

But instead of attacking the duellist and avenging their master's death, his opponents tried to escape.

I will not allow them to flee. Caspar shot them down with two quick balls and sheathed the firearms before hitting the last man in the shoulder with a thrown dagger. 'Too slow, demon servants!' Quickly, Caspar approached the wounded man, who was leaning against a wall, and pressed a blade against his throat. 'How did you find us?'

Dogs had started barking, and here and there, faces were becoming visible behind half-open shutters. Someone shouted for the guard: four shots in rapid succession were not the normal order of the day in Magdeburg; that would surely cause a ruckus.

Caspar wanted to be gone by then.

'We ... we watched you – we wanted to rob you,' the man shouted, his eyes wide with terror. 'Please, spare me! I'm only doing this for my wife and children.'

'Wife and children?' Caspar laughed at him. 'Are they from Hell, like you?'

'No, no. We are ... poor – and since we have no money ...' His gaze flew from the stiletto to his assailant's face and back. 'The money, good sir, we ...' He was talking a mile a minute, trying to save his life.

Never, ever did this fellow belong to the Venetian's men. Caspar stopped listening to him, went over to the plague doctor and kicked away the mask.

Underneath was a young face, just as undemonic as the wounded man's.

Now what is this? 'Are you a servant of Evil?'

The man shook his head so fiercely it made his blond hair fly. 'No! I am not in league with the Devil.'

'Who is this?' He pointed at the dead alleged Venetian.

'Christian – Christian Schwarz.'

'All right. And who are you?'

'Karl Schulzenmüller. We came—'

Caspar drew his dagger from the man's shoulder. Steps approached, several dark lanterns threw their light on the half-timbered walls. 'Where did you get that silver mask?'

'We found it! In a burned-down house on our way to Magdeburg, on the face of a charred man. Christian decided to wear it when we robbed people, so we'd get famous – as a gang – so people would sooner give us their money of their own accord because they were afraid of us. We wanted to call ourselves the Plague Brothers.' Karl was sobbing now, and pressing his hand against the wound. 'Please, good sir, don't kill me! From this night on, I will be a virtuous man . . .'

Caspar had heard enough. He hit him with his fist and the man collapsed, unconscious. Quickly, he took the mask, which was embossed with the three symbols of Vanth. The silver showed that a ball had hit the cheek, damaging the mask and one of the symbols. The blood on it came from 'Christian', the man he had shot.

'Shit,' Casper whispered. He collected his pistols before hiding in a courtyard, hoping to elude the approaching city guard. In his left hand, he held the plague doctor's mask.

While the armoured men with their pikes and lanterns passed him by, Caspar thought about what he had heard. The Venetian was gone – but why? Had he really been killed and burned? Or had he renounced Vanth and left the mask behind for some successor?

Caspar raised the mask to let the evening moon's light shine through it. One eye was covered in red glass, the other socket empty. Through the broken glass, the moon seemed more mysterious, powerful and dangerous. A blood moon.

Slowly, he raised the mask to his face to try it on.

As an experiment.

Out of curiosity.

I can easily take it off again if . . .

The loud bang of a detonation interrupted him and an enormous fireball rose into the black sky. Seconds later, small pieces of debris and stone rained down.

Dash it! Caspar hastily put away the mask and ran out of the courtyard into the city streets. He knew what had detonated and where.

The keg-mine had worked better than Jäcklein could ever have imagined . . . just at the wrong moment.

Nicolas turned from his view of the bank of the Elbe from the island and pushed his hat back to get a better glimpse of the walls. 'As far as ramparts and firepower are concerned, Magdeburg can't compete with Hamburg. But it is still remarkable. And yet if the Emperor and the Imperial League decide to attack the city, Magdeburg would be hard-pressed. At some point, they'll get fed up with the Protestants. Who knows what goes on inside that ultra-Catholic ruler's head?'

Posing as a noblewoman, with her maidservant Tahmina and Nicolas as her bodyguard, Aenlin left the city centre through the heavy gate to take a walk to the island in the middle of the Elbe. There, they planned to ask about boats and barges setting sail for Hamburg within the next few days, as they'd had only negative replies from the large ships in the city port.

Before the trio started, however, they decided to eat. They sat down on a bench in front of a small hut, where a fisherman's friendly wife sold them smoked eels and home-brewed beer. The mystic, convincing as an exotic servant in her blue robe and bearing the wrapped staff, asked for milk.

Aenlin studied the vessels moored at the bank outside the

ramparts. On some of them, light was visible through portholes or on deck; others looked deserted. Perhaps their crews had taken lodgings in the city, or preferred to spend the night behind the safe walls of the nearby bastion. 'I hope we can find a passage.'

'We could steal a boat,' Nicolas said, putting his hat back in place. 'No, just joking. I know we need somebody who's familiar with the Elbe.'

Aenlin grinned. 'Anything else would be too hard on Moritz.'

A fine lady's clothes were not unfamiliar, but she was not particularly fond of wearing such dress. It felt wrong on such an adventure. She was armed only with the stilettos she wore in her belt. *In case of emergency, I'll have to borrow one of Nicolas' pistols.* She tucked the midnight-black strand of hair which had escaped her headdress behind her ear.

'Poor boy. After what happened with the naiad it has become a bit of a challenge for him to travel by river.' Tahmina took a sip of milk and fell silent.

Aenlin waited a few heartbeats. *She's not speaking much.* 'You're concerned that we can't agree on what to do with Nica,' she said bluntly.

'My mind is occupied with the fact that I have not come to a solution. I am vacillating . . .'

'Between . . . ?' Nicolas looked around at a tableau of fishermen and basketmakers, shipwrights and mill wagons. The Elbe was a busy river, with several mills using the force of the water to grind grain into flour. The summer harvest meant the millers were pretty busy; as a Hanseatic city and trade centre for grain, Magdeburg always had plenty of commissions to fulfil.

'Between immediate death or interrogation of the Aztec.' Tahmina tasted the eel, then chewed happily after that cautious first bite. 'A little like snake,' she pointed out.

'You've eaten snakes?' Nicolas shuddered. 'What do they taste like?'

'Like eel,' Tahmina said, 'only better.'

Aenlin sighed. She felt just as torn as her companion. 'Nica is too dangerous for us to hesitate for long. We must assume she's the most powerful of them – and what kind of magic might she summon in battle, given that Agatha was able to call forth from the earth a creature like the Xolotl?' She touched Tahmina's arm. 'I say this in all respect and admiration for your art.'

'It is all right. I feel uncomfortable myself, not knowing what Fate has in store for us. I remember only too well the demon from the earth.'

'We shouldn't travel to Hamburg in this state,' Nicolas said. 'Will we still be arguing when we confront Nica? Or throw a coin?'

'Then let's determine what we are going do,' Aenlin demanded. 'Right now. Then it must be done.' *Enough arguing.* 'I say we interrogate her.'

'Too dangerous,' Nicolas objected at once, touching the hilt of his rapier. 'We need to kill her.'

Tahmina sighed, her blue eyes darting to and fro between the two of them. 'Me? Do I have to be the one to tip the scales? Great . . .'

'It's got to be up to you because you're the only one who can truly judge the situation,' Aenlin said gently. 'Well?'

Nicolas rose and put down the cloudy beer. 'Look! The little one over there.' He gestured discreetly to the left to draw their attention to a young woman wearing a simple shift, with a bright white bonnet on her hair. 'What's she wearing around her neck?'

Aenlin squinted slightly, trying to focus her gaze. *Lucifer, what a quirk of fate!* 'An obsidian necklace,' she said in surprise.

'She appears to be in a bit of a hurry to get away from the boats moored here – that might mean nothing at all. Or quite a lot.' Nicolas rose. 'You know what? I'll go and get her.'

'Ask her nicely,' Tahmina admonished.

'I'd better go too.' Aenlin followed the sprinting landsknecht.

Running in a dress was exhausting; it demanded quite some skill. *I really should have worn my breeches.*

'Do you think she stole it?' she asked once she'd caught up with him.

'Yes, I'd guess she's a thief.' Nicolas hung on to his broad-brimmed hat with one hand. The guns attached to his baldric clattered, but he didn't seem to notice their weight as he speeded up a bit. 'Who would wear such jewellery? And what might bring its owner to Magdeburg?'

Aenlin could guess the answer. *Have we discovered another secret Aztec priestess?*

'An ally of Nica's, travelling to Hamburg to aid her,' he said, speaking her own thoughts aloud.

'Or someone planning no good for the city.' Nicolas gestured at the stranger to wait for them, but instead, the dark-haired woman started to run, quickly outdistancing them. One hand was clutching the heavy stone necklace as it bounced about on her chest.

At last, she tore off the piece of jewellery and threw it away. 'Keep it,' she called. 'I don't want it.'

'Stop!' Aenlin ran past Nicolas and stopped the thief by grabbing her right arm. 'You have nothing to fear from us.'

'Just tell us where you got the necklace.' Nicolas picked it up. The small obsidian plates were engraved with the same symbols they had seen on the priestesses' jewellery. 'It *is* obsidian, just as we thought. And the symbols resemble . . .' He paused, unwilling to disclose too much to the stranger.

The dark-haired woman, tanned from the sun and with dirty hands, adjusted her bonnet. Up close, she smelled of smoke and cooking; they guessed she earned her living by smoking fish.

'Mercy,' she pleaded, cringing, clearly afraid of being beaten. 'I usually don't do things like this, but I . . . I couldn't help myself.' She lowered her gaze in shame.

'Where did you get the necklace?' Aenlin gently but firmly.

'What ... what is it to you? Have you come to punish me?' Furtively, she gazed at Aenlin's expensive dress. 'But a noble lady like you would not demean herself to do such work. Who are you?'

'We are the ones who will bring it back,' Nicolas answered with a grin, 'so you won't get in trouble. That is who we are.'

'Oh, thank you! Thank you, you are truly good people, and I will tell you everything!' She pointed to an unlit, bulbous barge that looked like a refurbished cog, a type of ship the Hansa rarely used any more. 'I stole it from there. When I delivered my fish, I saw the jewellery—'

'There's more?' Aenlin exchanged a glance with Nicolas. He really had found a good lead.

'Much more. They said they were merchants – they had all this jewellery and other stuff from the New World – stone idols, paintings, weapons and figurines of strange creatures. They've been moored here for a week now.' Guiltily she nodded at the necklace in Nicolas' fingers. 'It was constantly on my mind, whispering at me, calling for me – I'm not an evil woman, I promise you, good people! It – it must have been this cursed necklace.' She spat three times to avert the evil eye. 'It's cursed witchcraft!'

'How many people are there?' Nicolas signalled to Tahmina that let her know everything was all right. When she raised her glass to take a sip of milk, he saw her other hand was clutching her ebony staff.

'Four – two sailors and their wives. They said they wanted to get some sleep, then leave soon because the stars are bright at night this time of year. So I couldn't wait any longer – I didn't want to wait, because the necklace was calling to me, even in my dreams.' She sighed. 'Thank you for saving me from my stupidity. I feel so much better now.'

'You were very lucky, praise your lord,' said Aenlin, and sent her off with a friendly pat on the shoulder. 'We have this; back to town with you.'

'And in the future, stick to smoking fish.' Nicolas pocketed the obsidian necklace.

'Thank you!' the thief called in relief as she ran away.

'Off she goes, guilty conscience personified.' The captain turned to Aenlin. 'Do we check the ship?

'Yes. At once.' She *really* missed her baldric, her pistols and her practical clothes. The stilettos would have to suffice. 'It may give us new information.'

Tahmina joined them and agreed to investigate the barge with them. Her gaze followed the cornered thief, who was just disappearing behind the mill. 'Let us not waste any time.' She started unwrapping her staff to unveil its symbols. 'While the crew is sleeping.'

'Just a moment.' *I won't be able to move silently in these clothes*, Aenlin thought, shedding her dress; she'd be able to move easier in her undergarments. She already wore comfortable shoes, of a type seldom seen on aristocratic feet. Her expensive clothes landed in the grass, as did her hat. She used a ribbon to tie her long, black hair into a ponytail, before chopping off the hem of her underslip to reduce it to a less puffy, knee-length garment. 'Ready.'

Tahmina grinned and Nicolas sighed.

'I know it's neither proper nor fitting – but how was I to know that we'd have to undertake such an investigation today?' Aenlin nodded at them. 'Let's go.'

Together they hurried towards the dark boat, which had a narrow gangway leading to the deck. It stood out among the other vessels because of its bulging shape. The barges on either side were dark as well, which made their endeavour easier, especially with dusk falling quickly.

'Let's pretend to be visitors,' Nicolas said. 'Sometimes, being obvious is the easiest way.'

'Searching for a new tailor for me.' Aenlin grinned. 'No, we're customers looking for exotica. Quiet now.' She took the lead and walked carefully up the gangway, followed by Tahmina and Nicolas. The mercenary's weight made the wood sag and creak.

The deck of the ship remained quiet. The wind carried the smell of water and the threat of fall, as well as a chill from the Elbe. The boat bobbed slightly up and down.

'Go on,' Nicolas whispered, pulling his dagger. 'Let's take a look around.'

'For the people or the cargo?' Aenlin drew her own stiletto.

Tahmina clutched her ebony staff so she could use it to defend herself. The symbols remained dark, so there was no magical threat anywhere nearby.

'Cargo,' Tahmina answered. 'If it is harmless gewgaws, we can leave. No one must be harmed.'

'Are you sure?' Nicolas said. 'If a priestess—'

'We've been arguing about it for too long already,' Aenlin said, running ahead. The time for talk was over.

They went through the narrow door and found a creaking stairway that led belowdecks to an area smelling of spice, warm wood and water. The Elbe sloshed quietly against the hull of the moored barge. An oil lamp shed a dim light.

The three of them stood in the open cargo hold. Next to the stairs, two men and two women lay in hammocks and hinged beds attached to the walls with chains. The sleepers' breath was even; one of the women talked softly in her sleep.

'Fan out and look around. We'll meet back here by the stairs.' Nicolas disappeared into the ship's dark belly, his steps clearly audible. A landsknecht rarely had to move silently, which was a definite disadvantage for their illicit snooping.

I hope these people are sleeping really deeply. Aenlin stayed near Tahmina.

With a quickly whispered Yatu word, the runes on the Persian's staff glowed softly, lending them a dim light for their search. Carefully, they moved onwards, past crates, sacks and chests all secured with heavy locks. They each had a hand-written paper label attached.

'Exotica,' Aenlin whispered. 'There's something here.'

She tested some of the latches and managed to push one open – the merchants were either careless, or very sure that no stranger would dare come aboard.

Show us your secrets, if you have any. 'I need some light.' Slowly, she lifted the lid. The well-oiled hinges didn't creak.

Tahmina lifted her staff and looked at the contents. Their stench reminded Aenlin of oil, alchemy and blood. 'These are . . . hooks!' she whispered. 'Blood-smeared hooks and chains – scraps of skin and hairs are still clinging to them. This is probably not intended for a trader of exotica in Hamburg.' She rummaged around, the clinking of the metal seeming to echo loudly through the silence of the hold, but she found nothing.

There was a crackling sound in the darkness to their right and a board creaked under someone's weight.

'Nicolas?' Tahmina swept the glowing end of her staff towards the sound.

The dim light fell on the end of a mace covered in glittering black-green obsidian blades.

At first Aenlin thought the weapon was mounted to the wall in some sort of bracket, then a warrior with a naked torso stepped into the light. Instead of a human head, he had a jaguar's skull. His skin was painted with turquoise and green symbols and he wore a loincloth embossed with a stylised moon. With a snarl, he presented his long fangs and levelled his mace at the women.

A werebeast like Statius. Aenlin slowly reached for her

pistol – which wasn't there. *Where's Nicolas?* There had been no sound of battle. 'Ready, Tahmina?'

'Yes.'

Suddenly, the light in the cargo hold grew brighter, banishing darkness.

'Is that your doing?' Aenlin looked around.

Between the crates, sacks and chests, she discovered the menacing silhouettes of six more jaguar warriors, their fangs bared and their ears laid back. In their fists, they held the same terrifying clubs embedded with stone blades.

'No. No, it is not.' Tahmina looked at the lamp, which was shedding significantly more light now.

Aenlin was really hoping to see Nicolas standing there, two pistols at the ready, but instead, she saw the dark-haired thief sneering at her. The woman was standing next to the passengers, who had awakened. She had exchanged her shabby fishmonger's clothes for a luxurious turquoise robe with gold threads; in place of the white bonnet, she now sported a headdress made of exotic plumes. 'I knew my little charade would lure you on board.' Her attitude was that of a queen lording over her enemies. 'I assume you know who I am.'

'Nica.' Aenlin aimed the stiletto at her. *She has tricked us splendidly.* 'Have you come to start our conversation?'

'My true name is Mano. No, I came for an entirely different reason. We agreed that I would not attack you in Hamburg.' She smiled cruelly. 'Which is why I have travelled here – so I do not have to break my promise. It was easy to follow Tahmina on the spiritual plane after our encounter.' She glanced aside, looking bored. 'Nicolas. How long are you going to hide? I know where you are – my jaguar warriors can smell you. You can neither escape nor surprise me.'

The landsknecht rose from behind a chest, aiming his pistols at the priestess. 'I am angry at my own stupidity.'

'Do not worry. I will see to it that you will be justly punished.' Mano laughed. 'Of course, my warriors are in town as well, killing Jäcklein, Moritz and Caspar as we speak. We will sacrifice their blood and their hearts to the god of the underworld. When you are dead, I will retrieve the claw of Itzli.' She pointed towards the other side of the river. 'Now that I am here, I have great plans for Magdeburg: I will strike the city with the curse of complete annihilation.'

Lucifer, your help now would be timely. Aenlin didn't know what to do; she felt completely overwhelmed. Mano was the most powerful foe she had ever faced, and she had come unprepared and without a plan. She had only two stilettos on her and the obsidian knife was in her room, hidden in her luggage. Mano's henchmen would have no trouble finding it. *We have underestimated how evil she is.*

Something collided with the hull of the barge, making it sway. The wood creaked under the pressure, followed by a raw, grinding sound. Quite unexpectedly, the ship teetered to starboard.

'What was that?' Nicolas' weapon was aimed unwaveringly at Mano. 'Probably not a tree.'

'No, it was not. I have brought not only jaguar warriors with me, but also an incarnation of Xiuhcoatl, the two-headed fire snake, who is more fearsome than any pathetic dragon from your little fairy tales. If you offer resistance, if Tahmina fights back, or if one of you feels particularly heroic, Xiuhcoatl will attack. The boats, the mills, everything will be destroyed. No one would survive his attack. Perhaps you should bear that in mind.'

'What do you want from us?' Aenlin put away her stiletto. *The time to fight back would come.* For now, it was essential they stall, keep the priestess talking. Many a tongue loosened in the flush of victory. *She will tell us what she has planned – what she really intends to do with the claw.*

'Oh, it is really very simple: I want to sacrifice you.' Mano gestured at the two men and two women standing behind her to start preparing the ritual. 'For you have already brought me what I was missing.'

Quickly, her four helpers pushed together a few crates, forming a makeshift altar, and retrieved the chains with the hooks attached, which they threw over the rafters.

Aenlin watched the crew's trained movements. What had looked like a floating curio shop turned out to be a travelling sacrificial chamber to appease the deities of the New World and to sow the seed of evil unnoticed.

'We will stop you,' she said.

'And doom the innocents to die in Xiuhcoatl's fire?' Mano shook her adorned head, its jewels and plumes shimmering in the lamplight. 'You wouldn't dare.' She looked at the landsknecht. 'Not even you, Nicolas. Lower your pistols! They will avail you nothing.'

The jaguar warriors stood guard while Nicolas was disarmed and led to the altar. Tahmina and Aenlin quietly, unobtrusively, stepped backwards to be able to talk without being overheard.

'What shall we do?' Tahmina whispered. 'I am up for anything, love.'

'Do you believe she'll really set this snake on the city if we fight back? That this creature is really swimming around the barge right now? Or do you think it's just a lie to keep us from resisting?' Aenlin considered her chances. *Two stilettos, me and a mystic against such superior forces? This will be the hardest battle we've fought so far.*

Tahmina lowered her head slightly. 'I have never heard of such a creature, but I am afraid that the priestess is not lying. Imagine it attacking Magdeburg!'

'Can you stop it?'

'Mano will feel it if I use my powers.'

Nicolas let them undress him and push him face-down on the altar. The priestess stepped close to him, drawing an obsidian knife and praying softly.

The invocation began.

She's weaving the curse of total annihilation she intends casting upon the city. Aenlin grabbed the hilts of her stilettos. If she allowed Mano to finish her ritual, Magdeburg would be doomed.

The four servants drove the hooks through the mercenary's legs and arms. Nicolas moaned and gasped softly, but he gazed steadily at Aenlin and Tahmina, as if trying to convey a secret message to them. The servants jerked him up by the chains, the hooks firmly embedded in his skin and joints, until he was dangling in the air right in front of the priestess.

'We must not let him die!' *And neither must he let us die.* Aenlin was desperate. She thought about the snake in the river beneath her.

'He will not.' Tahmina clutched her staff. The carvings were glowing, but softly, as if trying to hide the fact that their magical power could be unleashed at any moment. 'Have you forgotten the things he has survived? He will laugh at Mano, free himself and subdue the priestess.'

'This is different. She knows how to kill him.' *How can he live without a heart? Without a head?* 'Remember what happened to Moritz.'

Aenlin's fingers tingled. She wasn't good at keeping still. She was *Aenlin Kane*, daughter of Solomon and Bess, follower of the Bringer of Light. She couldn't allow herself to be blackmailed by something that might never happen. Maybe this Aztec snake didn't exist at all – perhaps it was just an illusion, nothing but a rumbling and swaying of the ship. However, it was certain that she, Tahmina and Nicolas would die if they didn't fight back. Under no circumstances must this curse fall upon Magdeburg.

My training, my very existence as a member of the Kane family, everything has led me to this spot, to this moment. This is my Fate – my destiny. Lucifer, for you and in thy name.

'Will you be with me when I attack, beloved?' she whispered.

'I will. Whatever happens, we will face it together, whether it is death or triumph.' Tahmina breathed deeply. 'Say when—'

Unexpectedly, Mano stabbed her dagger into Nicolas' body, beneath the left side of his ribcage, ripping open his belly with a long cut. Blood spurted out, streaming across his skin, across countless old scars.

Nicolas' screams of pain echoed throughout the cargo hold, shaking the boards of the makeshift altar and jangling the chains: he sounded as if he were a god in extreme pain. The jaguar warriors covered their ears, and Aenlin felt dizzy.

Mumbling the summoning words, Mano suddenly pushed her free hand through the cut to grab Nicolas' heart and tear it out.

'Now!' Aenlin called out as she took a swing.

Caspar reached their lodgings and suddenly found himself in the middle of a crowd of people armed with buckets and every other conceivable vessel able to hold water, all fighting the flames threatening to spread from the debris of the ruined barn.

The inn's fire-bell was still clanging wildly, summoning helpers from all across the neighbourhood to the site of the accident; those already there were scooping water from barrels filled from the river to pour onto the hot spots.

Caspar studied the ruins, looking especially at the scattered remains of carts and crates. The blast had wreaked havoc, but it appeared to be the result of pressure and fire, not the deadly metal bits Jäcklein had intended using. The keg-mine must have detonated while it was being loaded. *What a wretched invention – an unparalleled crackpot idea.*

A boy ran past him, proudly carrying several feathers. Even

covered in soot, some of the quills scorched, Caspar could see they were unusually colourful. *They're from the New World!*

'Just a moment.' Caspar grabbed the back of his shirt. 'Where did you find these?'

'On the street! They was just lying around.' He broke away. 'Let go of me!'

'Did you find anything else?'

The boy kicked his shin and tried to bite him. 'You won't get nothing from me – go and find your own stones!'

Stones? Caspar shook him violently and an obsidian shard fell from his pocket. The boy covered it protectively with his foot. *Thought so.*

'Keep it, child. But don't cut yourself on it. Now, scram!'

Quickly, the boy retrieved his loot and disappeared into the mass of people still working on extinguishing the fire. Such an inferno was the biggest threat to any city.

Feathers and obsidian. A new story was emerging for Caspar: the keg-mine had not been detonated accidentally; his friends had obviously decided triggering the snap-lock was their only way to fight superior numbers and send their enemies from the New World to Hell.

'Jäcklein? Moritz?' Caspar shouted into the mess of collapsed walls, destroyed beams, cracked stone and pulverised bricks. He walked carefully across the smoking, smouldering debris, past helpers who had covered their mouths with kerchiefs and were trying to extinguish the embers. 'Jäcklein?'

'Here,' answered a weak voice from the half-collapsed wall the barn shared with the inn. Jäcklein was sitting with his back against the stones, pressing a piece of cloth to a bleeding gash in his forehead. 'I'm alive, but I feel horribly sick – I've vomited twice already, and the world's spinning in front of my eyes – tell me, has it really turned into a carousel?'

Caspar stalked across the debris to his friend and knelt next to him. 'Let me see.' He recognised the signs. 'I felt the same after a bad cropper from the Comte's back. The blow to the back of my neck was so hard that I couldn't walk straight for days.' At least the bleeding cut above the landsknecht's pale eyebrow would be easy enough to stitch up. 'Where's Moritz?'

'Somewhere over there, I think.' Jäcklein didn't try to hide the desperation in his voice. 'I wanted to look for him, but every time I try to get up, I puke.'

'What happened?'

'I came back into the barn with beer and there they were – eagle demons, half human, half griffin! Then the keg exploded . . .'

Just as I thought: young Moritz detonated it as an emergency measure. Caspar rose. 'Keep applying pressure to the wound. I'll take care of Moritz.' He found a pitchfork lying amid the debris that had somehow escaped being consumed by the flames and used it to push aside steaming remnants and heavy pieces of rubble.

The firefighting operations had calmed down now the last flames had been extinguished. People were now concentrating on pouring buckets of water onto the spots where smoke still rose until the embers finally surrendered, hissing as the last traces of fire died away.

'Moritz!' Caspar worked his way forward to the corner of the ruined barn, trying to ignore the heat rising uncomfortably through the soles of his boots. The leather wouldn't save him from burns for very much longer. 'Moritz, where are you?' he shouted.

Poking around in the debris, he found a smashed, human-sized eagle's head, its beak shattered. Blood had run across the blue tongue; the one remaining eye stared blindly from its socket.

Before anybody else noticed, Caspar pushed the severed head into a nearby pocket of smouldering embers. The feathers swiftly disappeared, producing an evil stench, while the heat bent the beak quite out of shape. *Now no one will find any trace of the supernatural.* He'd have to hope that the other warriors had been burned to ashes in the conflagration – otherwise, the fat really would be in the fire in Magdeburg – literally. That kind of discovery would cause a witch-hunt beyond compare.

After shovelling aside endless piles of steaming rubble, he happened across a hand. one he'd almost overlooked, so filthy, so covered in dirt and dust was it. Judging by its size, it had to belong to Moritz.

'Please, Almighty God, let it still be attached to the rest of him,' Caspar muttered. He knelt and started digging through the debris, paying no mind to his expensive clothes.

The hand led to a forearm, an arm, a shoulder – and then the neck and head of the missing landsknecht appeared. The fire had singed his eyebrows and his long black curls, and his skin had red burns from the heat. His pulse was weak. He was barely breathing.

'Over here!' Caspar called for help. 'Someone's alive here! Barely!' With a handful of strong men, he excavated Moritz, inch by inch.

The duellist didn't like what he saw: the young giant had grievous wounds clearly not caused by the detonation, but the explosion had widened the gaping cuts from the obsidian weapons – and the Passau Art protected only the outer shell, not the vulnerable insides.

When the helpers saw the wounds, they started working more slowly, muttering prayers and crossing themselves.

They've already given up on him, Caspar thought, and shouted, 'Hey! Keep working – he's not dead yet.'

'No one could survive this,' one man muttered.

'Unless he's in league with the Devil,' added another, crossing himself again.

'You'd be better thinking of the miracles of our Lord God,' Caspar retorted sharply, but he threw them some kreutzers. 'Come on, keep digging! The boy can't stay under the debris: he needs a good doctor, and decent care.' *And the assistance of his own god, Odin.*

Encouraged by the money, the men kept working and were soon able to free Moritz. Under the duellist's command, they loaded the battered landsknecht onto a wagon, one that had brought barrels of water to extinguish the flames. Caspar collected his battered friend, although he had to help Jäcklein, who still couldn't stand upright; he was lurching worse than a drunk, retching and cursing every few feet.

'Hey, coachman.' Caspar slipped a thaler into the man's hand. 'My name is Caspar von und zu dem Dorffe. These are my servants. Where would they be in good hands to have their wounds attended to?'

'In the Golden Sun, sir.'

'Then get them there, please, and make sure they are tended.'

'I will, sir.'

Caspar shook Jäcklein's hand. 'Take diligent care of Moritz – I'll trust you to come up with a way to save him.'

'Brandy and sutures and then some milk of the poppy to make him sleep and heal,' Jäcklein replied. 'We learned that on the battlefield.'

'It won't be enough . . .'

'I'll also pray for him. Can't hurt.'

Caspar slowly stepped away from the wagon. 'No, I mean, because of his skin – he's frozen, remember? So how is the barber surgeon supposed to patch him if his needle can't pierce the patient's skin?'

'Ashen tree, ashen tree, pray buy these wounds from me!' Jäcklein looked at the unmoving, grievously wounded Moritz. 'You're right: this is going to be hard.'

'Take care of him!' Caspar ran into Aenlin's room and grabbed the claw of Itzli. From there he hurried to the stables on the other side of the inn, which had not been hit by the explosion and fire, and without bothering with a saddle, mounted the snorting Comte.

There's no time to waste, he told himself. *To the others, and quickly!*

He galloped through the startled city of Magdeburg towards the harbour. If the Aztec had attacked them at the inn with her demons, Aenlin, Nicolas and Tahmina were probably facing similar problems.

Please God I'll get there in time to warn them.

Aenlin attacked the nearest jaguar warrior, who'd been too distracted watching the ritual to raise his mace in time to deflect her stiletto. The steel blade found the creature's heart and Aenlin twisted it to destroy the muscle utterly.

With a muted growl, the creature collapsed.

She yanked out her stiletto, muttering, 'Distract them!' to Tahmina. 'I'll finish this!' With her face set in grim determination, she leapt towards the praying priestess.

The mystic hit one of her enemies in the abdomen with the base of her staff, triggering a spell. The round butt glowed hotter than a blacksmith's hearth and burned a hole into her opponent's belly, melting veins and vaporising entrails, felling the jaguar warrior without a sound.

'Run,' Tahmina told her, 'I am right behind you!' She had already started weaving a new spell.

Aenlin's confidence that they would be able to defeat Mano was growing with every step she took towards the priestess – until the Aztec's four mortal henchmen, brandishing long daggers, blocked her way. The remaining predator demons lined up behind them, their obsidian blades gleaming.

Mano interrupted her invocation to say calmly, 'I knew you

would try.' Her right hand was still within the body of the landsknecht dangling from the hooks in front of her. 'Xiuhcoatl will rage and rampage and the city will perish in your name. But you have not—' She grimaced and stared at Nicolas. 'What . . . what is happening to you?'

The captain had opened his eyes wide. They suddenly turned all white, cold light flaring from them – and from the gash in his chest.

Mano tried in vain to jerk free her hand. 'No!' she screamed, 'no, don't!' She braced her other hand against his chest, pulling, then threw herself backwards, trying to free herself.

Aenlin looked at Tahmina, who was gazing at Nicolas as if ensorcelled. 'Did you do that?'

'No, this can only be the captain's doing.'

The light from his chest had spread to the priestess' arm. Her bones and veins became visible; her flesh turned translucent, like glass. The light spread past her elbow to her shoulder, where it split, as if about to engulf the woman completely.

Her henchmen looked terrified; even the jaguar warriors just stood there, not knowing what to do.

'No – please! I did not know that!' Mano, still pleading, tried to fall to her knees, but her hand was stuck in the body of the dangling man. She lost her headdress and her self-assurance: a ruler turned into a frightened subject. 'I pledge eternal loyalty to you! By all the gods of my homeland, *please*—' All colour had drained from her; she had turned into a crystalline being of red veins and white bones. The light spread to her neck, then to her head. 'I renounce them! Is that what you want? By my life: I renounce them to—' In her agony, Mano gritted her teeth so hard they splintered into ivory shards.

This is Lucifer's miracle. Aenlin didn't understand what was happening, but she recognised opportunity when she saw it. *Onwards!*

With her stiletto, she hacked her way through the shocked henchmen and hybrids; they all fell, bleeding, to the planks. Before anyone could react or try to grab her, she had moved through the gap and stabbed the priestess, who was turning into a creature of light.

At close quarters, Aenlin realised what the glowing light was doing to the woman. *She is melting from the inside!* Liquefied flesh and body fat was oozing from every pore. Her veins were melting like butter, her blood boiling without coagulating. Mano seemed to be made of glassy wax that was losing its structure because of the incredible heat raging through her.

With a crash, the barge shook, sending pieces of wood flying through the hold.

There was another crash and two dragon-like heads attached to one serpentine body pushed their way through a jagged hole. The two-headed snake hissed, its tongues darting in and out. Turquoise scales on the back of their heads bristled, rubbing against each other with a rattling noise. When the being opened its maws, a glow emanated from deep in the throats. A burst of fire was imminent.

When Aenlin raised her weapon, Mano wailed like a banshee.

I will finish this! The blade entered the translucent body of the priestess. When it pierced her heart, her screaming stopped abruptly.

As Mano's eyes grew dim, she lowered her gaze at Aenlin. 'You knew what he is,' she moaned. 'You know what he is and you ha—'

The light within her and in Nicolas suddenly died. The priestess' hand slid from the landsknecht's wound and she fell to the floor. Her bones broke with a noise like glass shattering, then she dissolved, her skin melting to nothing, until she was nothing but a puddle of pulp.

It's over! We made it—!

But a rumbling behind her warned Aenlin that it wasn't yet done. She turned quickly and grabbed Nicolas' rapier from the floor. The remaining jaguar warriors, overcoming their shock, now faced her. 'I'll finish you off, too,' she promised to them. 'You'll end up just like your priestess!' She lifted her stiletto and the rapier.

Tahmina had raised her staff, trapping the snakes' heads within a pearlescent sphere; they raged silently, spitting their flames in vain. 'Hurry, Aenlin,' she gasped, 'you must kill Xiuhcoatl – it's taking all my strength just to hold it back.'

'On it!' Challenged like never before in her life, Aenlin attacked, stabbing, slashing and impaling one enemy after another. *'For Lucifer!'* Her heart was racing, but she wasn't afraid and not once did she flinch.

The demonic creatures, weakened by the death of their mistress, were fighting less aggressively now, and when at last they turned to flee, overcome by their unstoppable opponent, Aenlin followed, stabbing into the backs of their necks and felling them all.

So much for werebeasts. Breathing heavily, she whirled, wiping sweat from her face, pushing back the midnight-black strand of hair.

The two serpentine heads were taking turns snapping at Tahmina. Her Yatu powers were obviously fading now, for she was defending herself with blows from her staff, rather than spells.

Aenlin ran through the cargo hold, fighting to keep to her feet, for the barge was rocking noticeably now. The vessel must have torn free from its moorings. If it was floating down the Elbe, it could run aground or collide with another boat or the riverbank at any minute.

The scaly heads showed clear wounds inflicted by the mystic. The turquoise scales were bloodstained and, in some spots, torn away or cleaved in half.

'Let's kill this thing!' Aenlin's arms were hurting from the constant fighting, but battle-lust and the sight of Xiuhcoatl re-invigorated her. She joined Tahmina and stabbed at the beast, which was squeezing itself further and further into the barge.

'What are we going to do?'

Xiuhcoatl had enlarged the hole; dark water was gushing in. The weight added to that of the beast was making the barge list, causing the Elbe to pour in even faster.

'I am exhausted,' Tahmina admitted. 'I have power for one last spell – but Ōrmozd himself will have to weave it, if it is to work.'

Aenlin's eyes fell upon the unused chains with the hooks attached. *That's it!* 'Get ready,' she called as she started running again. She threw her stiletto at the monster, crying, 'Hey! Come here!'

Roaring, the wounded creature turned away from Tahmina. It came rushing towards her through the rising water, which splashed and foamed around its scaled body.

When she reached a supporting beam, Aenlin turned sharply to the right, grabbed the hooked chains and hurled them at the beast.

The curved pointy ends pierced the hide like fish hooks, jamming themselves into the scales so tightly so that the beast could not free itself. Raging with anger, the giant snake thrashed about, trying to bite Aenlin. In its maw was a tell-tale glow.

I've got you hooked. Now for the rest. She deftly dodged the twin heads while tying one end of the chains to the beam, leashing Xiuhcoatl.

'Destroy the hull,' she yelled to Tahmina. She threw back her heavy, wet hair. 'Sink this barge!'

'But—'

'Do it before the beast burns us to ashes! Then get out of here!'

Tahmina raised her staff, the bottom white-hot with heat. Steam erupted as she thrust it through the knee-deep water and hit the wood; a large chunk burst outwards and the Elbe rushed in, foaming and seething.

The barge heeled at once, throwing Aenlin into the deeper water. As she sank beneath the surface, Xiuhcoatl's snarling heads darted around; they missed biting her by no more than a hair's breadth. Their maws filled with river water, quenching any ability to breathe fire. Smoke and hot steam rose, but the chains held, as did the massive support beam. The bound beast thrashed beneath the surface, squirming and coiling, trying and failing to escape its bonds. Every time it broke free of one hook, another immediately found new purchase on its turquoise scales.

Through the murky gloom, Aenlin saw a spot on Xiuhcoatl's lower neck where a hook was bending up several scales, revealing vulnerable pale skin beneath. *I won't let you harm this city.* Before the beast could turn, Aenlin extended the rapier, slicing open its unprotected flesh with her rapier. Turquoise-black blood flowed from the gash, which was as long as her arm, its bodily fluid colouring the water darker still.

The snake-demon intensified its attempts to free itself of the hooks and chains, fear and pain making it even stronger. The creaking and the groaning of the wood sounded muffled, but Xiuhcoatl's thrashing and screeching, the clanking of the metal chains, all added to the overall din.

This is the end of you, beast from the New World! Aenlin evaded the thrashing creature, seeing bubbles of air rise from it, but her lungs was screaming for air, too. *Damn it!* She was scared – for herself, and especially for Tahmina!

Forcing her way through the water, she tried to head to the surface, but once the lights in the cargo hold went out, there was no up and no down for her any more. Her attempt to free Nicolas from the beam died, like Xiuhcoatl, somewhere beside her, for she was running out of air. She choked, striving desperately not to breathe in the Elbe's icy water.

Suddenly, an unexpected current grabbed her, spinning her in circles. She scraped painfully against something sharp in the darkness, but when she instinctively opened her mouth to scream, she produced only a gurgling sound – and used up the last of her precious air.

But I did it! Aenlin coughed and water filled her nose, her mouth, her lungs, but the undertow was pushing her upwards, and there was light.

Lucifer, it's up to you now – save me!

One light turned into several shimmering, ghostly images above her, until she broke the surface. Someone grabbed her, pulling her out of the Elbe and over the side of a boat. She lay there coughing and retching among eels and fish, all jumping and twitching around her as if to welcome her to their number.

'There's our next naiad,' she heard Caspar say.

'Nicolas is still on board the barge,' Tahmina replied, her voice worried. 'He is chained up.' Then she was at Aenlin's side, supporting her. 'Together with the snake.'

My love is alive! Aenlin was wheezing and retching so hard that she couldn't speak. Death had come awfully close this time. Shakily, she embraced her companion, thinking, *But somehow, we are alive!*

'Of course. My pistols are especially suited to shooting underwater at two-headed fiends.' Caspar's voice moved slightly further away from Aenlin as he continued, 'Ho, good fisherman, I'll soon bring you the fattest eel you've ever seen.'

A loud splash followed. Obviously, the duellist had plunged into the Elbe.

Aenlin wanted to tell him that Xiuhcoatl was dead and that he had nothing to fear from the serpent, but she couldn't, for she was hovering on the edge of unconsciousness. Tahmina said something to her that she didn't understand, then she felt soft lips on hers – and for a few heartbeats, the world turned black.

When the darkness lifted, Aenlin found herself not in the boat but in a bed, in a room. After her experience in the river and the slippery fishy bodies in the boat, her surroundings were comfortably warm and dry, and smelled of good food. *I am not in Heaven, nor yet in Hell.* She sat up, clinging to the sheet covering her. At once, her dark hair fell loose over her shoulders.

'Ah, she's awake.' Jäcklein sat in his nightshirt on a bench next to the hearth. 'We've taken new lodgings at the Golden Sun.'

Aenlin looked around. Beneath the sheet, she was naked – so someone must have removed her wet clothes.

Nicolas was lying next to her on the bed, his eyes closed. A bandage was wrapped around his chest. Blood was seeping through the layers.

Caspar was sitting at the table. He too must have shed his soaked clothes, for he was wrapped in a blanket with a bowl of hot soup steaming in front of him.

He answered Aenlin's unspoken question. 'I pulled the captain up. He was shimmering, or I wouldn't have been able to find him. What a miracle that was.' He smiled. 'The big snake was dead – lucky for me, for I dived right into it. Well done, Aenlin. Otherwise, it would no doubt have devoured me. Now it'll rot – nothing but food for the fishes.'

Then it ended well after all, Lucifer be praised! Aenlin wrapped herself in the sheet, rose stiffly from the bed and limped to the table to find something to eat. She was suddenly very hungry. 'I killed it, but you saved Nicolas. Don't sell yourself short.' She was feeling terribly cold out of bed. 'Where are Tahmina and Moritz?'

'She took him out of the city.' Jäcklein summed up what had happened to them in the barn while the others had been fighting the priestess on the barge. 'She said there was only one way for him to survive, that she'd have to sacrifice something for it.'

Aenlin didn't know what that meant, but she trusted her

companion. 'Then all we can do is wait.' She looked at the sleeping Nicolas and immediately, Mano's end rose in her mind's eye. *How she looked at me.* She couldn't remember the dying woman's exact words, but when they had first met him, Tahmina had said that Nicolas was special. He was so special, in fact, that he had transformed the Aztec.

What are you, Captain?

She didn't want to discuss it with Caspar and Jäcklein; that would only lead to more questions she couldn't answer. However, if a mighty priestess swore allegiance to this man, renouncing her own powerful Aztec gods to serve him, there must be something truly unbelievable about him. *The light from his eyes and from his wound . . . Do you belong to Lucifer without knowing it? Are you his secret Lightbringer?*

'We'll just have to wait – and eat soup.' Caspar pushed a spoon towards her. 'We all need to regain our strength. Your dip into the Elbe has weakened you, but I hope you're not angry with me for interrupting your swim?'

Jäcklein laughed, stroking his beard. 'She'd make a rotten water maid. What would she do in the river?'

Aenlin smiled thankfully at the duellist. 'How did you find us, after all that?'

'I was riding to the harbour to meet you when I saw a light in front of me,' Caspar told them. 'It was your silhouette – as if you had turned into a ghost. That shimmering silhouette started walking, waving at me to follow it – so I reached the island and found the fisherman, who rowed me out onto the Elbe.'

That was Lucifer's miracle! 'A thousand thanks!' With her free hand, Aenlin grabbed his right hand. 'I owe you—'

Caspar stopped her, waving away her gratitude. He took the claw of Itzli from the chair next to him and put it on the table. 'What do we do with this?'

Tahmina, in dry clothes, sat on the box, whipping the two horses, though she hated doing so. But if she wanted to save Moritz's life, she had to hurry. Her long brown hair rippled in the breeze, which had set her robe flapping around her.

She thundered through the night, along a road that was taking her further and further from Magdeburg. But at least she knew Aenlin was safe. Behind her, in the wagon, she had improvised a bed of straw and blankets to absorb the shocks from the bumpy journey for the young mercenary. Her staff was secured to the wagon's bed, next to the unconscious man, for she needed both hands to drive the horses.

Without Caspar and the miracle of the shining silhouette, they would all be dead. He had dragged Aenlin and her from the Elbe like two wet cats, then dived into the depths of the river to find the captain.

Caspar had ended many a life in his duels. He had ruined families and enriched himself – but for Tahmina, he was a saviour. *For me, and for the love of my life.*

And once again, sacrifice would be necessary to thwart Death.

Tahmina steered the wagon into a forest, the lantern dancing wildly in its bracket, illuminating everything but the path as she thundered along. Finally, she stopped the team of sweating, panting horses and rose from the box.

The horses snorted with exertion, whinnying and turning their heads one way and the other, uncomfortable at being in the dark fir forest. All around, there was deep silence; not a breeze was stirring.

Let us see if this works. Tahmina took a deep breath, then put her hands to her mouth like a horn. 'Tännel!' she called loudly into the silence. 'Tännel! Tännel!'

Her voice quickly faded between the tree trunks, but a crackling sound came from somewhere nearby; startled animals, fleeing from the nocturnal disturbance, eroded the night's earlier silence.

At first, nothing more happened.

Did I not call loudly enough? Or did it not work?

Tahmina was about to turn the wagon around when a soft rumble shook the earth.

A rhythmical sound sounded in the distance.

The towering trees around the wagon shook softly, shedding some needles. The horses, whinnying in fear, tried to run, but Tahmina clung to the wagon's brake to stop them from bolting with her and the injured giant.

'By the djinni of the desert,' Tahmina whispered to Moritz, 'they really are coming. Can you hear them?'

The giants of old became visible as they approached from three sides. Tall like firs, mighty like the gods of the ancient sagas, they loomed around the wagon.

'Here I am, Hagzussa,' said the leather-clad Tännel. He knelt so she could see him better in the dim light of the lantern. His long brown beard and his wild hair framed his familiar face. 'I came with seven-league boots – I even brought friends to aid you.'

'It is not me who needs your help.' Tahmina took the lantern from its bracket and illuminated the bed of the wagon. 'I brought you Holder. He is in bad shape. If he is to survive, then his people must perform a miracle.'

'It is him, truly,' said the giant on Tännel's right. 'Praised be Odin!'

'The boy has suffered a lot,' said the one on his left.

'You called me? You sacrificed your wish to save Holder?' Tännel watched her with deference, then, bowing his head as if she were a queen, said, 'I never thought a human could be so magnanimous, Tahmina from the Orient.'

Moved by his gracious gesture, Tahmina replied, 'He has done a lot for us, and he has a kind soul. Of all the people I have met, he is the one who least deserves to die. One day, he will do good things.'

Tännel carefully lifted the unconscious young giant from the wagon and cradled him in his arms. In his giant hands, the gigantic landsknecht suddenly looked like the child he was. 'My people will never forget this, Hagzussa.' He stood, then disappeared from the lantern's weak circle of light. 'Never.'

Tännel turned and hurried away, followed by the other two giants.

Tahmina could still feel the vibrations of their steps for a while after they were gone. Only once the tremors had completely died down and the branches of the firs no longer quivered did she turn the wagon around and let the horses choose their own pace on the way back to Magdeburg.

Ōrmozd, we did the right thing. A good feeling spread through Tahmina. *We have overcome so many dangers, averted so many threats – and perhaps saved an extraordinary life.*

O peace, o noble peace! Everybody must confess that thou shalt rightfully be called the Mother of Wealth. Those who don't want to believe it may ask Germany how it was before this unfortunate war and how, alas, it is now.

Randolphus of Duysburgk
(a.k.a. Rudolph von Dieskau, steward and author)
1638

CAPITULUM XIX

Free Imperial City of Hamburg, October 1629

'You see it is not our fault that we stand before you empty-handed.' As evidence, Aenlin presented the list of those accused of witchcraft and wizardry in Bamberg.

She stood together with Tahmina, Caspar, Jäcklein and Nicolas in the writing room of the de Hertoghe brothers. The landsknechts wore their traditional flashy, multicoloured garb; the duellist was clad all in noble black and sporting a new wig. Tahmina once again played the exotic servant.

'Many of them were imprisoned in the House of Malefaction. Two had already been executed. We freed Agatha Mühlbach, Veronica Stadler and Ursula Garnhuber. We managed to escape from the Hauptsmoorwald by a hair's breadth when the Prince-Bishop's henchmen attacked it – that was when we lost Mühlbach and Garnhuber.' Aenlin's face was full of regret. She wore breeches, a blouse, a jerkin and a baldric without weapons. The adventuress had tied back her long black hair into a ponytail with a white velvet ribbon, but as usual, one strand had escaped. 'Near Magdeburg, the last of them died of the plague. That was Veronica Stadler.'

'We refrained from bringing you the corpse,' Caspar said in a friendly tone.

'Yes,' Nicolas added, 'we assumed you would be fine with this. The citizens of Hamburg, too.'

'Altona, on the other hand, would have been happy if the Black Death had visited its rich neighbours for a bit,' Jäcklein added with a grin.

Aenlin watched the blond-haired de Hertoghe brothers, clad in their regal capes and hats, who were sitting silently on their throne-like chairs. Hans wore his eyeglasses as if they helped him to hear and understand them better.

'What do you say?'

The brothers put their heads together.

For more than an hour, they had been retelling their adventures, first over water, then wine, beer and tea, explaining why they had returned without the people the brothers had paid them to bring back. They had agreed their version beforehand; it was far more harmless than everything they had actually experienced. They didn't even try to explain to the West India Company that Aztec priestesses from the New World had brought evil to Europe with their rituals and deities, let alone bringing long-extinct giants into the story. Or naiads. Or the undead. Or animal-headed demons. Or other things you might sometimes hear about but rarely saw.

'We already considered you dead,' Claas said at last, taking the talking part as usual. Hans had been making notes and watching them all, as if trying to read their minds. 'That much I will gladly confess. No news, no letter. Only a missive from an angry captain called Barthel Hofmeister.' He took some papers from the table's drawer. 'These explained exactly what route you had taken.'

Lucifer, help me. Aenlin perused the printed lines. The scribblers outdid one another with their descriptions of various atrocities, but she realised with relief that their names were never mentioned. A plague doctor wearing a silver mask was, though. Also, an eyewitness swore to them that he had seen a giant near Magdeburg, while a fisherman downstream of Magdeburg had dragged pieces of a giant eel or snake from the river.

'These tales are grossly exaggerated.' Aenlin smiled. 'But please see them as further proof of our adventure.'

'It is utterly regrettable that you could not save any of the people we sent you to rescue.' Claas stroked his trimmed beard, which touched his lace collar. 'Still, you shall be paid.' He nodded at his brother.

Hans rose and went to a strongbox at the wall behind his desk. He had to use half a dozen keys on various locks and bars before it finally opened. He came back with five heavy pouches.

One clinking pouch apiece landed in front of Nicolas and Jäcklein, one in front of Caspar and the last pair of them in front the two women.

'That is the pay you would have been entitled to,' Claas explained. 'There will be nothing for your dead. We will keep their shares until their relatives come to claim them.'

Hans laughed softly, and Aenlin raised an eyebrow.

'My! Very generous.' Jäcklein took the pouch before him at once. 'A little compensation for our . . . special adventures. That was not part of the contract.'

'Why is the Company so generous?' Nicolas, who had no visible marks any more – despite having almost literally lost his heart to a woman – wasn't trusting this result. 'You are merchants. You don't simply give away money.'

'A good question, Captain.' Claas reclined in his chair. 'And easily answered: this is not the Company's money; it comes from our client. We are only following orders.'

'You even consider the surviving dependents,' Jäcklein said, 'which is laudable.'

'Who wanted us to save these women?' Aenlin didn't care about her pay; she was waiting for her inheritance, which she would get only with the help of the de Hertoghes. Woe to them if they tried to trick her. 'Now that everything is done, you can surely tell us.'

'We don't know.' Claas took a sip of his port and pointed towards the exit with his crystal chalice. 'My dear landsknechts, would you be so kind as to wait outside? We have something to discuss with the ladies.'

'We know.' Caspar rose and patted his pouch. 'How I love the sound of gold!'

'We shall squander it all tonight,' Jäcklein suggested as they left. 'We have escaped the Reaper so often that I don't mind annoying him some more.'

Nicolas looked at Aenlin. 'We will be waiting outside for you.' He followed the other two men.

The door had barely closed behind them when another one opened.

A man entered. He wore a jerkin and breeches beneath a long robe that was extravagantly cut but still as boring as his face, his wig, even his way of walking. In his hands, he carried a strongbox that looked almost too heavy for him.

'This is Banker Kettler. He works at the Bank of Hamburg. He has come to deliver what you asked for, Miss Kane. We had stored it there at the request of Jacobus Maus.' Claas de Hertoghe looked at Kettler expectantly.

'Yes, certainly.' The banker produced a key from his pocket and opened the lock of the strongbox. 'We have checked the paperwork that the West India Company submitted. Since your father is dead, Miss Kane, and you are able to prove your lineage, by virtue of my office I hereby hand you his legacy.' He pushed the strongbox across the table. It screeched across the wood, leaving deep furrows.

'You will compensate me for this, Banker Kettler,' Hans commented, making a note.

Aenlin stared at the box. *My inheritance.*

'Go on,' Tahmina prompted. 'You have been waiting so long for this.'

Not in the presence of foreigners. There might be very personal things in there. Confidential things. Mysterious things. The only person she wanted to share this moment with was Tahmina. 'I will take it with me, Banker Kettler.'

'I will not stand in your way.' Kettler locked the strongbox and handed the key to Aenlin. 'There you go. Look inside whenever you want to, when you feel ready. But bring the box back to the bank at some point. It is not part of the inheritance.'

Aenlin rose and took one handle, Tahmina the other. 'Thank you, Banker Kettler.' She looked at the de Hertoghe brothers. 'My thanks to you, that you paid us in full. You could just as well have kept the other half of the fee and told us this was some loophole in the deal. We would never have found out.'

'We are serious businessmen, Miss Kane.' Claas and his brother nodded at her. 'May whatever you find inside bring you happiness. This is my wish for you.'

The women left the room and after Aenlin had collected her weapons from the guard at the door, the Company building.

'There she is: the fledgling heiress.' Jäcklein regarded her as if he were a doctor. 'Oh! I see no joy, no jumping, no rejoicing. Was it only gewgaws and clabber in the end? No gold, no wise writings, or whatever your father collected?'

'It is Pandora's box,' Caspar said, stroking his goatee.

'You have not yet opened it,' Nicolas guessed.

'No, I have not. I want to open it . . . alone.' She was a little afraid of the feelings that might lurk inside. *The time has not come yet.* 'But I would still like to celebrate.'

'To drink to the captain's resurrection!' Jäcklein slapped Nicolas on the shoulder. 'Baptised you have been already, in the Elbe.'

Aenlin winked at Nicolas. They had told no one what had happened on the barge; he could tell his friend and Caspar about it if he liked, but he'd already said that he had no explanation for the events on the river. Tahmina had no magical explanation, either.

It's still a mystery – and in the end, he might well be Lucifer's creature.

'I wonder how Moritz is,' she wondered aloud.

'You mean Holder.' Tahmina smiled. 'I am fairly sure he has survived. But I also know that he will not return. The world of the humans is not for him.'

'Hear, hear.' Jäcklein raised his finger. 'The mystic has spoken and it sounded very mystic.'

'Mysterious, even.' Adjusting his long-haired wig, Caspar pointed at the nearest inn. 'Should we drink now? How often will I have to ask?'

'I have one more thing to do first.' Aenlin took the claw of Itzli from a pouch on her belt and dropped the engraved obsidian knife to the cobblestones. When it hit the ground, there was a cracking sound, but only a small fragment chipped off it. 'Let's destroy this artefact.' She stamped on it with the heel of her boot and the dagger broke into three pieces. 'This way, it can never again be used for evil.'

'Ho, this is a nice task!' Jäcklein readily helped smashing the obsidian by stamping on it himself. 'Perish, demonic Aztec power!'

Caspar kicked some of the fragments, which rattled across the cobbled quay to disappear into the water. 'For ever.'

'And ever.' Tahmina struck the last intact piece of the blade with the butt of her staff and ground it to dark granules.

Aenlin watched the destruction with relief. *Another danger averted. This adventure could have no better end.* 'Gentlemen, as we say in England, now—'

'Caution,' Nicolas said in an abruptly serious voice. He touched his rapier. At once, Caspar grabbed his pistol and Jäcklein reached for the hilt of his dagger. 'Someone is approaching.'

'I daresay it's some shady figure.' Jäcklein laughed involuntarily.

'How foolish can you be, to ambush landsknechts who are armed to the teeth? What we are should be obvious!'

'But he does not know that we are the best.' Tahmina leaned on her staff without letting go of the handle of the strongbox.

The clean-shaven man wore elegant clothes; his face was that of diplomats and merchants who would do anything under the rubric of business. He stopped in front of the group and made a perfect courtly bow.

'I have waited so long for the day that I would see all of you together.'

'*Verdammt!* He talks as if he knows us.' Jäcklein lifted his hat with a grin.

'Or as if we were famous.' Caspar looked at the man and suddenly his face lightened. 'He has to be a nobleman! It would probably be best if I challenged him directly, before he thinks twice about it and runs away.'

Aenlin remained relaxed, just like the others and tipped the brim of her hat. 'What do you want?'

'You are Aenlin Kane, daughter of Solomon Kane.' The man bowed once more. 'Your reputation precedes you. I assume this is your team? The people you have travelled with to Bamberg?'

'He has eyes like the Devil,' Jäcklein stated. 'Return to Hell, Sulphur-hoof!'

'How do you know about our journey?' Nicolas stood next to Aenlin, half protecting her. 'You don't belong to the Company – which means you must be our real client.'

'I didn't hear your name. The whistling of all those balls must have made me hard of hearing.' Caspar tapped the studded hilt of his pistol with his fingers. 'Do me a favour and introduce yourself again.'

'I am Grand Duke Mikhail Alexandrovich Fjodorov.' Another bow. 'In the name of the Tsar of all the Russias, I would like to buy your services. We have heard some of the things that happened to you on your way. Considering what the Tsar is planning over the next two years ...'

'The Tsar?' Jäcklein blurted. 'The *Russian Tsar* sent us to collect the Aztecs?'

'I never would have thought that.' Caspar let his hand fall from his weapon. 'Why did he—?'

The Grand Duke laughed noncommittally. 'I do not wish to talk about this in public. Hamburg is very attentive. If someone should ask you what we talked about, your answer should be that I wanted only—'

An armed figure sprang from behind a wagon that stood at the side of the road. A shabby red hat concealed much of his face and a light scarf covered his mouth and nose. The pistols in the man's hands were pointed at Aenlin and Caspar. A glow emanated from the barrels. 'In the name of Vanth: give me what is mine!'

'What are you thinking?' the Grand Duke shouted at the man, taking him for a common robber. 'How dare you—?'

The masked man swivelled his barrel slightly and fired.

With a *bang!* the Grand Duke plummeted to the cobblestones; after a moment's delay, the ball that hit him exploded within his chest, sending blood, flesh and bone splinters flying.

'Never!' Caspar drew his pistols and stepped forward. 'You will die like your companions!' He fired.

The ball made a hole in the masked man's clothes, exactly where his heart should be, but despite the precise hit, he didn't fall – he didn't even stagger.

Aenlin had heard the gunshot, followed by a metallic sound. *A breastplate!* Their enemy was wearing a thick iron plate beneath his clothes to protect him from common musket balls.

The masked man fired in response and the glowing projectile hit the duellist's shoulder. This shot had been less well-aimed, but the ensuing detonation of the demon ball destroyed the joint, laying it open.

'You fraud. You miserable . . .' Caspar fell, silenced by pain.

The masked man drew two more firearms from beneath his cloak. 'Don't move. If even one symbol on that staff starts glowing, I will fire a ball into the mystic's mouth. Stay away from this fake Count.' The man looked at all of them in turn. 'Where is the mask?' They looked at one another, questions in their eyes.

'The plague doctor's mask! Tell me where it is!' He waved his pistols about. 'Quickly! Otherwise your friend will die, and afterwards, I will kill the rest of you, one by one.'

'In my bag,' Caspar gasped. 'Take it, you fucking pig, then piss off. My next ball will be aimed at your head.'

'Give it to me.' The masked man pointed at Aenlin. 'Get it out and toss it to me.'

She did as the unknown man demanded, thinking, *We should have destroyed it.*

The silver mask with its long beak rattled across the cobblestones and came to rest at his feet. 'Now you can attend him.' The stranger bent down, keeping an eye on his four opponents. 'Yes, that's it!' In perverse delight, he pulled down the scarf.

Aenlin recognised his face, even if it had aged considerably. *How can that be?*

Caspar cursed. 'Bracke? Bracke, you undead piece of shit! *You* were the Venetian who made our life a living hell?' Carefully, he lowered himself to his right side; blood seeped from the wound into his black clothes. It was visible only when it dripped down onto the cobblestones. 'Oh, damn. This is not going to end well.' He slowly exhaled and closed his eyes. 'But I hit him. Right in the heart.'

With one hand, Bracke placed the mask onto his face and took a deep breath. 'Vanth, hear my prayer! Now I am a part of you again! Give me back my full power! Grant it to me so I may do your will!' He laughed as the remaining red glass began gleaming. 'Yes! Yes, you have answered my prayer! Let me be your harbinger! Let me eliminate the hordes rampaging about the Dark Lands – you alone shall rule! No Egyptian cults, no sorcerers, no servants of Satan, no Aztec woman can match you! Vanth – I pray to thee!'

Aenlin touched Caspar's throat, trying in vain to find his heartbeat. 'He is dying,' she screamed in terror, still trying to find a pulse. *Dead!* The look that she gave Bracke was full of hatred. 'You killed him, you murderer! His life was a thousand times the value of yours!'

'You will not leave Hamburg,' Nicolas vowed in an ice-cold voice.

'Call me what you like.' The glow in the muzzles of his weapons was redder than ever before. 'He shot me a few months ago. I am only repaying his meddling. I should have killed you, Aenlin Kane.'

'I didn't simply watch and wait for my end last time round,' Aenlin said darkly. Secretly, she drew the stiletto from her boot. 'I will not do so now.'

'Be my guest!' Bracke raised his pistols and pulled the triggers. 'Vanth help me!'

'Lucifer help me!' Aenlin leapt forwards.

Kingdom of England, London, October 1629

'What ill, ill weather.' Henry Rich, First Earl of Holland and Baron of Kensington, looked out through the long windows of his reading room into the garden. A storm whipped through the night, blowing sheets of rain against the windowpanes. He looked over his shoulder to the fireplace, wondering whether he should have his servants add more wood.

His day's work done, he had exchanged his long, tailored

brocade jacket and his puffed-sleeve shirt and breeches for a silken nightshirt and dressing gown. His goatee beard and moustache were bristling rebelliously, and he had taken off his long curly wig, revealing his own short blond hair. In his left hand, the slim man held a full wine glass.

'This weather is fit for neither man nor beast,' added a dark voice, coming from nowhere.

Startled, Henry looked around for an intruder. 'Who is it?'

'Melchior Pieck, your Lordship.' The man stepped from concealment between the cupboard and the curtain. He wore the black robe and brown leather apron of a plague doctor; on his head, he had a round hat. 'You should invest more money in your guards. If I were an assassin ...'

'You are an assassin, for all you are serving me.' Henry looked at the man, whose face was hidden behind a dented and deeply scratched silver mask. One red glass was missing, showing the man's own eye behind it. 'What is this? Your latest camouflage? A little conspicuous, don't you think? Also, it will constantly force you to tend to things about which you know nothing. In times of the plague, everyone will want your counsel.' He waved him closer. 'Since you have come to my humble home, I hope this means you have fulfilled your task?'

'I have, your Lordship.' Melchior stepped before the man at the window and bowed. 'Although the inheritance proved to be nothing but an empty strongbox.'

'An empty strongbox?' Henry exhaled. 'You jest, surely, Pieck. You've kept the inheritance for yourself.'

'What did your Lordship expect inside that strongbox?'

'Everything. Nothing.' With a sigh, he emptied his glass. 'We are talking about Solomon Kane's legacy. I expected gold, mighty artefacts, treasure maps, mysterious things not of this world. This man experienced so much – he was able to collect so many things! But he left nothing to his daughter?'

'In truth, the contents of the strongbox were meant for his beloved Bess, your Lordship,' Melchior said, his voice dull from behind the mask. 'To be exact, it was a flower.'

'A flower. Dried, I assume?'

'Yes. A forget-me-not.'

Henry laughed aloud. 'What nonsense. That cannot have been all. Where is this box now?'

'In the Lower Port. In Hamburg.'

'Bring it to me.'

'Your Lordship?'

'It *must* have contained some inheritance. Written somewhere – on a side, or engraved or ... A man like Solomon Kane would never have bequeathed the love of his life a dried flower. That's ridiculous! Or maybe it was a special flower with magic powers? Dash it all, Pieck!'

'You, a wealthy man, wished me to kill Aenlin Kane in the hope of gaining wealth and artefacts? To acquire her inheritance?' Melchior laughed incredulously.

'But what if he had found the Holy Grail? The water of eternal life? Imagine something no man other than he could have found. Moreover, the Lodge was afraid Kane might have had information on it.' Henry tapped the long silver beak. 'Take this thing off. It looks frightening. With me, you need no disguise.'

'You could be afflicted with the plague, your Lordship. Then I would at least be well prepared.'

'Your jokes are worse than the king's.' Henry regarded his empty glass. 'The envelope?'

'I gave it to the little Persian.' Melchior still hadn't removed the mask. 'What did the message mean?'

'Oh? You read the letter?'

'It opened by accident. But I did not understand it.' Melchior put his hands behind his back, the leather of his apron creaking as it tightened. 'What is so special about the mystic that she is invited here? Did you want me to bring her along when I delivered the strongbox to you?'

'Are you studying mysticism and alchemy these days?' Henry put his hands in his pockets. 'You surprise me, Pieck.'

'No, I am not. But I listened in on a conversation about the Persian's former master. He is, I believe, in London, and would very much like to talk to her—'

Henry laughed again. 'That fellow's done. I believe he fell foul of the wrong people.'

'Ah. I understand.' Melchior tapped his nose. 'I can smell how that went. These "wrong people" killed him, but afterwards found his knowledge so interesting that they decided to invite his student.'

'More or less, Pieck. More or less.' Henry sniffed and looked out of the window. 'Not a bad idea.'

'Your Lordship?'

'The mystic. As soon as you have recovered the strongbox from the basin, see to it that this ... this ... Lalila ...'

'Tahmina, your Lordship.'

'Whatever. She received the friendly invitation. Now you will be the urgent invitation.' Henry turned to face the mercenary again. 'How much will that cost me?'

'You – or your friends? You are giving this order on their behalf, are you not?'

'We are an alliance, my dear Pieck, and we all contribute to the Lodge's war chest. So?'

'Hard to tell. She understands spells and curses that are second to none. She uses Yatu, an Oriental magic – that could be deadly for me. I would not put it past her to have a pet djinn. You know—'

'You are a good negotiator, Pieck. You always were.'

'Your Lordship, what do you think about a counter-offer?'

Henry raised his brows now. 'Don't forget your status, man!

You may be floating on the surface of the scum, but you are still far beneath me.'

'I will never forget that.' Slowly, Melchior took off the mask and showed his familiar stubbled, aged face to the Earl. 'Still, this is a face-to-face offer.'

'Are you drunk, Pieck?'

'No. I do not drink any more.' Melchior gave him a wry, miserable smile, almost uncanny. 'Mark my words, your Lordship: you and the Lodge must forget that Tahmina the mystic and Aenlin Kane ever existed. In exchange, your Lordship may continue living.'

Henry took his hands from his pockets. 'Pieck, if you're not drunk, you have lost your mind!'

'I am not Melchior Pieck.' The old mercenary pointed at his scratched mask. 'These symbols that I rendered useless belonged to a dark goddess, one Pieck worshipped, and from whom he got his power. My friends and I killed him, your Lordship, and now I have used his corpse to set a trap for you, to trick you into revealing the information I needed. I have heard enough. For now.'

Henry recoiled from the man. 'I . . . I am talking to a corpse?'

'Put me to the test.' Melchior Pieck raised his arms. 'Stab me, shoot me, let loose your dogs upon me. I will not fight back.'

'You are . . .'

'Please, do try, your Lordship.'

'I shall!' Henry hurried to the fireplace, grasped the poker and smashed it against Melchior's temple, shattering the bone.

The mercenary staggered sidewards, dropping the silver mask.

'Well swung, your Lordship. Do you play the Scottish game of golf?' Melchior's skull was caved in, but the deep wound wasn't bleeding. 'You stand in the presence of an Oriental miracle.'

'You . . . you are this Tahmina? By the Almighty! You are a necromancer!' Henry dropped the poker and stepped back. 'Servants—!'

'Act against Aenlin and me one more time,' Tahmina said through Melchior's mouth, 'and you will die. The Lodge will die. Everything and everyone related to you and it will die. Then I will make you my puppet, and I will *utterly* disgrace your name. Never forget that, your Lordship. I can be *everywhere* – and I can let the dead haunt you.'

In a heartbeat, Pieck's body flopped to the priceless Persian carpet covering the library floor. His left eye hit the upturned tip of the mask and without a sound, the metal beak punched its way through Pieck's head to emerge from the back of his skull.

Henry screamed in terror as the doors flew open; his servants had heard his call and had come to their master's aid.

'An assassin!' Henry called, pointing at the corpse. 'Trying to kill me! Call the guards – have them search *everything*.'

'Your Lordship, there is a thunderstorm that—'

'*Search everything*,' Henry shouted, and he fled from the room.

The message had been delivered and he had clearly understood it.

But I am still silent about what is worse than death,
What is worse than the plague and embers and famine:
That the treasure of souls was also forced from so many.

Mourning for a Devastated Germany (1636)
by Andreas Gryphius

CONCLUSIO

Free Imperial City of Hamburg, November 1629

'To Caspar!' Jäcklein lifted his brandy. 'May he challenge the Devil in Hell to a duel and kill him. He'd come out fine!' He raised his glass to his lips.

'To Caspar,' echoed Nicolas, Aenlin and Tahmina and they emptied their goblets in unison. Even the mystic drank the strong alcohol in salute to the duellist.

They had rented the back room of the Thirsty Roper and had just washed down a delicious meal with plenty of good beer. Outside, an autumn storm was howling through the Hanseatic city, presaging a frosty winter as it chased people into their homes or Hamburg's many inns and taverns.

'We owe him so much.' Aenlin looked at Tahmina and then at Nicolas. 'He was worth more than his weight in gold.'

Jäcklein refilled his goblet from the bottle the tavern keeper had left at their table. 'But in the end it was you who killed Pieck – with a stiletto, before any of us could even move.'

'I couldn't have done it without Caspar's help.' Aenlin remembered how the flaming lead balls had missed her by a hair's-breadth. *The heat.* She had slit Bracke's throat with her stiletto and torn off his mask to rob him of Vanth's power. *There'll be no immortality for him.*

In his death throes, Pieck had tried to fight back, grabbing for the mask, but Aenlin had stabbed him a second time, through the back of his neck.

Nicolas, Jäcklein and Tahmina had desperately tried to save the duellist, but he had long since bled to death.

Later, they had rendered the mask harmless and put it and Melchor Pieck's corpse to good use.

'To Caspar,' Jäcklein repeated, promptly emptying another goblet, then immediately refilled it. 'Lord in the heavens above, how much have we suffered, Captain? Statius dead. Caspar dead—'

'Moritz!' Tahmina said happily.

'Many thanks for the reminder. Dead, too.' Jäcklein spoke darkly, downing his brandy. 'I can barely keep up with the drinking.'

Nicolas followed the mystic's gaze and rose from his chair. 'By the old gods!' he exclaimed, and gave the young giant, who had quietly approached their table, a bear hug. 'Here he is, the man himself!'

'Huzzah! Not dead at all!' Jäcklein emptied his goblet again. 'You always find a reason, yes?'

Aenlin hugged Moritz, then Jäcklein jumped at him like a little Jack-in-the-Box, kissing his forehead loudly. Tahmina and the young giant held each other tight for a long time.

'Yes, here I am,' Moritz said, and he laughed loudly. Black curls surrounded his head, just as when he and the landsknechts had first met, but now a thick beard graced his face. He was dressed like a hunter, in leather and skins. On his belt, he wore a sword-sized dagger. 'I have come to thank the woman who has saved my life.' To everyone's surprise, he knelt before the delicate Tahmina. 'Call my name to the wind three times.'

She tried to object: 'But—'

'You sacrificed the favour owed to you for my survival. This way, I can repay you.' He rose and kissed her hands. 'Never forget. Wherever and whenever you need me. You know what we can do.'

Aenlin saw the tears of emotion in Tahmina's eyes and her throat constricted. 'At least with you, everything ended well,' she whispered. *Lucifer, I thank thee.*

'Captain Nicolas, I am signing off. Keep the pay you owe me as a compensation. This is not my world, even if I thought so at first.' He shook Nicolas' hand. 'I will live my life elsewhere on this earth – not on the battlefields, where I went looking to live it first, and not as an adventurer.'

'Yes, go back to your Paradise lost, you giant child. May you live in peace.' Jäcklein waved his mug. 'I'd like that as well.'

'Who would not?' Aenlin said.

'I hereby release you, Moritz Mühler.' Nicolas saluted him, then threw a leather pouch to the giant. 'However, you've more than earned your pay. Now sit down, eat and drink with us, as a farewell.'

'And I'll fill you in on what you've missed,' Jäcklein added. 'Poor Caspar is dead.' Quickly, he drank another brandy, then told Moritz at length about the battle of Magdeburg, about Melchior Pieck and his unexpected attack. The two of them became lost in conversation.

'What are you going to do now, Nicolas?' Aenlin smiled at the inscrutable, enigmatic man. 'What will you do with your uniqueness? Or is there some Paradise lost waiting for you, too?'

'I'll go to war,' Nicolas answered airily, 'because that's all I can do, and all I want to do.' He touched the spot on his chest where the Aztec had tried to rip out his heart. 'That's my destiny. Someone else thinks so, too.'

'Who is this someone who made you a ... ?' Aenlin lacked the right word. 'Made you what you are?'

Nicolas shrugged. 'Does it matter? He clearly wants me to rush from one battle to the next.'

Even though he'd heard only half the conversation, Jäcklein interrupted, 'Yes, from battle to battle – with loyal Jäcklein by your side! We won't stop before either the Cathotants or the Prostelics have won!'

'Oh, listen to him: he's talking in tongues!' Moritz laughed.

'Do you have a new mission, then?' Aenlin would have wished for the man to find peace, a place of contemplation, but he didn't know about such things. He was driven, excited by the banging of drums, by war cries, by the noise of pistols and muskets, the waving of flags. *It probably really is his destiny, so who am I to disagree?*

'We'll soon be on our way again. You'll see.' Nicolas raised his mug of beer to her. 'The Swedes and the Poles have signed a truce at Altmark. It's for six years. Gustavus Adolphus secured riches from the wealthy cities; that'll fill his war chest.' He drank deeply. 'And when the spring comes, the Swedish army will be there to kick the Emperor's ultra-Catholic arse with their heavy boots.'

'I've told you: they'll attack via Stralsund!' Jäcklein crowed.

'Pomerania,' Nicolas argued, raising his hand. 'Want to bet?'

'Sure, Captain!' In his intoxicated state, Jäcklein needed several tries before he could shake Nicolas' hand. 'Listen to me!' He quickly rose from his chair. 'I've got it!'

'What have you got?' Moritz teased him. 'An inspiration? Divine Epiphany?'

'I've got – enough.' Laughing, he dropped into his chair again, then he hugged Moritz, convulsing with laughter at his own joke.

Aenlin looked at these men who had become her friends. Tousled Jäcklein. Indulgent Moritz. Nicolas, whatever he is. *A man blessed by Lucifer.* With a twinge of melancholy, she took the coffer, unlocked it with the key and quickly kissed Tahmina's cheek. 'It's time.' She raised the lid.

'Well?' Jäcklein prompted, waving his goblet. 'What can I drink to next?'

Weird. Aenlin picked up drawings. 'Look – maps. Instructions. Drawings of alien creatures.' She flicked through a hodgepodge of records from her father's travels. Among the parchments and papers, there were a few heavy gold coins of unknown minting, a pouch stuffed with black pearls and another filled with cut and uncut gemstones. There was a weirdly shaped bone dagger, an engraved wooden disc, various tusks and a hat buckle.

Thanks to the pearls, jewels and coins, Aenlin had it made. *But Mother should have inherited this when she was still alive, not me.* Thanks to the Company, she had more than enough money.

'There's also a letter,' Tahmina said, putting a hand on her lover's back.

'It's not addressed to me. I'll read it to my mother at her grave.' Aenlin put everything back into the coffer. *So this is it.* It had affected her less than she had expected. *Maybe because nothing in there was actually meant for me.* Her father remained a stranger to her, though; that was what she truly regretted.

'Satisfied with your inheritance?' Nicolas pushed a mug of brandy towards her.

Aenlin nodded hesitantly. 'His true inheritance lives on in me. That is his legacy.'

Her adventures across the Empire had taught her a lot, but there was still much more to learn. She raised her brandy high in the air. 'Cheers!' Inconspicuously she touched Tahmina's leg. She remembered Jäcklein's words. 'But now, to Paradise lost! May we all find ours.'

'To Paradise lost!'

AFTERWORD

Fantasy and history – two things I enjoy mixing in my novels.

I have been preoccupied with the topic of the Thirty Years' War for a while, and I knew it was the perfect setting for a fantasy novel. Reading the pertaining literature and studying the sources, you get an idea of what the people of that time had to suffer and endure, of the atrocities that took place, even beyond the witchcraft trials and the mood of the time.

It was an easy job for the powers of darkness to extend their influence and make offers to desperate people that they couldn't or didn't refuse – at least in my interpretation.

The adventures of Solomon Kane, a Puritan fighting evil, were conceived by Robert E. Howard, who also created Conan the Barbarian. They take place some time earlier. Unlike Conan, not everyone knows Solomon Kane, and the movie version of his story some years ago was a terrible flop.

The character appealed to me at once, but I didn't want to simply continue Howard's stories. I needed something new, something that held a little echo of him, a memory.

So I invented his daughter as a homage to him: less Puritan and with her own ideas concerning faith.

The band Blind Guardian, veterans of the German power metal scene and always open to fantasy, were similarly enthusiastic about the Thirty Years' War as a setting. As a role-player and gamer, I've been listening to the group's music for many, many years, as our characters travelled through adventures with a background of Blind Guardian's songs.

I would never have dreamed that one day I'd be collaborating with Blind Guardian on a shared project! With the song 'Children of the Smith' for the game *The Dwarves*, they'd already made me incredibly happy. In a way, this new album is the next level. It's a concept album with a strong orchestral influence, on which I had substantial input. It tells the story of what happened to Nicolas after this adventure, and where his travels took him.

I found this musical/artistic approach extremely exciting and was curious how Blind Guardian would tell this story. It is truly a great honour for me, to have had a little bit of input into this album.

Of course, I want to thank Hansi Kürsch, Blind Guardian's lead singer, for asking me to collaborate.

I also thank Hanka Leo, my editor, whose red pencil flitted across the lines of this novel, hunting down my inconsistencies.

Let us also not forget my test reader, Yvonne Schöneck.

And of course thanks a lot to Jo Fletcher, who supported me and my works from the beginning of my very first steps in England.

Will there be a sequel to *The Dark Lands*?

Will you ever know what happened to Aenlin, Nicolas and all the others?

Well, I don't intend to write one about them.

Basically.

But as they say – never say never . . .

Markus Heitz
Germany
Fall/Winter of 2018

BLIND GUARDIAN
LEGACY OF THE DARK LANDS

Almost twenty years have passed and still there is no peace. In 1648, the mercenary captain Nicolas is still firmly caught in the clutches of the Thirty Years' War.

The story continues with *The Legacy of the Dark Lands*.

First, author Markus Heitz published his novel, *The Dark Lands*, and now the power metal band Blind Guardian follows suit with its orchestral album. What mysteries surround Nicolas? How can he shake off the chains of war? And what happened to his loved ones?

In a special collaboration, this bedrock of heavy metal and Germany's most successful fantasy author tell a unique story, in their own, distinct ways, both extraordinary and inimitable.

With this orchestral metal album, Blind Guardian fulfils its long-cherished wish to focus on imposing choral singing and a classical orchestra like those used in movie production.

ABOUT THE AUTHOR

Markus Heitz studied history and German language and literature before writing his debut novel, *Schatten über Ulldart* (*Shadows
over Ulldart*), the first in a series of epic fantasy novels, which
won the Deutscher Phantastik Preis, Germany's premier literary
award for fantasy. Since then he has frequently topped the
bestseller charts, and his Number One-bestselling *Dwarves* and
Aelfar series have earned him his place among Germany's most
successful fantasy authors. Markus has become a byword for
intriguing combinations: as well as taking fantasy in different
directions, he has mixed mystery, history, action and adventure,
and always with at least a pinch of darkness. Millions of readers
across the world have been entranced by the endless scope and
breadth of his novels. Whether twisting fairy-tale characters
or inventing living shadows, mysterious mirror images or terrifying creatures, he has it done all – and much more besides.